'*Tender* is an amazing novel, gripping, completely compelling, and at once demanding and satisfying. Belinda McKeon has an inimitable, to-die-for writing style, and a sublime talent for constructing a clear, often poetic exposition of the complexities of friendship and love, of the unfathomable nature of human relationships.'

Donal Ryan, author of *The Spinning Heart*

'*Tender* rises above every other book on the shelf for its language alone; the beauty of each sentence will break your heart. But the story, full of the pleasures and terrors and betrayals of youth, will do that anyway. There is no way around it: you will weep. Spectacular.'

Andrew Sean Greer, author of *The Story of a Marriage*

'Utterly exquisite, unflinchingly observed, *Tender* is the story of a specific obsessive love, but also the story of youth itself, the blinding needs of heart and body, the illusion that one can change reality to suit one's desires – just by wanting to enough. McKeon's intelligence and insight shine through every page, and the words themselves perform miracles of revelation as they dance from one sentence to the next.'

Robin Black, author of *Life Drawing*

'It's a great pleasure to read something so acute and beautifully written – especially the dialogue, the voices spring off the page – and also so subtly subversive. It's a story of self-realisation and artistic freedom told by the person who was realised upon. So many women will recognise themselves in Catherine.' Kate Clanchy, author of *Meeting the English*

TENDER

Also by Belinda McKeon

SOLACE

Belinda McKeon

TENDER

PICADOR

First published 2015 by Picador
an imprint of Pan Macmillan, a division of Macmillan Publishers Limited
Pan Macmillan, 20 New Wharf Road, London N1 9RR
Basingstoke and Oxford
Associated companies throughout the world
www.panmacmillan.com

ISBN 978-1-4472-5217-7

A CIP catalogue record for this book is available from the British Library.

Printed and bound by CPI Group (UK) Ltd, Croydon, CR0 4YY

Visit **www.picador.com** to read more about all our books
and to buy them. You will also find features, author interviews and
news of any author events, and you can sign up for e-newsletters
so that you're always first to hear about our new releases.

For K

He was the friend of my life. You know, you only have one friend like that; there can't be two.

James Salter, *Light Years*

AWAKE
(1997)

Dreams fled away, and something about a bedroom, and something about a garden, seen through an open window; and a windfall, something about a windfall – a line which made Catherine see apples, bruising and shrivelling and rotting into the ground. *Windfall-sweetened soil*; that was it. And, the flank of an animal, rubbing against a bedroom wall – though that could not be right, could it? But it was in there somewhere, she knew it was; something of it had bobbed up in her consciousness as she lay on the lawn in front of James's house, a wool blanket beneath her, one arm thrown over her eyes to do the job of the sunglasses she had not thought to bring.

The French windows were open. They were to the left of the front door, which seemed a bit strange, or pointless or something – if you wanted to walk out to the front of the house, wouldn't you just use the door? Still, they were nice – elegant, that was what they were, and modern – and through them now came the noise of James and his parents, talking in the loud, excited way this family had. His mother shrieked at something James had said, and James swore at her – the fond, gleeful kind of swearing they did all the time, this family; Catherine could not get over them. They were talking, probably, about the local wedding James's parents were going to that afternoon; James was also expected to go, but James was staying home, using Catherine's visit as an excuse. Catherine was not sure how she felt about this: a mixture of panic and guilt and flattery, which did not make it easy to relax, lying here in an old bikini belonging to James's sister, not that the fact of lying here in a bikini made relaxation easy in the first place. If her parents knew . . . But her parents did not know, she reminded herself once again, and once again she put the thought out of her mind.

Arrah, for fuck's sake, Mammy. That was James now, really roaring, and next came Peggy, her Cavan accent laying the words down like cards: *I'm telling you, Jem, I am telling you.* James was a desperate wee shite, that was something else Peggy had said to him a moment ago; Catherine laughed again at the thought of it. *Desperate wee shite*; she'd say it to him when he came back out here. It would become another of their lines. Already they had their own way of talking, their private phrases, their language, and they'd only known one another since that morning in June; though it seemed like so much longer, it was only six weeks ago that James had shown up in Catherine's flat on Baggot Street, the flat she shared, during term time, with James's old schoolfriends, Amy and Lorraine. It was them he had been looking for, of course, when he had arrived that morning, back from his time in Berlin, but instead he had found Catherine, because Catherine had moved into the bedroom he had left empty the previous October. He had been working for a big-shot photographer over there, someone Catherine, at the time, had never even heard of, but someone big, someone with whom James, despite not even being in college, had managed to get himself a job as an assistant – and this was so typical of James, that he could just go and get something for himself in this way, and it was so unthinkable for Catherine, the guts it would involve, or at least it had been, before meeting James . . .

There, now, was James's father, wry and lovely and long-suffering, asking James if he would not get back out into the garden and give James's mother and himself a bit of peace. *That lassie*, he said – and Catherine knew he was referring to her, and she thrilled to hear herself mentioned – *That lassie will be dying of the thirst.* Then he added something in a lower tone, inaudible to Catherine, and Peggy shouted his name, sounding outraged, and James told him he was very smart, very fucking smart, and *Now for you*, James said then, and Catherine knew that he had done something – maybe had clipped his father on the ear, or pretended to, maybe swiped the last piece of ham from his father's plate. Something, anyway. Some little moment of contact. The previous evening, she had seen James bend down to where his father was sitting at the table and plant on the crown of his head a quick, firm kiss, like a kiss for the head of a baby; just in passing, just as though it meant nothing at all. Catherine had actually blushed. She had felt as though she had done something wrong, something too much, just by having witnessed it. This family. They were just so – they were *amazing*. They were just *brilliant*. And it was so strange, because in so many ways they were so much like Catherine's own family – farmers, the house on the hill, the kitchen smelling of the same things, the bedsheets in the spare room the same sheets that Catherine's parents had on their bed – and yet, they were so—

Extraordinary. That was what they were. That was a James word; that was one of the words she had got, over this summer, from James. From all the talking they had done, firstly in Dublin, those intense days after he had returned from Berlin, and then – after Catherine had returned to her parents' home in Longford for the summer and James had reclaimed his old Baggot Street bedroom – over the phone, James had given her so many new ways of saying things, so many closer, sharper, more questioning ways of looking at the world. They had talked on the phone almost every evening this summer; Catherine would call the payphone in the hall-way on Baggot Street, and James would be there waiting with a cheery *hello*, and they would be off, sometimes for hours, and in those conversations James had given her so much, so many new things to think about. And so many new things to worry about – or, not new things, just things it had never really occurred to her to think about before. Like how little she knew about, well, everything, really. That had been obvious all this past year – college had made that obvious – but James, her conversations with James, had forced her to see it so much more clearly. James had not said this to her directly – James was not like that, not blunt in the way that, say, her classmate Conor was, ripping the piss out of her, making her feel humiliated and small. It was more that in talking to James, listening to him talk, Catherine had come to realize just how much more carefully she needed to think about everything: about her life, about what she was doing with it, about what she was doing at college, about what she was doing with these summer days. About her relationships, of which there were none; Conor was not a relationship, no matter what James said, however often or hilariously – she loved the way he insisted on talking about the dramas of her life as though they were actually interesting, as though there was actually something happening where there absolutely was not. She even loved when he insisted on talking about her relationship with her parents, which was something she had never even thought about in such terms before – she really needed, James had told her, to start thinking about her parents as *people*, instead of just as her parents – and about the way things were with them, and about how this influenced pretty much everything she did. Psychology; James was not at college, because James, as he had told Catherine that first day in Baggot Street, had not wanted to go to college, had wanted to do something different, had wanted to go his own way, but if James *had* gone to college, he told her, it was Psychology he would have liked to study. That or Theology, he had added, and Catherine had burst out laughing, assuming the Theology part to be another of his jokes, because he was hardly religious; but James had insisted: he wanted to understand, he said, what it was, exactly, that people believed.

James hardly needed to go to college, anyway; James already seemed to know about everything. Art, obviously; Catherine was a year into a degree that was half Art History and he knew ten times more than her. He seemed to know more about her other subject, English, too, though on poetry she thought she had the advantage. But when it came to people and the way they behaved, James could talk for hours, and when it came to other things, too; politics, for instance. One night a couple of weeks previously, Catherine had found herself lying awake for hours, thinking about the North – or rather, thinking about the question of whether, if you talked about the North on the phone – as she and James, or rather James, had for a long time that night – your call was likely to be picked up on, to be noted, along with your name and your whereabouts. Because James had said that this often happened; at the end of the call, James had mentioned, as casually as though it were nothing at all, that he and Catherine were probably on some list now, the two of them, that phone calls all over the country were monitored for conversations just like theirs.

Catherine had rung off as quickly as she could, pleading some obligation or other, and she had sat for a long moment afterwards, staring at the phone, at the cord pulled through from the hall, at the plump, cheerful-looking digits on the buttons, her head feeling as though it was pulsing in and out of something unreal. Then she had gone into the sitting room, where her mother was watching television with Anna, Catherine's six-year-old sister, and she had been unable even to look at either of them, worrying about what could happen to them now, because of what she and James had done. Which was the height of paranoia, of course it was, but James had had an answer for that too, the next night, when she described to him the stress she had gone through. And it was true. It didn't make it any less real, all of that; that she thought they were being paranoid didn't make it any less real at all. Catherine had not been able to change the subject quickly enough, that night, to get on to something that was not dangerous, and she did not want to think about it now, either. She did not want to think about it anytime. She wanted lemonade, which was what James had gone into the house for, glasses of cold lemonade for the two of them, and he would be back out with them now, she thought, squinting up at the sunlight; he would be back out any minute. The glasses would be gorgeously cool, would be glistening with ice, and Catherine would sit up on the blanket to see James as he came towards her from the house, and *you desperate wee shite*, she would call out to him, and he would pretend to scowl at her, stepping through the metal archway his mother had set down at the edge of the lawn. Roses – or at least Catherine thought they were roses – were trained up the archway, a vivid red against the paintwork, and now she heard him; she heard, close to the patio door and now coming across the driveway, his footsteps, and yes, there it was, the ice, the clinking, and Catherine clenched all the muscles of her arms and her shoulders and her thighs, just for the pleasure of it, just for the loveliness of releasing them again, stretching out on the blanket so that her fingers and toes touched the grass now, its cool, clipped pile. She sighed, as the sun bleached white the world shut out by her eyelids, and once again she tried to train her vision –

was it still vision if your eyes were closed? – on one of the tiny black floaters swirling in and out of view. But there was no holding them; they came and went like birds.

This was her second day in Carrigfinn.

*

James's hair had grown over the summer; it rose in an unruly quiff over his forehead. He had the reddest hair of any boy Catherine had ever known, which was probably down to the fact that, until James, she had had such a dislike of red-haired boys that she had not even wanted to look at them, let alone talk to them. They made her think of misery, somehow; of small houses and V-neck jumpers and of that helpless, defeated look that came over the faces of some children in primary school when the teacher was humiliating them and there was nothing the child could say or do to change this. She had not articulated this to James, actually, this association; she thought now, as she watched him duck down under the archway of roses, that she must say it to him, that he would find it fascinating, would find it, probably, quite clever, quite funny. Analysing it, picking it apart, he would make it, of course, much funnier still. *And what's so offensive about V-neck jumpers?* she imagined him asking, and she laughed in anticipation of it, hugging herself a little with the pleasure of it, so that James looked at her suspiciously now, his lips pursed in a manner that set her laughing harder still. He was so funny, James; it was probably the thing that was most brilliant about him. He was funnier than anyone she'd ever met. Everything about him was so lit up by this brilliant, glinting comedy; he was so quick, and such a good mimic – so good it was almost disturbing, sometimes – and he had this gift for getting right to the truth about people with a single,

9

seemingly casual line. And he was so loud, and he cared nothing for what other people thought of him; more than once during those first days in Dublin, Catherine had cringed at the attention paid to them by people on the street as James, marching along beside her, had held forth energetically on whatever was grabbing – seizing – his attention at that moment. Passers-by had glanced at him, or stared at him, or raised a withering eyebrow in his direction, but James never seemed to notice; he just charged on. It had been the same, even, in Carrick the previous evening, as he and Catherine had walked from the train station towards the road for Carrigfinn. No thought to who might be listening. No care for who might say he was a right dose, a right pain in the head, that Flynn fella with the hill of red hair. Even as they thumbed a lift, then – Catherine feeling ill with nerves in case they might be seen by someone who could report back to her parents – James had had her in stitches, and when they finally got a lift, from two old women who were neighbours of James's parents – two old women who made sure to get a good look at Catherine, as the girl James Flynn was bringing home – it had actually hurt, the effort of keeping the laughter in. James, all the way home, had stayed straight-faced, keeping up a jolly, newsy patter with the two women, gossiping with them about other neighbours, agreeing with their assessments and their complaints; but the whole time, he had been kicking Catherine's foot, trying to make her laugh, alerting her to intimations, innuendoes, in the things he was saying. Catherine had barely been able to breathe by the time the car had left them at the bottom of the lane.

Catherine was back in Longford until October partly because she had got a summer job – at the local newspaper, where she spent her time making press releases look like news stories – but mostly because her parents wanted her home for the summer, because her parents did not see any reason for her to stay in Dublin when she did not need to go to classes or to the library. When she had been going to Dublin in the first place, her parents had wanted Catherine to move in with her father's sister in Rathmines, rather than get a place with friends from school, and when the place with those friends had fallen through in Freshers' Week, a year of living with her aunt Eileen had seemed unavoidable, but then on the student union noticeboard, Catherine had seen an ad for a room on Baggot Street, and had scribbled down the number, and that number had led her to Amy and Lorraine. They were also first years at Trinity, but studying science subjects rather than arts, and this guy James had gone to Berlin just before the October rent had been paid, and so they needed, badly needed, someone new for his room. Would Catherine be interested? She said yes, her heart racing, and she moved in that evening. They were from Leitrim; that was the detail she used as a bargaining chip with her mother, or as a kind of security clause; Leitrim, after all, was a neighbouring county to Longford, so it was almost as though she was living with people from home; it was not as though she was moving in with Dublin people, or with English people – or with boys. To Catherine's amazement, her mother had agreed reluctantly, and had said that she would come up with some way of explaining it to Catherine's father, and Catherine had spent a happy year living with the girls, who were such fun, and so easy-going, and who treated the flat as a home, not just as somewhere to stay a couple of nights a week before going home again for the weekend. They were both up there for the summer, of course, and she envied them so much, getting to live with James; she envied them even the month they had lived with him before she knew any of them, even the years when they had all been together at secondary school.

How could you envy a time of which you could not possibly have been a part? And yet she did. She looked at James now, as he knelt beside her on the blanket, passing her a glass of lemonade. It was cool and solid in her hand.

'You're going to burn,' she said, her gaze on his bare arms.

'We're all going to burn, Catherine,' he said sternly. 'Sure look at the get-up of you, sitting out where decent people can see you, and your naked body on display.' He shook his head. 'Pat Burke is watching, Catherine. Pat Burke is scandalized, that's what he is.'

'Oh, shut up about that old bastard,' Catherine said, taking a mouthful of lemonade.

'Chin-chin,' James said, making it sound somehow like a warning, and he clinked his glass against hers. He drank deeply and looked down the hill to the canal. A boat, a small cruiser, was moving away from the lock. Catherine could hear the noise of the gates as they closed again.

'That's right,' James shouted down in the boat's direction, although there was no way the people could hear, and, quite apart from that, he had no idea who they were. 'Bate on now, ye fuckers! We don't want your type around here!'

'You're terrible, Muriel,' Catherine said, which was one of the lines which had become theirs over the past few weeks; it was from a film they both loved. *You're terrible, Muriel.* The right way to say it was in an Australian accent, with a wide-eyed expression of shock and dismay, but Catherine was too hot and lazy to bother just now, and anyway, James, attempting to squeeze onto the blanket beside her, was not even listening.

'Shove over, Reilly,' he said; they were shoulder to shoulder, hip to hip. The physical contact was a jolt for Catherine; her mind was casting about frantically for a way to break what she felt to be the tension of the moment. But her mind could not be trusted; her mind responded to the request to divert attention from his body by dumping attention onto it even more crudely than if she had reached out and stroked it from top to toe.

'Your skin,' she said, her voice sounding weird and insistent. 'Your skin will be destroyed in this sun. You need some cream for it. You need to rub in some of that cream your mother gave you.'

'Oh, for fuck's sake,' James grunted. 'That stuff is ancient. You'd be as well off covering yourself with jam.'

'Well, I have it on, and I'm not burning.'

Which had been another stupid thing to say, because now James was up on one elbow, peering at her body, taking it all in: her bare thighs, her stomach, her cleavage, such as it was in this ridiculous eighties bikini. She felt an impulse to wrap herself, hide herself, in the blanket. James was really staring at her now; she tried to laugh, but it came out as a gasp.

'You're turning blue, Catherine,' James said, settling down again as though this was nothing. 'You look like you're coming down with cholera. It must be something in the cream.'

'What?' Catherine said in another gasp, and she sat up in a rush, stretching her arms out in front of her. Instantly she saw that he was not serious, that this was just another of his jokes, and he was convulsed with laughter beside her now, but still she found herself making a show of checking herself – stomach, thighs, calves, and then she lifted her hips and examined what she could see of her arse cheeks, for good measure. There was no blueness, obviously; her freckled skin stared back at her, still bright with the sheen of the lotion, the tiny fair hairs shining in the sun.

'Fucker,' she said, shoving James.

'Ha ha,' he half sang, one minor chord following another, and he did not even open his eyes. She thought about doing something to him, something to get revenge on him; she wanted something, she realized, to make him sharply aware of her again, even though she had been wishing for just that kind of awareness to slide away from her only a moment ago. The cold lemonade, maybe, all over his T-shirt and onto his rolled-up jeans; all down his long, thin legs, over his knobbly feet, white and uncalloused and naked. Or maybe a couple of ice cubes, tipped out of her glass and slapped onto the exposed length of his throat, gone down under his collar before he had the chance to realize what it was she had in her hand.

'Reilly,' James said, in a drowsy undertone, and he let the back of one hand flop onto her stomach before taking it away again. 'You're blocking my sun.'

*

Pat Burke; it was extraordinary how red-faced, horrible old Pat Burke had become one of the private jokes between her and James, one of their lines, but he had. Pat Burke this, Pat Burke that. *Pat Burke is watching; Oh, that's one for Pat Burke, now; Good God, Catherine, what would Pat Burke say?* His name was shorthand for pretended moral indignation, and Catherine loved it, though when they used it she always felt, at the same time, the quickened heartbeat of guilt and of unease at doing something at which her parents would be so horrified. Burke was recovering from a heart attack the previous summer, and on the first Friday of every month he still had to take the train to Dublin for treatment; each time, he came back with a store of gossip about other Longford people who had been heading up to the city and coming home again. At the bar in Leahy's, he would unveil the tasty particulars of what he had seen and heard: the shoppers, the holiday-makers, the sibling-visitors, the ashen people facing tests and diagnoses and tubes and machines; the goners, the chatters, the chancers. And in the city itself, and in the train station, there was also so much to see, which was how on the first Friday in June, Pat Burke happened upon a great morsel, which was the sight of young Reilly, Catherine or whatever her name was, Charlie Reilly's eldest girl, sitting on a bench in the middle of the day, holding hands with some young fella, a huge haystack of red hair on him, bold as brass and without a whit of concern for whoever might be looking their way.

They had not been holding hands. They had been sitting on one of the wooden benches in the gloomy space facing the train platforms, and their heads had been close together, each of them with a hand up to an ear. And yes, maybe, Catherine thought afterwards, maybe their hands had been touching, because they had been listening to her headphones; she had wanted James to hear the Radiohead song she loved, the miserable, beautiful one from *OK Computer*. Catherine had been taking the train back to Longford for the summer, and James had insisted on walking her to the train station, and she had been feeling sad and shaky at the prospect of leaving him – Longford was over two hours from Dublin, and it was unlikely that she would be back up very much during the summer – and shaky, too, at the fact of this, at the fact of this all having come upon her so quickly – three days previously, she had never even met him – and at the fact of it rattling her, now, so deeply, and embarrassed by it, and confused – and worse still, she knew that James was feeling sad about their parting also, because he had told her, and because, in fact, he kept saying so, and Catherine had no idea what to do with this, how to take this, this openness, this unbothered honesty, which seemed to cost him nothing to hand out to her – no blushing, no shiftiness in his eyes or around his mouth – and yes, the fact was, their hands had been touching, or more like their wrists, the press of his wrist and the press of hers, skin against skin, bone against bone, and it was so strange, it had struck her, that a wrist could be such a boring part of someone and yet so massively, overwhelmingly *them*. And the grim lament of 'Exit Music (For A Film)' plunged into this feeling so perfectly, so intimately, that she felt weird about sharing it with him, actually; felt as though it might be saying something somehow dangerous, and the fact that he was nodding, that he was closing his eyes, offered no comfort to her, no breeze of reassurance, and then Thom Yorke was droning, telling someone to breathe, and in that moment Catherine glanced up for some reason, and there, in front of her, was that old weirdo Pat Burke from home, wearing a black suit and a black tie as though he was coming from a funeral, a splattering of small silver badges on his right lapel, and he gave Catherine a wink; a slow, delighted wink.

'Hi, Mr Burke,' Catherine said before she could stop herself, her head jerking upwards, which caused James to jolt beside her and follow her gaze.

'Miss Reilly,' Burke said with heavy emphasis, as though he was a butler announcing her arrival to a room, and with a little bow and a long look at James – a look, Catherine thought, that was more like a leer – he walked away.

'Who the fuck was that?' James said, taking the headphone from his ear and watching as Burke made for the Sligo train.

'A neighbour,' Catherine said. Her heart was thumping; the blush was searing itself into her cheeks, postponed by the shock but coming on fully now.

'He looked like he was coming to claim your soul.'

'Don't look at him.'

'*We hope – that you choke – that you cho-o-oke*,' James sang in a low, rasping whisper, and Catherine elbowed him.

'Stop,' she said. 'It's bad enough.'

James snorted. 'What's bad enough? Those trousers? Did you see the state of them? The arse like an old turf bag.'

'It's just bad enough,' Catherine said, and she lowered her head to indicate that she was giving all her attention, again, to the song.

Sure enough, two mornings later, which was Catherine's first summer Sunday at home, she noticed her mother looking at her awkwardly, in the way that meant she had something to say. Catherine braced herself. She was sitting at the kitchen table with a bowl of Cornflakes and Coco Pops mixed together the way she liked them. It was after eleven, and because she had not dragged herself out of bed earlier, she would now have to go with her father to one o'clock Mass; the others had already been. Catherine had been out the night before, in Fallon's and then on to Blazer's with some of the girls she had known in school, but it had been the usual shit: bumping into people she never saw anymore, and having bitty conversations with them, and then worrying whether her ID would be enough to get her into the club – it was just her luck that now that she had finally turned eighteen, all the clubs in town had adopted an over-nineteens policy, and getting in depended on whether you knew the bouncer, or on whether he decided he fancied you, or on whether you could plead with him, as Catherine had eventually had to do the night before, pointing out to him that she wasn't even drunk, that she could never get properly drunk in Longford, because her father always insisted on collecting her, no matter how late she was out – parking, sometimes, right outside the nightclub door. She reckoned the bouncer had felt sorry for her; that that was why he had let her in. Certainly he had looked at her, just before nodding her through, with something like pity in his eyes.

And then Blazer's had been rubbish, as usual. Cringey dancing to songs from *Trainspotting*; girls who'd been in her Science and Geography classes trying to look like they were off their heads on E when all they'd had was eight bottles of Mug Shot. Clodhopper morons asking if you wanted a shift, the saliva already flecking and bubbling at the corners of their mouths. Anyone half-decent-looking already getting the face worn off them in a corner, and David Donaghy, who'd ignored Catherine's attentions on the school bus from September 1991 to June 1996, ignoring her all over again, and then shifting Lisa Mulligan, who Catherine was pretty sure was his second cousin. Catherine's old schoolfriend Jenny screaming, 'You need to get pissed!' at her, over and over, and then falling asleep slumped against the mirrored walls, and then shifting David Donaghy when his cousin was finished with him. Two o'clock could not come quickly enough. Catherine had almost been glad of the sight of her father's Sierra pulled up tight to the steps at the front.

But then he had been silent all the way home, so Catherine knew that Burke had said something to him. There was no danger of her father raising the subject with her himself – the rules might come from him, but that did not mean that he had to articulate them, at least not with Catherine and Ellen, and definitely not when they related, in even the most peripheral of ways, to what Catherine and Ellen might get up to with boys – but in the morning, Catherine's mother would pause at the kitchen counter, just as she was pausing now, and she would glance in Catherine's direction, and she would clear her throat: a short, almost apologetic rev.

Catherine looked up to meet it; her mother, folding a tea

towel with great precision, looked away again. On the radio, a Shannonside presenter said something about the button accordion. *Fuck the button accordion*, Catherine thought.

'Are you seeing any of your friends from college over the summer?' her mother said.

'Doubt it,' Catherine shrugged. 'Most of them are gone travelling to Germany and America and stuff.' This was not true, but it made some point that Catherine had suddenly found herself wanting very badly to make: that her friends had actual lives. That people her age were out there, doing things for themselves, living independently and freely. This was not actually true, for the most part, since most of her friends from college were also spending the summer working in the towns closest to where they had grown up, and were back living with their parents, but this detail, Catherine had decided, was completely irrelevant. They *could* have been travelling; that was the point. If they had wanted to travel – *this* was the point – they would have been able to. Allowed to. Zoe, that girl from Catherine's Art History tutorial, was in Italy, for instance – Zoe was the kind of person who would think nothing of heading off to Italy by herself for the whole summer. And Conor had made noises about bar work in Chicago, though he had not actually gone in the end due to lack of funds, but he had intended to. And James: James had been in Germany for the entire year! Her mother needed to know that Catherine had friends like this. Except that she did not need to know – it would not be helpful or useful for her to know – the actual details, at least not about Conor and James, because that would lead to too many questions – which was precisely, Catherine remembered, what was about to happen now. She sighed heavily.

'What's wrong with you?' her mother said, her suspicions raised.

'Nothing.'

'I'm just trying to make simple conversation, for God's sake.'

'I'm not stopping you.'

Her mother took a deep breath. 'I was just wondering,' she said slowly, clearly having to work to stop the words coming out sharply, 'whether you have any other friend? Anyone in particular?'

'*Other* friend?' Catherine said mockingly. She could not stop herself. When she was home, when she was talking to her mother, she turned into a fifteen-year-old again. It was ridiculous; she needed to snap out of it. She cleared her throat. 'What do you mean, any other friend?' she said, more evenly.

Her mother shrugged. She had on the striped navy and white top that Catherine loved on her, its vivid white, its dark navy bands; the sleeves were pushed up on her arms, which were already growing brown – Catherine wished she had inherited her mother's olive complexion rather than her father's gene for sunburn. On her mother's wrist was the Swatch watch that Catherine and the others had given her for her last birthday, her forty-fifth, the strap splayed with colours, the tiny mirrored face glinting, now, as she turned the tea towel again in her hands, laid it down on the table to be folded the other way. Forty-five; her mother was *forty-five*. It seemed impossible, but it was nothing beside the thought that in another handful of years, she would be fifty. Fifty. Her mother, slim and tanned and brown-haired; her mother who wore jeans and runners, who had recently bought a new pair of sunglasses to wear in the car. How could she be nearly fifty? And as for Catherine's father, that was completely outrageous – he was ten years older, and sixty was not even an age Catherine was willing to countenance for one of her parents. Sixty was, was it not, the point after which nobody much remarked if something happened to you? If, one morning or one evening, you simply slipped away? What the hell was she supposed to do if that happened to one of her parents? It panicked her, the thought of it; it kept her awake at night, staring at the wall. She had told James about this, of course, but James had come nowhere close to understanding; James had thought she was mad. Or, actually, it was not madness of which he had accused her, but something else – something she had forgotten now, a word she had not heard before – dependent somehow, dependent on them in the same way they were dependent on her – anyway, he had given her a right lecture over the phone that evening. He did not even know exactly how old his own parents were, he had said; sixties, maybe? Late fifties? Catherine had been astonished. For his parents to be that old, and for him not to be riddled with the anxiety of their mortality, with the knowledge that the clock was counting down on the very fact of them – how could he go around like that? How could he have felt relaxed enough, for instance, to have gone off to Berlin? *Oh, for fuck's sake, Catherine*, James had spluttered, and then Catherine had changed the subject. They were so alike, the two of them, so alike in every way – and yet, there were moments when she saw the ways in which they were so different. And she did not like those moments. She found herself moving quickly to chase those moments away.

'Well,' her mother said now, more pointedly; Catherine had not given her any answer to her question. 'Well? Is there anything you want to tell me? Is there anyone you—'

'No,' Catherine said, pushing back from the table.

'Are you *sure*?'

'Yes, I'm sure,' Catherine said. 'And I think that tea towel's folded now.'

'Don't be so bloody smart!'

'I'm not being smart.'

'I'm only trying to have a simple conversation with you!'

'About Pat fucking Burke,' Catherine spat.

'Catherine!' Her mother glanced, horrified, towards the open back door. 'Watch what you're saying!'

'Well? That's it, isn't it?' Catherine said, crossing to the sink angrily. 'He saw me with my friend up at the train station, and he told Daddy, and now I'm in trouble, and I didn't even *do* anything.' Forget fifteen: she sounded ten, now, and she was dismayed at how easily this had happened, at how automatically her voice had become this babyish whine; but in the next moment, she had decided that she was perfectly entitled to whine, and that she might as well go the whole hog, and she banged down her bowl. 'It's not *fair*,' she said, folding her arms.

'Stop that, Catherine,' her mother said warningly. She put one hand on the table and the other on the counter, blocking Catherine's way to the door. 'I just want to talk to you.'

'I didn't *do* anything,' Catherine said, and she tried for a contemptuous laugh which would make clear her feelings about all of this, but as soon as she started it she realized that it would come out as a sob, so she swallowed it back down. 'Pat Burke is nothing but a creep. Everyone hates him, and yet you all still listen to him.'

Her mother raised an eyebrow, as though to say she could not argue with this, but nor could she openly agree. 'He says he saw you with your boyfriend.'

'He's not my boyfriend.'

'Well, you were seen holding hands with him, whatever he is.'

'We were listening to my Walkman, for Christ's sake!'

'Well, if you're going to be so public about it, you can't be surprised when somebody sees you.'

'Oh my God. Oh my God. We weren't doing anything! He's a friend! He's an old friend of Amy and Lorraine's, and he was going in the direction of the train station anyway, and I wanted to tell him about this song – this song I like—'

She stopped. She could hear how unconvincing it sounded. And, also, she was reeling a little, in shock a little, that already she had pushed an untruth into the story; James had not, after all, been going in the direction of the train station anyway. He had gone there especially for her. To sit with her. To hug her goodbye. To wave her off from the platform, with his arms going madly, not giving a shit who was seeing him or laughing at him, doing it with such glee and enthusiasm that Catherine had cringed. But she could not tell her mother this; she could not tell her mother any of it. Her mother would not understand. Her mother, like her father, had surely never known this kind of friendship, the kind of friendship in which you did not want to waste a single minute, in which every minute was a chance to talk about something more—

'Look, Catherine,' her mother said, shaking her head. 'We don't expect you not to have boyfriends. You're old enough for that now. You don't have to tell me lies.'

'Oh, thanks very much,' Catherine said, the words tart with bitterness. 'That's very good of you.'

'I told you not to be so bloody smart!'

'I'm *not* being smart,' Catherine said, and she slammed her hands down on the edge of the sink. There had to be a better way to do this, she thought; there had to be a better way to argue and protest and stand up for yourself. A dignified way; a grown-up way. She would ask James about it the next time she talked to him, she decided; James would know. James would know how to keep your voice level in a situation like this, and how to sound confident, and how to come out the winner with just a few carefully chosen words.

'I *hate* that old prick!' she shouted suddenly across the kitchen, and then she burst into ragged, jerky sobs. Her mother rolled her eyes.

'Oh, for God's sake, Catherine. Get a hold of yourself. You're eighteen years old.'

'I *know* I'm eighteen!' Catherine wailed. 'That's my whole point! James is my *friend*! He's a friend of the girls, and he was in Germany all year, and he's back now, I mean just for the summer, and we were listening to music, and I was just saying hello to him at the train station, and I'm *sick* of not being able to do what I want!'

'Catherine,' her mother said, and she actually laughed. 'Stop being so ridiculous. Of course you can' – she made a face – '*listen to music* with whoever the hell you want. Or *say hello* to them, or whatever it is that you call it now. Daddy was just upset that he had to hear about it from Pat Burke. That Pat Burke was able to tell him something he didn't already know. And something *I* didn't know.'

'Oh my God,' Catherine said, putting her hands to her head. 'Oh my God. I can't take this. I can't—'

'Well,' her mother said, laying the tea towel flat on the table and smoothing it as though it was a map she was intending to read. 'You're getting very bloody worked up about something you claim to be nothing at all.'

James was not her boyfriend. No one was her boyfriend. There had been no boyfriend while she was at school, and there had been no boyfriend during the long summer after her Leaving Cert, and there had been no boyfriend during the first year of college, and there was no boyfriend now. How could there be, when she was back living at home? Which was not an acceptable excuse, according to Catherine's sister Ellen, who was sixteen, and who therefore lived at home all of the time, and who did not let this stop her from having boyfriends, and as many boyfriends as she felt like. It was not that their parents were any less strict with Ellen than they had been with Catherine; it was just that Ellen ignored their strictness, or rather worked around it, with the skill of someone dis-mantling a bomb. Especially now that she was going into her Leaving Cert year, she explained to Catherine, there were simply certain experiences she refused to go without. So, if she wanted to go to the pub where the people her age drank, she made up a story about maths grinds at a friend's house, and when their father collected her four or five hours later, she was ready and waiting, chewing gum to hide the bang of cider and equipped with a perfect explanation for why her clothes smelled of smoke. She was never asked for the explanation. Their father, Ellen told Catherine, needed so much to believe that she would not do such a thing, would not go boozing and smoking and shifting fellas in an alleyway in town, that he simply went on doing that: he believed. Their mother knew; their mother, Ellen said, had come into the bedroom and ranted at her on more than one occasion, but Ellen had gone on denying everything, and doing everything, and she suspected, deep down, that their mother respected her for that.

'If she saw Shane Keegan, she'd *want* me to go with him,' she'd said, setting out her case to Catherine earlier that year. 'He's a complete ride. You couldn't pass up a chance like that.'

'Yeah, right,' Catherine had scoffed. 'If they found out you were shifting one of the Keegans, they'd ground you until you were twenty-five.'

'They could try,' Ellen had said, bouncing a tennis ball off the bedroom wall. 'Anyway, one of us has to be shifting fellas. It's a complete waste of time you being up at college if you're not even going to get together with anyone. *I* would have got together with that Conor fella ages ago if I was you.'

'No, you wouldn't.'

'Yeah, I would. He sounds like good craic.'

'Yeah, well,' Catherine said weakly. 'It's not that simple once you get to college.'

'Course it is,' Ellen said, the ball slapping against her hand. 'You just don't know how to do it.'

You're not even ugly: that was something else that Ellen had said about Catherine's ongoing celibacy. Or, not celibacy – when she was out, she often shifted guys, or acquiesced to their requests to shift her; she took their tongues into her mouth and let their hands roam over the cheeks of her arse – but whatever it was. Singlehood. *Gomhood*, Ellen had called it when Catherine had described it that way. Catherine was tall, Ellen pointed out, and she had some nice clothes, and long hair, and her skin was all right, and so what? What was stopping her? All she had to do, Ellen explained, was to go to the cinema with someone, or to the pub, and shift him, and talk to him, and then, once she got tired of him, she could break up with him. It was just what you did. Unless you were ugly, that was.

Not even ugly: for Catherine, in a strange way, this was enough. In college this past year, it had become clearer to her that boys found her attractive; boys looked at her, they flirted with her, they told her where the parties were going to be. And living with Amy and Lorraine had meant that she had met lots of boys, too. The whole business with Conor they disapproved of; Conor, who was in one of Catherine's English tutorials and over whom she had been stupidly mooning all year, and with whom she maintained a friendship which consisted mainly of him slagging her, and of her thinking of suitable retorts half an hour later.

The problem – although Catherine herself did not see it as a problem – was that she did not want something real. Shifting someone you actually knew; she could not imagine it. How would you look them in the eye the next day? There was just so much – liquid. Slither, that was how she thought of it; slither that had been allowed into the space between you. It was appalling. Undignified. It was way too close a range. And sex: no. Just no. She was not going there; not until she worked it out somehow, how she could do it without dying of shame. Which would involve doing it, obviously, or doing some of it, at least; but this was a glitch in her own logic which Catherine felt perfectly entitled to ignore.

It was the morning after things had finally come to a head with Conor that Catherine had first met James. She had been drinking in the Pav, which was the bar at the back of campus for the cricket players, but in which everyone drank at the end of exams – or indeed, as in the case that evening of Amy and Lorraine, before exams were over. But Catherine had sat her final paper, a disastrous Art History one, and to obliterate the memory of it she had been getting good and plastered, which was hardly the best of ideas when Conor was around. By half past nine, she was slumped in a booth beside him, pulling her oldest trick, the trick she had been pulling unsuccessfully with boys she fancied for years, which was to pretend to fall asleep on the boy's shoulder, and to hope that he would notice, and react by putting an arm around her and pulling her close.

Conor did not put an arm around her. Conor moved away from her, so abruptly that she almost smacked her head on the wood of the booth, and Conor began making jokes about Catherine to the other guys at the table, and Conor reached over and nudged Catherine – who was still, mortifyingly, pretending to be asleep, her head hanging, because she could not think what best to do – and told her that she had to get up, now; that she had to go home. And then Conor was calling Amy over, which was the last thing that Catherine wanted, because she knew that Amy would kill her stone dead for being so pathetic, and sure enough, she opened her eyes and there was Amy with a face like thunder, and there, on Catherine's elbows, was Amy's strong, angry grip.

'Take this kid back to Baggot Street, will you, Ames,' Conor said, 'or put her on a bus or something.'

Catherine pouted, another of her old tricks, with an equally low success rate. 'I don't *want* to go home.'

'I'm not taking her home,' Amy said. 'It's not even ten o'clock.' She shoved Catherine in front of her, in the direction of the tiny bathroom at the front of the bar. 'And my name is not Ames,' she shot back at Conor.

'Whatever, sweetheart,' Conor replied.

'Dickhead,' Amy said, as she poked Catherine in the back. 'Come on, keep going.'

'To do what?'

'To puke, and then to have cold water splashed all over your silly little face by me,' Amy said. 'Are you wearing mascara?'

'I told you, I don't wear eye make-up.'

'Well, that's another thing we're going to need to discuss,' Amy said, as they reached the bathroom, and she pushed Catherine into a cubicle. 'Bend,' she said. 'Think of something that disgusts you.'

'Conor disgusts me.'

'Shut *up* about Conor,' Amy said. 'Think of vermin or something. Worms.'

'I don't have any problem with worms,' Catherine said. 'I grew up on a farm, remember?'

'Shut up about that fucking farm as well,' Amy said.

'Nobody cares that you grew up on a farm. Anyone would think you'd crawled to college straight from the famine, the way you go on. Cows and tractors, for Christ's *sake*. So what? My dad has a ride-on lawnmower. Do you hear me going on about that? No, you do not. Now, come here.' She pulled Catherine closer, so that their faces were inches apart. 'Open your gob.'

'What for?' Catherine whined.

'Open your *mouth*,' Amy said, and when Catherine obeyed, Amy shoved two fingers down her throat, so that it came right up, the lunch from that day, and quite a lot of the cider from that evening.

'That's better,' Amy said, her hand on the nape of Catherine's neck. 'Good girl.'

'I *hate* Conor,' Catherine said, coughing and rubbing at her mouth. 'I *hate* him.'

'Then act like it,' Amy said, and she turned the cold tap on. 'Now you and I are going to get plastered all over again, and when James gets home from Berlin tomorrow, we are going to spend the whole day getting pissed with him, and you are not going to waste another fucking minute of your glorious state of drunkenness talking to Conor Moran. Or even thinking about him. Now splash.' She pointed to the sink, and then, moving to the toilet, she hitched her skirt up and began to ease her knickers down.

'Do you need me to leave?' Catherine said, embarrassed.

'Splash, Catherine, and look lively about it,' Amy said, and she leaned back her head as her loud, easy flow began to come.

*

In Baggot Street all that year, James had been a photograph, blu-tacked to the mantelpiece mirror; in the photo he was all legs, sprawled out on the carpet in front of the couch, with

Amy's arms around his neck, and his hair a mop of red curls and waves and cowlicks; his expression was one of suffering, but in an ironic, delighted way.

Also, James was a set of drawings which every night in her sleep Catherine was keeping pressed like so many dried flowers, without even knowing she was doing so for the first couple of months. If it had not been for a film she and the girls had been watching one night close to Christmas, a film about an artist whose drawings, Amy said, were very like those of James, Catherine might never have known what she was sleeping on, but Amy went into Catherine's bedroom and pulled the large, flat folder out from under the mattress. Lorraine cleared a space on the carpet, moving aside the tea things and the cigarette packets and the *Evening Herald* that had been there for a fortnight, and Amy laid down the folder and opened it up.

Nobody was looking directly at him; that was what Catherine first noticed. He drew with charcoal, in strokes which were careful, which seemed to leave nothing to chance, going after detail – the ring on a finger, the rib of a cuff, the hard skin on an elbow – as though it was something threatened, something which had to be caught and preserved. And yet, for all his obedience to detail, it was the expressions – not just the faces, but the moods and preoccupations travelling through those faces, running under their surfaces like hidden streams – which came up out of the pages torn from a sketchbook and which set going in Catherine an anxiety which she could not understand.

'Nobody knows,' she said then, surprising herself; she had said it before consciously realizing it. 'Nobody knows he's drawing them.'

Beside her, Amy nodded. 'That's what he does. He catches people unawares.'

'He's a little stalker,' Lorraine said. 'A little paparazzi fucker.'

'See this one of Lorraine,' Amy said, and Lorraine gave a protesting wail.

'I have a double chin!'

'No, no, it's you,' Catherine said, taking the drawing. 'I mean, you, except with a double chin.'

'He's a sneaky little bastard,' Lorraine said, reaching for her cigarettes. 'He did not have my permission to do that.'

Catherine looked at Amy. 'Has he done you?'

She nodded. 'Somewhere in there. It was while we were in Irish class last year.'

'She was staring out the window deciding whether or not to give a hand job to Robbie Fox,' Lorraine said.

'Shut up, you,' said Amy, laughing. She went through the drawings more quickly now, lifting them up at the right-hand corner, separating them carefully; about fifteen or so in, she stopped. 'Here I am,' she said, pulling the page out slowly.

'It's lovely,' Catherine said quietly.

'Lovely for Robbie,' Lorraine snorted.

'No, really,' Catherine said, above their laughter. She leaned in to look more closely. It was Amy, in a school jumper, with a tie loosely knotted beneath a shirt collar, sitting with her knuckles pressed to her chin. Lorraine had remembered correctly: she was looking out a window. James had drawn the wooden frame, and an outline of the buildings outside, and he had drawn the small hoop in Amy's right earlobe, and the biro in her hand. As with the other portraits, he had caught something in the eyes, and something about the mouth, which brought on a feeling of – Catherine could only think of it as worry, a kind of unease. Even though this Amy in charcoal, her attention on something outside or on something deep within her mind; even though she looked beautiful, soft-eyed – even for all this, there was something about the portrait that made Catherine feel that it was somehow wrong to be looking at it. Then it struck her: how direct the angle was. James would have needed to have been sitting almost right in front of Amy, only slightly to her right, to capture her like this; he would have needed to have been two desks or so in front of her, and turned fully around.

'How did you not *see* him?' she said to Amy, and Amy just shrugged.

'That's the thing about the way he does them. He has some way of not letting anyone notice him. I don't know how he manages.'

But on the morning James came back to Dublin, Catherine had quite forgotten about him – or rather, Catherine was too preoccupied with other matters to remember that he was coming. The other matters related to the night before, which had ended on Grafton Street not long before dawn, with Conor taking hold of her shoulders and telling her that she was a great chick, a great chick, over and over, while still, so enragingly, failing to actually put his arms around her and hold her, which by that time she had wanted so badly, for so long, that she felt as though she might just vaporize, standing there in front of him, with his useless fingers on her useless skin, or that she might instead just knee him in the balls, which was what she *had* done, come to think of it – she could hear again Amy's voice saying, *Oh Jesus, Catherine* – but not even that successfully, because Conor had stood upright far too quickly afterwards, and he had been pleased, she could see, and now he was gone home to Wexford for the summer, to work in his uncle's pub, and it would be October before she would see him again. About this, she felt miserable, but also relieved: there would be no more of his snideness, no more of his mockery, no more of his moods. She could recall asking him, before they left the Pav for the club – she had not stayed away from him after Amy's lecture in the bathroom, or had managed to do so for only about twenty minutes – for advice on her situation, or indeed non-situation, with her summer job at the *Longford Leader*: since January, she had been meaning to phone the editor and remind him that he had told her, the summer before, to come back when she was in college. But she had not phoned him, for various reasons.

'One reason, Citóg,' Conor had said, when she told him. 'One reason. Visceral fear.'

'I'm not afraid of him,' Catherine had said, delighted, as usual, to hear Conor referring to her with the nickname he had given her. It made no sense; it was the Irish word for left-handed people, and she was right-handed. But she loved it, anyway, and she tingled every time he said it. 'How could I be afraid of him when I don't even know him?'

'Right. Because that's really stopped you being afraid of people before.'

'Fuck *off*.'

Then Conor had dragged someone else into the conversation, had humiliated her in front of someone who was a virtual stranger: Emmet Doyle, a quiet Dublin guy who Catherine knew vaguely from editorial meetings for *Trinity News*. He wrote mostly about dull student union politics, and he dressed in a slightly odd combination of smart shirts and scruffy cords, and his hair fell in soft brown curls around his face, and he blushed whenever anyone spoke to him. The blushing ought to have endeared him to Catherine, who suffered from precisely the same affliction, but instead it irritated her. She wanted men to have faces which showed not a flicker of what was going on in their minds. But now here was Emmet Doyle, blushing, and looking a little bewildered, while

Conor outlined to him the farce of Catherine's inability to call the *Leader* editor, and while Catherine yanked at Conor's arm, and shoved him, and told him to stop making such a big deal out of it, Emmet proceeded, in his nice, polite, South County Dublin sentences, to suggest ways for Catherine to approach the task – what she should say to the editor; how she should make her case.

'I mean, just tell him you have, like, experience, and that you've done news, and that you've done layout, and that you've done different kinds of features and stuff. I mean, you've done stuff for *TN*, haven't you? I've seen your name.'

She shrugged. 'A few—'

'Tell him you got the last interview with Jeff Buckley,' Conor cut in.

'Jeff who?'

'Oh, for Christ's sake, Citóg,' Conor said, putting his hand to his face, and it went on like that, a catalogue of mortification and stupidity, until daylight was hitting the red stones of Grafton Street, and until there was nothing else for it but to go home.

The next morning: a thumping skull, trembling skin, a stomach like seasickness. Amy and Lorraine were at the exam halls, with hangovers of their own for which, they made clear as they were leaving, they held Catherine entirely responsible, and a bag of peas from the freezer was the best thing she could find in the way of relief; she took it back to bed and fell asleep a second time with its coldness pressed above one ear. That sleep was a sinkhole of utter oblivion, in which dreams were out of the question because her body had a great deal of work to do, and when her eyes opened two hours later, what she noticed firstly was that the pain was gone, and secondly, that the noise from the street outside was much louder than it ought to have been, and thirdly, that it was not actually the noise from the streets, but the noise of someone in the sitting room, someone moving around, lifting things and putting them down. Sitting now, they were: the creak of the leather armchair. One of the girls, Catherine thought. Home to kill her for having kept them out until six o'clock in the morning.

'Hello?' Catherine called out, without raising her head from the pillow. 'Hello?'

In response, there was only another sound from the armchair; it protested like that when you sat forward. A shifting, now; the scrape of something on wood.

'Hello?' Catherine called again. 'Who's there?'

The voice shocked her when it came. It was a man's, sharp and wary. 'Hello?' it said, and Catherine heard again the creak of the armchair; he was standing up. 'Hello?'

'Hello!' Catherine said, almost shouting, trying to push authority, a lack of patience for nonsense, into her tone, but her heart was slamming, and she knew she sounded scared. She was sitting upright now, and conscious of the fact that, apart from her T-shirt, she was naked, and that the guy, whoever he was, was walking to the sitting-room door, which was directly across from the door to her room. Her mind scanned the possibilities; Cillian, Lorraine's boyfriend, was already gone to London for the summer, and Duffy, their landlord, had a nasal whine she would know anywhere.

'Who's there?' the voice said, even more sharply this time. He was out of the sitting room now; he was in the hall.

'*I'm* here!' Catherine shouted, angry now.

'Who's I?' he said, sounding equally angry.

'Don't come in, don't come in!' Catherine shouted, and she

knocked the bag of peas to the floor, and the little green orbs scattered, and the door handle turned, and a head topped with red curls and cowlicks appeared.

'You must be Caroline,' was what he said, while Catherine sat there, the duvet snatched up around her, one naked leg sticking out, and the now-thawed peas having spilled onto the carpet below. She stared at him. She stared at his hair, and at his face sandblasted with freckles, at the amused little twist of his thin-lipped mouth. He was wearing a jumper, old-fashioned and patterned in dark greens and greys, and faded jeans, and black Docs, shoes rather than boots, the leather scuffed and scratched. He was fully in the room now, having pushed the door wide open.

'Catherine,' she said, in a tone intended to shame him – she had worked out who he was by now, she had remembered what Amy had said the night before, but still, how dare he just let himself in here? How dare he burst into her bedroom like this, as though it was still his? It was *not* his; it was not his for another couple of days yet, and she was nearly naked, and he was completely out of order, and this was something he needed to realize, this was something for which he needed to make amends—

But James was not paying Catherine, or Catherine's tone, the slightest bit of attention. James was looking around the room, taking in everything Catherine had done to make it her own: her desk, covered now with books and lecture notes and balled-up clothes; her CDs, stacked high on the window-sill; the wardrobe, decorated now not just with his black-and-white postcards, but with things she had put there: a photocopy of a Patrick Kavanagh poem she had loved from her Writing Ireland course; a photograph of her sister Anna with muck on her T-shirt and a scraggy chain of daisies in her hair; a *Muriel's Wedding* poster, showing Toni Collette in a shower of coloured confetti; the picture from the cover of *Beetlebum*, showing the guy or girl or whichever it was lying passed out on a pile of leaves.

He looked to the peas. 'You're getting your greens, anyway, Caroline,' he said. 'That's good to see.'

'Catherine.'

He glanced at her. 'Why, what did I call you?'

'Caroline.'

'Oh, no,' he said, shaking his head as though appalled. 'Oh, no. That's not you at all, at all.'

He stepped over towards her, extending a hand. 'I'm James. I hope Amy and Lorraine told you I was coming.'

'Oh, yes,' Catherine said, as briskly as though they were in a boardroom. 'I'm sorry the place – I mean – I just finished my exams yesterday, you see. I was out – ' She stopped, gesturing by way of explanation at the peas. 'So.'

He burst out laughing, a high, delighted peal. 'Oh, Catherine,' he said, shaking his head again. 'What you do with your frozen vegetables is none of my concern.'

'I need to get dressed,' Catherine said, pulling her leg back under the duvet.

'Right you be,' James said, and he strode towards the door. He glanced back at her.

'Tea?' he said, and he was gone.

Tea, Father, actually; that was what he had said, a perfectly pitched imitation of the mad housekeeper in the sitcom about the three idiot priests. So he was funny, like the girls had said; he was clearly also a bit weird, or lacking normal manners, or something – the way he had just opened her bedroom door like that and let himself in. She took her time about getting dressed, not because she wanted to do it with any degree of care – she could not be bothered to shower just yet, for one thing – but because she wanted to postpone the strangeness, the inevitable awkwardness, of being out there with this guy when nobody else was home. She could have hidden, could have stayed in bed for the rest of the afternoon – what could he do about it? – but she was hungry, and anyway, she was not at all sure that he would not come barging in again, maybe bearing tea, maybe making himself comfortable at the end of her bed, talking her head off for hours. That was another thing Amy and Lorraine had said about him: that he talked. Talked and talked; there was nobody else like him for that, Amy had said, meaning it as a good thing, and Catherine had found herself quite looking forward to meeting him, then, this talkative James. To see what that looked like: a boy who could talk. But now, standing in the mess of her bedroom, buttoning her old flannel shirt and stepping into a pair of shorts she had found at the bottom of her wardrobe, she felt wary. Wary not so much of him, but of herself – how would she handle this? What account would she give of herself? What would he think of her, when she was forced to actually talk to him? But then, it struck her: what did she care? He was a redhead, wearing the wrong kind of Docs and a jumper like something her mother would buy for her father. What did she care what he thought of her? She tied her hair up into a ponytail and headed barefoot down the hall.

'How are you now, Catherine?' he said without looking up, as she came into the kitchen. On the counter, the little transistor radio was going; *Doesn't make it right*, a woman was singing in a kind of wail. Catherine turned it off. James was sitting at the table, leaning over a newspaper, which had not been there earlier that morning; he must have brought it. He pointed to the teapot, to a plate of toast.

'Help yourself,' he said.

'Thanks.'

He clicked his tongue and she glanced at him in alarm, but it was only something in the newspaper, it seemed. He was reading it intently, his cheek pressed into his knuckles.

She sat. The butter was still visible on the toast, which was something she hated; she preferred it melted in completely. Still, she took a slice, and poured herself a mug of tea, and then she sat there, watching him frown over the paper, wondering if she should go to the sitting room and get something to read herself. But maybe that would be abrupt, or something; probably, he was just finishing that one article, and then he would be ready to talk to her. She ate her toast, and she looked around the kitchen, and then she looked at him. Considered him. His hair was longer than it had been in the photograph, and really quite wild; he looked a bit insane. His freckles went everywhere, even behind his ears; his eyes were a light, cold-looking blue. He wore a silver digital watch, and he bit his nails, she could see – the tips seemed buried in the underskin. This made her shudder, the thought of how tender it was there, and just as she was pushing the thought away, his gaze shot up to meet hers.

'You're like a cat we have at home,' he said sharply.

'Sorry,' Catherine laughed, pretending confusion. 'I was miles away.'

'You were not,' he said. 'You were having a good ould look.'

She felt herself blush. 'I was *not*.'

'Arrah, well,' he said, shrugging. 'Look away, Catherine. Sure beggars can't be choosers.'

She laughed again, but he ignored her, turning back to his paper, and really, she thought now, he was a bit bloody rude.

After all, this was her house, at least until Friday, and he was only visiting, and so he should be putting in a bit of an effort, shouldn't he? And yet it was very clear to Catherine that he was not at all interested in talking to her, not trying at all to think of topics for conversation. Instead, here she was, her mind clacking through possibilities like a panicked secretary, instantly discarding each one: too stupid, too boring, too bland, not something she knew anything about. And there he was, turning the pages of his newspaper. Like he was the only one in the world who could read the fucking *Irish Times*.

'So, Catherine,' he said, and he closed the paper swiftly and folded it over. 'Tell me how your year has been.'

'My . . . year?'

He nodded, leaning back in his chair, looking at her encouragingly. 'Have you enjoyed your first year of college?'

Catherine stared at him. How was she supposed to answer a question like that? Was there any need for him to be so blunt? There were other ways in, after all. There was such a thing as small talk.

'You sound like one of my aunts,' she heard herself saying.

He looked taken aback. 'Well,' he said, after a moment, and there was a high, presumably joking, primness in his tone, 'what's wrong with that? I'm sure your aunts are very respectable women.'

'You haven't met them,' she said, nonsensically. What was wrong with her? What was she even saying to him?

'All in good time, Catherine,' James smirked, and he rapped on the table. 'So. College. Tell me. What are your subjects?'

'English and Art History.'

He looked at her more closely. 'Really?'

'Yeah. I know you're—'

'So you know your art.'

'Not really,' Catherine said, which was an understatement; Art History might as well have been Theoretical Physics for all the headway she felt she had managed to make with it this year, and English even more so. It had been a tough year, a year in which most of what she had had to study, and the ways in which she had been expected to study it, had come as a shock. The exams this past fortnight had frightened the life out of her. Probably, she had passed them, but in some cases this would not be by very much; she had written a mortifyingly bad answer to the *Pride and Prejudice* question on her Literature and Sexualities paper, three pages of waffle, mainly about the fact that Darcy had not seemed bothered by Elizabeth's tan. All through school, Catherine had pulled in As and Bs without much effort, but the weeks before these exams had made her realize that she knew hardly anything about, well, knowledge, at all. In school, she had been able to learn reams of stuff off by heart, and to throw it down on paper when necessary, but in college, that was not how the business of learning worked: in college, they expected you to use your mind. Did she even *have* a mind? she had found herself wondering, this year, on more than one occasion. It was so disheartening. To discover that, actually, what you'd had all this time, been praised for all this time – what had got you off the hook all this time – was not, after all, intelligence, but a shallow robotic skill.

'I mean, yeah, I've enjoyed it,' she said now with a shrug. 'Not the fucking exams, though.'

'My God, Catherine,' he said, feigning shock. 'I hope you don't talk like that to your aunts.'

She laughed. There was a pleasure in hearing him use her name; it was so direct. It was somehow a higher level of attention than she usually got from people; almost cheekily personal. Intimate, that was what it was. And yet pulled clear of intimacy, at the last second, by the reins of irony which seemed to control everything he said, by his constant closeness to mockery. She found herself wanting more of it, and she found, too, that it held a challenge: to edge him away from that mockery towards something warmer. To make him see that he was wrong in whatever decision he had made about her, about her silliness, about her childishness, about whatever it was he had, by now, set down for her in his mind.

He yawned. 'Jesus, I'm knackered,' he said, hanging his head.

'Did you have a long flight?'

He looked at her. 'Flight?' he almost spat.

'When you came—'

'I didn't fucking *fly*. I've just spent three days in the cab of a lorry.'

'Three *days*?'

'The driver had to go all over Europe making deliveries.'

'Oh.'

'Holland. Every back road in Belgium. Sleeping in the cab at bloody rest stops. The snores off the fucker. France. And then pegged out on O'Connell Bridge half an hour ago like a Bosnian refugee.'

'Oh.'

'I fucking *wish* I'd had the price of a flight. A friend of my ould fella arranged the lift for me. That's how I got over there in the first place, and it's how I'll be going back. It's free.'

'Oh, well,' Catherine said. 'I've actually never been on a plane.'

He looked at her. 'I can well believe it,' he said.

She felt a blush sting her cheeks. *Fuck off*, she wanted to say, but she had only just met him; she could hardly say that, could she? Or, *How many planes have* you *been on?*, but that would just let him know how much he had bothered her.

She sat there, stewing in her own silence. After a moment, he looked at her and sighed.

'Ah, don't mind me, Catherine. I'm sorry. I'm just grumpy from the journey. It was a nightmare.'

'It must have been awful,' she said, carefully.

'It *was* awful. You'd want to have heard your man, the driver. Blacks, blacks, blacks. Faggots, faggots, faggots. Women. The tits on that. Oh, he says to me, I had a great little Italian whore where you're sitting, right there, the lovely little arse on her. And you know, I was sure she'd give me something, you know, crabs or an oul' itch or something, but no, she was clean as a whistle. Great little girl.'

'Oh my God,' Catherine said.

'Dirty fucker.'

'*Jesus.*'

He glanced at her. 'I hope I'm not shocking you.'

'No!'

'Talking to you about Italian prostitutes and you trying to eat your toast.'

'I've finished my toast,' she said, a little too brightly; she sounded like a toddler, she realized.

'Well, then,' James said, stretching his arms high. 'Let's retire to the parlour, shall we?'

The sitting room was huge and high-ceilinged, with cornices and corner mouldings and a big front window; it was the flat's only remnant of the grandness which must have once been in evidence through the whole house, a Georgian three-storey over a basement, with stone steps sweeping up to the front door. Now the girls rented the ground floor, and two other flats upstairs held what seemed, from the noise levels, a combined population of about twenty people, and downstairs in the basement lived a couple in their thirties, who complained whenever the girls played music too loudly and who acted like martyrs if, on a Monday morning, they had to wheel the other bins out for collection as well as their own.

Duffy, the landlord, was a thin, bald man from somewhere in Westmeath; he drove a black Mercedes and always wore a suit under a shabby raincoat. The rent was due on the first of the month, but he called for it whenever he pleased, and he expected it to be waiting for him, sitting in cash in a little wooden box on the mantelpiece. When he came, he looked around the rooms to make sure that everything was in order, checking the oven, checking the shower, checking in the bed-rooms with an air of long-suffering forbearance.

'You'd want to keep that tidier, now,' he'd say, pointing to some corner of a room, some mountain of clothes or tower of dishes. 'It's not nice, now, to see girls not looking after a place like that.'

Catherine had been nervous around him at first, but had taken her cue from Amy and Lorraine, and now she talked to him the same way they did, in bored-sounding monosyl-lables that provided only the barest minimum of information. Duffy had been pleased to see Catherine move into the room which had been occupied by James; he had not, he had told them, liked to see a 'young fella' living in among girls, and he had not, anyway, liked the look of this particular young fella.

'And he couldn't find work in Dublin?' he had said, when Amy and Lorraine told him that James had gone to Berlin. 'Well, and I suppose he couldn't. The get-up of him. I doubt one like him will get on any better out there, either.'

'Prick,' Amy had mouthed to Catherine across the room.

Now James was checking the rent box for cigarettes; he found none there but came across a packet of Marlboro on the bookshelf. He lit up and took the armchair, kicking his Docs off.

'It's good to be back here, I have to say.'

Catherine, settling on the couch opposite him, nodded. 'I know the girls will be glad to have you home.'

'Can't wait to see them.'

It surprised her, the little twinge of jealousy she felt hearing him talk about Amy and Lorraine this way; she had only just met him, for Christ's sake. And yet she knew what it was, why it made her feel somehow wistful, hearing him talk that way: she herself had drifted away from her schoolfriends, the girls who had been her closest confidantes not even a year ago, and she often envied Amy and Lorraine the way they had remained so close. And now here was James, someone else they had remained close with, and beside the three of them – even though Amy and Lorraine were not yet here, even though it was just her and James – she felt her outsider status very keenly.

'Berlin must have been cool, was it?' she said, wanting to change the subject.

'*Cool*,' he said, imitating her. 'Yeah, it was grand.'

'And did you like your job?'

He smirked. 'You sound like one of my aunts.'

'Very funny.'

James gestured over to Catherine for the ashtray, which was on the floor under the couch. 'Ah, no,' he said, as she passed it over to him. 'I did. Old Malachy is as odd as bejaysus. But the work is interesting. Certainly a lot more interesting than anything I'd have a chance of getting here.'

'How did you get the job?'

He shrugged. 'I wrote to him.'

'Wow.'

He raised an eyebrow. 'Well.'

'And what do you do?'

'I assist, Catherine,' he said, arching an eyebrow. 'Which

means I do everything. Well, Malachy presses the shutter. Most of the time.'

'Amy says he's pretty famous. I haven't—'

He glanced at her. 'You haven't heard of Malachy?'

She shook her head, the blush pricking her cheeks again. Why had she said that? She should have kept her mouth shut and just let him talk; there had been no need to expose her own ignorance like that. But James looked delighted; he was laughing to himself.

'Poor oul' Malachy would take to his bed for a week if he heard that. He thinks he's on every college curriculum going.' He took a drag of his cigarette and exhaled a thin plume. 'There was a piece of his in a group show at IMMA this year, with Wolfgang Tillmans. You didn't see that?'

She shook her head. 'I'm always meaning to go to more stuff at IMMA.'

'Oh, well. And he had a thing at MOMA too, though I presume you didn't see that?'

Catherine opened her mouth to reply, but he talked over her.

'And in September we start getting ready for a big show in Madrid, at the Museo Nacional, and then I think Rome, then Tokyo.' He frowned. 'No. Tokyo first. Tokyo in February. That'll be a fucking nightmare.'

'Do you get to go to all these places?'

'Oh, no. I'm just a studio assistant. He has special slaves to go travelling with him.'

'That'd be *amazing*.'

James winced. 'I'd take being on the road with yer man in the lorry over Malachy any day, to be honest with you.'

'Oh, right,' Catherine said, with a laugh that quickly slid into nervousness, because James was regarding her very closely now. He was stubbing out his cigarette in the ashtray, and staring over at her, and he was smirking slightly, and he was looking her up and down. He nodded to himself.

'Hmm,' he said.

Catherine twitched; her left leg shot out in front of her as though a doctor had tapped her on the knee. 'What?'

'No, no,' James said, as though she was mistaken about something. 'Just thinking.'

'Thinking about what?' she said, sounding breathless.

'I'm just trying to think how our Malachy would do you.'

She lurched sideways, as though he had made a grab at her, and he burst out laughing.

'Oh, I love seeing what people's self-consciousness looks like,' he said, grinning. 'Everyone reacts differently when you point a camera at them. All I had to do with you was mention the idea, and you nearly went through the wall.'

'I did *not*.'

He squinted. 'Still. I can see how he'd do it. Dead on.' He framed Catherine with his hands. 'And very close up. Close enough to see your pores.'

She shook her head vigorously. 'I don't like—'

He waved a hand. 'Nothing to do with it, what you like or don't like.'

'I hate close-ups,' Catherine said. 'I always have spots, or blackheads, or something. And my teeth.' She clamped her mouth shut.

'What's wrong with your teeth?'

She shook her head.

'They work, don't they?'

She shrugged.

'You can chew things?'

'Obviously I can *chew* things.'

'Anyway. He's not interested in people being beautiful. That's not what old Malachy is about. So you can rest easy.'

'Thanks very much,' she said, almost sullenly; she did not like the way this conversation was going. Had he just insulted her? Had he just implied that she was ugly?

'You're welcome,' he said, flashing her a smile. His own teeth were not that great, actually; a bit crooked, and quite yellow. She was suddenly very tired, looking at him; she found herself wishing that Amy or Lorraine would come home now and take over with him; that one of them would come back to relieve her. He filled her with curiosity, but at the same time, there was only so much of this kind of conversation that she could handle with anyone she didn't know well, especially with a boy. She was getting better at it after a year of college, but it was still so difficult for her, having to come up with things to say and then having to come up, immediately, with ways to answer; she felt it like a physical weight. Now, for example, as he sat there, lighting up another of Amy's cigarettes, what was she supposed to say to him? Ask him some more about Malachy's photographs, what they looked like, probably, but she did not trust herself to do this properly: she could not be sure of having the right words. He'd said portraiture. He'd said abstract. There had been some photography in her Twentieth Century course, but she had clearly not paid close enough attention. Are they sad, or are they serious? she thought about asking, but that sounded so simplistic; she imagined James giving her some lecture about the irrelevance of emotion. Were the people Malachy photographed naked? That seemed like something she could ask, maybe, but then that was probably a question that would be asked only by someone who did not understand art at all, someone who was, basically, perving on the idea of naked people.

James pushed out a long sigh. 'So, Catherine.'

She swallowed. 'So,' she said, making a last, desperate grab at a possible topic with which to divert him from whatever it was he was going to say to her. But nothing came. She nodded, as though accepting her fate.

'So,' he said again, winking at her. 'Any fella?'

A sort of dull queasiness washed over her, like a trace of the hangover she had just about shaken off, but it was nothing to do with booze, this feeling. It was to do with something else, and there could be no denying that she had walked herself right into it. This guy, this guy she did not even know, except from a photograph, except from some drawings which were, come to think of it, still under the mattress of her bed; she had let this guy in – or, more precisely, she had let this guy let himself in – and she had got up to talk to him, and she had drunk tea with him, and she was sitting here, now, watching him smoke, and she was wearing these ridiculous shorts that she never wore, that exposed far too much of her legs, and her shirt was not even properly buttoned, and so of course he thought she was up for it; of course he did. She cursed herself. How was she supposed to talk herself out of this corner? She stared out the window, to the oblivious blue sky. From the armchair came a pointed throat-clearing. Out of the corner of her eye, she saw him wave.

'Hello?'

'Sorry,' she said, glancing back to him. 'Sorry, I heard you.'

'So that's a no?'

She swallowed. 'It's just not something I really have time for at the moment, being in a relationship.'

He blew out another plume. 'Ah, sure, who'd have you? The state of your teeth.'

She stared at him in disbelief. 'Oh my God!'

'Ah, sure, you're as bad as Shane McGowan, Catherine, let's face it. Worse again. Half of them broken. The other half rotten.'

'*Fuck* you,' she said, sitting bolt upright. Her heart was thumping. 'Fuck you, you fucking redhead!'

He threw his head back and laughed in huge, heavy peals, his throat long and exposed, his mouth open as though he had turned his face up to the sky to drink in the rain. He roared with laughter. He thumped the floor with the heels of his hands. He inhaled hard, and he dropped his chin, his eyes tightly closed, looking as though he was trying to steady himself, and then he was off again. He could almost have been crying. As soon as that thought struck her, Catherine could not stop seeing what he would look like if he actually was crying; could not but see him in the grip of a sobbing fit. It was so strange. She had never seen a man cry. She was not seeing one cry now, either, she had to remind herself, but still. She felt a weird thrill at the sight of him; a squeamish sense of staring where she was not supposed to stare. When he finally stopped, gasping for breath, sort of moaning, as though it had all been too much for him, this torture she had put him through, she had forgotten what it was they had even been talking about.

But James had not. 'Oh, Catherine,' he said, shaking his head. 'Catherine, Catherine. Your teeth are lovely.' He was picking up his cigarette; he gestured, now, with it up and down the length of her. 'The whole lot of you is lovely. Sure the fellas must be queueing up for you.'

'No,' she said vehemently, and then instantly worried that this was the wrong answer. 'I mean . . .'

'Oh, come on.'

She decided to take a different tack. To sound less available.

'Well,' she said, feigning hesitancy, 'I suppose I have spent the year messing around with someone, but it's nothing, really. Nothing worth talking about.'

'Messing around is good. We like messing.'

'No, really, I don't even mean that kind of messing around. I don't know what I mean, really. I don't mean anything.'

'O-K,' James said slowly.

'No. I mean, it's just someone. It's nothing. Nothing happened. It's no one.'

He raised an eyebrow. 'I don't think you should say any more without the presence of a lawyer.'

'Fuck's *sake*,' said Catherine now; why had she even needed to bring Conor up? She was such an idiot. She was not to talk about Conor. She was not to make an embarrassing situation even worse.

'What's his name?' said James, tipping his ash.

'Conor.'

He shook his head. 'Not a good name.'

'No,' she said, still cringing.

'Forget him.'

'Good idea.'

'We can't have Conors going about the place. Conors are barred from this establishment now. Conors are now the outcasts of society.'

'I feel better already,' she said, laughing, and strangely enough, she realized, it was true.

'Very glad to hear it,' James said with a solemn nod.

'And you?' Her voice jumped high on the question, worrying about the territory into which it might be pulling her, but she had to ask; it was only polite to ask, after he had shown an interest in her love life, her whatever it was.

'What about me?'

'Any nice German girl?'

His eyebrows shot up. 'No,' he said firmly. 'No nice German girl.'

'No not-nice German girl?'

'No not-nice German girl either.'

'Oh, but you'll have to do something about *that*,' she said, trying to borrow the teasing tone he had used on her. 'I mean, when you go back,' she added, hurriedly.

'We'll see,' he said, sounding bored of the subject.

'Oh, come on.'

He looked at her sharply. 'Come on what?'

She stammered. 'I mean, meet someone. You know. German girls, I mean. They're good-looking, aren't they? Blonde.' She took a breath. 'Some of them, like.'

He sighed. 'That they are, Catherine. That they are.'

'*So.*'

'So,' he shrugged, and he stubbed his cigarette out. 'So here we are,' he said, looking at her. He took a deep breath, and Catherine's mouth went dry.

'I . . .'

'Both of us lonely,' James burst into song. 'Longing for . . . something . . .'

And now what the fuck was happening? What was she supposed to do with this? She spluttered out a laugh, just for the sake of getting some other sound out into the room, something other than his weirdly passionate – what was that, a baritone? No, a baritone was lower, gruffer; his must be a tenor voice.

'You can't really sing,' she said, which was not actually true, but she had needed to say something to break the tension, the mortification of him singing at her; she needed him to stop. What was he doing? What was *she* doing? Her mother would kill her – *kill* her – if she could see her right now, if she could know how she had spent the last hour.

'The summer,' he was saying now, having stopped with the singing, at least, but what was he saying about the summer? Catherine blinked at him.

'What?'

'I said, what are you doing with yourself for the summer?'

'Oh,' she said, relieved. 'Going home. Back to Longford. I'm meant to have got a job.'

'*Meant* to?'

She sighed, remembering that she still had not made that phone call. 'I was going to ask the editor of the local newspaper for a job.'

He looked impressed. 'Oh.'

'I've been writing a bit for the college paper.'

'About what?'

'Art,' she said, feeling almost triumphant as she saw the effect this had on him; he pursed his lips as though conceding something. 'And literature.'

'*Literature*,' he said mockingly, and the heat rushed back to her face, but in the next instant, he was nodding approvingly. 'Very good. Very good, Catherine. So that's what you want to do?'

'I think so.'

'Do you write anything else?'

She swallowed. 'Poetry,' she said, and instantly regretted it; his eyes had lit up with something, and she was pretty sure it was scorn. 'I mean, it's shit, obviously.'

He frowned. 'Why obviously?'

'Never mind.'

He was regarding her steadily. 'I think it's a very good thing that you write poetry. A very good thing indeed.'

She squirmed. 'Don't be ridiculous.'

'What's ridiculous about it?'

'*It's* ridiculous. This is ridiculous. My point is, I'm meant to have called up the editor of the local paper at home, I'm meant to have done it six months ago, and I told my mother that I would, and I never did it.' She took a breath. 'And now I'm going home tomorrow, and she thinks I have a job, and I want to have a job, and I don't. And I'm dead when my mother finds out.'

He frowned. 'Is your mother a very violent woman, Catherine?'

She burst out laughing. 'Fuck off.'

'Will she beat you? Will she lock you in the shed?'

'Fuck *off*. I should have done it. I shouldn't have put it off.'

He looked at his watch. 'It's half past two,' he said. 'How many hours behind is Longford?'

She stared at him. 'Oh, very funny,' she said, after a moment. 'Sure you're from Leitrim.'

He shrugged. 'Leitrim's another time zone entirely.'

'*Stop*. It's not funny.'

'Indeed it is not,' he said, and he got to his feet. 'Come on,' he said, reaching a hand out to where she sat, looking up at him.

'Come on what?'

'Come on up,' he said. 'There's a phone in the hall, isn't there?'

'I can't call him *now*.'

'Now is better than tomorrow.'

'No,' she said, shaking her head. 'It's too late. It's months too late. I'm going to have to forget about it.'

'And what? Live all summer on the proceeds of your poems? Come on.'

'*No*,' she protested, as he pulled her to her feet; he stepped back to make room for her, and in the next moment they were standing in the middle of the room, clasping hands. James was looking at her with an expression of resolve beneath the surface of which a fit of laughter seemed to be twitching, but he did not laugh; he did not even smile.

'Number?' he said briskly.

'It's in my room,' she said, with an air of misery.

'Change?' he said, and he rooted in his jeans pocket. 'Here you go,' he said, handing her a fifty-pence piece.

'Oh *fuck*,' Catherine moaned. 'I'm not even dressed.'

'It's a *phone*, Catherine. Come on. We're getting this over with, and then we're going to drink some stolen wine.'

'Some what?'

'From the back of our Eddie's lorry,' he said grimly, as he pushed her towards her bedroom door. 'I think I earned that much. Anyway, I'm fairly sure he was stealing it in the first place.'

As she was finding the editor's number in her address book, a new thought occurred to her. 'I don't want you standing beside me while I'm talking to him,' she shouted out to James.

He appeared at the door. 'You're terrible, Muriel,' he said, nodding towards the poster on the wardrobe.

'Seriously,' Catherine said. 'You're not standing beside me.'

'I haven't the slightest interest in standing beside you,' he sniffed.

'And no listening at the door.'

'No listening at the door? No getting back *in* the door if you don't do what you're meant to do. Now go on.' He pointed. 'And don't come back in here without a job to your name. Do you want our poor children to starve?'

'Oh, God,' Catherine moaned through her laughter as he marched her to the outer hall. 'Why did you ever have to come home?'

*

That night was for all of them. Amy and Lorraine came home from their exams, and they launched themselves at James, whooped and cheered and even cried because he was home, and there were moments when Catherine felt, again, like an outsider as she watched them, as she saw how easy and how happy they were with each other, but that went away; the way that James behaved towards her sent it away. That night was for all of them, cooking dinner together in the house and heading out into the night afterwards, down to Searson's and on to O'Donoghue's and on to dance in Rí-Rá, and stumbling, laughing, home through the streets. And the next day – Catherine postponed her journey back to Longford – was for her and James, wandering around the city, going to IMMA and St Patrick's Cathedral and into the gardens behind Dublin Castle, all the places she had not been to yet, all the places it had not occurred to her yet to go, and through campus, where she felt as though she was showing the place off to him, and on towards the National Gallery, except that they did not end up in the National Gallery; they ended up, instead, in a strange little pub called the Lincoln Inn. And that night was another night for all of them, and the next day was not a day, either, when Catherine felt like taking the train home, and that day she and James stayed in Baggot Street and talked again for hours and hours, and that night was another night of drinking and dancing, and the next day was Friday, and Catherine finally had to face up to Longford, and to the long, empty months ahead, and, feeling really heartbroken, she packed her rucksack, and she said goodbye to the girls, and James said he would go with her as far as Connolly station, that he would help her with her bags. And at the station, as they waited, Catherine said, *I want you to hear something with me; I want you to listen to the lyrics of this song. Listen. Listen.*

——

'Dreams fled away. What's the rest of that line?'

'What line?' James said lazily, from the other end of the blanket.

'You know, from the Thomas Kinsella poem, the one about September.'

'*I* don't know.'

'It was on the Leaving curriculum. You have to have done it. Everyone had to do it.'

'I don't *know*, Reilly. You're meant to be the poet.' He pulled his legs towards him, let them drop back again. She felt him wriggle in closer to her.

'I don't know what's happening to my memory,' she said, trying to ignore her heart, the way it was going faster.

James sighed. 'Dreams fled away. And the fire brought a crowd in?'

'Those are two completely different poems! The second one's Austin Clarke. Did you seriously think that was the line?'

'I don't *know*, I told you,' he said impatiently. 'I don't remember my bloody Leaving Cert homework.'

'When night stirred at sea—'

'Lookit, can you stir over a bit on the blanket there, please, while you're speaking of stirring. I've got far too much of the grass.'

'We need two blankets, really,' Catherine said hopefully.

He made a noise of exasperation. 'Well, I'm not going into the house again. I just got another earful from my mother about this fucking wedding.'

'Really?'

'Yeah. She's still nagging at me to go. And to bring you with me. Fuck's sake.'

'Well, I don't mind.'

'You must be joking.' He sat up; his shadow dropped onto her. 'Whose side are you on?'

'OK, OK,' she said, holding up a hand. 'I just don't want to cause trouble.'

'Trouble?' he almost spat. 'You're not causing trouble. You're helping me out.'

'Well, good, then,' she said uncertainly.

'Good,' he echoed, and seeming satisfied, he sank back down.

*

James, when Catherine had phoned him earlier that week, had announced that she was going to join him at his parents' house in Leitrim on Friday evening and stay for the whole weekend. It was a masterful plan, he declared, because it would mean that he could go down home, which it was about time he did anyway, having been back in Ireland for over a month, and having Catherine with him would mean that he could visit his parents without having to go to the awful neighbour's wedding to which he had been invited, because Catherine's presence would get him off the hook. At the same time, it would mean that the two of them could see each other again, because there was only so much you could talk about on the phone. Catherine lived on the same train line that he would be taking to Leitrim, so they could meet half-way and travel down together, and on Sunday they could leave together again, and she would get off the train in Longford, and he would go on to Dublin.

'So it's the perfect solution,' he said, sounding very pleased with himself. 'God, I would have been great to have around during the Cuban Missile Crisis.'

'I can't come,' Catherine said, hoping that none of the

journalists in the office around her would hear. She covered her mouth with her hand. 'There's no way I could get away.'

'What do you mean?' he said impatiently. 'There's a breaking Longford Missile Crisis, is there? I thought they only let you write the Births and Deaths section?'

'It's not work,' she said, as quietly as she could. 'It's just home.'

James said nothing.

'Hello?' she said, a little desperately. 'I mean, I'd love to. I just wouldn't be able to get away for—'

'Catherine,' James cut across her. 'Not this again. Not this complete shite about your parents. I'm tired of listening to you talking this nonsense. You're not in primary school anymore. You can do what you want.'

'I *can't* just up and go to your house for the weekend. What would I tell them?'

'Why do you have to tell them anything?'

'I just have to.'

'So you tell them that you're going up to Dublin. You *live* in Dublin, remember? You're just visiting Longford for the summer.'

'No I'm not.'

'Sorry? What are you telling me? You've decided not to go back to college?'

'No. You know what I mean. I mean, yeah of course I live in Dublin, but this is my actual home.'

'Catherine,' James said sharply. 'You have a flat in Dublin. As far as your parents are concerned, you have a reason to be in it this weekend. Tell them – I don't know – tell them it's Amy's birthday.'

'I stayed up the weekend for Amy's birthday in May.'

'Lorraine's birthday, then. Lorraine's engagement party. Lorraine's funeral. I don't care. Tell them whatever you have to tell them. Tell them that you're getting the half six train to Dublin, and get yourself to the train station. Then wait for the train passing through *from* Dublin and get on it. I will be on it. I will be keeping a seat for you.'

'I don't know, James. Someone might—'

'Pat Burke? You're not using the Pat fucking Burkes of the world to get out of this, Reilly. I want to see you on that train. I will see you on the train. In fact, just to make absolutely sure that you get on the train, I will see you on the platform in Longford. Never before in the history of this country has that sentence contained such excitement and anticipation.'

'I don't know,' Catherine had begun to say. But James had hung up.

When she got off the phone, she went into the kitchen, where Anna was filling in a colouring book at the table while their mother stood at the sink, rinsing lettuce and radishes for a salad.

'You were talking on the phone an awful long time,' Anna said without looking up from her page.

'Was I?' Catherine said, glancing at her mother's back.

Anna nodded, a twist of distaste suddenly taking over her face; it looked almost grotesquely adult on her little features. 'How the hell can you have that much to say to anyone?'

Catherine burst out laughing; it was so clearly a mimicry of something their mother must have said while the phone call was going on. Now her mother said Anna's name sharply, but she did not glance with a grin at Catherine, her eyebrows raised, the way she did whenever they both heard the child say something funny or precocious or endearing. She kept her back turned, looking out the window at the lawn, or at the meadows, or at the hedgerow or at the sky; at the young calves, bucking and leaping, or at the plastic swing, drifting, or at the white garden chair, upturned by Anna or by a gust of wind. Catherine had left a book out there, she remembered; she went out to bring it in.

In truth, it was not just the question of how to get to Carrigfinn for the weekend which bothered Catherine; it was also the question of what going to Carrigfinn for the weekend meant. Days with him. Nights with him, without the company – the buffer – of the girls. That day in Dublin, the Pat Burke day, they had hugged goodbye at the station, and Catherine had wondered if she was meant to understand it, what was going on between them. Because something was going on. She felt so close to him already by that stage, and the phone calls that followed confirmed it; the way James spoke to her during the phone calls confirmed it. The directness. The openness. That first afternoon in Baggot Street, it had shocked her a little, to hear him talk about how much he was looking forward to seeing Amy and Lorraine again, about how he could hardly wait to see them; outside of television, she had never heard a boy talk so sincerely, so emotionally, before. She had actually squirmed, listening to him. If he had been joking, if he had been being ironic, that would be one thing, but this was not irony; this was a strange, unafraid openness. And now, during their phone calls, it was the same, and again, she felt herself wanting to scuttle away from it somehow; from the way he told her that he missed her, that he wanted to see her, that he wanted to have her company again. Always she listened for the irony, for the trace of mockery, but it was never there; he was serious. He was saying aloud the stuff that, Catherine now realized, she had always thought you were meant to keep silent.

And of course the real irony was in her own reaction. Because she had wanted this, for so long, or had believed she wanted it; she had spent so long trying to get close to various boys in this way. And now she had it, apparently. Now she had someone who talked like this to her. And what was she meant to do with it? Because James was not her type. The way he talked so much. The way he looked. The red hair, clumped, untamed. The freckles like cowshit spatters. The clothes: baggy jumpers, worn-down Docs, navy socks ribbed and faded, jeans bunched in with a canvas belt. He was grand, he was fun to talk to – but beyond that, no. And yet, she was enjoying him so much, so much more than she had enjoyed anyone before. She felt her brain grow, talking to him. She felt herself wanting to live her life so much more fully. There had been nobody like this for her before. So did that not mean something? After all, what did she really know? Of it, of being with someone, of being – was this what it was? – in a relationship with someone, of actually being in love, instead of just thinking you were? Instead of all the things she was, by now, so accustomed to doing: storing up every sighting of them, counting the moments of eye contact as though they were coins, as though they could get you somewhere, buy you passage to somewhere? This was not how it was with James, and so maybe this, after all, was what it was meant to be like. Maybe she had misunderstood this, as she had misunderstood so many things, all these years. That first night he had phoned her, the excitement and gladness she had felt at hearing his voice had unnerved her, and she had heard it in his voice, too – and something more in his voice, as well: a kind of relief. A relief that she was glad to hear from him. And what did that mean?

It was Lorraine's birthday, she told her mother, and Amy was throwing her a small party; at 'small party', her mother shot Catherine a look which made clear not just that she did not believe her, but that she was disappointed that Catherine, in lying to her about her reasons for going to Dublin for the weekend, would come up with so pathetic an offering. But getting her mother to believe that she would be staying in Baggot Street until Sunday evening was all that mattered. She left the *Leader* office at six, and walked to the station, and she watched as the half six train to Dublin departed, and she sat and waited for the one coming in the other direction. As it pulled in ten minutes later, James was standing with his head out the carriage door, waving; Catherine was immediately mortified. He looked insane. He was doing, she knew, some kind of regal wave; pretending to be royalty arriving into Longford. She saw people on the platform notice him, raise their eyebrows at him warily, or with bafflement, or in outright disgust. A man in the uniform of the train company shook his head slowly as he waited for the carriages to come to a stop. He put a hand to James's door.

'That's not safe,' he said.

'He's—' Catherine started to say, coming up next to him, but she was interrupted by James, leaping out of the carriage to hug her, all arms and tightness and laughter and saying her name, over and over. Her name.

'Hi,' Catherine said, her voice a high-pitched, awkward trail.

'Can you let these people behind you on there, please,' the Iarnród Éireann man said angrily.

'Oh, we're getting on as well,' James said, still with his arms around Catherine.

'Well, will you make up your mind, please,' said Iarnród Éireann.

'James,' Catherine hissed.

'Oh,' he said, squeezing her again. 'It's so good to see you.'

From beside them, a click of the tongue. 'For *fuck's* sake. Fuckin' . . .'

Carrigfinn was a farmhouse, whitewashed with black window-sills, a lawn stretching out in front of it. A long tarmacadam drive came down to meet the lane.

'God, I was always so jealous of people who had tar-macadam around their houses when I was a kid,' Catherine said as they walked through the gates. 'They could cycle or do roller-skating or whatever they liked.'

'Really?' James said, considering this. 'Well, we don't have any roller skates, but feel free to cycle around the house all weekend if you like.'

'Ha ha.'

'There's the ould fella. Tidy yourself up a bit.'

'What?' Catherine said, alarmed.

'I'm *joking*, Reilly, for crying out loud.' He raised a hand. 'Well, Daddy!' he called.

A man turned from the garage door, which he was paint-ing, Catherine now saw, covering its brown planks over with a vivid green.

'Ye got this far,' he said, putting his brush carefully down and coming towards them. He was tall, with a head of white curls; he wore a pair of navy overalls smeared in several places with green, the sleeves rolled up. His arms were tanned. He came a few steps towards them and stopped, one hand on his hip, the other reaching out, she saw with a jolt of shock, to James.

'Well,' he said, as James, repeating the same word, went right up to him and planted a kiss on his cheek. His father's hand stayed on James's shoulder a moment, held the bone of it, then fell away.

'We got a lift out with Fidelma McManus and the mother,' James said, stepping back to where Catherine stood.

'Jaysus, I hope you had plenty of news for them,' his father said with the trace of a smirk. He nodded to Catherine. 'Hello.'

'Hi, Mr Flynn,' Catherine said, sounding yappy and absurd. 'Nice to meet you,' she added, in a cooler tone.

'Who's this lassie?' he said to James. 'Tell her not to be calling me names like that.'

'This is Catherine, Daddy,' James said. 'Catherine, this is my father, Mick.'

'Very nice to meet you, Catherine,' his father said, and they shook hands.

'Catherine lives with the girls above in Dublin.'

His father made a face. 'What girls?'

James made a noise of exasperation. 'You know what girls, Daddy, for fuck's sake. The girls I went to school with. Amy and Lorraine.' He rolled his eyes at Catherine, who tried to laugh. 'What girls,' he shook his head.

His father shrugged. 'Ah, sure,' he said, and he winked at Catherine. 'Sure I can't keep track of you.'

'You can keep track of what you want to keep track of,' James shot at him.

'And where are you from, Catherine?'

'You went far,' he said drily to James, when she told him. He looked back to the garage door. 'And what do you think of my labours?'

'You're turning the place into a post office, is it?'

It was true: it was that kind of green.

'Ah, get in to your mother and don't be annoying me,' his father said, swatting a hand to send him away.

James's colouring was from his mother, Catherine saw. Peggy. Her accent was almost Northern; that singing affection in her

65

words. She had a kind face, and when she saw James she put her arms around him, just the way James had done to Catherine at the train station, and when she was introduced to Catherine, she put her arms around Catherine too. They were just in time for dinner, most of which Peggy spent playfully upbraiding James for not having come down from Dublin to see her and his father sooner, and for hardly ever phoning them, and for not having sent her any postcards from Berlin.

'What in the name of Jesus do you want with postcards from Berlin?' James said, his mouth full.

'Well, I'd just *like* them, Jem,' his mother said.

'You've enough rubbish coming into the house as it is,' James said. 'All your bloody catalogues and everything.'

'Oh, Catherine,' Peggy said, looking to her with a face of mock dejection. 'He's an awful boy.'

'He is,' Catherine laughed.

'An awful, awful child. I don't know where we got him, I'm telling you. All the rest of them are as pleasant as can be.'

'Ah, poor mother,' James said, getting up from his chair and putting his arms around her shoulders; he buried his face in her neck. 'You're an awful bollox, do you know that?'

'Oh, Catherine,' Peggy said now, laughing, her eyes wet. 'Do you see what I have to put up with?'

'Ah, you love it,' James said dismissively, kissing her hard on the temple; he slipped back into his chair.

'Oh, God help me,' Peggy said, still laughing, and she pointed to the plate of vegetables in the middle of the table. 'Catherine, pet, help yourself there, won't you now.'

'Oh, by the way, Mammy,' James said, scraping with a knife at the pat of butter, 'I can't go to Edel's wedding now. Catherine is here.'

'Ah, Jem!' his mother said, putting her cutlery down. 'Sure you can't do that. Sure you can bring the wee girl. Sure they'd all be delighted to meet her.'

James shook his head, not looking up from his plate. 'Catherine hates weddings,' he said. 'I can't do it to her.'

'Ah, Jem,' his mother said with a sigh, and that was it; the matter was closed.

Dreams fled away. She just could not think of the rest of that line, but anyway, it did not matter; anyway, within an hour or so, with James's parents gone off to the wedding, Catherine had other things to think about. She and James had lain out on the lawn for another while, and then James had suggested a walk down to the canal, and it was down by the canal that things became clear – finally, as Catherine thought of it afterwards, although at the time, this clarity did not feel like anything which was continuous with the things which had gone before. At the time, it felt like swimming, which was not something Catherine had ever been able to manage – her arms got tired, and her legs moved wrongly, and her breath got trapped inside her body and thumped its frightened wings – which was to say that at the time, it felt like drowning. What did it matter, she snapped at herself afterwards, whether she felt like drowning, or whether, indeed, she drowned, when it was James who was struggling, James who was speaking, James who was pushing the words out with that strained, clipped sound?

A boat was moving into the lock as they reached the canal, a gleaming white cruiser, on its deck a tanned and patient family – mother, father, two young girls – speaking French, and pointing at the rush of water, and wearing orange life jackets high and blocky on their bodies. Catherine and James waved at them, and smiled at them, and then for a while they sat on the stone bank to watch them, legs hanging down over the lock as the boat rose up below. The children were shouting, and the father was nodding, and the mother was busy with something close to the boat's controls. The released waters plummeted in from the other side, like so many eaveshoots giving up their store of rain.

'Daddy's giving you the eye,' James said.

Catherine glanced at him. 'What?'

'Your man, Catherine,' he said drily. 'Not my poor ould fella. Jesus Christ.'

'Oh,' she said, laughing. She looked down to the Frenchman; he was occupied with one of the children.

'No, he's not,' she said, but as often happened whenever she became aware of a man's attention, or even of the possibility of it, her hands went to her hair; she fixed her ponytail.

'Oh, yeah,' James said with a smirk. 'And *Maman* is not too happy about it, I can tell you. Look at her, shooting daggers at those long legs of yours.'

Catherine blew out through her lips. 'Don't be ridiculous. Sure her legs are miles longer than mine anyway.'

'Look, look,' James said out of the side of his mouth, and it was true, the man was gazing up at her now, his hands on his hips. The woman said something to him, and he busied himself with something on the side of the boat.

'Now, Reilly,' James said, nudging her. 'Bloody homewrecker, that's what you are.'

'Stop,' she said, laughing.

'You know, you don't keep your eyes open at all, Catherine,' he said, and he sat back from the edge of the bank, pulling up his knees and leaning against them. 'So you don't.'

Catherine shrugged. 'It's not really *worth* noticing that kind of thing.'

'Is it not?'

'To be looked at by some old French guy I've never seen before and will never see again? Big deal.'

'It is a big deal, if you ask me.'

'How?'

James just stuck out his lower lip.

'*How?*' Catherine said again. 'I mean, look at his wife.' She pointed down to the woman, who had dropped now to her hunkers and was winding the ropes, her legs brown and strong, her sunglasses pushed up on her blonde hair. 'I mean, if that's what he's into, then he's not going to be into me.'

He rolled his eyes. 'Oh, for Christ's *sake*, Catherine.'

'What? I'm nothing like her.'

'You're a woman,' he said flatly.

'I'm not a woman.'

'You're not a woman?'

'I'm a girl.'

He shook his head impatiently. 'Makes no odds.'

'Well, I don't agree.'

'Well,' he said, and now his tone seemed almost angry, 'you have the luxury of not having to agree.'

Startled, she attempted a laugh. 'What's got into you?' She nudged him. 'James?'

'Nothing's got into me, Catherine,' he said, his voice thick with something. 'Nothing at all.'

He got to his feet, and she followed him, confused and embarrassed; what had she done? Was he pissed off with her for being so naive, the way Conor had seemed so often during the year, making snide allusions to her virginity, giving her the full force of his derision when she had got something wrong? But James was not like that – but was he? What was he to her, really? she found herself worrying again, as she got into step beside him; what was this? Being down here with him had done nothing to quieten the questions that had been bothering her. She was alone with James. She had been alone with him several times that day. Now here they were again, side by side, shoulder to shoulder, on a beautiful day, sunlight glinting on the water, the sky giving them its acres of blue – so was this something? She could not get a handle on it. Was this *them*? Suddenly she felt the urge to laugh, although nothing was funny. The word *this* was slamming itself against her consciousness; *This! This! This!* bouncing off the walls of her mind, and when James stopped, now, and began to turn to her, she stopped in her tracks, panicked. Was this how it happened? If he tried to kiss her, she thought, she would want to throw herself into the canal. It would be like one of her uncles, turning to her. And yet what else had she brought it to, this thing between them? Coming down here. Talking to him, confiding in him, the way she did. If this was happening now, who was she to refuse it? Who was she to dispute it? This must be how it happened.

'Catherine,' James said, and she jumped. He noticed, and burst out laughing.

'Are you all right?' He reached out and took her arm; she felt it twitch.

'Sorry,' she said. 'I was just . . .'

'Are you worried I'm going to murder you?' he said, and he moved his hands to her neck. 'Oh, Catherine,' he said, grinning, shaking his head. 'I'm sorry. I'm so sorry to have to do this to you—'

'Stop,' she said, managing to laugh; she felt paralysed by the sensation of his fingers at her throat.

He moved away from her. 'You're very jumpy.'

'Am I?'

He sighed, putting his hands in his pockets. 'Listen, Catherine. There's something I need to say to you.'

She inhaled sharply, and he looked at her, his gaze suspicious – but something else in it, too; something like hurt.

'Sorry, sorry,' she said. 'It's just – it's so fucking hot, isn't it?'

He shrugged. 'It's warm.'

'Well, I'm hot,' she said, almost panting.

'Catherine,' he said, hunching his shoulders high. 'You know the way I was saying to you earlier, about my mother really liking you?'

She nodded; on the way down to the canal, he had told Catherine how taken his mother was with her, how she had really, really wanted him to bring Catherine as his guest to the neighbour's wedding. Catherine had laughed it off, uncomfortable, but he had insisted; his mother was really crazy about her, he had said. It had been a relief to be able to change the subject to the French family and their boat, but then that, in turn, had become something uncomfortable, and now this, whatever it was. Under her arms and on the palms of her hands, Catherine felt sweat collect.

'Oh, your mother is so lovely,' she said, nodding eagerly. 'Your whole family. I mean, the ones I've met, and I'm sure the others, as well—'

'And in her head, you know, Catherine, my mother will already have us married off.'

Something punched its way out of her, some incredulous, horrified noise. It sounded like a laugh, sort of, she told herself; it had not been a laugh, but it might pass for one. She might get away with it. The sky, the grass verge, the glint of the canal waters seemed, for a moment, to spin.

'That's ridiculous,' she said, laughing more normally. She waited for James to return the laugh, but he just shook his head.

'I've seen the way she looks at you. I could hear the two of you downstairs this morning, chatting away a mile to the dozen.'

'It was just small talk, for Christ's sake,' Catherine said, in her tone now a kind of pleading. What the fuck was happening? 'She was asking me about my family.'

He nodded curtly. 'She likes family. She likes new generations.'

'Oh, well. I mean, your eldest brother is married, isn't he? And Breege is practically engaged, your mother said.'

'Oh, yeah,' he said grimly. 'All doing their duty.'

'Well, then.'

'No, no, my mother is delighted with you,' he said, giving her a strange, unreadable smile. 'I can see it very clearly. She's looking forward to the day.'

Catherine took a breath; raggedly, it found its way through her, and raggedly, it pushed out again. What was happening could not, surely, be happening, she told herself; they were eighteen years old – well, James was nineteen, but nineteen was *young*, too young – and they had met not even two months ago – and she did not, did *not* think of him that way – so this could not be happening, *could* not – but what had she stumbled into, what had she caused? *This! This! This!* was beating inside of her, a pummelling in her blood; and what was that way he was, now, looking at her? What was that look in the blueness of his eyes? It looked like anger, looked almost like hatred, but he could not, surely, hate her – not if he was bringing this up with her, not if he was trying to haul this future down on top of her; but was that what he was doing? Was that possible? Was this some kind of hallucination, some voodoo?

'But I'll never be getting married, Catherine,' James said then, and he shook his head.

'Oh, Jesus, me neither,' Catherine practically shouted.

James held up a hand to dismiss this. 'Oh, no, you will, you will of course,' he said, clicking his tongue. 'Of course all that will happen for you.'

'No, no, I never want to get married,' Catherine said, feeling the need to stamp it truly down. 'I want my freedom. And I can't see myself ever meeting that person. You know?'

Then came a laugh, the very thing she had been wanting from him, but it was not the light laugh she had hoped for; it was hollow. It was hard. 'Oh, yes, Catherine,' he said. 'I think I know what you mean.'

Better not to speak at all, she decided now; nothing she could come up with could work for her, none of her words could carry her through. She had never known confusion like this; it had such infuriating depths, so many levels opening and sliding into one another. James was seething, it seemed to her; he was rigid, beside her, with a darkness that appeared to have come upon him from nowhere, and she was its landing ground, it seemed – or, maybe, she was its cause? It was in his eyes, and it was in the set of his shoulders, and it was in the lock of his jaw, and she saw all this, and she wanted to run from it, wanted to protest; how had she provoked it?

'All of this is a way of saying something, Catherine,' James blurted.

'Yes?' she said, her heart pounding.

'It's a way of saying I won't be giving my mother a wedding. I'm not that kind.'

'OK,' she said, dumbfounded.

He looked at her. 'I'm . . . different,' he said slowly.

'OK.'

'So that's how it is.'

She nodded; a rapid one-two. She knew but she did not know. She knew but she could not trust herself. She was so often wrong. She was so often sloppy, melodramatic, blurting her exaggerations like a fool.

'OK,' she said again.

James bit his bottom lip, pressing the teeth in hard. 'I decided a while ago that I wanted to tell you, but there was never the chance – over the phone wasn't right.'

'Oh God,' she said, picturing the front room at home, the cord across the hall. 'Of course not. No, no.'

'So I asked you here.'

'Yes.'

'Because I feel so close to you. And because I wanted to tell you in person.'

'Oh, yeah! I'm so glad you told me, James. I'm so glad . . .'

'You're not the first person I've told, obviously.'

'Obviously,' she said, feeling, despite herself, a little offended.

'I mean, Amy and Lorraine know. I told them a few weeks ago.'

'OK!' she said, nodding, desperately trying for the right note of brightness. 'OK!' she repeated, and she sounded like some annoying bird.

'Of course, they said they already knew.' He laughed properly for a moment. 'Fuckers.'

'Ha!' Catherine said, with the same stupid brightness.

'But the big thing for me now, you see, is to tell my mother. Because she doesn't know, needless to say. And I think it's time for her to know.'

'Oh—' Catherine started, but James shook his head to indicate that he did not want her to speak.

'I've been needing to tell her. This weekend has just confirmed that for me. The way she's been around you. You know? It's time.'

'OK.'

'And it's not going to be pretty, Catherine,' he said, kicking at the dust of the path as he walked. 'I know that much.'

'Ah, no,' Catherine said quickly. 'Ah, James.'

'No, no,' he said firmly. 'I know that much. She's not going to take it well.'

Catherine swallowed. She tried to find the right thing to say, and when it came to her, she felt a rush of gratitude. 'But your mother is so *brilliant*,' she said, taking James's arm. As she said it, she was picturing Peggy as she had been at the kitchen table that morning, cigarette in hand, gold bangles jangling, freckles on the bridge of her nose, the V-neck of her cotton top. That was a nice top, a modern top, a top that not many women Peggy's age, Catherine thought, would wear. None of this she said to James; none of this could be helpful to him. But still, she said again, she was sure that his mother would be fine. Would, she said again, be *brilliant*.

He shook his head. 'I don't think so, Catherine.'

'But *why*?' Catherine felt almost stung; this seemed to her, suddenly, like a battle she wanted to win. 'Why do you say that? Initially, maybe, she'll be surprised. But she's so *great*, James. She's so mad about you.'

'How she is *now* is not what we're talking about, Catherine,' James said, snatching his arm away from hers, and his tone was as sharp as she had ever heard it. He stepped ahead of her, his hands shoved in his pockets again. 'How she is *now*,' he said over his shoulder, 'is not the problem. The woman she is now is a woman who is seeing her son in a certain way. With you, for instance – well, I've told you.'

'She was just being friendly to me, for Christ's sake!'

He stopped and looked back at her. For a moment she thought she saw tears in his eyes. But no, he was not crying. He was grimacing. He looked truly disappointed in her; he looked utterly sick of her. He sighed, staring past her now to the fields on the other side of the water. 'Maybe I should never have let her believe even as much as she does.'

Catherine said nothing. Tears of her own were ready to start up, given half a chance, she suspected; she did not trust herself to speak.

'I mean, all of this, can't you see, all of this – the way she sees the two of us, the way she's so delighted with you – all of this, Catherine, is *why*.' He shook his head, and it was not dampness she had seen in his eyes, Catherine realized; it was pain.

'James,' she said weakly.

'You know, I was always close to Amy – you know that.'

She nodded. He had told her that Amy had been his best friend all through the last years of school; he had told her how, since Amy had started college and he had gone to Berlin, they had grown apart a little, and that this had been sad for him, but that it had felt natural. And anyway, he had said, now he had her. Now he had Catherine. Catherine had not allowed herself to think it through, what James had meant by this. Catherine, like the frightened child she was, had not allowed herself to ask. Now she felt a stab of envy at the thought of how much better Amy would have been at handling this situation, this conversation; how much better, it struck her, Amy very possibly already had been. Had he told Amy and Lorraine that he wanted to tell his mother? Probably. And probably they had not reacted anything like this; probably, they had reacted with common sense and calmness.

'And, you know, I think my mother had ideas about me and Amy too, is what I'm saying, but it didn't matter so much back then,' James said. 'We were kids. And Amy was never out here with me, not the way you are now.'

'OK,' Catherine nodded.

'I suppose what I'm saying is that I've never had to see the way my mother looked at a girl before now. At the way she looked at me with a girl, I mean.'

'Right.'

'And so, *no*. No more. It's bad enough. I'm nineteen years old, Catherine. I have to put a name on it. I need her to know.'

'Of course you do,' Catherine said, and she reached out to touch him, but could not land on the right place; every part of him seemed to be some kind of force field. She let her hand go to the top of his arm, near where she had seen his father touch him the day before; she rubbed him there. He seemed to start at the feeling of her hand on him, as though he had not known it was coming, but then he relaxed. But then he sighed heavily, so maybe it was not relaxation at all; maybe it was exhaustion.

'I'm scared shitless about it, to tell you the truth,' he said, shaking his head.

'It'll be all right,' she said, and she closed her fingers around his shoulder as she had seen his father do, and she thought he might come to her for a hug then, but he stayed where he was.

'It'll be all right,' she said again, and with that, he seemed to decide something, and he nodded, once, briskly, and he took a step ahead.

'So now for you,' he said.

'Well,' she said, working to keep her voice steady; to keep it cheerful, even. 'I'm glad you – I'm glad.'

He nodded. 'Me too. I felt it was important. I felt it was time.'

'It *is* time,' she nodded eagerly. 'It *is* important.' If she just repeated the words he used himself, she thought, if she just bounced them back to him, then surely she could not go far wrong. *First, do no harm.* Because what she had to concentrate on, she felt now, so strongly, was her face; what she had to put all her work into was the expression in her eyes, was the business of what she was doing with her mouth. Smile. Smile. Breathe through her nose – not too deeply, not like she was fighting for it. Widen her eyes; force them full of brightness. Show none of the riot going on inside; the bafflement, the confusion with all its stupid roars and plummetings, the astonishment, this weird temptation to stare. Show none of the fact that *This! This! This!* had now become *Gay! Gay! Gay!* – because that was wrong of her, utterly wrong. Nothing was more urgent now than to keep all of this out, to keep her face soft with calm and with intelligence and with openness, the face of someone wiser, someone better, the face of someone that she wanted, so badly, to be. He was reading her; he was watching her face for the story of how he would be received – for the story, almost, of what he was. And she would not give him a face by which he could justify a tone any darker than the one in which he was speaking to her now. She was Amy, she decided in that moment. She was Lorraine. She was able. She was knowing. She was for telling; she was for trusting; she was for shelter and for comfort and for relief. Still it banged in her brain, and silently she roared it away, because she should not even be thinking it, should not even be seeing it; she should just be seeing James, her friend, her best, best friend, and now he was walking, and Catherine was following, and the stone of the canal bank was so weathered and bird-stained and grey, and it led on to a path trodden down through this grass by who knew how many feet over who knew how many years.

*

Still, she was excited. There was this feeling – and she was far from proud of it – of having been given something. Or rather, of discovering that she'd had something all along, without realizing it; like those priests in Dublin who'd had no idea that the painting in their dining room was a Caravaggio. She had never before known anyone who was gay. Nobody real. Nobody Irish, really, other than David Norris, the senator who had fought for the law to be changed, and it was not as if Catherine actually *knew* him. It had almost been a fantasy – a fantasy upon a fantasy – men who were not just loving, but so loving that they were able to love other men. Ridiculous, of course, but that was how she had thought of it; that was how she could not help thinking of it now. Feeling so warm towards James as he walked beside her; feeling such tenderness for him, such – it felt almost like gratitude. Because now – now what? Now she had one of her own? There it was, her own shallowness, and it was so depressing, and it was something that James could not know. That she was not good. Not – what was it? Not neutral. Not this solid ground for him, not for him this safe, trustworthy shore.

But this was something he would not know.

And anyway, maybe she could snap out of it. Maybe, when the novelty faded, maybe then she would become a better friend. Not this silly tourist, trotting beside him up the lane, trying not to stare.

He was talking about David Norris now, she realized; or rather, about that summer, four years previously, when the decriminalization had gone through. He had been fifteen then, and going into his Junior Cert year, and it had been hell, he told her; it had been horrible. Everyone around him talking about it, jeering about it, in school, on the school bus, in the shops in town, at the church gates, and on the radio programmes, especially on the radio programmes – listening to everyone else talking on the subject, it seemed endlessly, it seemed everywhere you turned, and being petrified that they would work out, somehow, that they were talking about you. That you were one of them.

'Exhibit A,' he said, as they reached the gates, and for a moment she thought he was talking about the house, or about his father's freshly painted garage door, the vivid greenness of it, which was the thing which had caught her eye, making her think back to the babbling innocence of the night before; but he was talking about himself, she realized.

'But nobody found out,' she said, to try to comfort him, seeing immediately then what a stupid thing this had been to say. 'I mean, then,' she said hurriedly. 'I mean, nobody found out before you wanted them to.'

'No, they did not, Catherine,' he said, crossing to where they had left the blanket on the lawn; he gathered it up and tucked it under his arm, handing her a glass to carry into the house. 'No, they did not. I made damn well sure of that.'

'Well, then,' she said, uncertainly, as they passed under his mother's painted arch.

Then they had a night that Catherine would remember, she thought, until the day she died. Nothing much happened, except that everything was perfect. The night was perfect: it was warm enough to sit outside, and the sky was on fire as the sun went down, and then it was the coming of a delicate blanket of stars. James's mother had left stuff for dinner in the fridge for them, and they made it together; Catherine fried steaks on the pan and James went out to the vegetable garden for salad things and came in with lettuce and scallions and radishes, caked with dry muck, and, from his mother's greenhouse, tiny tomatoes which were a deep, shining red, and sweeter than any tomatoes Catherine had tasted before. In the dining-room cabinet, James found a bottle of wine.

They ate outside. As he filled their glasses, a tractor passed on the main road below. It was travelling fast; someone in a hurry to get home. Out of habit, Catherine craned her neck to see.

'What the fuck are you looking at?' James said, following her line of vision.

'Tractor!' Catherine said, in the tone she and her sister had always used at moments like this: it was the tone in which other people might shout 'Fire!' It was an old joke between them. Now James stared at her.

'OK, darling,' he said, shaking his head slowly. 'Now we're going to have to give the doctor a call, and have a little chat with him about your tablets.'

She laughed. 'It's a thing Ellen and I used to do. When we were younger, and at home during the summer; we had a thing for men in tractors. Young guys, obviously. Boys. Not ould fellas. We weren't that desperate.'

'Ah,' James said, nodding. 'I see.'

'When one of us would hear a tractor coming up the lane, we'd roar out to the other, and the two of us would race to our viewing spot.'

He whooped with laughter. 'Your *viewing* spot?'

'Yeah. This bit of high ground behind the hedges at the front of our house. In the rhubarb patch. The two of us would crouch down there and look out through the hedge. It was the perfect height for spotting someone in a tractor cab.'

'My *God*. The planning that went into that.'

'Oh, yeah.'

'I mean, meticulous. I mean, military precision, Catherine.'

'A fine art.'

'I love it,' James said, biting into one of the tiny tomatoes. 'Of course it's true, too. You can't beat a young fella in a tractor cab.'

'You can not,' Catherine said, and she felt again the thrill of this new state of being between them. She marvelled at it; how much they had now – and how much more, stretching out ahead.

'Oh God, there are *so* many fellas I want to show you,' she said, sitting up in her chair with the force of the excitement. 'Honestly, James. I can't *wait*. All the spotting we'll do.'

'Yes, indeed,' James said, reaching for his glass. 'Rhubarb patch, here we come.'

'But in Dublin, I mean, in college, and . . .' Catherine shook her head. 'It's just so brilliant, James. It's just . . .'

The wine was at her already, she knew; it was the reason she was gushing at him like this. But she was glad of it. It was allowing her to move. It was giving her the words – or at least, some of them – which had refused to come to her before. 'And there must be guys you want to show me,' she said, reaching across for him; she squeezed his hand – which was not, either, something she would have felt able to do before. 'I can't wait to see them. I mean, who are you into? At the moment?'

'Oh, *into*, Catherine,' he said drily, and it felt almost like he was mocking her; she blinked at him for a moment, uncertain. 'Who am I *into*?' he said again, staring at the salt cellar.

'Yes,' she said, trying to sound encouraging. 'There must be someone.'

James's mouth twitched, but he did not speak. After a moment during which Catherine began to panic that he was angry with her, he put his cutlery down and slid a hand into the pocket of his jeans. He pulled out his wallet, a worn brown leather billfold, and opened it.

She laughed nervously. 'Are you going to pay me to shut the fuck up?'

'I fucking might,' he said, but he was looking for some-

82

thing; he flicked through the sections where his cards were held. He stopped, and pulled out what looked to Catherine like a small white square. He frowned at it for a moment, then handed it to her. 'Here,' he said, shrugging as though it was nothing much.

It was a photograph, or part of a photograph – it had been cut out of a photograph. It had been taken at a black-tie event; the boy was wearing a tuxedo, though with the jacket off and the bow tie hanging open around the shirt collar. He was dark-haired, and he was smiling, and he was probably a bit drunk – that wobbliness to his features – and his arm was thrown loosely around someone, but the someone was gone.

'His name is Keith,' James said quietly.

'I don't think Armani does a navy-blue taxedo,' Catherine said, one of the lines from one of the films they had laughed over, those first nights in Dublin; one of their lines, now, and James laughed to hear her use it, but only a little.

'Indeed,' was what he said.

Keith was not beautiful; that was what struck Catherine about him. He was not ugly; he was just not anything much, really. He was slight, and ordinary-looking, and his smile was not a smile at all but a laugh; someone had said something to him to make him laugh just as the shutter had been pressed.

'Nice,' Catherine said, and she hoped it sounded convincing.

'It was taken at our grad dance last year.'

She tapped the right side of the photograph. 'Is this his girlfriend you cut out here?'

'Oh, no,' he blurted. 'No, no. Though I suppose it does look like that. No, just some of the other lads from our year.'

'You didn't like them in the same way.'

'No, I did not,' he said pointedly.

'And did you take this photo?'

'*Please.* Are you trying to insult me? It's barely even in focus.'

'Plus he's looking at the camera.'

'Smart-arse.'

'But do you not have any proper photos of him?'

He shook his head briskly. 'No. No. That wasn't an option.'

'Oh, well,' Catherine said, as she passed it back to him. 'He looks nice.'

James took it from her, and he touched the edge of the photo, and she thought he might run his finger across the surface of it, but he did not. 'He has this . . .' he said, and then he shook his head.

'No, go on,' she said, and her heart was beating faster, and she ordered it to cop itself on. She was not going to do this; she was not going to sit here and perv on the sight of James talking about a boy. She was not going to entertain this in herself; she was not going to feel this on her skin, in her mouth, on the tips of her fingers, the way she did. She cleared her throat. 'Go on,' she said again, leaning across the table for his hand. 'Tell me.'

Delicacy. That was how James described it; that was how he described the boy's face, and what he had loved about it. He was gazing at the photograph as though he had entered once again into its world: a hotel ballroom on a summer night last year, balloons sagging and streamers fallen and cider slick on the floor; 'Live Forever' blaring over the speakers. Girls in long dresses and boys in rented tuxes; everyone getting messy and plastered and, eventually, upset. Catherine had photographs just like this one from her own grad dance; for Catherine, too, there had been a boy in a dishevelled tux. That boy was long forgotten now; that boy had, anyway, been completely oblivious of her stares.

'Did he know?' she asked James now.

He looked at her. 'Are you mad?'

'Where is he now?'

James slid the photograph back into his wallet. 'England,' he said. 'He did Pharmacy. Easier to get onto the courses over there.'

'Oh, a pharmacist,' Catherine said, and she could have been her mother, approving of someone's choice of a husband. She laughed at herself, and she thought that James might join in, but he did not seem to be listening.

'I should really get rid of that photo. If I was hit by a bus, and they found a photo of Keith Murray in my pocket. Jesus Christ.'

'I'd get there first and make sure nobody saw it,' Catherine said, and then, because she worried that this had not sounded like enough of a joke, she added, 'and I'd take all your money as well.'

'You'd be made up,' James said, refilling their glasses.

She hesitated, and he noticed, eyeing her sharply.

'Go on,' he said, imitating her tone from a moment earlier.

She laughed. 'I was just wondering if there was anyone in Berlin.'

'No,' he said immediately, shaking his head. 'No, no.'

'I mean, German guys are good-looking, aren't they? Some of them.'

He smirked. 'Some of them. Oh, yeah, some of them.'

'Well, then. There must have been someone.'

'What do you mean, someone? Was I *with* someone? I've told you, I've never been with anyone.'

'No, I just mean, were you interested in anyone? I mean, was there anyone like Keith there?'

He shrugged. 'There was a neighbour. Stefan.'

'Nice name.'

He raised an eyebrow. 'Nice everything.'

'Oh, yeah?'

'He has the studio upstairs from Malachy.'

'And you got to know him?'

'He'd come in to us a few times a week, just for a chat or whatever. He and Malachy have known each other for years – he's older, thirty-something.' He smirked again. 'I think old Malachy has a thing for him and all.'

'Oh,' Catherine said, surprised. 'Malachy's gay?'

'Malachy's nothing,' James said shortly. 'Or, I mean, what Malachy is is not up for discussion. With him, I mean. There's no question of talking about such things.'

'Oh,' Catherine nodded, not quite understanding what he meant, but not wanting to show this. She was feeling again her inadequacy, her childishness in the face of this world in which James had existed, a world she could not imagine: these older people, their studios, their being gay or not quite gay or whatever it was he was talking about. Her life – college, home, now the long days at her corner desk in the *Leader* office – was so narrow and ordinary by comparison. She would change this, she resolved now, whipped into determination by the wine. She would hunt out for herself a more interesting life. A more varied one. James was already helping her with this, she thought; she felt a rush of gratitude towards him again. He was eating now, so she did not bother him with this, and anyway, she was not sure she could put it into words – what could she say to him, thanks for being gay? – without sounding like an idiot.

'And there's no chance with Stefan either?' she said instead.

James shook his head. 'Stefan likes the ladies. Most of his sculptures are of the ladies. Or of parts of the ladies.'

'Oh.'

'Oh, it's awful rubbish. Basically Rodin getting high with Koons. But it sells.'

'I can't believe he's not gay,' Catherine said, feeling very keenly the injustice of it. 'Can he not be persuaded?'

'Oh, well, Catherine,' James said, in a tone which implied that things were very far from being as simple as all that.

'Isn't there anyone?'

He glanced at her. 'Anyone?'

'Anyone who *is* gay? There, I mean.' She stammered; she could not find the right way to say this. 'In Germany, I mean. In your—'

James put his head to one side as though considering this very carefully. 'Is there anyone who is gay in Germany? Hmm.'

'Stop it,' she said, laughing to cover her embarrassment. 'You know what I mean.'

'I know what you mean, Catherine,' he said, so warmly that she felt guilty, for some reason. 'I know what you mean. But no. There's nobody. At least nobody I've met.' He pointed to her plate. 'Finished?'

'Not yet.'

'You look finished. Are you going to eat the fat? Longford savages.'

'I mean, not yet, you haven't met anyone just yet,' she said, passing him her plate. 'I mean, when you go back, you'll be meeting someone.'

He spluttered. 'Oh, will I now?'

'I mean, you *can*,' Catherine said, embarrassed again. 'I mean, you *might*. I mean—'

'Jesus, you're giving me worse odds by the second. I think you'd better stop.'

'Come on, James,' she said, laughing. 'You know what I mean.'

'I do,' he said, and he rocked back on his chair. 'Here's hoping.' He lifted his glass, which was empty now, as was Catherine's, but they clinked anyway.

'I have a feeling,' she said. 'You'll get a fella, and I'll get a fella, and we can compare notes.'

'Hmm,' he said, his eyes on the night sky.

'Compare photos, even,' Catherine said, and she let something suggestive enter her tone, so that he looked at her, to check, and she winked at him to let him know that she had intended it, and they both laughed.

'God, I love wine,' Catherine said mournfully. 'I wish there was more.'

'More wine!' he said, mock-aghast. 'Where do you think you are, Clarence House?'

She pouted. 'Do you have *anything* else to drink?'

'There might be whiskey,' he said doubtfully, standing with the dinner plates and leaving them on the windowsill by the front door.

'Then bring on the whiskey!' she said, thumping the table. She had never had whiskey before, actually, but it would be exactly right for now, she decided; it was exactly what was needed. She threw her head back and stretched her arms wide, and as she did so, James, passing by her chair, leaned down to put his arms around her. She could smell him; the shower gel he had used before dinner, mostly, and something warmer, too, something more muggy and slightly sour; the food, probably, or the wine, maybe a trace of sweat from under his arms; maybe he had been sweating, telling her all that he had. Poor darling. She hugged him tighter, her arms on his arms. James made a sound like growling, and with one last squeeze, he pushed his lips hard and quick to her jaw.

'Oh, Catherine,' he said, standing again. 'Look at it.'

She looked: the garden in moonlight, the stars sharp and

sure of themselves, the sweep of silent meadows down to the canal.

'I wish it could always be like this,' he said.

'Me too.'

'Just you and me, and this weather, and this quiet.'

'Yeah,' Catherine said, and then she found that she was holding her breath, and she realized why: so that she would not say something else, something rash or foolish, to spoil the moment, the way she usually did. This was new. This was something else he had given her: this pause.

'Yeah,' she said again, and above her, she heard James sigh.

'Now, drink,' he said, heading for the front door. *'Drink!'* He went into the house, closing the door behind him; through its glass, she saw him move through the sitting room into the kitchen. She felt rising in her a shiver of gladness and of excitement, and she savoured it as it ran through her. Already, in the half-minute since he had gone, she had thought of so many things she wanted to tell him.

*

Catherine had said that everything would be all right, and a month later, after James had come out to his mother, Catherine kept saying that everything would be all right. She had to say this. She needed to say it. She needed to believe it, because James seemed to have gone to a place where such belief was not merely naive, but irrelevant.

'Yeah,' he would reply when Catherine tried to reassure him. There was no anger in his tone, no sarcasm; just this flatness which suggested that he was taking in her words, and all words, to be considered later, sometime later, when he could spare the energy to listen to them, and to decide whether to keep them or cast them aside. They were in Carrigfinn again; James had come down from Dublin to be with his parents for his last days before going back to Berlin. Catherine had come to Carrigfinn to be with him on short notice; he had phoned her at home in Longford right after the conversation with his mother.

'Catherine,' he had said. 'I need you to come. I need you to come down here to me, Catherine.'

Catherine had been waiting for the call; she had told him to call her as soon as he had spoken to his mother. It would be all right, she had told him over and over; everything would be all right, she had been telling him now for weeks. OK, his mother might be taken aback, might not know how to respond at first, but she would come round, Catherine knew that she would. She would be great, Catherine told James; she would be brilliant. James had never believed her; James had disagreed with her every time, muttering about wishful thinking, muttering about things being more complicated than Catherine realized, and Catherine had argued with him – fought with him even – telling him that he just *wanted* to be pessimistic, that deep down, he must *want* his mother not to be OK with what he was going to tell her – and when she thought of that now, she felt so ashamed. She felt so – what had she been doing, with all of her big, clever theories? Who had she been trying to fool?

'Catherine,' he had said on the phone when he had called to tell her how it had gone, and his voice had been only a whisper. Only a trace.

No, he had said, not well, it had not gone well, and there had been the shock, then, of hearing tears in his voice, and of feeling – before the flood of sorrow for him, before that – of feeling a mean, indecent stab of discomfort at this; that he should cry, dissolve into crying, and that she should hear it. But he did not dissolve; he kept going, kept his voice going, and kept it clear. No, not well, he said, not well at all. And Catherine asked for the details, for the when and the how, asked whether the set-up had been as he had planned it, whether the words had been the words he had rehearsed, they had rehearsed; asked about timing, asked about location, as though it was a proposal she was asking him about, rather than what it had been. As though it had been an asking, rather than a telling – but then again, had it not been an asking? Had it not been an appeal? Asking his mother to hear him, to see him, to regard him the same way she always had; and his mother, sitting there in front of him, had put her head in her hands.

'She put her head in her hands, Catherine, and she cried and she cried. And she pulled at her hair. She took hold of her hair, and she pulled at it, as though she was trying to pull it out from the roots. Which I think she was.'

'No, no,' Catherine said, trying to soothe him, but he did not want to be soothed.

'I need you to come down here,' he said simply. 'I can't be here by myself. Please, Catherine. Please come.'

She nodded. 'I can come in the morning. I can tell them I have to go to Dublin for something to do with college. I can get the train—'

'No, not tomorrow, Catherine. Tonight. The late train. Please.'

'James,' she said, his name sticking in her throat. 'Tonight's impossible. How would I explain it? They know there's no train that late going to Dublin. They'd know—'

'I don't *care*, Catherine. I don't care what you have to tell them.'

'I just don't know. It's so difficult.'

And it was his silence after she had said that that had

made up Catherine's mind for her. It was the sound of his breathing, shallow and slow.

'I'm coming,' she said. 'I'll thumb a lift out from the station when I get there.'

'*Catherine*,' her mother said in disbelief when Catherine walked into the kitchen and told them that she was going to her friend James's house for the night. She had not come straight off the phone; she had wanted to take a shower, first, and to wash her hair, so that she would be presentable when she got to Carrigfinn later. She had shaved her legs, too, because she had noticed, while she showered, that they needed to be shaved, and she had nicked herself in a couple of places, as she usually did, but the bleeding had stopped now, she thought. She was in her dressing gown, with her hair in a towel, standing just over the threshold of the kitchen door.

'*Catherine*,' her mother said again, and she looked almost as though she might laugh, so impossible was this thing that Catherine had just done. To have said it just to her mother would have been one thing, but she had come in and made the announcement while both her parents were in the room; her father had just come in from the fields, and was sitting at the table, that week's *Leader* open in front of him. He was in his overalls still, and he looked tired. The paper came out on a Wednesday, but he liked to keep it for Friday evening. He liked to sit at the table and read it from cover to cover and talk to her mother about anything that caught his eye.

Now he was looking at Catherine's mother with the same expression with which Catherine's mother was looking at her: an expression that said that this had to change, that this idea which had come into the air of the room needed, very quickly, to dissolve.

'I need a lift to the train station,' Catherine said, tying the belt of her dressing gown more tightly. 'Or I can get a taxi, if you don't have the time to drop me in. I'll be back tomorrow evening, or Sunday.'

'Patricia,' Catherine's father said; Catherine's mother's name. He sounded like he was pleading. Still he had not looked to where Catherine stood.

'*Catherine*,' Catherine's mother said again. She was standing at the counter; she was pouring tea. The teapot was old, and prone to leaking, and Catherine's mother was the only one who knew how to use it without letting hot tea spill out of the sides, but it was leaking now, Catherine saw; her mother frowned at it, as though it was something she had not even known she was holding, and put it down.

'James asked me to come down this evening,' Catherine said. 'His mother is sick. I want to keep him company.'

'Patricia,' her father said again, more insistently.

Catherine's mother held up a hand; whether to him or to her, Catherine did not know. 'Catherine, darling,' she said, gently. 'It's not a good idea for you to go to that lad's house like this. Can't you go tomorrow for the day? I'll drop you off and pick you up, if that's what you want.'

'No,' Catherine shook her head. 'He needs me now. I have to—'

And that did it for her father. *Need* was the wrong word to have used, of course, it struck Catherine immediately – too much like desire, too much what the body did, not the mind – but it was out now. He turned to her. His eyes, the blueness of them – he had given those eyes to her. She had looked at those eyes, not five minutes ago, staring back at her from the bathroom mirror. *I dare you*, those eyes had said to her; and these eyes were saying precisely the same thing.

'Now listen, Catherine,' her father said, and just as her

mother had done, he held up a hand. 'Your mother and I cannot let you put yourself in danger. Your mother and I know things that you don't know.'

'You don't know anything about James,' Catherine said, and her mother gasped. This was not done, this way of talking; not in this house. This was not how conversations happened here. Her mother said her name again, not in warning this time but in shock, and her father stared.

'We know plenty,' he said slowly. 'We know that Pat Burke saw the pair of you on top of each other above in Dublin.'

'Charlie!' her mother said. 'Leave that.'

'No, no,' her father said, planting an elbow on the table. His jaw was working. 'So you needn't think we don't know what's going on between you and this fellow.'

'There's nothing like that going on between us,' Catherine said. She kept her voice even; she kept it calm. She was determined not to do any of the things she always did when she fought with her mother; this was not a fight with her mother. This was not something she had ever done before, standing up like this to her father, and if she was going to do it, she was going to do it right. Their eyes were the same blue. Their minds went to the same places; she could see, now, where his had gone. 'James doesn't think about me that way,' she said, 'so there's nothing to worry about. Even if I felt that way about him, which I don't—'

'Ah, for God's sake would you stop talking nonsense, Catherine,' her father said, sitting back in his chair. He looked to her mother. 'Patricia. Can you put a stop to this? She won't even get going there in the morning if she's not careful.'

'Catherine,' her mother said, coming around the counter towards her, her eyes full of imploring, full of the silent language that was spoken between them: *Just do what he wants, and we can work something else out later. Just do what he wants now. Just say no more.*

'I need to be at the station by eight,' Catherine said, shaking her head, but her mother's attention was somewhere else, now, as she neared her; Catherine glanced down to where she was staring, and saw a thin trail of blood snaking down her bare calf.

Her mother said her name quietly, too quietly for her father to hear. She nodded towards the blood. 'You need to—'

'It's nothing,' Catherine said, irritably. 'I just cut my legs shaving them.'

'Now,' her father said, nodding. 'Didn't I tell you?'

'Tell me *what*?' Catherine said.

'Catherine,' her mother said, grabbing her by the elbow. 'Get down to the room and clean yourself up. We're not talking about this any longer.'

'You can't go down to stay with that fellow and that's the end of it,' her father said. 'Sure we couldn't allow that. Sure don't we know well what that would lead to? What kind of idea do you think you're going to give him, going down there like that for the night?'

'I'm not going to go like this,' Catherine said, witheringly. 'I was planning to get dressed.'

Her mother looked at her as though she might slap her. 'Catherine,' she said, her mouth tight.

'Are you just going to keep saying my name?'

Her mother sighed. 'Don't be smart, Catherine.'

'I'm not smart,' Catherine said, rubbing the blood into her leg. 'I'm eighteen years old, and I don't even live at home most of the year, so this doesn't even make sense, what you're saying to me.'

'You'd live here the whole year round if I had anything to do with it,' her father said.

'Well, I don't. I live in Dublin, and I'm only visiting here.'

The way he looked when she said this, the way he looked down to the floor, gave her a stab of guilt – a stab, weirdly, of something like loneliness – but she stood her ground.

'So it makes no sense, trying to control me now,' she said. 'I'm old enough.'

'That's *enough*,' her mother said. 'You can go to Leitrim tomorrow, and come back tomorrow evening. That's plenty of time to visit your friend. What more can you do for him anyway?'

'I told you,' Catherine said. 'His mother is sick.'

'And what are you going to do about it? You're not going to make her better.'

'What's wrong with his mother?' her father said.

'She's . . .' Catherine swallowed, casting about for a condition; why had she not thought of something before now? 'She's depressed.'

Her father looked at her mother as though this confirmed something. Her mother clicked her tongue. 'Jesus Christ.'

'What's *that* supposed to mean?'

'What's this fellow dragging you into that for?'

'You know bloody well why he's dragging her into it,' her father said.

'It's not *like* that!' Catherine said. She was shocked at how fluent she had found herself to be in this language, this register, of standing in front of her father and telling him how it was. 'It's not *like* that,' she said again.

'That's enough, Catherine,' her mother said, trying to steer her towards the door.

But her father was in the mood for an argument now, too; he was standing up. 'Look, Catherine,' he said, and for a moment Catherine worried that he was going to come towards her, but he stayed where he was. 'Look, Catherine, I was young once too. I know what it's like to be your age, and I know what it's like to be that young lad's age, too. I can understand the way he must feel about you.'

'Oh my God. I've told you this a thousand times before! I've told both of you. James doesn't—'

'And if you go down to Leitrim to stay the night,' her father said, 'you may forget about it. That's it. What kind of account of yourself are you going to give, going down to Leitrim like that? What kind of message are you going to give to that young lad?'

'It's not *like* that,' Catherine said, rolling her eyes. 'We're not boyfriend and girlfriend.'

'Pat Burke—'

'I don't *care* about Pat Burke!' she shouted. 'Why do you care so much about Pat Burke? What has Pat Burke ever done for you? He's not even really your friend!'

'Well, he was enough of a friend to tell me what he saw.'

Catherine snorted. 'He saw nothing.'

Her father shook his head at her. 'He saw enough.'

Her leg was bleeding again; she rubbed at it with the sole of her foot. Beside her, her mother clicked her tongue. 'How did you do that to yourself? Couldn't you be more careful?'

'She's hasn't the sense to be careful, Patricia. That's the point.'

'Don't talk to me like that.'

'*Catherine*,' her mother said. 'I'm getting you a plaster, and you're getting dressed, and that's the end of this. It should never have gone this far. You know better than—'

'She doesn't know anything, Patricia,' her father cut in. 'You don't know how the world works yet,' he said to Catherine. 'Sure how would you? It's only natural. But your mother and I know, and it's our job to protect you. A young fellow has natural instincts, and if you go and put yourself in the way of them—'

'Oh, for Christ's sake, that's *it*,' Catherine said. It was not a tone she had ever used before with her father, but it was possible, she now realized, and it was somehow addictive. 'For Christ's sake,' she said again, and she looked at them both as they stared back at her. 'James is not interested in me. There's a very simple reason for that.'

'You might think—' her father began, but Catherine held up a hand.

'James is not interested in me because James is gay.'

There was silence in the room for a moment; for a moment, there seemed not even to be, in the room, any breath. But that could not be, because beside her, her mother was taking a very long breath now, Catherine could see, and letting it out again, like it was something she had to hold on to to keep herself steady on her feet, and at the table, her father had to be breathing too, because her father was shaking his head.

'Oh, Catherine,' her mother said quietly. 'Why did you—'

'Now,' her father said, and his tone sounded triumphant. He was speaking to her mother, Catherine saw. 'Now. Now do you see how little she can be trusted to keep an eye on herself? Now? Didn't I tell you there was more to this than she was letting on? Didn't I tell you?'

'Jesus Christ,' her mother said, shaking her head.

'What?' Catherine said, turning to her. 'What's the big deal? Lots of people are gay.'

'Well, I hope you don't know any more of them,' her father said.

'Charlie,' her mother said sharply. 'Stop that.'

'Is this the way you're going on in Dublin, going around

with people like that? Is this what we sent you to Trinity for, so you can meet up with this kind of crowd?'

'James doesn't go to Trinity,' Catherine said.

'Then how the hell did you meet him? What the hell are you doing going around with him?'

'Catherine,' her mother said. 'This boy is troubled.'

'He's trouble,' her father said.

'He's troubled. It's no good getting close to him.'

'It can't be cured,' her father said.

'Charlie,' her mother said. 'Please.'

'Well, it's stopping here,' her father said, and he sat down to his paper again, and he opened it and closed it. 'It's stopping here, I can tell you that. You're not to go next nor near that place. Or you needn't be coming back here.'

'Don't say that to her,' her mother said, and her voice, Catherine heard in dismay, was on the verge of breaking. 'Don't ever say that to any of them.'

Her father hesitated.

'Charlie,' her mother said. 'Please.'

'This is your home and it always will be, Catherine,' he said, his eyes on the newspaper. 'But I don't want you associating with the likes of that fellow. I want that to be clear.'

'I'm only going for a couple of nights,' Catherine said, and she left the room.

In the bedroom, Ellen was waiting for her, her eyes wide with disbelief.

'What the fuck was that?'

'I'm sorry,' said Catherine, as she pulled clothes out of the chest of drawers. 'It had to be done.'

'You did that and now you're just leaving me here to deal with it?'

'You don't have to deal with it.'

'Fuck you,' Ellen said, pushing past her, and Catherine was horrified to see that she was in tears.

*

That night in Carrigfinn was not a pleasant one. The next day was not a pleasant day. They were a night and a day passed in the tension of inhabiting rooms, listening for who might walk into them. On the surface, it was the same house she had visited a month ago, or it might have been: Peggy, so welcoming to Catherine, embracing her, telling her how delighted she was to see her again. Calling her *pet*. Calling her *wee darling*. But she was not the same person to Peggy now, Catherine knew that, just as Peggy was not the same person to her. This Peggy was the woman who had reacted to James in the manner that she had, in just the manner that James had predicted she would, in just the manner of which Catherine had said, *Oh no, no, no, that won't happen. Everything will be all right. Everything will be more than all right.*

All right; that was not what this was. There were moments, that night, that next day, when Catherine looked up to see that Peggy was staring at her, on her face an expression that was not very far from blame. They were in trouble, she and James. They were in so much trouble. Being in trouble in this way made Catherine wary of moving; wary, even, of meeting anyone's eye. James's father was confused by the quiet and the caution, she knew; James's father did not know what James's mother now knew. He kept trying to joke with them, to draw them both out, and he kept giving up, flashing curious looks in Peggy's direction, going outside to the farm, where things could be managed, where reactions could be trusted to be what he expected them to be. He thought that they were miserable, all of them, over James's imminent departure, Catherine thought – and he was right about that, actually, because if there was one thing that she dreaded more than heading back to the house out of which she had walked the evening before, it was not having James to phone up and James to visit; it was the thought of James being a thousand miles away, in a city and a country to which she had never been, not that it would have made a damn bit of difference if she had been there. He would be gone, and she would be here, and that was what she was facing into, and the thought of it made her breath feel as though it was going to refuse to come. But that was not the thing to think about now, she knew; that was not the important thing. The important thing was James. The important thing was to be with James, now. On his bedroom walls, it struck her, there were no posters – they were, in that respect, so different from her bedroom walls at home, still covered with the school years collage of pictures from *Just Seventeen* and *NME*. His walls were covered with wallpaper, a pattern of ivy, or something else rising and green. Catherine sat propped against one side of the wall, and James sat propped against the other, and they sat there waiting for the hours to pass, James seeming absorbed in *Mrs Dalloway*, Catherine having tried and given up on *Orlando*. Outside, it was sunny, but outside was not a matter for them. Catherine lay down now, feeling the urge to sink into sleep, and James shifted in his seating, so that his legs were still draped across her, the weight of them pinning her just above her knees. Soon, it would be dinnertime, and they would have to go up to the kitchen, to the table, where James's mother would smile and sigh across the table, at once pretending that nothing was the matter and making very clear that something was, and James's father would try to get everyone laughing, and James would be monosyllabic and sarcastic, and Catherine would end up overcompensating, and chattering, and thus betraying him, the way she had done at breakfast, the way she had done at lunch. What was she meant to do, stay quiet and hurt and angry also? They could not both be that way.

But sleep; all she wanted was sleep. She felt so tired. She felt, for a moment, a longing to go home, to run home, but she could not do that either, and even the thought of it struck panic inside her like a match. Ellen's face; her mother's face; her father's face – she pushed them away. Tomorrow was the day for leaving. Tomorrow was the day for home.

'Are you asleep?' James said, nudging her with his leg.

'No,' Catherine said, the word all in a drowse.

'Don't go to sleep,' he said, and she heard him turn a page.

MOONFOAM AND SILVER

(1998)

1

Half of each can was a curving block of red, the familiar font of the brand name swooping over it, and at the bottom, in yellow-piped block capitals, the word SOUP.

ONION MADE WITH BEEF STOCK sounded vile. PEPPER POT; what, even, *was* pepper pot soup? And barley was some kind of crop, wasn't it? A crop grown in places where the land was good enough to hold it.

These were the *actual* soup cans; that was the thing to understand. That gold circular canvas over there was an actual Marilyn, and in another room were the actual Jackie O paintings, the canvases washed over with an eerie blue. And somewhere else in the gallery was the actual Mao, smug and bleary and bloated. Or, one of the actuals, actually. One of the Maos, six of the Jackies, one of the Marilyns, her lipstick glossy even in monochrome, her beauty spot like a sharp bud of dirt in the paint. Not *the* actual. That was the point. That was the—

'Let me guess, Citóg,' said a voice from behind her. 'You're mulling over the layers of irony. You're thinking of how they're themselves and yet at the same time not themselves. You're thinking, what am I looking at, actually? What am I—'

'Why am I looking at you, Moran, is the question?' Catherine said, turning to face him. 'What are you doing here?'

'On a date,' he shrugged. 'What do you think of this stuff?'

'I think he was at his best in the mid-sixties, really, wasn't he?' she said evenly.

'Oh, no doubt,' Conor said. 'Sixty-five to sixty-six, I'd say, to be even more precise about it.'

'Pretty downhill after that.'

'Mmm,' Conor said, nodding vigorously, and together, they drifted on to the huge silkscreen of the dollar sign.

In truth, Catherine didn't have a clue when Andy Warhol had been at his best, but the mid-sixties seemed a likely possibility, and it seemed like the kind of thing that would be said about Warhol; so she had put it out there, as she often did now, and as often happened now, it had worked. She had got away with it. She was still not quite able to believe that this happened, but it did. You said something, sounding confident as you said it, keeping your voice level, and people nodded, and people agreed with you, and people looked at you as a person who apparently knew their stuff. That was it. It was so easy.

This was what she had discovered this year at college: that when you gave the world the impression that you were up to it, ready for whatever it wanted to throw at you, the stuff the world threw at you turned out to be not that big of a deal after all. It turned out, actually, to be kind of comically manageable. Essays. Reading lists. Meetings with her lecturers. Writing articles for *Trinity News*; she was doing loads for the books pages of *TN* now, and getting on nicely. Also, boys, there had been lots of boys, once she had copped herself on and stopped mooning over Conor, who was just a mate now, and actually not a bad one; one among many. This was one of the things of which she was proudest about this second year at college: that she had so many friends now. Maybe too many. Or maybe they were acquaintances, rather than friends, but she didn't think about the distinction. She just liked it. She liked the way that it was no longer possible, when she walked through Front Arch in the morning, on the way to her class or to the library, to get to where she was going without bumping into at least a couple of people she knew, and maybe more, depending on the time of day; sometimes, if she was not in a rush, not on her way to a lecture or a tutorial, it could take her a full hour to get where she was going, such was the volume of people she would bump into, such were the chats to be had. It gave her a buzz, the feeling that her days were teeming, that there were never enough hours to talk to all the people she wanted to talk to, let alone for all the books she wanted to read, all the poems she wanted to write, all the things she wanted to know about, and talk about, and add to her store.

'Anyway,' she said now, joining up with Conor again. 'Who's the lucky lady?'

'Alice from Modern Theatre,' he said. 'Great girl.'

'Aren't they always?'

'Don't be jealous,' Conor said. 'You here with Rafey?'

'I'm meeting Zoe. Rafe and I broke up.'

'What?' Conor said, looking shocked. 'But you were together on Valentine's Night!'

'Yeah. And I decided that was that.'

'Ah, Citóg. After all the trouble I went to, introducing you to him?'

She shrugged. She was enjoying this, she realized: Conor looking crestfallen because she'd dumped the guy he'd set her up with. She should do this kind of thing more often.

'Jesus, you're hard pleased,' Conor said, shaking his head. But then he grinned, and Catherine rolled her eyes; she knew that something lewd was coming.

'Don't, Moran,' she warned.

'I'd say it was a good experience, though, all the same?'

'Moran!'

'Clitóg no more, I'd say. Made a woman out of you at long last, did he, Rafey?'

'Oh, would you ever just *fuck* off,' Catherine said, but she was laughing; she could not help laughing when Conor slagged her off.

'The Doyle's having a party in his rooms later,' he said, leaning against the wall. 'You coming?'

The Doyle was the nickname which had been bestowed this year on Emmet Doyle, the boy who had the previous summer so earnestly – so sweetly, really – counselled Catherine on how to bluff her way into a summer job. He was no longer, though, that same shy boy; over the last year, he had transformed himself into a fully fledged House Six hack. *Muck*, his satirical column for *TN*, was a nod to the generations of American journalists he had learned about in his History of the Media class, and it framed itself as an exposé of hypocrisy, pomposity and dishonesty on campus – but it was more muck-slinging than mud-raking, chiefly an exercise in ridicule and mischief, and it frequently got things appallingly wrong. In November, for instance, Emmet's gleeful account of a senior lecturer's very public night on the tiles at the History Ball had turned out to be a blow-by-blow account of the man's very public fall from the wagon after seven years of sobriety. A diatribe against the college's practice of awarding honorary doctorates to 'lazy and irrelevant wasters', meanwhile, which called for students to picket the next conferring ceremony, had run in February, on the very day that Nelson Mandela was announced as that year's chief honoree. Mostly, though, *Muck* took aim at various college societies and at the students' union, as well as at various other local targets: the tutors, the security guards, the chaplains, the American tourists who lined up to see the *Book of Kells*, the Freshman girl who had dyed her hair blue. He had a nickname for everyone; 'Poetess' was what he called Catherine, having filched two of her poems from the slush pile for *Icarus*, the college literary magazine. Catherine tended, as a result, to avoid him when she saw him coming, and she was not in the mood for one of his notoriously chaotic parties tonight.

'I can't,' she told Conor. 'James is coming home tomorrow.'

'Tomorrow? I thought he wasn't coming home until the summer.'

'Well,' Catherine shrugged. 'He changed his mind. He's home tomorrow. And so I don't want to be wrecked in the morning. I'm meeting James early at the airport.'

This was not true; James was once again getting a lift home from Berlin in the cab of a lorry, and he had written to Catherine and the girls saying that he would make his own way to Baggot Street when he arrived, probably sometime in the early afternoon. It shocked her a little that she had told this lie so easily just now, and so readily, without having in any way planned it or decided that it was necessary; she blinked at Conor, feeling a little breathless, worrying that he would pull her up on it, that he would expose her dishonesty and, worse still, the motive behind it. Which was – because Catherine did not know – which was what, exactly? Why had she felt the need to make up a story? Why had she felt the need to disguise the extent of her excitement about James's homecoming, to throw Conor off the scent of the preparations she wanted to go home and make? Because he would laugh at her? But Conor always laughed at her, and she liked it – but no, she realized, this time she did not want Conor to have the opportunity to laugh at her. This time there was something that she really did not want Conor to know. This time was different, she realized, watching him; this time was something somehow truly private.

'I just can't come,' she said apologetically. 'I'll go to the next one.'

'Go to whatever parties you like, Citóg,' Conor said, shrugging. Then something seemed to occur to him. He frowned. 'Here. This doesn't have anything to do with you and Rafe breaking up, does it? This guy James coming home?'

'Rafe and I broke up because we'd run our course. We had nothing in common. And anyway, you know James is gay. I told you that.'

'Yeah, I know, I know, your precious gay friend. You've mentioned that. Once or twice.'

'Shut up,' Catherine said, laughing, but she could not suppress a wave of unease; James was unaware that Catherine had, over the course of the last term and a half, outed him to several of her college friends, none of whom he had actually met. It had just happened; it had just come out, so to speak, when she had been telling people about her friend the photographer in Berlin, and about how brilliant he was. Drink had usually been involved, and she had always felt bad the next morning; but then, it was not as though James was *not* out. He was out to Catherine, out to Amy and Lorraine, out to his mother – but still. It was something she had yet to tell him, the fact that people like Conor and Zoe knew. It was something which would have to be almost immediately addressed, given that she was so much looking forward to bringing him onto campus this week and introducing him to everyone. It was a bit of a problem, probably. It was not something, for instance, that she had mentioned in her letters to him. She felt her stomach twist with anxiety, and she must have winced, because Conor looked at her more closely.

'What's up?'

She shook her head. 'Nothing.'

'Not having regrets about old Rafey?'

'Jesus!' she burst out. 'Why don't *you* shag Rafe, if you're so obsessed with him?'

'Now, hang on,' Conor said, holding up his hands. 'I mean, I'm glad you're getting your own Private Idaho back again, but that doesn't mean the rest of us have to be lumped in with him.' He jerked his head towards the girl he had come with, who was now lingering in front of the Marilyn piece. 'I'm laying my pipe the way any man with eyes in his head would.'

'You can't say that!' Catherine spluttered, her heart slamming in her chest. He laughed, and she stared at him, feeling confused. *Could* he say that? Was that an insult to James? She thought so, but she could not be sure – much of what Conor said to her, to anyone, could be perceived as an insult, if you decided to see it that way; but surely it was not just about *deciding*? She felt she should know; she felt she should, on this question, be so much clearer, so much more solid. It was not as though Conor had a problem with gay people; he had nodded almost respectfully when Catherine had told him, one night early the previous term, about James. He knew gay people himself, he had said; there was a guy he had been to school with who he was pretty sure about, and obviously a few people in his theatre class. *Obviously*, Catherine had said in response, feeling the surge of pride she so often felt when she talked or thought about James, about how close she was to him. But now, here, in this moment, should she be standing up for him? Should she be angry on his behalf? She was glaring at Conor, trying to get a handle on him, and he was grinning back.

'You know it makes sense, Citóg.'

'Oh, fuck off, would you, Moran,' she shot at him, turning

pointedly back to the soup cans, and he laughed again, and he walked away.

'Give him a kiss from me,' he said, as he went.

James was coming home early. He had planned to stay in Berlin until June again this year, and possibly even over the summer, but he had not made it that far. He had made it up to Christmas, and he had made it through January, but a week ago Catherine had had a letter from him, telling her that he had had enough. He had had enough of Berlin, and he had had enough of working for Malachy, and he missed Dublin, and said that he wanted to take photographs there again, and because he missed the flat on Baggot Street, and missed Amy and Lorraine, and because he missed Catherine. He missed Catherine most of all, and most of all he was coming home because he missed Catherine. Catherine knew that. James told her that in his letters; he had told her that in every letter since the end of August. *I miss you. I miss you so fucking much. I miss you all the time. I miss your voice. I miss your company. I miss your God-awful jokes. I miss your obsessions with ridiculous men. I miss talking to you and listening to you and sitting with you and bursting like the Milk Tray man into your room like I did that very first morning. I miss you. I mean it. I miss you. I miss you all the time.*

And Catherine said the same to him. *All the time,* she wrote in her letters, *every single day* – and that was not lying, because every single day, Catherine thought about James, and every single day there was at least one moment when she wished he was with her, and almost every single day, she added to her latest letter to him. There were weeks when she sent him more than one letter, and there was one week, soon after Christmas, when she got three letters from him, each as long and detailed as the next, but it was still not the same as actually having him with her, and she told him that; she told him that all the time. Email was more immediate, but James did not have much access to Malachy's computer, so they did not tend to correspond that way – and anyway, with email you did not have the heft of the pages, the life of the ink woven tight into the paper, rushing across it, a thing that had come directly from the other person's own hand. Or from the pen in their hand, which was almost the same; which was almost like touching them for yourself.

In her letters, Catherine described everything that happened to her, putting a net over everything she had seen and heard and read and experienced, so that she could capture it for him, so that it could be as though it was happening, just for him, a second time. Because she did miss him; *I miss you I miss you I miss you I miss you* was how she closed her letters to him often – she loved the rhythm of it – and then she would sign them, and add a line of kisses, the *x*'s so easy to lay down, so much easier than the reality of his kisses and hugs. Writing that she missed him, actually, was also so much easier than the thought of saying it face to face, and easier, indeed, than the experience of reading the same words when they came from him; the admission, the declaration was still too emotional for Catherine to be entirely comfortable with it, too nakedly open in its affection and its need. James and she were just different on that score. He was so much more able to express himself emotionally; it was for him so much more natural to be verbally and physically demonstrative in that way.

Or at least, it was so much more natural for him to be like that with some people. With others, Catherine knew, it was another matter entirely – with guys. Because there had been no guys for James during his time in Berlin this time around, either; there had been no expressions of affection, verbal or physical or of any other kind. They had been a failure, these six months, he had written to her; they had, he had said in more than one letter, been a torment. *Lonely*: that was the word he had written, over and over. *Alone*: that was another. *Never*: that had been another, and whenever Catherine read him using that word, looking with it grimly into a future the nature of which he had already decided upon, she had known it was her job to argue, to reason, to come back at him with words that were softer, and sweeter, words like *Someday* and *Someone* and *Soon*. Telling him, once again, that everything would be OK. That everything would turn out OK, turn around, turn into the kind of life, the kind of lightness, that he deserved to have. That this had happened, after all, for her; this was how she had built her argument, using as a comparison the way things had turned around for her so brilliantly this year. The previous year, she reminded him, she had been so so scared, so awkward, so shy; the previous year, nothing and nobody around her had seemed like they could belong, in any way, to her. Her college subjects had intimidated her, and this year she was mad about them; this year, she spent hours every day in the library, devouring novels and essays and poems. Her love life had been non-existent, and now it seemed never to have a dull moment; there had been Rafe, and there had been others, just kisses, or in some cases just flirtations, but great kisses, fucking *great* kisses, and flirtations that had set her whole body tingling with giddiness and a barely containable impatience, that had charged the air, hard, with the hugeness of possibility, the sense of her own fresh power. The first of the guys had been Aidan, the older guy from one of her tutorials – a mature student, for Christ's sake, thirty-one years of age, constantly talking a blue streak about Chaucer: in other words, the least likely candidate imaginable for a snog. But when he put his hand to Catherine's cheek at the Visual Arts Society party, and said her name, and pulled her to him, his hips square against hers, Catherine had felt like she had never felt before, the shock of her own skin, of her own body and its hunger. So *that* was what all the fuss was about, she had realized, as Aidan's tongue had pushed through her lips. *That* was the point of kissing someone you actually knew, as opposed to a random stranger in a club with whom you were only going through the motions: the jolt. The surge. The way you could stand, pressed up against them, kissing them, laughing with them, and not notice that hours were passing, that it was two in the morning, that your friends had gone home, that the wall behind you was damp and was cold. Someone's hands in your hair, and someone's hands moving up and down your back, under your top, under your waistband, and someone's lips and someone's tongue, and someone's smile, when the two of you stopped – when the two of you paused – and the things someone might say to you, the things they told you about yourself, about how, maybe, they had watched you for so long, liked you for so long, about how you were this and you were that – none of it true, Catherine thought, all of it too flattering and too idealistic, but still. And the taste of someone; the smell of them; the feeling of their frame, of their flesh, of their bones. With Rafe, months after Aidan, it had been more complicated, because with Rafe there had been sex, and shagging someone was not like kissing someone – shagging someone was not, it seemed to Catherine, something you just knew naturally and automatically how to move through, how to build on, how to do – but Rafe and the responsibility of sex with Rafe were over now, and they were not things about which she had to worry anymore. *Dusky dick?!* James had written to her in that letter after her and Rafe's first time, the letter which had made her laugh so loudly that Amy had called down the hall, demanding to have the passage read aloud to her. *Dusky dick. I've heard*

them called some things, he had written, *but that's a new one on me.*
And he had gone on: praising Catherine, and congratulating
her, and ribbing her, and making her snort, and making her
blush. She had not used the actual phrase, of course – she
had been trying to find a way to describe the lovely colour
of Rafe's skin – but that did not matter; James liked to take
something and to run with it until it had become something
else entirely, and Catherine loved to watch him, loved to read
him – she could always hear his voice saying the lines, see his
eyes full of mischief, sarcasm, delight.

But she could also see the darkness in them; she could see
the pain. Early on, he had written to her that maybe this had
not been such a good idea, this second year working with
Malachy in Berlin; that maybe it had been a mistake. Yes,
the city was beautiful, he wrote, but there were days when its
beauty seemed like a taunt, like an insult. When it was so hard
not to take its beauty personally. And Catherine knew, when
he wrote like this, that he was talking not just about the city,
not just talking about the streets and the galleries and the
squares, but about the people who walked through them;
about the guys. He had met nobody. He had not broken
through in that way. There had been people – of course there
had been people – but they had been other people's people;
they had not been for James. After the first couple of months,
almost every letter had come to have a sense of this, sometimes so vivid that Catherine felt as though she could see
the scenes he was describing, the disappointments – felt,
too, as though she could still do something to change them.
As though she could just reach out and put her hand on
James's shoulder, for instance, as he stood in a doorway near
Malachy's studio, talking to a German boy called Florian,
and saying to the boy that no, he was busy later, that he could
not join Florian and his friends in a bar – Catherine, reading

about this, wished that she could just reach out and push. And say, *No, go; you have to go; you have to see what this might be.* But he never did. He always just watched these boys that he longed for; he always just longed. And when the proof came, as it so often did, that he could not have them, that there could not be even the glimmer of a chance – the proof of a girlfriend, or even just of a sighting with a girl, his heart was always broken. *Sometimes, Catherine,* he had written in one letter – and in other letters variations on the same line – *it is just too fucking hard. Too fucking hard. I don't know. I try not to, but it is so hard not to feel . . .*

Over Christmas, he wrote her a sequence of short notes, the days and dates floating in as headings, looking almost unreal by the time, well into January, that Catherine saw them – *Christmas Eve, 4 p.m.; Christmas Eve, near midnight; Christmas morning, 10 a.m.; New Year's Eve, sunset.* Almost all of those days he had spent in the studio; the Tokyo show had been looming by then, and every hour had been precious to Malachy. It was overwork, Catherine had decided, which was making James's tone so deadened, his words so rambling; it was, she decided, a kind of homesickness, no matter how vehemently he might have insisted that he was happy not to be coming home. How could he, he had written, face Christmas dinner with his mother? But his loneliness, during those last days of the year, had been seared into every word he had put down on those pages; even when he had only been writing about Malachy, and about what a slave-driver he was, Catherine could see the panic and the fear in the very shapes of his letters, in the stretch of his lines. He looked forward so much, he told her, to her letters; he wished he could have a long letter from her every day. Her letters to him, he wrote at one point, were all that he had, all that he looked forward to; and this was a line that so unnerved – and, in fact, so frightened – Catherine that she found herself skipping forward to the next page, hoping for something easier, hoping for something to make her laugh, or make her hungry to know the same things about art, about light, about Berlin, that James knew – or to make her forget. To make her forget that he was in some kind of trouble, her lovely, her wonderful, her so-brilliant friend; that he was going through a thing that she did not know how to help him with, that she worried sometimes – often – would lower itself down on him and claim him, once and for all. Her life, with her manic romances and her friends and her burrow in the library, with her notebook of poems, or half-poems, and her rattled-off articles for *TN*, with her visits home, where everything was still so uneasy, so awkward, between her and her parents, but where nothing was really badly wrong, really badly unbearable, the way things seemed like they would be for a long time between James and his mother – her life seemed like something harmless, something weightless, in comparison. And yet she liked her life; she loved her life; she did not want to think of her life in this way. And so, if she was honest – if she was blunt – the truth was that actually, lately, she had not really been writing to James as often as she ought to, or had been writing the letters without always actually sending them. She had been enjoying the writing of them as much as ever, but something had been stopping her from putting them in the post. Some of her letters to him lately had functioned more like diary entries, and she had kept them, because by the time she had got round to finishing them, they had been so woefully out of date – she had sent him the letter about the first time with Rafe, but the next letter, about what it was like to be Rafe's girlfriend, and what the second time having sex with him had been like, and the third, had turned into the letter in which she had wondered about breaking up with Rafe, and then that letter had become the letter in which she had described the break-up, and Rafe's unbothered reaction, and how it had all felt like a bit of an anticlimax, really, if James would pardon the pun. James would not have to pardon the pun, because James would not get to read the letter, unless she took it out of her desk drawer and handed it to him when he arrived in Baggot Street tomorrow afternoon. James, over the last few weeks, had noticed the lag in her correspondence, while there had been no lag in his; more than once, she had come in to college to find an email from James, teasing her, needling her, pretending to be very disappointed in Catherine and her negligence – but of course not actually pretending, not actually teasing, when it came down to it, at all.

Still. He was coming home. That was the thing to remember; that was the thing that made all of this feel as though it would be OK. He had written to her of the decision earlier that week, and in fact maybe just the knowledge that he was coming home, that they would soon be together in the flesh, had been a factor in the fall-off in urgency, for Catherine, of sending him the long letters that had been the hallmark of their separation – for that was how they had both thought of it, especially during those first difficult weeks: a forced separation, a hard, mirrored exile – but now that he had decided to close up the distance between them, the physical chasm, maybe she had decided at some level that there was no need to write at such length to him anymore. Maybe she had felt, from the moment she had read his announcement – *I'm coming home. I've had enough of this place. Get the couch cushions ready for me* – that he was in some sense already home, and that to share things with him, all she had to do was write them down for herself, and because in some sense he was already here with her he could see them without needing them to be flown across the miles. He was home. Or, he was not home, not just yet, but he was as good as home, and when he was home, Catherine decided, none of that darkness which had come on him in Berlin could get to him, none of that loneliness would have a chance, not a moment, to sink its misery into him, to pull his days and his nights to shreds. Catherine would be with him. Everyone would be with him. Life would be with him, this teeming, booming, multiplying thing, and she and he could do everything together, and everything would once more be OK. Everything would be more than OK.

Zoe showed up at half three, complaining of a hangover and a broken umbrella and a bus that had failed to arrive. Catherine had already seen the whole exhibition by then, but she went around it with her again, standing for a long moment in front of *5 Deaths*, the piece made from the crime scene photograph which showed an actual corpse, a dead woman, staring blindly out from beneath a massive overturned car.

'It's too much,' Zoe said, her face screwed up in distaste. 'I don't give a shit about how powerful the effect of it might be. I still think it's wrong.'

'It's such a long time ago,' Catherine said.

'What difference does that make?'

'Don't you think that detaches it from any real emotion?'

'She's still a dead person,' Zoe said. 'She's not any less dead now than she was forty, or whatever, years ago.'

'I don't know,' Catherine said. 'I think the whole point is to be unsettled. It's not actually a photograph of a dead woman.'

Zoe squinted at her. 'You what, Citsers?'

'It's a piece made out of a photograph of a dead woman. Or, of a death scene, actually. Of the mechanics of someone dying, I mean. The actual person isn't even the point. I mean, the photograph would be as important to the police, or whoever, even if the woman wasn't lying there. Or even if there were twenty dead women lying there.'

'Well, Warhol wouldn't have wanted it if there hadn't been any dead woman,' Zoe said.

'Come on,' Catherine said, deciding to change the subject. 'You need to see the pillows.'

'Pillows?' said Zoe, who claimed to have had only two hours of sleep the night before. 'There are pillows?'

'Silver pillows,' Catherine said, and she led the way.

The silver pillows were actually foil balloons: fat, elongated tubes of helium, making a gentle, sleepy trail through the air. A gallery assistant sat on a chair in one corner, reading; she did not even glance up as the girls came into the space.

'So lovely,' Zoe said, lifting a hand towards the drift of silver. 'Look, we're in every one of them.'

The foil of each pillow was, by now, shabby and tarnished, presumably from the months of being bashed around; all of the reviews of the Warhol show had talked about this piece, about the fact that viewers were allowed to touch it. As the pillows clipped one another, kissed one another, they made a noise like so many slowed-down, ticking clocks; there were maybe twenty of them, some of them very clearly diminished, unable to lift themselves and steer themselves as confidently as the others did. Others of them were already fully deflated, reduced to rags of silver on the floor, and Catherine wondered whether their sad scattering was intended as part of the piece.

'Catch,' Zoe said then, slapping at one of the pillows; the silver fled her, and, calling out in delight, she hit at another, and then at another, leaping at them and laughing at them, calling to Catherine to do the same. She hesitated a moment, but then set to, and then all around them, the silver was glinting and swooping and falling, and she and Zoe were reaching and spinning and swiping, and they were like children, bumping into one another, bumping into the white walls, breathless with laughter, red-faced with it, and the noise was like a thunderstorm; no, the noise was like a shower of hail; no, the noise was like a waterfall on a mountainside, crashing another kind of silver onto stone, and then there was someone in the doorway, someone in the doorway that led to the soup cans and the Jackies and the Marilyns, and at first Catherine was embarrassed, because here she and Zoe were, eighteen and nineteen years of age, throwing themselves around an art gallery, attacking the works of art, and surely this person in the doorway would think oddly of them, would think less than warmly and approvingly of them, and for a moment Catherine almost stopped, but in the next moment, she felt instead delighted, delighted in a defiant kind of way, because why *not* do this; why *not* feel such glee and abandon in just this way? And then came the next moment, which was the moment when she saw who the person in the doorway was, and if her breath seemed to have gone as she danced under the helium pillows, as she wove and jumped and shouted in the silver stream, then it had not gone at all, there had been plenty of it, because it was gone now, and it was really gone, and she had gone still and the silver was plunging around her, and Zoe was still leaping, and James was there, a young, thin boy in the doorway, no, a boy who looked somehow at once both young and old, his red hair grown high and grown messy, into huge, tumbling curls, his skin pale, his freckles faded, his smile nervous, and hesitant, and moving, now, his lips were moving, as he said her name.

2

'What the fuck? What the fuck?!'

'Surprise. Surprise. Surprise. Surprise.'

'You were meant – tomorrow! You were meant – it was tomorrow, wasn't it? You said tomorrow! You said Sunday!'

'I know. I know. I wanted to surprise you.'

'Oh my God, James. Oh my *God*.'

'Sorry.'

'No, you're not sorry. No, you're not sorry. You fucker. You *fucker*.'

'No, I'm not sorry. Yes, I am a fucker.'

'How did you get here? How did you—'

'I got a lift. I told you. In another lorry. I just left on Wednesday instead of on Thursday.'

'No, how did you get *here*? How did you know I was here?'

'Oh. Amy was in Baggot Street when I got there. She told me where you were gone. Off on your cultural expedition, like a good little girl. I got the bus. Which took nearly as long as the lorry from Berlin, I might mention.'

'You *fucker*! I can't believe you did this! I can't believe you're here!'

'I can't believe I found you engaged in a Dionysian orgy in a room full of priceless Andy Warhols, but there you go.'

'Oh my God. Oh my God. Seriously, James, this is un-believable. How can you be *here*?'

'How can you not be in handcuffs?'

'Stop it, James, seriously. I can't believe this. I can't believe this. You're actually *here*.'

'I'm here.'

'You're actually *here*.'

'I'm home.'

'You're actually *here*.'

*

By the time they got home from Emmet Doyle's party that night it was after three o'clock, and they both staggered in the door for different reasons: James because he was exhausted, Catherine because she was plastered. The house was in darkness; Amy and Lorraine were either still out themselves or long in bed.

Everything was all right now; booze and dancing and the company of everyone had made everything, every single thing, all right. James had not really wanted to go to Emmet's party, of course; he had protested to Catherine that he would know nobody, that he was not in the mood yet for such full-on socializing, that he just wanted to go back to Baggot Street with her, and spend the evening catching up properly, talking about everything. But Catherine and the others had persuaded him; the others had wanted Catherine to come anyway, and Catherine, after a couple of drinks, had decided that she wanted to go. James had resisted for a while, but she had talked him round, had persuaded him that it would be fun, that it would be a good introduction to everyone else she wanted him to meet, that it would be full of good-looking guys. Zoe had agreed, egging James on, nudging him, leaning in conspiratorially as though she had known him as long, as deeply, as Catherine had, as though they knew what he needed, knew what was good for him, and Catherine – Catherine had felt a pang of irritation, seeing this, and a pang of jealousy, seeing how readily, how laughingly, James had responded to her pleas, but mostly, she had been relieved, that they would all be going out tonight, and going out with everybody, instead of going home to face up to the seriousness of what had been in James's letters. And of course she felt terrible about this, of course she felt like a horrible person, but it was just that she could not face up to it yet, not just yet, now that he was here, now that he was beside her, leaning into her, clutching her hand, so often, underneath the table of the pub they had all gone to in Thomas Street after IMMA. She could face it tomorrow, she told herself, but not tonight. Tonight she needed to have fun; tonight *they* needed to have fun, the two of them, as a celebration, a launching upon Dublin of the force that, together, they were going to be. They drank in Thomas Street and then in the Buttery bar until it was time to make their way to Emmet's rooms, by which time Catherine was tripping and rambling, and James was – she did not, exactly, remember how James was – and she and Zoe were manic and Conor had somehow met up with them again, and Conor had said something to James – she could not remember what it was, but she knew that she had wanted to *kill* Conor for saying it at the time. Maybe she had tried to kill Conor, or anyway tried to give out to him – she could not remember; had she said something to him, shouted something at him, on their way across Front Square?

'Did I say something to Conor about you?' she asked James now, from the armchair into which she had slumped as soon as they came in the door of Baggot Street. James was fixing a bed for himself on the couch cushions, wrestling with the grey, saggy duvet that Amy or Lorraine had left out for him. The room was in half-darkness; Catherine had turned on the main light, but James had complained instantly about its brightness, shielding his eyes, and had fumbled with the switch of the lamp beside the television until it had come on. He had stripped, by now, down to his polo shirt and his boxers – she had not even noticed him taking his jeans off, which meant that she must, for a minute or so, have dropped off – and he had his back to her, so that she could take a good look at the thinness of his legs, the way his back was threaded with the jut of his spine.

'You're so *skinny*,' she said now, which felt suddenly much more important than the question of whether Conor had said or had not said anything to him, and anyway it did not matter, apparently, which of them was the more important, because James did not seem to be listening to her; he did not seem to plan on turning around and giving her any kind of answer.

'James,' she said, and she threw her hand towards him, which did not work, because her hand, of course, was attached to her arm and to the rest of her body, so she reached down to where her foot was and she took off her shoe; '*James!*' she said again, more insistently and more loudly, and she pulled the shoe back into the air behind her head and she pushed it forward and she let it go.

She missed. But James, his face almost unrecognizable with tiredness, turned around anyway.

'I was calling you,' Catherine said, and her head was very floppy, for some reason; her head kept falling back and falling forward, and the cushion of the armchair behind her could not hold it, which was surely what the cushion of the armchair was supposed to do. 'I was *calling* you. I wanted you.'

'Go to sleep, Catherine,' James said, his mouth a funny, cross straight line, and he came over to where she sat, and he pulled her out of her chair by both elbows, and walked her towards the door.

She pouted. 'I don't *want* to sleep. I want to talk about the party. Wasn't it brilliant? Wasn't everyone so cool?'

He opened the door. 'Go to sleep, Catherine. I don't have the energy. Go to sleep.'

'I'm so glad you came to the party,' she said, but he was closing the sitting-room door.

*

Sunday was a write-off, but on Monday morning Catherine's head felt clear again, and although it took much persuasion to budge James from his bed on the couch, by eleven o'clock they were both on campus, sitting on a bench by the lawn outside the arts block, drinking coffee and surveying the talent.

'There's Shane,' Catherine said, grabbing James's arm. 'Remember I wrote to you about him?'

'Shane *Russian* Shane?' James said, looking around in every direction. 'Where?'

'Over there,' Catherine said, 'but for fuck's sake don't be so obvious!'

But it was too late: James was staring at him. Shane was not someone she knew personally, but he was someone she had described at great length in her letters to James; he was a fourth year, and studying Russian, and both she and Zoe agreed that he was one of the best-looking guys in college. *You should see him, James*, she had written, back in October or November, *you'd love him. He's unbelievably sexy.*

'Him?' James was saying doubtfully now. 'With the grey hair?'

'I told you about the grey hair! The grey hair is what makes him so sexy!'

'What is he, forty?'

'No!'

'He looks forty. Are you sure that's not Aidan?'

'James!' she said, thumping him on the arm.

'When am I going to meet the famous Aidan, by the way?'

'Never you mind meeting Aidan. Concentrate on Shane.'

'I don't see it, Catherine,' James said, shaking his head more firmly. 'I don't see it at all.'

'But he's gorgeous.'

'He's all right. I wouldn't say much more than that.'

'Wait until he stands up. He's tall. You might change your mind.'

'Ah, Catherine. Now you're just forcing things.'

'I'm *not*,' she said mock-petulantly, pretending to be offended, but the truth was that she was slightly offended, actually. Shane was a ride. For James to so bluntly deny this now, to so bluntly refuse Catherine's invitation to admire him, to light-heartedly stalk him and trade pithy, funny comments about him: she felt almost robbed. She looked around the lawn, hoping to see another of the guys she had so looked forward to showing him, but there was only the usual late-morning spread of unremarkables, smoking their cigarettes and drinking their coffees and reading their yellowed paperbacks in preparation for their afternoon classes. Which, come to think of it, was something Catherine should be doing herself right at this minute; she had a Romance tutorial at three, and a *TN* article – an interview with Pat McCabe – due that evening. But it seemed wrong, somehow, not to spend this time with James. He was just home. He was *finally* home. He was *here* – here, and now. She could not waste that. She could not behave in a normal manner, as though it was just a normal Monday, with James far away in Berlin, and everything needing to be saved up for a letter to him.

'I can't believe you don't think Russian Shane is gorgeous,' she said. 'I've been looking forward to showing him to you for months.'

'Oh, well. Sorry.'

'I don't feel like showing you any of the others now.'

'Ah, Catherine,' he said, taking her arm. 'I'm dying to see them all. Sure I feel like I'm after walking onto a film set or something. I'm going to meet Dusky Dick next, I assume?'

'Oh my God,' she gasped. 'Don't you *dare* call him that if you do meet him!'

'If? *If?* It's a matter of *when*, not *if*, I hope.'

'Rafe doesn't come in to college much these days. I think he prefers to study at home. Or smoke weed there.'

He frowned at her. 'You've killed him, haven't you, Reilly? You've chopped him up and buried him under the patio. That beautiful langer, the colour of a Longford sunset, gone forever.'

'Oh my God, *stop* it,' she said, swatting at him, but the truth was that she did not want James to stop. This was what she had wanted for so many months: for James to be here with her, gossiping about boys, reducing her to helpless laughter with his jokes and his mutterings and his outrageous innuendoes, the way that only he could come up with them; the way that she remembered him from the summer. She felt so lucky, having him here beside her; she felt luckier than anyone else sitting around this lawn, anyone else walking around this campus, anyone living in this whole city: they only had the stupid city, and she had James.

'Now *he*'s more like it,' James said, sitting up suddenly, and it was Catherine's turn to look about wildly.

'Who?'

'Him,' James said, pointing straight across the lawn, his arm held high; Catherine gasped and batted at him to put it back down.

'Jesus! A bit of discretion!'

'Ah, sure who gives a fuck? Sure he's not looking at me.'

Yeah, but plenty of other people are, Catherine thought, but she was too concerned with trying to work out who he was talking about to nag him further. There were no guys she even recognized around, except Emmet Doyle, opening a Coke can beside the bin, and the sight of him gave her a rush of guilt about the way she had dragged James to his ridiculous party, so she cast about for someone else, but there was nobody else, and by leaning into James's line of vision, she landed once again on Emmet.

'You're not talking about The Doyle?' she said, incredulously.

'Oh, yeah,' James snorted. 'I forgot about that ridiculous nickname. Yeah, I was impressed by him at the party the other night as well. He's very nice. Very nice indeed.'

'Oh, come *on*,' Catherine spluttered. 'He's The Doyle.'

'What does that mean?'

'He's a messer,' Catherine said. 'He's a *TN* hack.'

'So are you.'

'Yeah, but he *really* is. He practically lives in the publications office. And the rest of the time he's just swaggering around campus, doling wisecracks and insults out to everybody.'

'Sounds like your friend Conor.'

'No, he's worse,' Catherine said. 'He saw some of my poems up in the publications office and he's been slagging me about them ever since. *Quoting* them at me. He's a fucker.'

'Well, I don't care about his taste in poems. I just think he's a right little bit of stuff.'

'Ah, James.'

'I do. Those lovely ruddy cheeks of his.'

'James!'

'You have a filthy mind, Reilly. What did you say his real name was again? Or are we only allowed to use his *nom de plume*?'

'Emmet,' she said sulkily.

'Ah, after Robert Emmet the patriot, presumably. Well, I'll write your epitaph for you, Sonny. Come over here to me and I'll write you a lovely one.'

'I don't think he's a patriot, exactly. He went to Gonzaga.'

'Come up, you fearful Jesuit!' James said then, in a roar, which horrified Catherine – she covered her face with her hands, the sight of which only served, of course, to encourage James, and by the time he had finished with his commentary, Catherine was almost falling off the bench with a mixture of laughter and mortification, and James was holding on to her, helplessly laughing himself, and in the next moment he was hugging her, his arms tightly around her, his breath hot on her neck. His body was still quaking with the laughter, and against her shoulder he was making a noise like crying, and for a horrified moment she thought that he actually might be crying, but as he gave a long, low sigh she knew that he was all right, that he was just recovering, just steeped in the enjoyment of how funny he himself had been.

'Oh, Catherine,' he said, without pulling away from her. 'I'm so glad you're home.'

She snorted. 'Glad *you're* home.'

He went very still. 'Why? What did I say?'

'You said you were glad *I* was home.'

'Arrah, you, me, who gives a fuck which one it is,' he said, and he hugged her more tightly, and though she felt terrible about it, she wished that he would let go of her now: she knew that he liked to be physically affectionate, that it was just his way, but this was such a long hug, and in such an exposed, public place; she felt herself cringing at the grip of him around her now, and to try to bring it to an end, to try to wrap it up in some way, she patted him on the back with her right hand, gently but firmly: once, twice, three times. And in her arms, James burst out laughing, and with his own hand, he did exactly the same thing, except that he did not pat her back but really clapped it, almost belted it, as though they were two hurlers embracing on the pitch after one of their teams had beaten the other.

'Very funny,' she muttered into his shoulder. 'Nothing gets past you, does it, Flynn?'

'Not a thing, Reilly,' he said happily, and he planted a round of quick, light kisses all down her neck.

They spent the whole day together, having coffee after coffee, one endless conversation, Catherine introducing James to as many of her friends as she set eyes on, and arguing with him over the attractiveness, or lack thereof, of various boys. There was no sign of Rafe, to Catherine's relief, but in the evening Aidan sauntered up to them on the ramp, fresh from a Romance lecture, his Chaucer under one arm, mad to talk about the Wife of Bath. But once Catherine introduced him to James, it was James's time in Berlin he wanted to talk about; he had heard from Catherine, he said, shooting her an unreadable glance, so much about James and what he was doing over there, about the great time he was having; it must have been such a rush, living there, was it? He himself had been there, but years ago, before the wall had come down, and he had heard such good things about the city now, about how hedonistic it was, how alive. In typical Aidan form, he did not pause for long enough to have this question actually answered by James; he continued on. James was watching him in amusement, Catherine saw, but also with something else, something more guarded.

'What did you think of him?' she said, after Aidan had taken his leave of them a few minutes later.

But James just shrugged. 'I'm ready to go home,' he said. 'Will we head?'

'Oh,' Catherine said, uneasily. 'I have to write my article.'

'What article?' James said almost crossly.

'The McCabe interview. I told you. Tonight's production night and I have to get it in.'

'Oh well,' he said, leaning back against the railings. 'Will I wait for you?'

'No, go ahead,' Catherine said, frowning as though she could not countenance causing him such an inconvenience. 'I'll run up and get this done, and I'll be home in an hour or so. I won't be long.'

'Promise?' said James, in a tone of mock pleading.

'Promise,' Catherine said, and they embraced as tightly as two people who would not see each other again for weeks, or months, or years. Then she was crossing Front Square at a fast clip, thinking how lovely it was, the evening air. The moon was out, and the cobblestones were a shimmering lake of grey. For a moment, she thought she heard her name being called, but that was someone else; that was someone calling someone else's name.

She wrote the McCabe interview up quickly once she got a desk in the crowded publications office, chopping a couple of hundred words out reluctantly when it was finished – all the good quotes he had given her were long ones, and she wished she could fit them in, but with them in there was no space for anything about the actual novel – and printed it out. Seeing it emerge on the tray, Emmet Doyle crossed the room to pick it up for her, looking at the first page as he brought it to her desk.

'"Patrick McCabe strides into the bright surroundings of Cafe Irie in Temple Bar, looking like a man who is at once distracted and intense",' he read aloud. 'What's this, a novel?'

'Give me that,' she said, snatching it from him. He was grinning at her, and for a moment she could almost see what James had meant – he was kind of attractive, his skin clear, his eyes a dark, striking blue, his lanky frame perched, now, on the edge of her desk, but it was so conventional, his attractiveness; it was not the kind of thing she had imagined whispering over with James.

'There's a letter for you, by the way, Poetess,' he said, nodding towards the mailbox on the opposite wall. 'Did you get it?'

'No,' Catherine said, getting up. 'How long has it been here?'

'A couple of days,' Emmet shrugged. 'It's probably McCabe's wife, warning you to stop stalking him.'

'Fuck off,' she laughed, taking down the envelope. It was handwritten, and bearing a Dublin postmark; she tore it open to find a curt note from the publicist of the novelist Michael Doonan, granting her the interview with him that she had been chasing for months. She was, the publicist explained, to be given forty minutes on a Friday afternoon the following month, and the questions were to focus on Doonan's new novel, *Engines of Everything*, not on the earlier trilogy which had recently been made into a controversial television series. This gave her a few weeks for preparation, which was just as well, because she had read only one of Doonan's books, and she wanted to do a good job on this interview, because he so rarely granted them.

'Restraining order?' Emmet said, coming up to her at the mailbox. He was grinning as widely as ever, but the blush was back again; she watched its progress across the smooth skin of his face.

'Very funny,' she said, stuffing the envelope into her pocket. 'Well, enjoy production night. I have dinner waiting for me.'

He gave her a disbelieving look. 'What, has your mother moved in with you or something?'

'No,' she said, laughing. 'Just my friend. James.'

'Oh, *James*, is it?' Emmet said archly. 'That's the ginger I saw you hugging outside the arts block this morning? I was heartbroken, Reilly. I thought the time we spent together on Saturday night meant something. You came back to my place —'

'With about a hundred other people.'

'And then this morning, I'm coming out of my Politics tutorial—'

'You were not coming out of a Politics tutorial at half eleven in the morning.'

'. . . to see you – I resent that statement, by the way – to see you with your arms around another man. I'm heartbroken, Reilly. Devastated.'

This was Doyle's usual routine, this layering of sarcasm onto mockery onto brazen cheek, onto what, deep down, might even be a trace of genuine honesty, until it was impossible to tell which was which and what was what. It was a code, deep irony by means of the pretence of sincerity, in which he and a few of the other *TN* guys frequently spoke, and Catherine could not get her head around it. Talking to them, she tried to imitate it, but her efforts always seemed to come out just sounding bitchy.

'Fuck off, Doyle,' she said now, and exactly that thing happened, but Emmet seemed not to notice.

'You brought your friend to my party the other night, right? I was talking to him for a while.'

'Yeah. He'd just arrived from Berlin.'

'Very strong culchie accent for a German.'

'Hilarious,' she said, as she gathered her things from the desk: her notes, her jacket, her bag. 'Right. I'm off home,' she said, making for the door.

Emmet followed her. 'Does your friend go to college here?' he said, as they reached the hallway. 'I don't think I've seen him before Saturday.'

'No, he's not a student,' Catherine said. She turned slightly, and Emmet stopped abruptly, so that he was standing very close to her. He stepped back. Catherine stepped in the other direction. There was silence between them for a long moment; Catherine did not know what to do with it.

'Don't you have a newspaper to put to bed?' she said eventually, her tone sharp.

For a second, Emmet looked as though he did not understand the question, but then he rolled his eyes at her, and the grin was back. *Put to bed?* he said mockingly. 'Where'd you learn that, the *Longford Leader?*'

'Goodnight, Emmet,' she said, waving without looking back at him, as she took the first flight.

He leaned down over the banister. 'Goodnight, Poetess,' he called.

3

Sometime after nine the next morning, Catherine tiptoed into the sitting room to wake James up in the same way she had woken him the morning before: by bouncing on his couch cushions until he groaned. But this time, instead of jumping on him, she stood and watched him for a long moment as he slept. He was on his side, with his arms raised over his face, his head pushed forward into the crooks of his elbows; it was a position she remembered from Carrigfinn during the summer, from when she had crept into his room to wake him. Now the air was thick with the smell of his sleep, the stale, slightly sickly smell of a night of dreaming breath.

James gasped and dropped his arms to his chest, and his eyes shot open, wide; they were staring right at Catherine, staring through her. She was startled by his expression, which seemed almost terrified, and she took a step back, but in the next instant James was blinking sleepily, stretching, and he looked like himself again.

'Morning,' she said brightly, reaching down to stipple her fingertips on his bare shoulder.

'No, no,' he said, burying his head in his pillow. 'It's not morning, Catherine. Go away. It's still the middle of the night.'

'It's getting-up time,' she said, crossing to the window and opening the shutters. 'God, this room is always so stuffy the morning after we have people round.'

He raised himself to his elbows and frowned at her. 'Oh, so I'm a "person round", am I?'

'What are you going to get up to today?' she said, coming back to the couch.

'You tell me,' he shrugged. 'Another day of staring at the older men you have a Daddy fetish about, presumably. God, you've no taste at all, Reilly, do you know that?'

She pushed his head into the pillow until he bawled in protest, and then she released him, laughing. He twisted around and grabbed her, his hands tickling her waist, inching towards her belly button; she squealed and tried to wriggle away from him, but he had her. He pulled her down, and pressed his face into the back of her neck, growling, squeezing her so tight that she could hardly breathe. She pushed back against him, but he had stopped tickling her now; he had stopped moving altogether, and now his body against hers was solid and still. He sighed.

'So what are we doing today, Brain?'

It was one of their routines, a quote from a cartoon they both found hilarious, and Catherine responded without missing a beat. 'The same thing we do every day, Pinky. *Try to take over the world!*'

'Oh, Reilly,' he said, nuzzling her, 'we're awful eejits, do you know that?'

'I know,' she said, happily.

'So, what are we doing today?'

'Well, I have a load of lectures. And I have to meet up with Dr Parker to ask him about my Plath essay.'

'*Daddy, Daddy . . .*'

'Shut *up*,' she said, kicking back at him. He snorted.

'All right,' he said, and on her neck she felt the scrape of his stubble. 'Will I come in with you, then? Or what do you want to do?'

'Oh,' she said, surprised. 'You want to come in to college with me again?'

'Oh,' he said, sounding embarrassed. 'Was that not the plan? I thought—'

'No, no,' she said, feeling embarrassed herself now; she was actually blushing, and so glad that she had her back to him so that he could not see her, 'Of course you can come in to college with me. I just thought . . .'

'Oh, well, I won't if you don't want me to,' he said, and she could feel the pillow jolting as he shook his head. 'No, no. Of course. You have your lectures. Sure if I wanted to go to lectures, I'd have gone to college myself.'

'It's just,' she said, and she turned around now to face him. His morning breath hit her; she reeled for a second but managed not to let her reaction show. 'It's just, yeah, I thought you'd have your own stuff to do. You said you wanted to find a darkroom this week, and look for a job, maybe, and—'

'Yeah,' he said, quietly.

'I mean, we can meet up later.'

'I'll walk in with you anyway,' he said, 'and then we can make our arrangements for later. Does that sound OK?'

'OK,' she said, but uncertainly, and she knew he heard the uncertainty in her tone, and she saw him react to it – a sort of wincing, a sort of tightening and thinning of his mouth, a darkening of his eyes – so, to try and change the mood, she shook him, and bounced on him, and tickled him until he begged her to stop.

'Now, *up*,' she said then, getting to her feet and heading towards the kitchen. 'It's a new day. New dawn.'

'Fuck the dawn,' she heard James mutter from behind her, as he snuggled back into his makeshift bed.

—

Once again, it took ages to get him out of the house, and by the time they reached college she was running late for her Expressionism tutorial, but as they came through the Nassau Street entrance, James grabbed Catherine's arm suddenly and pulled her over in the direction of the security booth.

'Come here for a minute,' he said. 'I want you to see something. I want to show you something.'

'James. I'm late.'

'It'll only take a second,' he said, and then he was jabbing at the long, curved window of the booth, tapping a finger on the glass. 'I love this. Look.'

All Catherine could see was the white-haired security guard, looking as though he was ready for war in his uniform of epaulettes and peaked cap. He regarded James with suspicion for a moment, before yawning and looking away.

'All these *faces*,' James was saying, from beside her, and then she saw what it was that he was talking about: the long row of student ID cards slotted into the frame behind the glass. Each of them had been found on campus, or somewhere in town, and handed in here; they stared grimly out at the passers-by, a line-up of missing people who were actually not missing at all.

'I love these things,' James said, running a finger along the glass slowly, as though he was reading braille. 'I love the way people always look in these kinds of photographs,' he said. 'The way they're got.'

'*Got?*' she repeated, uncertainly.

'Yeah. The way people are caught in them. Before they have a chance to arrange their expressions the way people always want to when you photograph them. Before they even get a chance to think.'

'God, they're ugly as sin, I think,' Catherine said, standing back from them a little; a guy from her American Poetry class passed by, and she smiled a greeting at him.

'No, no,' James said, hunched down at the window. 'They're perfect. I mean, look at this one.'

He was looking, now, at a card depicting a dour, pallid-looking girl; he was gazing at it with as much admiration as if it was the original Botticelli Venus. The girl was someone Catherine knew from around, actually, and in the flesh, she was quite pretty; probably, she hated this photo of herself. Possibly, she had lost her ID card on purpose, in the hope of getting a new, updated one, with a much more flattering headshot, but as Catherine herself had discovered the previous year, that trick did not work. They kept your photo on the computer system; you were stuck with it for the entire length of your degree. In her own, Catherine looked like a junkie: lank-haired, slack-mouthed, wearing the sloppy denim jacket she had worn almost every day since buying it for herself at the age of fifteen; she had only recently got rid of that jacket, by donating it to the Oxfam shop on Great George's Street. Someone else was probably walking around Dublin in that jacket now, which was a strange thought; someone who was unaware of the previous life it had led. These days Catherine wore a brown suede jacket she had bought second-hand in Harlequin; its lining was ripped and stained in places, but the suede was soft and lovely, and she liked to stroke the collar of it when she was wearing it, while she was talking to people – a habit which Emmet Doyle, come to think of it, had picked up on and had mimicked laughingly on the ramp a couple of times.

'I'd love my photographs to look like these,' James said now. 'I'd love them to be this truthful.'

'But they look like mugshots!'

141

'Not mugshots,' James said, shaking his head. 'With mug-shots there's a definite style. And in mugshots they need you to be recognizable, for the next time you're caught with your trousers down. With these, though, nothing matters. The second you're within sight of the camera, that's it. *Boom*. Got you. Don't care what you think of you. Next!'

'I hate mine,' Catherine said sullenly.

'Oh!' James said, thrusting his hand out to her. 'Can I see it?'

She snorted. 'Not a hope!'

'Ah, come on. Please. Please. I want to see it. I want to make a photograph of you like these ones.'

'You must be *joking*!' she said, covering her pocket with her hand, just in case he decided to delve in there. 'Now I have to go, or Roberts will have the door locked. Do you know what you want to do later?'

'Oh, I'll be around,' James said, almost dreamily, still immersed in the IDs.

He was around. He was around for coffee after her tutorial, and for lunch after her next lecture, and when they had fin-ished their lunch he insisted that they go to Café en Seine, for a 'proper coffee', and Catherine agreed, guiltily and a little grouchily, because she was meant to be in the library prepar-ing for her meeting with Dr Parker, but still. How many times had she walked these streets and gone to this cafe without James, wishing that he had been with her in just this way? How many letters had she written to him, talking about her lectures and what she had got up to on her lunchtimes and what she had seen and what she had thought? And now he was right here, talking a blue streak about his new philosophy of portraiture, and linking her arm the way he always liked to do when they walked, and what did she have to be complaining about, exactly? What did she have to be moaning about? She could prepare for the meeting about her essay when they got back from their coffee. All she had to do was come up with a title, and five minutes glancing over the poems would be enough for that. She leaned into James, feeling again the giddiness of his still-strange presence beside her, and she nodded at something he was saying about angles, and she smiled. And then she saw him. A beautiful specimen; there was no doubt but that he could only be described as a beautiful, an absolutely fucking stunning, specimen coming towards them. A guy, their age but dressed in a suit and tie, meaning that he was probably, actually, a couple of years older, that he was probably on his lunch break from an office job. He was breathtaking: tall, and skinny, his short hair slightly scruffy, and with perfect, olive skin, and with a lovely kind of preoccupied look in his dark eyes, and with lips so full they looked as though somebody had punched them to make them that way, or kissed them, maybe – kissed them until they were swollen; and he was coming towards them now, rapidly, his hands in the pockets of his gorgeous, navy suit, his steps rushed and urgent, and Catherine did not even have to jerk James's arm, or elbow James in the side, to get James to stop talking, to pay attention, to see what was there for the seeing, right in front of them, because James, beside her, had simply stopped walking.

'Holy shit,' he said, right there in the middle of Dawson Street, staring at the guy as though he was his long-lost brother. 'Holy fucking shit.'

Catherine was mortified. '*James!*' she said, looking down at the red slabs at their feet. 'Jesus!'

But James was not listening to her. He was staring; he was staring at the guy now as the guy came closer to them, and as the guy – who was somehow, mercifully, oblivious, his eyes still fixed on a point in the direction of college – passed them by.

'Do you know him?' Catherine said, stupidly.

James did not even acknowledge the question. He had turned to watch the guy go, and his mouth looked grim and his eyes almost angry, and he was saying nothing. Catherine looked at him, baffled. Was he joking? she wondered. Was this some kind of act, some kind of parody he was putting on?

'James,' she said, trying to laugh. 'Are you OK?'

The guy was changing course up ahead, she saw. He veered to the left, weaving his way through the crowd, and he disappeared into the bookshop.

'Come on,' James said, and he headed back the way they had come.

Nothing Catherine said to him as they stood at the Irish fiction section, pretending to look at novels but actually watching the every move of the guy – who was further down in the same aisle going through the new releases – could persuade James to be any more subtle. He stared; he frowned; he banged and messed up and dropped the books so that practically everyone else in the shop looked their way, irritated, but still the guy's focus did not waver; he had obviously come in here looking for something, and he was going to keep searching until he got it.

'He is *lovely*,' Catherine offered, hearing how ineffectual the words sounded, how somehow naive and unworldly; it seemed beside the point, suddenly, that the guy was actually cute. James's reaction had filled the space around them with a much starker, much more forceful energy; beside him, glancing towards the guy, she felt like a kid looking for another glittery sticker to add to her collection.

'Just look at him,' James said. 'With his book.'

He said *book* as though it was something shameful, Catherine thought; as though it was something for which he was mocking the guy, rather than admiring him.

'He's too fucking lovely altogether,' he said then, more loudly.

'James! He'll hear you!'

He cut his eyes at her. 'He'll hear me staring?'

'No, but . . .'

'Well, then,' he said, and as the guy moved down the aisle now, James moved too.

'For fuck's sake!' Catherine said, exasperated. 'This is—'

'This is *what*, Catherine?' James said, turning back to her. 'This is what? Do you need to go? Do you want me to meet you in the cafe?'

Her mouth dropped open. She felt heat sear her face. 'No, but, obviously . . .'

He frowned. 'Obviously what?'

'I don't know,' she said, stammering now. 'I mean, he doesn't . . .'

'Oh, for Christ's sake, Catherine,' James said through gritted teeth, and she felt again the shock of it – that he seemed really, truly angry. Angry with her. Angry *at* her. But what had she done? All she was doing was trying to talk to him. Reason with him. He couldn't just *stare* at people in this way. He couldn't just talk at such an obvious volume about them, doing nothing to hide his interest. He just had to be more artful about these things. He had to be more discreet.

'I really need to get back to the library, I think,' she said, and she realized she was holding her breath as she waited for his response.

He looked at her for a moment as though he was about to really explode at her, really scream at her, but in the next moment, all the anger seemed to have gone out of him, seemed just to slide out of his shoulders and out of his eyes, and he nodded. 'All right,' he said, tiredly, putting down the novel he had been holding. 'Will we go?'

Relieved, Catherine led the way, but as she neared the exit, she glanced back to say something to him, something light-hearted, something on a completely different subject, and she stopped short, because James was no longer behind her. She looked around in confusion, back to where they had been standing, and then to the door, in case he had slipped ahead of her, somehow, but he was in neither place. She looked to the till; could he be buying something? But no, and he was not at any of the tables, either, and not on the stairs; he was nowhere to be seen.

Neither was the guy, she saw now, her heart thumping, her cheeks once more blazing; neither was the guy in the suit standing where he had been standing a few moments ago, looking at the new releases. She moved back into the centre of the floor, looking left and right; the other customers seemed to swim around her, the shelves and the stacks of books and the crinkling green carrier bags. She pushed back further, to the section marked TRAVEL, the section hung with posters of beaches and skyscrapers and medieval side-streets, with blue-bubbled maps of the world. She swept through it, her heart still clattering, in places the dampness of sweat on her skin, but she saw no trace of them, of James and the boy – the boy she had so stupidly, so cluelessly, pointed out to him. In a question, in a bewildered, injured question, she heard herself say James's name aloud. A woman looked at her strangely. *Mind your own business, you old bitch*, Catherine thought, but already she had forgotten about the woman, and was looking again for James; why would he do this to her? Go somewhere without her – go with—

With a single step, she was into the next section, and James was standing right there, leaning against a display table, his thighs pressed against it, in his hands a book with a cover washed in bright, abstracted colours. It was *Birthday Letters*, Catherine saw; Ted Hughes's new collection of poems about Plath. It was a book Catherine had been meaning all month to buy, and to read for her essay research; to now find James apparently immersed in it seemed surreal, like a jagged before and after in her life forcing themselves on top of one another as some kind of practical joke.

'Oh,' she said, working to steady her voice. 'You found that.'

He blinked, seeming surprised. 'What?'

'The Hughes. I wanted to buy that, actually.'

'I'll buy it for you,' he said brightly, snapping the book shut, tucking it under his arm, but as he gave her a quick, strange smile, something in his eyes snagged her suspicion; something in the way his glance hovered over her shoulder. She turned, and there was the guy, standing maybe ten feet away, also holding a book. He was also leaning against a table, and one arm was slung over a low bookcase; he looked as though he had been precisely arranged for a photograph. Everything about him was studied, perfect. He did not look up as she stared at him – and as James, behind her, presumably stared too – but she felt quite sure that he knew they were watching him, and that he was enjoying it. He reached up, apparently absent-mindedly, to run a finger over an eyebrow, and Catherine felt her throat close up – what was that? Did that mean something? Was that some kind of signal? She felt sweat bloom again in her armpits, and on the palms of her hands. The room felt as though it was at once coming towards her and rushing away. She put a hand to the table.

'Come on,' James said, from behind her, and he walked at a brisk clip to the till.

And she could have cried. She felt it like nausea. That something had tilted like this between them; that something between them was off. What had just happened? She could not even begin to put it into words, to try to understand it; what was this anger and distance that had come and unfolded itself in the space where her self touched on his? All afternoon as she tried to work in the library, her mind reeled when she thought of that moment: turning to say something to him and finding that he was not there, and seeing, then, that the guy, the stranger, was not where he had been either. What had she thought? What had she imagined? Body pressed to body, mouth to mouth, crotch pressed to crotch, in the poetry section of Hodges bloody Figgis? Had she honestly believed in any part of herself that that was going to happen? Had she honestly, worse still, feared it? And if she had feared it – for there could be little doubt, from the thumping and sweating and panic of her reaction, from the way that she had bolted through the shop, calling his name, like a mother suddenly finding herself without her toddler, that she had in some way feared it, dreaded it, dreaded even the thought of it, losing him to this guy, seeing him even just walking off to a cafe with him – then what did *that* mean? What did that say about her, about what kind of friend she was?

Nothing good, anyway. Nothing that could ever be allowed.

*

James was waiting by the railings of the arts block when she and Zoe came out of their Modern Painting lecture that evening; Zoe spotted him first, and ran over to him, waving and calling his name. Catherine held back, still shaken from what had happened that afternoon, still unsure of herself and of how James would be with her, but he was smiling, laughing as Zoe put her arms around him, kissing him; he looked at Catherine over Zoe's shoulder, and winked.

'Surprise,' he said, as Zoe released him, and he stepped over to kiss Catherine.

'How was your day?' she said, too brightly, and she thought she saw a sneer or a smirk in his eyes for a moment, but no, she was imagining things; he was smiling just as before, and he was nodding.

'Good, good,' he said, indicating his camera bag. 'I found myself a darkroom. It's here on campus, actually. I bumped into your old flame Aidan this morning and he put me in touch with someone in the Photography Society.'

'*Aidan* did?'

'Yeah. He knows the treasurer quite well, apparently.'

'Don't you have to be a student here to use the PhotoSoc darkroom?' said Zoe.

'*Well . . .*' James looked at her, raising an eyebrow. 'Technically, of course. But the promise of sexual favours always opens a door or two, I find.'

Zoe screeched with laughter at this, grabbing James as though she had to hang on to him to stop herself from falling, and James, laughing himself, took in her reaction with obvious satisfaction. Catherine felt again the odd stab of jealousy she had felt in IMMA on Saturday, watching the two of them getting on so easily, so readily, but it was stronger this time, and it felt like real irritation; she had a sudden desire to step in and knock Zoe away from James, to turn the conversation around to something entirely different, something that was not fuelled by this stupid, cheap innuendo. She hated the way Zoe fed on it, and asked with her eyes for more of it, as though that kind of talk was all that James was good for, the only language that he was capable of speaking—

'So I'm going to be on campus a good bit, that means,' said James, who had by now detached himself from Zoe anyway. 'Which is good news, I think? Isn't it?'

'Yeah,' Catherine managed to say.

'*Of course* it is,' Zoe added enthusiastically. 'We can have coffee all the time! We can have lunch! I can introduce you to Simon!'

James raised an eyebrow. 'Who's Simon?'

'He's my *gay friend*,' said Zoe, making a show of fluttering her eyelashes.

James shot a look at Catherine. 'Oh, yeah?'

'He lives in England,' Zoe said, more bluntly. 'But he sometimes visits! He might be visiting sometime this year!'

'Oh, goodie,' James said drily. 'I'll put it on my calendar.'

'Ah, come on,' Zoe said. 'Don't be like that. We'll find you another man in the meantime. Won't we, Catherine?'

'Yeah.'

'I mean, there's always the LGB Society!'

'Oh, yeah.' Catherine turned to James guiltily. 'I actually meant to say that to you. There's a society—'

'Thanks, girls, but I'm all right for now,' James said curtly, and for a moment Catherine thought he was annoyed, but when Zoe cosied up to him again, he took her arm without hesitation, laughingly mimicking the purposeful face she was giving him.

'But first of all, James,' Zoe said. 'Are you coming to the Buttery?'

'What's in the Buttery?'

'Booze, at Tuesday night prices. And boys. Lots and lots of boys. Are you coming, Cits?'

'I have my meeting with Dr Parker.'

'What meeting?' Zoe said.

'About the essay I want to write. About Sylvia Plath.'

Zoe grimaced. 'Jaysus. OK, well, when you're finished with your Dead Poets Society, you can catch up with James and me? OK?'

'OK,' Catherine nodded, and she watched them walk away.

'So, Citóg,' Conor said, coming up to her as she stood at the bar of the Buttery an hour later. 'I hear you're laying your pipe with The Doyle now. Jesus, there's no stopping you.'

'What? Did he tell you that?'

'Sure he didn't have to tell me. Sure the pair of you were spotted sneaking out of publications together yesterday evening.'

'For fuck's sake! We talked for about a minute!'

'*Relax*, Cits.' He put a palm to her forehead. 'You're very agitated. A bit like your friend over there.'

He indicated the table at which James and Zoe were sitting; several other people had joined them now, including Aidan and Liam, a Northern Irish guy Aidan had befriended lately in the library, and James was being the life and soul of the gathering. He was describing something now, wildly gesticulating, his face frenetic with hilarity and excitement; he was almost shouting, breaking down frequently with laughter, and Zoe, too, was shrieking with laughter, which was only egging him on all the more. He had been high like this when Catherine had arrived from her meeting, and in truth, he was slightly getting on her nerves; she had come up to the bar not because she needed another drink, but because she needed some respite from the noise. Still, it was one thing for her to feel like this about James; it was quite another for Conor to comment on him. She looked at Conor warningly now,

151

hoping that this would deflect him, but as usual with Conor, it had the opposite effect.

'I'm glad you told me he was gay,' he said, smirking. 'Sure I'd never have been able to work it out for myself. Sure look at him.'

'Sorry?' she said sharply.

'"Notes on 'Camp'"', Citóg. Ever read it? Cause I'm pretty sure your mate has.'

She saw from his reaction then – his eyes widened, his mouth frozen in the act of saying whatever it was next going to say – that her face contained everything that she felt in that moment. She was shaking with anger, and she saw him take this in, too; saw his eyes read this and decide something about it.

'Fuck off, Moran,' she said, the words spitting out of her. 'Fuck. Off. Do you hear me? Are you listening to me?'

He tried to laugh, but the sound fell out of him, hanging in the air awkwardly a long moment. 'Jesus, Cits,' he said, and he reached for her. 'Here. Listen—'

'No,' she said, pulling away before he could so much as touch her. 'I will not listen. I will not fucking listen. You listen to me. James is my friend. James is my *best friend*.'

Conor's expression changed then, hardening, mockery pinching itself into it. 'Ah. That's sweet, Citóg.'

'And you can take the piss out of anyone you want,' she went on, clenching her fists now, 'but you will not take the piss out of him. Not like that.'

'I'll do and say whatever I like, love.'

'No. Not when I'm around.'

He laughed; a single, shocked peal. 'Cits. Get a hold of yourself, for Christ's sake. This is just embarrassing.'

'I am not fucking joking, Conor. I mean this.' To her horror, she found that she was close to tears; they were there as a pressing, growing fullness at the back of her throat, and now they were pricking her eyes. Conor, she saw, had noticed them, and at the sight of them, his scorn slid into something else – not concern, but astonishment – and he glanced over to James and back to her.

'This is insane,' he said, and for a moment he looked as though he was almost going to cry himself, but that was not Conor, that would never be Conor, and instead he lifted his chin and gave a short cough. 'Fuck this,' he said, and he shrugged on his rucksack.

'He's not out, Conor,' she said, a whine in her voice. 'He's not—'

'I don't give a shit what he is. What business is it of mine?'

'He's not fair game for that kind of slagging in the same way that everyone else is. That kind of public slagging. Slag me as much as you want, and slag Zoe and Emmet and Aidan . . .'

Conor's face creased with irritation. 'I couldn't be bothered slagging any of you,' he said. 'I'm gone. I have better things to do than deal with this nonsense.' As he strode out of the Buttery, he met Emmet at the door, and Catherine saw Conor shake his head, and say something to Emmet, and in the next moment Emmet's eyes shot to her; she leaned in to the bar and wiped, with her thumb and index finger, at her eyes. She had recovered by the time he reached her, and she was able to turn to him, narrowing her eyes with pretended displeasure at the sight of him, ready for whatever wisecrack he was getting ready to roll her way.

'Come on, Poetess,' he said. 'Let's go somewhere we can get a pint that's not made up from the dregs. Are you barred from the Stag's?'

4

Emmet, out of his usual environment – not, of course, that the Stag's was out of his usual environment, but it was not, at least, on campus – was different. Not radically different; he still called Catherine 'Poetess', and when he was not calling her that he was goading her about being a culchie, and before they'd even been served their pints he had made several statements about people which, in print, would almost certainly have constituted libel, but he was different. He was more hesitant, somehow; that was how Catherine would have put it, if she had been asked to – and she realized that, automatically, in her mind, she was shaping this thought about the difference in him as she might have written it in a letter to James. She could tell James about it in person later, naturally – she would have to tell him, since she would need to explain to him where she had suddenly disappeared to – but that was not the same. She preferred the idea of putting it in a letter, the story of how Emmet had come up to her in the Buttery (she would, of course, leave out the part about James sitting, laughing, at a nearby table), and about how she had walked with him, keeping up a wry, sarcastic banter, across Front Square and up Dame Street and down the little tiled alleyway that led to the Stag's Head, and about how they had found a table in the snug, where there were hardly ever any free tables, and about how the decrepit taxidermied fox had looked down on them, and how Emmet had gone to the bar and come back with two pints.

It was a kind of holding back, she thought, this new hesitancy; a kind of pause. He was not actually holding back – he was not sitting there, tongue-tied, or boring, or having decided that he did not want to talk to her after all – but there was something; she could not put her finger on it. It was as though, even as they spoke, he was not fully listening to her, or talking to her, but watching her – watching her in the way you might watch someone if they were talking to someone else, if they were part of a conversation on the other side of the table from you, safe to look at, safe for you to think your thoughts about, without them having to know.

He smiled more often, too; that was something else about him. And not the manic grin of The Doyle as he marched around campus, trailing trouble, but a smile she did not remember seeing him smile before. What did he need with that grin, she found herself wondering, when he had a smile like this? It was almost sweet. It was almost shy. Although you could not say that of Emmet Doyle, really, no matter how nicely he smiled after a few mouthfuls of Guinness, no matter how his blush might sometimes betray him.

'So,' he was saying, and now the smile had disappeared again and the grin was back in its place. 'I read the rest of your interview with the guy from Monaghan. It was actually pretty good.'

'Thanks,' Catherine said, surprised.

'He sounds like fun.'

'Yeah. He's gas.'

'*Gas*,' he repeated, in an exaggerated rural accent. 'Did he mind that you hadn't read the book?'

She glanced at him. 'What?'

'You were *obviously* winging it! The poor guy clearly didn't know where to look.'

'Listen, Doyle,' Catherine said, pointing a finger at him. 'Unlike you, I don't actually just make stuff up.'

'Well,' he said, 'that's your first mistake,' and, lifting his pint, he made as though he was going to toast her, but switched instead, just as her glass was approaching his, to the fox.

'So,' he said, after they had gone through what publications office gossip they could muster, Emmet recreating in vivid detail the 5 a.m. panic attack of Derek Galvin, the *TN* editor, as the entire sports section had deleted itself before his eyes, 'did your mate have your dinner ready for you when you got home last night?'

'Well, there was toast,' Catherine said, which was a lie – James had made shepherd's pie for everyone the night before – and one she had not intended to tell, but it had just come out for some reason, perhaps because it had seemed funnier, because it would make Emmet laugh, the way he was laughing now, his face lit up with pleasure, his eyes bright.

'He must have had an amazing time in Berlin, did he?' he said after a moment. 'Your mate.'

'James.'

'James,' he said, with a mock-formal nod. 'What was he doing over there?'

'He's an artist,' Catherine said, hearing how her voice had thickened with the importance of the phrase; she cleared her throat. 'He was working for a really famous photographer over there. Malachy Clark.'

'Well, I've never heard of him, and I'm a very well-known patron of the arts, so he can't be that famous.'

'Do you ever talk seriously about anything?' Catherine said, frowning at him over her glass. She had meant it as another joke, but as soon as she had said it she realized that he would probably not take it that way, and she saw already the blush on his face, a bloom and blotch of crimson at the tops of his cheeks, and she felt bad.

'Sorry,' she started to say, but he cut across her.

'Sorry, you're right. Well, did James have a good time over there? It must have been an amazing year for him, was it?'

'Well,' she said, swallowing. 'I mean, I think it was all right.'

'Only *all right*? I'd fucking love to spend a year in Berlin. How could it be only all right?'

She shook her head, feeling a rush of annoyance with herself; how had she walked right into this? 'It's complicated,' she said, waving the question off. 'I don't really want to talk about it. I mean, James is gay, for one thing.'

Guilt flooded her instantly; she had done it again, and silently she started to berate herself, but her attention was distracted by Emmet's wide-eyed, enthusiastic nodding.

'Oh,' he was saying. 'OK. OK. So your friend's gay. That's – great. That's cool! That's really great, Reilly. That's cool.'

'He's going to be gay whether you think it's great or not, Doyle.'

He looked uncertain. 'What do you mean?'

'I mean, you don't have to give him your approval.'

The same uncertainty lingered on his face then, but in the next instant it had vanished, replaced by his grin. 'He doesn't have my approval, the deviant,' he said, archly. 'Running around hugging innocent culchies and taking photographs of, what, probably naked men, is it?'

'Very funny.'

'Not one bit funny, Reilly. Does your mother know you're gadding about with homosexual men?'

She grimaced. 'Well you may ask,' she said, finishing her pint.

She got another round in, and then, maybe because Emmet had mentioned her mother, they were talking about their families. He told her about his older brother, a fourth year studying Medicine, who was not much impressed, it seemed, with *Muck* or with Emmet's reputation on campus; Emmet said that he had just that past weekend received a lecture from him on the need to mend his ways.

'So he wasn't at the party?'

Emmet scoffed. 'Saturday night. He was probably playing bridge.'

'Do you see much of him?'

Emmet shook his head. 'What's your family like?'

'Mine?' she said, surprised. 'They're fine. I mean, they're down in Longford.'

'Do you go down much to see them?'

'The odd time. Not as much as last year.'

He clicked his tongue. 'The life of the degenerate Poetess up in Dublin.'

'Any chance you might stop calling me that?'

'I'll consider it,' he said lightly. 'You have a little sister, don't you? You told me.'

'Did I?'

'Yeah,' he grinned. 'One day last year up in publications. You said she was a right little rascal.'

'Anna. Yeah. She's seven.'

'I wish I had a brother or sister that age,' he said. 'I'd say she's some craic to go home to, is she?'

'She's hilarious. She'd give you a run for your money in the mimicry stakes, I can tell you. You should hear her doing our mother.'

He laughed in what seemed like genuine amusement. 'So when are you going to see her again?'

'Soon. I'm due a visit. Though they're in the process of knocking down my bedroom at home to put up a new extension, so it might not be the best time.'

'They're knocking down your bedroom?' He looked at her as though waiting for a punchline. 'Jesus. They must be *really* pissed off with your degenerate lifestyle.'

'Something like that,' she said. And then her name was called from the doorway, and Emmet's name, and when she looked up, Zoe and James were coming towards their table, waving, grinning, looking very plastered, and very pleased with themselves for having found her, and very much in the mood for more booze.

But on the walk home two hours later, James was quiet. He did not take Catherine's arm; he did not talk about the night and how it had gone; he did not ask her any questions about her drinks with Emmet; he just looked at the ground, as though he was walking home alone, and he kept walking. Catherine attempted to make light conversation, but most of his answers were monosyllables, and by the time they were past the Green, she had pretty much given up and lapsed into silence herself.

It was when they got back to Baggot Street, into the light of the hallway, that she saw how pale he looked, and how hard-eyed with what looked like exhaustion, and she felt almost frightened, looking at him; she wanted just to go to her bedroom, and leave him to his bed in the sitting room, and close the door. But she could not do that, it turned out, because it was one of the nights when Lorraine's boyfriend Cillian was staying over, and because Lorraine and Amy shared a bedroom, the only way for Lorraine and Cillian to have sex was for them to drag Lorraine's mattress into the sitting room and spend the night there; James's sleeping things had been left in a heap outside the door, and on the kitchen table Lorraine had left a note reading *Sorry, J! Kip in with C?*

'Oh, for fuck's sake,' James muttered, sounding furious.

'Well, of course you can sleep on my floor,' Catherine said, filling a glass of water. 'It'll be fine.'

'For fuck's sake,' he said again, his fingers to his temples. 'Dumping my bedclothes outside the door. This is my fault. This is my own stupid fault. I should have a place of my own.'

She spluttered her disagreement. 'You've only been home a couple of days! It's no big deal. Come on. Let's go to bed.'

But he sat down heavily at the table, snatching up one of the girls' packets of Marlboro, and lit himself a cigarette with a grim, heavy sigh. 'I'm sick of this,' he said, looking out the window to the night's darkness. 'I'm sick of this shite already.'

Maybe if she had not been so tired herself; maybe if she had not been drunk – not as drunk as he was, but drunk anyway, four or five pints along – Catherine would just have let him sit there, moaning like that; she would have known that it was only the booze talking, and the tiredness, and whatever else was eating at him – things that she had not, after all, really tried to talk to him about yet, things that any real friend would probably by now have encouraged him to talk about: Berlin, whatever had happened there or had not, all the darkness of his letters, all the sadnesses that he had hinted at, that he had run from, surely, coming back here – and that the best thing to do would be to leave it all until the morning. To leave her bedroom door open for him, so that he could come in and settle himself down on her floor after he had finished his cigarette; to put a hand on his shoulder, maybe, and say, *It's OK, it'll be OK*, and then kiss him on the top of the head and say that she would see him in a few minutes. Maybe, if she had not still been angry with herself over the scene that had taken place in the bookshop that afternoon, or angry with him for the way he had, in the Buttery, become everyone's best friend, or angry with Conor for what he had said about him, or angry with James – again – for his silence and brooding on the walk home; maybe, if she had been a version of herself who was free of all that anger, of all that residue of a day that seemed to have so many parts to it that it could not, surely, have been only one day, she would have been able to do the sensible thing.

But she was not that version of herself. The bile rose in her; the anger sparked again to her fingertips. 'Oh, would you *ever* stop fucking whining,' she said, and she lifted the glass of water she had just filled, and she tossed its contents into the sink. 'Would you ever?'

James stared at her. 'Sorry, Catherine?' he said, sounding incredulous, which just made Catherine angrier; she shook her head with an incredulity of her own.

'Why do you have to be so negative about everything?' she said. 'Moaning about your bedclothes, as though it's part of this big fucking conspiracy the whole world has against you.'

'My bedclothes,' James said, slowly and carefully, as he stood up from the table. 'Oh, Catherine. This is not about my bedclothes.'

Her heart was racing; they were too drunk for this, she knew. But neither could she stop herself.

'This is not about my bedclothes, Catherine,' James said again, coming towards her. 'This is about what happened in the pub tonight, isn't it? You were having your nice cosy date with Little Emmet—'

'Little Emmet?' Catherine cut in. 'The guy must be six foot tall!'

James smirked. 'Is he now? Is he now? Well. Lucky you.'

'Oh my God, you're being ridiculous. Are you actually—'

'Am I actually *what*, Catherine? Am I actually *what*?'

'I don't give a fuck about Emmet Doyle!' she shouted, and she flung out her arms as though to illustrate how true this was. 'You can have Emmet Doyle if you want him. You certainly fucking behaved like that tonight in the Stag's. *Oh, tell me more about yourself, Emmet,*' she imitated him, tilting her head, widening her eyes. '*Tell me more about your theory of satire.* For Christ's sake. Have him! Go on!'

He stared at her. He was somehow even paler than he had already been. He had been standing close to her, but now he stepped back – now he stepped back so that he was leaning against the kitchen counter, not, Catherine knew, because he needed the support of it, but because it was the only thing that was stopping him from backing away from her any farther. His mouth was a thin line. The cigarette was hanging out of his right hand, and its column of ash was growing longer and longer.

'James,' Catherine said quietly. 'I didn't mean it like that. I know you—'

'You know *what*?' James almost spat at her. His eyes were huge.

She shook her head rapidly. 'I didn't mean it.'

'You know nothing, Catherine,' he said, not to her, but to the ash from his cigarette as it fell to the floor. 'You know *nothing* about me. What do you know about me? What have I told you?'

Again, she shook her head. 'I know plenty,' she said. 'I

know we haven't talked about Berlin yet; but I read your letters – I know it was hard for you. I've wanted to talk to you about it; but we can't do it now. We can't do it tonight. Let's go to bed. Can we? Let's go to bed, and—'

He coughed out an angry laugh. 'So you're telling me now when to go to bed as well as when to get up?'

'*James,*' she said, the word barely sounding like his name at all; in her shock, it had slipped out before she had even finished saying it.

'What?' he snapped, glaring. 'What do you want from me? You want me to be funny for you? You want me to be great fucking fun?'

'James!'

'I'm fucking exhausted, Catherine. I'm completely worn out. I'm only three days home, and I can already remember why I left here, and it's not as though I can go back to that other hole either – so tell me, what the fuck is it, exactly, that I'm supposed to do?'

'Just be here,' she said, uselessly.

'Be here,' he nodded, as though seriously considering this. 'And listen to everyone's plans for me, is it? And look at all the gorgeous fucking fellas that everyone wants to giggle over with me. And look with you all at these fellas, and know that while you can disappear off to the pub with them, for me, there is not a chance, not a single fucking chance . . .'

His voice cracked. Catherine, almost crying herself now, tried to go towards him, but he held up his hands to tell her to stay where she was.

'I watch everyone, Catherine. I watch them live their lives, and I watch them meet the people they can love, and I watch them go on their dates, and take over sitting rooms to have sex with them, and I – what am I supposed to do?'

'James, you're only just home! There'll be—'

'There'll be what? There'll be *what*, Catherine? There'll be Zoe's friend from England coming for a visit sometime, maybe this year, maybe next? There'll be some poor fucker as pathetic as I am from the *Society* – oh, thank you so much, Catherine, by the way, for pointing me towards the *Society* – because sure if I can use the college darkroom, I can use the college queer society, and sure then everything will be just perfect, won't it, just as long as I can remember not to let anybody outside the *Society* see. Isn't that it? Isn't that how it goes?'

'What about that guy in Hodges Figgis today?' she blurted, not quite believing she was bringing him up. 'He seemed . . .'

James looked at her, seeming astonished. 'He seemed what?'

Catherine shrugged helplessly. 'He scratched his eyebrow – I thought maybe . . .'

'Are you trying to mock me, Catherine?' he said, his face screwed up horribly. 'Is that meant to be funny?'

'No! I didn't know – I thought that maybe you and that guy were giving each other the eye or something. You disappeared.'

'I disappeared to stare at him, Catherine,' he said coldly. 'To stalk him. That's what I do; that's what I've been doing for five years now, and what I made into a fucking art form in Berlin, and what I'll be spending my time doing here, too, by the looks of it. I stare at them, and they're either completely oblivious to me or they're completely disgusted.' He shook his head. '*He scratched his eyebrow.* Jesus!'

'James,' she said, finally humiliated into tears; she sobbed like a child, holding her fists up to her mouth. 'Please. It's not like that. It'll be OK here, I promise you. It'll get better, I promise.'

But he bent his head, and put his own fists to his forehead, and he pounded. And Catherine felt so desperate for him, so frightened for him, that she knew she could not go towards him. She knew she could not put her arms around him. She did not try to comfort him; she knew he did not want to be comforted. She knew he did not want for her to attempt to cover over his aloneness. He pounded his own skull, and he clutched at his own hair, and when he was finished, his breath long and ragged, she told him that it was time for them to sleep.

He shook his head. 'I don't want to be taking up room in your bed.'

She had not meant that he would come into her bed; she had meant that he would sleep on her floor, but she could hardly point this out, she felt now, and anyway, it did not matter. It was sleep. It was James. He was not going to jump her; he was not going to wake her up in the night, pushing his impatient dick into her thigh. He was going to rest, and she was going to help him, and in the morning everything was going to be better – of this Catherine was more determined than she had ever been of anything before.

*

Later in the night, she woke, and instantly realized why: she was freezing. James had taken all of the quilt. Gently, she tried to pull it from him, and he grunted; she tried again, and he shouldered her away. In the half-light, shivering now, she peered at him, holding on to her duvet – as determined a sleeper, it struck her, as he was determined in everything else. His face was so delicate as she watched him: the fineness of his cheekbones, the fullness of his lips, the dark slice of shadow beneath his chin. He was beautiful, it struck her, something she had never seen in him before; he was not handsome in the way that she usually found men handsome, but he was something else, something fuller, something so much more solid. It was not right, that nobody should look at this face the way she was looking at it now, from this angle, in this intimacy; it was not right that nobody should lie beside James and watch him while he hogged their pillow and their duvet. She shivered again and this time grabbed at the quilt much more forcefully; but still James would not yield it, so she nudged him, hard, with her elbow. He cried out, and it was a sound so full of disbelief and outrage that Catherine could not help laughing.

'What did you do to me?' James said, lifting his face to her; he sounded as panicked and confused as though he had woken on top of a moving train. 'What did you do to me?'

'Give me the duvet,' Catherine said, tugging it away from him. 'You're keeping it all to yourself.'

'You didn't have to *hit* me,' he said, in a tone of deep grievance.

'I didn't hit you,' she said. 'I couldn't wake you.'

'You hit me.'

'Go back to sleep,' she said, and he did.

5

'Come on.' Zoe's voice interrupted Catherine as she sat in the library the following week, trying to prepare for her Michael Doonan interview. 'You've been hunched up at this desk all day. Time for a cuppa.'

'I can't,' Catherine said, gesturing to the books on her desk.

'*Engines of Everything*,' Zoe said, picking one of them up. 'What a pretentious bloody title. I'm taking you away from it. You look like you haven't had fresh air in days.'

It was not that she had gone days without fresh air – quite the opposite; she had spent most of the last two weeks slacking off to spend time with James – but it did not surprise Catherine to hear Zoe say that she looked unwell. She felt heavy, and sluggish, and as though she was dragging herself around – and yet at the same time, she felt in her limbs the constant jitter of something like panic. She had been sitting here, trying to read Doonan's books, but on each attempt a line was all she had been able to manage, or two, before the words and the page in front of her had dissolved. She did not know what was wrong with her; it was as though she was restless and yet paralysed at the same time. James was in the darkroom, developing photographs he had taken of Aidan that morning outside the Old Library, and she was meeting him at four o'clock to head home, but for ages now she had not been able to stop looking at her watch, seeing how long was left to go; she was getting absolutely nothing done. Just when Zoe had come up to her, she had been considering whether she could get away with going over to the darkroom, letting herself into House Four and up the stairs, into the PhotoSoc offices; could she think of some plausible reason for showing up like that? That she had wanted to see how the work was going? But she could not, surely, just go into the darkroom; she would let the light in, and destroy the photographs, and – no, she could not do that, of course she could not do that. But why did she even want to go up there at all? And yet she did; she wanted to see him. It was ridiculous. She would see him at four o'clock, which was, now, hardly even an hour away. She would have the whole evening with him. And she had had pretty much the whole week with him, and the week before that; they had spent most of every day sitting in cafes, or on the Green, or going to exhibitions, or looking around the shops. And not much more than a week ago, she had been feeling crowded by him; not much more than a week ago, she had been wishing that he would do more of his own thing, and leave her to hers. And now – this. But what was this? What was this feeling? What were these feelings, because there was more than one of them: there were several of them, and it was by them, now, that she was crowded; it was by them, now, that she was feeling cornered, feeling overwhelmed. James—

'Come on,' Zoe said again, pulling her up by the shoulders. 'I'm staging an intervention, Citsers. Tea.'

As Catherine had known she would do, Zoe steered the conversation around again to the subject of Emmet, and to the question of how things were between Emmet and Catherine, as Zoe put it, 'post-Stag's'.

'Which is not *quite* as promising as "post-shags",' she said, arching an eyebrow, 'but it's a start.'

'I'm telling you, Zoe. You're barking up the wrong tree. It was just a drink. We were talking about *TN* stuff. There's nothing more than that happening. How could there be?'

'Why wouldn't there be?'

'Because he's Emmet. He's a messer.'

'He's cute. And he clearly likes you. He's been flirting with you all year.'

'I told you, Zoe, it's not flirting. He's *Emmet*. He's The Doyle. It's just the way he goes on. Everything is a joke with him. Everything is a parody.'

'You seemed to be having a perfectly nice time with him in the Stag's.'

'Yeah, but only because we were messing. That's exactly my point. There can only be so much of him slagging me about being a culchie and me slagging him about having gone to a private school.'

'Well. You don't have to talk. You can just shag.'

'Oh, God,' Catherine groaned. 'Can we talk about something else, please? Do we have to spend all of our time talking about boys?'

'We *don't* spend all of our time talking about boys,' Zoe said, but the accusation seemed to rattle her, because she stirred her tea for a long moment, staring at its milky surface. She sighed. 'How's James, then?'

Catherine coughed out a laugh. 'James is a boy.'

Zoe made a face. 'Yeah, but you know what I mean. How did his photoshoot with Aidan go? Any chance of a bit of hot boy-on-boy action there?'

'Oh for fuck's sake, Zoe!' Catherine said, more forcefully than she had intended; she had caught the attention of several people at nearby tables, and Zoe's eyes were wide with injured surprise. 'Sorry,' she muttered, but Zoe did not even blink.

'What was that for? You're not seriously feeling possessive of Aidan, are you?'

She spluttered. 'Oh my God. Zoe!'

But Zoe's expression had suddenly changed; she was looking over Catherine's shoulder, and had assumed a huge, cheeky smile. 'Stop talking about him,' she said, out of the corner of her mouth, waving now, and Catherine turned to see Aidan striding down the steps of the coffee dock, waving back in his laconic way.

'Oh, great,' Catherine said, reaching for her tea.

Aidan was looking well today, even handsome, wearing a checked shirt she hadn't seen before and a pair of black jeans, and he had shaved, which was not something he always bothered to do, and she wondered if he had cleaned himself up because he was getting his photograph taken, which was an idea that ought to have made her laugh, but that instead, like almost everything at the moment, just made her feel a strange mixture of irritation and anxiety. She wondered again if she could sneak off and meet up with James at an earlier time than the one they had arranged; she felt intensely the desire to be with him, talking to him, rather than here with Zoe and Aidan. But she pushed it back. It was not something she should listen to.

The shoot had gone well, Aidan said, though he did not really think of it as having been a shoot, just a half hour reading on a bench in the rose garden while James stepped around him with a camera clicking. James, Aidan said, was a bit of a perfectionist – which translated, upon further cross-examination from Zoe, into James having insisted on continuing to take photographs even when it had started to rain, and into his having asked Aidan not to put his copy of Housman away even though it was getting wet.

'What a *monster*,' Zoe said, sniggering. 'You should sue.'

'Oh, I'm sure the end result will be worth it,' Aidan said, putting a boot-clad foot up on the chair in front of him. 'He seems to know what he's doing.' He glanced at Catherine. 'He's photographed you, I presume?'

Catherine hesitated; in fact, while James had photographed her several times the previous summer, he had yet to take her photograph as part of this new series; several times he had mentioned his intention to do so, but had not yet got around to it. But she found that she did not want to admit this to Aidan. 'Yeah,' she said casually, as though this was the most obvious thing in the world. 'A few times. Mostly back in the flat, you know. There's good light there.'

'Oh, he said to me this morning that he doesn't really like shooting indoors,' Aidan said. 'Still, you work with what you've got, I suppose.'

'Yeah,' Catherine said, not looking at either of them.

'James says he's hoping to get his own place soon, actually,' he said, and now she looked at him; now she looked at him as though he had insulted her. 'I said I'd keep an ear out for him. My landlady has a couple of houses up around the Liberties. Bought them for a pittance ten years ago. If only we'd all had that kind of foresight.'

'I was nine ten years ago,' Catherine said, because she was feeling a sudden, very angry urge to dig at Aidan, and a dig about how much older he was seemed like the easiest way to get at him. It also carried with it, she realized in the same moment, a reminder of how much younger she was, and therefore an intimation of his sleaziness and lack of scruples in having come on to her that night the previous term. Which was ridiculous, because this was not at all how she felt about having snogged Aidan, but right at this moment, she found, she did not much care for the facts of the thing. She cared about the jagged bolt of shock and distress he had sent hurtling into her with his remark about James moving out of Baggot Street, and with his casual declaration that he intended to help James move out of Baggot Street, and she wanted to hurt him.

But it did not work: Aidan merely shrugged. 'Could have used your Communion money,' he said, flashing her a grin. 'The pair of you could probably have got a cottage on Cork Street if you'd gone in together.'

Zoe laughed. 'What do you think, Cits? The pair of us as flatmates? We could rent a bedroom to James and insist on vetting all his gentleman callers.'

'I have to go,' Catherine said, pushing up and away from the table. 'I forgot, I have a *TN* meeting.'

'*Oooh*,' Zoe started to croon, but Catherine did not stay to listen to the rest of it.

The morning after the argument with James, Catherine had woken to discover the bed empty beside her, and to find that Lorraine and Cillian were still asleep in the sitting room, and Amy alone in her bedroom, and that there was nobody in the kitchen or the bathroom or even in the hall; James's bed-clothes were just where Lorraine had left them the night before, and it was half past eight in the morning, and James was gone. She had paced her room, and then the kitchen, and then the corridor; she had stared at the payphone in the hallway, willing it into usefulness. But who could she call? He would not have gone home to Carrigfinn; he had told her on Sunday as they had walked in the park, Catherine still hungover from the party, that he had no intention of going home to Carrigfinn. They did not even know that he was back in Ireland. Zoe? Would he have gone to Zoe's house in Stillorgan? That was impossible. James turning up on Zoe's doorstep, before nine in the morning; there was no way he was going to do that. So then where? Was he just wandering the streets? Checked in to a hostel? He still had some money left over from the wages Malachy had paid him, but it was mostly in marks; he had not had the chance to convert it yet, and anyway, it was not much, and he had been meaning to look for bar work to have something else to live on—

The sound of the front door had startled her; she had been so caught up in obsessing over where he had gone that she had not considered the possibility that he might not, after all, have gone anywhere, or that he might be coming back. She had rushed to the hall door to meet him, and when she had thrown her arms around him, he had laughed, letting her hug him a moment but then holding her back from him with a look of bafflement on his face; he had only gone to the shop to buy breakfast things, but because it was so early the nearest shop had been closed, so he had walked to the next one, and that had been closed too, and the one he had found had been close to town, and what was she *talking* about, she thought he had gone?

She had laughed about it too, after a while, and at the breakfast table Amy and Lorraine and Cillian had laughed, and everyone had teased her, and she knew it was a story she would be teased about for ages; but at the same time, in James's eyes, she had seen something that was not laughter. Something that was not the enjoyment of how silly she had been, and how melodramatic. It had not been a coldness; that was too strong. He was still James, he was still right beside her, draping his arms around her every couple of minutes, still saying her name with that rich, layered affection. But it had been a change. There had been something – a carefulness – in the way he had looked at her. A decision, it seemed to her, about how he was going to be with her from now on, and about how he was going to be with, and for himself.

And it had driven her mad.

That was the only way she could see this, this thing that had happened to her over the last ten days: a madness. James had done exactly what Catherine had wanted him to do – he had stopped crowding her, stopped needing to be with her, beside her, every single minute – and she had reacted by becoming exactly as he had been. By clinging. Craving his company. Demanding it. For quite a few days now, the coffee breaks, the lunch breaks, the trips to the galleries, the long walks, had not been James's idea. The irony was – everything was irony now, it seemed to Catherine – James had found it difficult to get away to do these things with her, because James had other things on now – he had got himself work in O'Brien's, a pub near Christchurch, three evenings a week and two afternoons, and he was beginning, on top of that, to take his photographs, to put together the series he had talked to her about that afternoon – which now seemed so, so long ago – of the ID cards. He was approaching people in the street and asking if he could photograph them; he had also started to photograph some of the people Catherine had introduced him to in college. He was in the darkroom any chance he got, making prints, and Catherine had seen them all, and they were brilliant; they were wonderful – stark and strange and disorienting. They did not look like the ID card photographs – they were much more beautiful than that – but they had the same sense of people being caught in their unguarded moments, accessed in the pureness and vulnerability of who they really were: a man in construction gear, his gaze sliding warily to the side, an old woman in an apron, her hands clasped in front of her, her eyes closed, a boy their age – a boy who was cute, which should have been a source of pleasure to Catherine but felt instead like a scourge – in a football shirt, leaning back against a car, glaring at a point in the middle distance.

And no, James had not yet taken Catherine's photograph, but she was determined that this would happen over the coming weekend.

And this was part of what had changed, too: Catherine being determined that James would act, and act towards her, in certain crucial ways. That he would come with her when she wanted him to go for coffee or to the National Gallery, for instance, or to O'Donoghue's for an early-evening pint, even if he was working in another pub himself later and said he would prefer not to arrive there with booze on his breath; that he would walk with her on St Stephen's Green or along the canal; that he would, now, take her photograph.

He was bemused by it, Catherine thought. He did not seem to see it the way she did, as something to worry over, as something about which she should feel ashamed; those ways of seeing it, she suspected, would never even have occurred to him. For his part, the things he had told her that night in the kitchen, the experience of telling them, had seemed, to some extent, to have lightened the load he was carrying, to have freed him up in some way. He was up early in the mornings now, and unless she was quick about getting up herself, and getting ready, he was often out the door before she was, and it could be difficult to track him down during the day. On the evenings he was not working in the pub, he was mostly at home with her and the others in Baggot Street, but one evening he had wanted to go for a drink with Zoe and Aidan and Aidan's friend Liam, and Catherine, who had only wanted to stay in and watch television in front of the fire with him, had not been able to leave him to it; she had trailed along, and had not been very good company – Zoe, the next day, had made a comment about PMS.

He was going from her; that was how she kept thinking of it. He had made the decision, because of what she had said to him that night, or because of what she had forced him to face up to that day, to pull away from her slightly, to carve out his own space, to start living his own life. And Catherine could not understand where these feelings were coming from; she could not understand why they had such a hold over her, gripping her by the hair it seemed sometimes, clasping her by the throat – but she felt them. She felt alone; or she felt, at least, the threat, the spectre, of her own aloneness. She felt the panic of his going, and the emptiness with which it would leave her. He was not going anywhere, and yet she felt it. And there were no letters now; there were no fat white skins bulging with words through which to feel close to him, through which to feel that there was someone, out there, always, listening to her. There was only him, and there was only the distance from him to her. And Catherine was scrabbling across it now. Catherine was thrashing in it as though it was drowning her. And there was, too, the fact of what was happening to her body, now, when James put his arms around her, when James put his lips to her forehead, his lips to her cheek – but Catherine did not want to think about that part of it anymore. Catherine did not want to think about the second night, the previous week, that Cillian had stayed over, so that he and Lorraine had once again sequestered the sitting-room floor; Catherine did not want to think of her own gladness that night, or of what it had felt like to have James once more in the bed beside her, or what it had felt like to drift off and to awaken with him nestled so close.

There were things it was not good to think about. There were questions it was not useful to ask.

James was finished in the darkroom, as it turned out, when Catherine went up to find him; he was in the PhotoSoc office, chatting intently with a girl holding some kind of old-fashioned, box-shaped camera. If he was surprised to see her arrive, he did not show it; he just beckoned her over, and began telling her about the girl's camera, which had belonged to her grandfather, and which was, he said, a Rolleiflex, the camera that Richard Avedon had used, and Diane Arbus, and Robert Capa. He mentioned some other photographers of whom Catherine had not heard, and the girl beside him nodded enthusiastically and added some more names. Catherine glanced at her. She was plump and short, with blonde curls; she held the camera below her large breasts. Her fingernails were painted a glittery purple. James introduced her, but Catherine instantly forgot her name; all she could think about was how keenly she wanted to get James away, and home, and to herself. But he kept talking, as was usual; now he was explaining the workings of the camera, how you had to look down through it from above, as though through a tiny trapdoor, and at this, the blonde girl demonstrated and then, smiling, looped the leather strap from around her neck and passed the camera over to Catherine to try for herself.

'Oh, no, I'd be afraid I'd break it,' Catherine said, but the girl insisted, and so did James. She took it; it was lighter than she had expected, but sturdy, its silver dials jutting out against her palms, its pebbled black plastic surface pleasingly rough against her fingertips. She looked down through the neat square chute which topped it, and she staggered in surprise a moment; the picture was sharp and clear and moving, like a tiny television in her hands, and in it was a tiny, frowning James, now a grinning James, now a James who was calling out to her, waving at her, saying her name. She found herself staring at this James; she found herself transfixed by him. He was just the same as the real James, as the James who stood not two feet away from her, but he was different. When she moved, he moved. When she turned one of the dials on the side of the camera, he went out of focus a moment, but when she turned it once more, he was back again, crisp and perfect and real; there was a short, curved handle on the other side, and when she turned that, winding it like a clock handle, the camera gave a lovely, satisfying click, and the blonde girl cheered.

'You took him!' she said, clapping her hands. 'Well done!'

'Catherine,' James said much less warmly, 'you're wasting Lisa's film.'

'Oh, no,' the girl said, 'sure how would it be a waste? Sure this way I get to have a photo of you!'

'Jaysus,' James said, pulling a face. 'You're made up.'

'I bet it'll be worth a fortune twenty years from now,' the girl said, laughing. 'After my show kick-starts your glittering career.'

'Show?' Catherine said, frowning, looking from one to the other.

'Lisa's asked me to give her a few photographs for her group show,' James said, taking the Rolleiflex from her.

'You never told me!' Catherine said, hearing the whine in her voice.

'I've just found out myself,' he said.

'Myself and a few friends from NCAD are putting together a group show of new artists on an old factory floor in the Liberties at the end of the summer,' Lisa explained.

'The Liberties?' Catherine echoed incredulously. In her mind she heard, as though it was the shutter release of the

178

Rolleiflex, the neat, smooth *click* of parts coming together and working just the way they should. 'I've heard of there,' she said.

'Yeah, it's a great spot,' Lisa said. 'So many amazing spaces that are derelict now. I love James's portraits, and they'll be perfect for this show, I think—'

'We'll see,' James said, holding up a hand as though to suggest that this line of talk was dangerous, and needed to be deflected. He turned to Catherine. 'Anyway. Now that you've taken your masterpiece.'

'Sorry?'

'Will we head?'

It had started to rain, so they took the bus, climbing upstairs to find a seat together, and they had been sitting less than a minute when Catherine, moving to rest on James's shoulder, noticed that he was asleep, his head hanging, his hands lying slack and open in his lap. She tried to rest on him anyway, but he jerked away, though it might only have been the motion of the bus, going over a pothole or a bump, or swerving, maybe, to avoid someone on a bike. As he slept, she studied his face: the delicacy of his cheekbones, the fullness of his lips, the sheen of his stubble, golden and glinting at moments in the evening light. She felt it again, the sensation she had been having for days: that although he was beside her, even awake he was as far away, really, as he was now when asleep, and that she could not hold him, and that she could not even really know him.

Then they were nearing home, and she put her hand to his, to wake him, and as he had done that morning on the couch, he gasped his way back to consciousness, regarding her, for a startled moment, as someone he did not know and had not seen before.

'Our stop,' she said, her eyes pleading with him, and he nodded.

'Down we go,' he said, and they lurched towards the stairs.

Then they were home and he was himself again. Or his public self, or his social self; Catherine was beginning to have trouble remembering all of his selves. Amy and Lorraine were there, and Cillian had brought hash, so the air was giddy, the night seemed young, and in their excitement James was in the middle of them, chatting and teasing and making everyone snort and shriek and double over with laughter; he was witty and wizard-tongued and quick as a trap. And he was all sweet, mischievous physicality: all hugs, all nuzzles, his arms thrown so happily around the girls.

It was beautiful. It was whirlwind. He was full of laughter, and Catherine saw it softening his face: the sheer joy of being with these people, the way it lifted something, clear and clean, off of his heart. And she hated herself in that moment, because she felt jealous of them; she wanted him back to herself. Not the dark, quiet version, not the version she had been with all day, the James who had worried her and exhausted her, the James with whom things had, impossibly, become tense and strained; she wanted *this* James. She wanted the brilliant, funny, vibrant James, lit up with enjoyment, teeming with it, and she wanted him to be only her friend. She did not want him to love the others this much, to take such unbridled pleasure in their presence. It was not that she did not want him to be happy; it was that she could not deal with the idea that it was *others* who could make him happy, as he seemed to be now. She wanted him to be only her friend. She wanted the best of his attention; she wanted the highest pitch of his energy; she wanted to be the reason he was fascinated, delighted, amused. And here were all the others, stealing this ground from her, and she resented them for it, and she resented James, for being taken in.

And yet they were his oldest friends.

And yet she was his closest friend; she knew that.

And yet.

And yet?

The following Thursday, she came home late from the *TN* office to find James alone in the house, sprawled on the couch. He was watching *No Disco*; something hazy and bleached-out flickered on the screen as a man strummed a guitar, singing something about a shoreline. James lifted a hand in greeting.

'You shouldn't have waited up,' Catherine said, dropping her bag.

He shrugged. 'I didn't. I'm watching this. Listen to this fella.'

'What?'

'His voice. Listen to it. I've never heard of him before.'

'I don't know any of the music they play on that programme.'

Finally now he looked at her. 'How's our Robert Emmet? Any more rebellions in the pipeline?'

Catherine shook her head. 'I didn't see much of him. It was crazy in there – they're three days late going to print.'

'Did you not go for a drink afterwards?'

'Afterwards?' Catherine said with a snort. 'They're still at it. They'll be there all night.'

'Oh. Some other time, then.'

His attention was fixed again on the television, his head

lolling back. The guy was singing now, about shining, repeating the word over and over. Had James meant that sarcastically, that thing about going for a drink with Emmet? Was he actually talking about it as casually as this? She watched him, but he seemed absorbed in the music video, locked onto the man's voice, its throaty, gentle whine. She wondered if he was drunk, if he had been drinking wine with the girls, maybe, or if he was stoned on some of Cillian's hash, but there were no glasses in evidence, just a mug of tea on the floor in front of him, and no smell on the air. The music video ended and the programme presenter came on with his eager patter; James sighed and clapped a hand down on the couch.

'Fuck, I'm worn out.'

'What did you get up to?'

'I went over to Thomas Street, actually, to see a place.'

'A place?' she said dumbly.

'A place to rent. Someone Aidan knows told him about it, and he told me. It's in a woman's house, but I'd have the whole upstairs.'

The words seemed to come apart in front of her as though on a wet page. 'Sorry, what? What do you mean? Like, a place to live?'

'Yeah,' he said, looking at her as though he was waiting for her to deliver a punchline. 'Sure, you knew I—'

'I thought you meant next month,' she said, hearing herself babble. 'I thought you'd stay until the end of this month anyway.' She cast about for the rationale she knew to be in her head, somewhere, and then she found it, and she almost shouted in triumph. 'The rent on any place is going to be from the first of the month. You can't move in somewhere before the month is up.'

'Ah, no,' he said mildly, shaking his head. 'The woman's

fine about that. She says I can move in tomorrow if I want to. She's just keen to get someone in. The last fella bolted on her, I think.'

'But you're not going *tomorrow*, are you? I have my Doonan interview tomorrow!'

He looked at her, frowning. 'What difference does that make?'

She stammered. What difference did it make? 'I won't be able to help you with your stuff,' she blurted. 'And then I have to go home for the weekend afterwards, because it's Mother's Day.'

'Oh, yes, Mother's Day,' he said drily. 'I must remember to give my old darling a call.'

'James, you don't have to move tomorrow,' she said desperately. 'Please don't go that soon.'

'Well, I'm not *going* anywhere. I'm just moving into my own place. Sure I have to do that. I have to get out from under your feet.'

'You're not—'

'Yes, I am,' he cut across her. 'Catherine. I'm under everybody's feet.'

'Nobody minds!'

'I mind. And I mind sleeping on a couch, too. I wake up sounding like my ould fella, moaning and groaning in the morning.' He stretched his arms up high. 'So. You got the paper sent to bed.'

'Well. My part of it, at least.'

'And yet you didn't take the opportunity to stick around and maybe go to bed with anyone yourself?' He clicked his tongue. 'What are we going to do with you?'

'I wanted to come home. *Jesus.* Am I not even allowed to do that now?'

'You're allowed to do whatever you like, Catherine,' he said, stretching his arms out wide now, yawning. 'That's the whole point.'

'Yeah, well.'

'*Yeah, well,*' he mimicked her. He flashed her a smile. Catherine stared at it. *Moonfoam and silver*, the guy on the television sang.

6

Michael Doonan was already in the bar of the Central Hotel when Catherine got there, ten minutes before the appointed time. He was sitting on one of the long couches by the fireplace, wearing a brown polo neck and faded jeans, and he was pouring tea from a pot on the low table in front of him. His grey hair was shoulder-length, and though he was bald on top, the tresses were surprisingly thick and full; they also looked freshly groomed. Catherine, who had come racing into the room, intending to set herself up at one of the more private tables in the corner, came to a stop and backtracked a couple of steps, and it was at that moment that he noticed her, and clearly realized who she was; he gave her a cool, appraising nod, and patted the couch cushion. Catherine waved, too eagerly, and lurched forward.

She had spent all morning and all afternoon in the library, frantically trying to extract a set of coherent questions from the dozens of pages of notes she had accumulated. Though the publicist had told her only to concentrate on the latest novel, Catherine had wanted to appear very familiar with Doonan's work when she met him, and so she had tried, in the week gone by, to cram all of the books, from his debut novel *Cunningham* onwards, and very quickly she had become overwhelmed, and instead of paring back she had piled even more material onto the fire – calling up critical essays on Doonan from the stacks, looking up old interviews with him on the microfilm machines, emailing one of her lecturers, even, to ask his advice (the lecturer had not seemed to take her seriously, sending her a short note warning her not to be too easily charmed by 'the great man') – and by the time she was leaving the library and walking the five minutes to the Central, Catherine had wanted only to run home to Longford and dive into one of the hiding places she had had as a child. Longford had come to mind, probably, because Baggot Street would no longer be the haven it had been with James there; he would have moved into his place on Thomas Street now, and while Catherine would visit him there often, and while he had promised to call on Baggot Street a couple of times a week, it would not be the same. At the end of the visit he would always have to go home, or she would. And so she wanted, now, to hide somewhere she would not have to leave. Somewhere from which she would not be expelled.

'Miss Reilly,' Doonan said, his tone sounding wryly mocking or ironic, and her surname sounding like an accusation, somehow, and Catherine nodded, and sat down too heavily beside him.

'Thank you so much for meeting me,' Catherine said, all in a rush.

He looked surprised; almost, she thought, offended. 'Why wouldn't I?'

'Oh, well,' Catherine shook her head, attempting to push her bag under the couch so that the carbuncle of scribbled notes protruding from it might not be so visible, but of course Doonan saw it immediately, and of course immediately understood her reason for hiding it; as his writing made excruciatingly clear, Doonan missed nothing. It was what Catherine had come, over the hours of rereading him, to dread: the prospect of sitting in front of him, in the full glare of those famous powers of perception.

'So you're in Trinity,' Doonan said, and he gave her a strange, bright smile. His eyes were an arresting, deep blue. His nose was heavily pitted, and flushed in the way she knew to suggest heavy drinking, though maybe it was just one of those things that came with age: Doonan was sixty-one.

'Yes,' Catherine said cautiously, conscious of how, in his novels, he seemed to have only scorn for people who went to university, or who devoted themselves to activities even vaguely artistic or intellectual. In a short story, the name of which she could not, right now, remember – her mouth went dry at this realization, as though Doonan had actually remanded its title – a graduate student at Trinity had died a horrible death, alone and pathetic in his bedsit, and the writing had been utterly devoid of sympathy for him. 'English and Art History,' she added, in an apologetic undertone.

'That must be nice for your parents,' he said, gesturing towards the cup and saucer which had been laid out for her; she nodded to say that yes, she would like some tea.

'I suppose,' she laughed nervously, and Doonan laughed too.

'Well, you're in it now whether they like it or not, says you,' he said, winking, and he poured her tea.

'No, no, I don't take milk, thanks,' she said then to his silent query, which was a lie.

Michael Doonan had twice been nominated for the Booker Prize, and had once been described as a Booker winner anyway by a profile in the *Sunday Independent*, an error which had been picked up as fact and repeated by several other journalists. In the photographs which accompanied these articles, he always looked furious, glowering out of the page with his arms folded, which for Catherine, doing her research in the microfilm room this week, had only made the mistakes funnier, and she had intended to ask him about this, but now that he was beside her, with what looked like the same glower crossing his features every couple of minutes, she felt less inclined. She should stick to biography instead, she decided, and so, she asked Doonan the questions to which she already knew the answers, and she fiddled with the *TN* Dictaphone while he recited them.

Doonan had been born above his father's butcher shop in Glasson, a village in County Westmeath. He had trained as a butcher, and until he was almost forty, he had made his living from the trade. He wrote in the evenings and on Sunday afternoons, and it was the success of *Let Her Go*, in 1978, that allowed him to retire and write full-time. He was married, to Julia, and they lived in a lovely mews house close to the city centre, which was lovely, he said, because his 'lovely Julia' had made it that way. He was the author of seven novels and two collections of stories. He wrote every day, including Sundays, and he did not see what all this nonsense was about writing being difficult. It was, he said, about putting your arse on the chair and getting on with it. It was, in that respect, the same as any other trade, except that it was in fact much easier, because you were sitting down while you were doing it.

'I interviewed Pat McCabe last month, actually, speaking of butchers,' she said as soon as he had finished telling her his philosophy of writing. '*The Butcher Boy*, you know?' she added, as though it was necessary. 'He was gas.'

There was a long pause, during which her heart began a horrible, dread-steeped thumping.

'Mmm,' Doonan said eventually, cracking his knuckles. 'I hope you didn't believe everything Mr McCabe told you about carcasses.'

'Oh, we didn't really talk about carcasses,' Catherine said hurriedly. 'We talked mainly about writing, actually.'

'And are we going to talk about writing, I wonder?'

'Oh,' Catherine stammered, and he laughed.

'You're attractive when you blush,' he said, his eyes on her throat. 'Do you know that?'

'Well, I don't know,' Catherine blurted, feeling, now, quite miserable; ostensibly, yes, what Doonan had said had been a compliment, but not really, she knew. Really, he had been letting her know that he saw how flustered she was, and how young and unprepared and incapable of handling this thing properly – and yet, with others she had handled it properly: with McCabe, for instance, she had been completely fine, clear and to the point, and even able to laugh with him, so what was wrong with her now? Why was she not even confident of lifting her teacup, in case her hands would shake so much that she would splash it all over Doonan's awful, too-tight jeans? Why could she barely even remember the plot of *Engines of Everything*? She did not even trust herself to mention the name of the main character now, in case she got it wrong. Mickey Donovan, he was called, she was almost certain; but what if it was actually Mickey Donaghy? What if it was Mikey, not Mickey? How could she be unclear on something so basic?

And now she was blushing even more furiously, she knew, and Doonan was enjoying the sight of it, even chuckling to himself now, the prick, as he was stirring his second cup of tea, and asking her with his eyes whether she was ready for her second cup too, but no, she hadn't even touched the first one; why would she, when it had no milk? *Get a grip*, she told herself, gritting her teeth, and she took a deep breath and she looked him in the eye.

'Mr Doonan. In *Engines of Everything*, you return to a theme which has preoccupied you throughout your career.'

'Getting the damn thing finished, you mean?'

'No, no,' she said. 'The theme of self-reliance.'

'Well, I suppose—'

'Well, you see, what I was thinking,' Catherine said, cutting in – at this, he glanced at her in surprise but allowed her to continue – 'What made me think about this was actually Whitman's poetry. You know, Walt Whitman?'

'Yes, I know of Walt Whitman,' Doonan said levelly.

'Well, of course. Well, you see, in "Song of Myself", he has a line *so* similar to what one of your characters says to the other when they're breaking up.'

'Does he?'

'Yeah. I'll find it, I have it here,' Catherine said, and she dug into her bag and riffled through her pages for the place where she had written down his protagonist's words and underlined them in red pen, adding, beside them, the Whitman line. 'See, here,' she said, as she found it, and she thrust her foolscap pages towards Doonan, but thought better of it at the last moment, and took them back to herself. 'Leona says, "I have this feeling, this fear, and it's in me, Tommy, and I don't understand it."'

'Yes.'

'And the Whitman line is, "There is that in me – I do not know what it is – but I know it is in me."'

There was a silence. Catherine looked at Doonan, and she put the notes back in her bag, which took a couple of moments, but still he did not say anything.

'It just really struck me,' she said excitedly, as she sat back up.

'I can see that.'

'And did you, um – did you think about Whitman at all when you were working on *Engines of Everything*?'

He stared. 'Why would I think about Whitman?'

'Oh, no, I mean—' Catherine said, and she stopped. What the hell was she doing? Why was she throwing all of this nonsense at Doonan instead of asking him a simple question? 'I suppose you wouldn't,' she said then. 'Necessarily.'

He looked at her for a long moment, then leaned forward to take a sip of his tea. Sitting back, he indicated Catherine's cup. 'That'll be spoiled on you shortly,' he said. 'Drink up.'

'Oh, thanks,' she said, and she took a sip: bitter, and lukewarm. It took effort not to spit it back into the cup.

'Would you prefer a proper drink?' Doonan said, sounding concerned.

'Oh, no. I'm OK.'

'You're certain?'

She nodded.

'And you like Whitman, do you?'

'Well, I'm doing this course on American poetry—'

'I'm more of a Dickinson man myself,' Doonan said.

'Really?'

He nodded. 'I like the way she kept to herself, and then left them word to destroy every scrap of hers that they came across after she was gone. That's the way to do it.'

'But surely you wouldn't like that to be done with *your* work?' Catherine heard herself say, and she could almost have shouted with relief: it was actually something amounting to a question.

'Well, it's out there now, I'm afraid.'

'Oh, yes, I know, I know,' Catherine said. 'But I mean, the immortality question, I suppose.'

'Oh, we're talking about immortality now?'

'Well, if you don't mind,' said Catherine, vaguely.

'Do I mind immortality?' Doonan mused. He glanced at her. 'Would I have someone like you for company, though? There's the rub.'

'I think your wife might have something to say about that,' Catherine said, with a hectic laugh. Doonan's expression, intense and unsmiling, did not change.

'Would I, though? Would I have that luck?' he said.

'Oh, now,' Catherine said, managing to laugh, and he liked this, she could see, and a thought occurred to her. 'Sex,' she said, knowing instantly that she had blurted the word out too abruptly, too randomly, but if Doonan was taken aback, he gave no sign of it.

'Go on,' he said.

'You write it very well,' Catherine said, in another blurt. 'You write it brilliantly.'

'Well, thanks very much,' Doonan murmured. 'That's interesting to hear.'

'I'm just wondering, though, whether it takes a lot of consideration?' Catherine said. 'To do that, I mean.'

'Consideration?' Doonan said.

'Yes,' Catherine nodded eagerly. 'I mean, if you have to think about it a lot? Or try the scenes out in different ways?' This was not what she had come up with in her notes; what *had* she come up with in her notes? Why had she brought them at all, for Christ's sake, if they were so unreadable and unusable?

'I mean, do you have to work especially hard at those scenes in your fiction?'

He looked offended. 'Do they read like that?'

'Oh, no,' Catherine said quickly. 'Not at all.'

'That's a relief.'

'It's just, the challenge from self-consciousness that I'm interested in, I suppose,' she said.

He twitched an eyebrow, raised a hand to get the attention of the waitress. 'I can see that, darling,' he said.

———

'Look, it probably wasn't as bad as you think,' Emmet said half an hour later. He had been at his usual desk in the publications office when she had arrived, still in a state of shock, and one glance had told him all he needed to know about how the interview had gone. He had laughed at her, of course; he had thrown his head back and guffawed, but then he had seemed to register the fact that Catherine was actually upset, and now he was trying to talk her round.

'No,' Catherine said, slamming down the Dictaphone. 'It was horrific. It could not have been worse.'

'Well, no, it could have been,' Emmet said. 'By the sounds of it.'

'What do you mean?' Catherine said, wretchedly.

'Well, that you could have actually . . . I mean . . .' Emmet shrugged, to indicate that he preferred not to say any more.

'Oh, for fuck's sake, Emmet. Of *course* I wasn't going to sleep with him. Thanks very fucking much.'

'I'm not *saying* you were. I'm just saying, it could have been worse. And it sounds like he was an arsehole to you.'

'No, not really,' Catherine said. '*I* was – I mean, *Whitman*, for Christ's sake.' She let out a low wail. 'Oh my *God*.'

'You've lost me now, Reilly, just for your information,' Emmet said, glancing back to his screen.

'Why did I have to open my mouth?'

'Ah, relax, Reilly. I'm sure you'll listen to the tape and it'll be grand.'

She looked at the Dictaphone as though it was an active grenade. 'I'm not fucking listening to that,' she said. 'I can't even look at it.'

He grinned. 'I'll gladly listen to it, if you want me to.'

'You must be joking,' she said, clamping a hand on it. Then something occurred to her. 'Here, you better not write about this in your column.'

193

'I've better things to be writing about,' Emmet scoffed.

'I doubt it,' Catherine said miserably. 'I doubt you could come up with anything better than me sitting on a couch beside Michael Doonan and saying "So! Sex! Do you like it, do you?"' She shook her head. 'Basically.'

'Well, when you put it like that.'

'Anyway,' Catherine shuddered. 'I'm going home for the weekend. I'll see you next week sometime. If I ever come back to this city.'

He looked at her, surprised. 'Oh. You're going down home?'

She nodded. 'Yeah. It's Mother's Day on Sunday. Don't you know that?'

'Well, make sure to tell your mother all about your affair with whatshisname. That'll make a nice present.'

'I hate you.'

'Here,' he said, leaning over his desk for a sheet of A4 paper; he folded it, before scribbling something on each side. He handed it to her. 'That's for your mother.'

In blue biro on one half of the page, Emmet had drawn a vague squiggle, and on the inside, in block capitals, he had written HAPPY MOTHER'S DAY, MRS REILLY. YOURS, EMMET DOYLE.

'It's a card,' Emmet said.

'You are actually insane.'

'Did *you* get your mother a card?'

'I'm getting her one at the train station.'

He clicked his tongue scornfully. 'Shop-bought. You're a great daughter.'

'You're nuts!'

'At least I don't go around propositioning sixty-year-old men,' he said, turning back to his computer.

'You shouldn't proposition anybody, Doyle,' she said,

trying for wryness, and she waited for his retort, but to her discomfort, nothing came; he kept looking at his screen, clicking now a couple of times on his mouse. Maybe he hadn't heard her.

She thought about him as she walked to the train station. She had thought about him plenty; she had thought about him for weeks. She had not gone out with him since the night of the Stag's, not that the night of the Stag's had been a night of going out with him, in any real sense; it had just been a drink, no matter how excitedly Zoe might insist otherwise. And yet, it had not been just a drink. The way he had looked at her today when she had walked into the office; the way he had looked at her every time they had seen one another since that night. Something was different. He blushed, but then again it seemed to her that he always blushed; that his blush was just something he had not been able to get rid of, and that it dogged him all the time, not just when he was talking to her. It was not the blush; it was the way he sort of . . . wavered. A waver that, when they saw one another, came into his eyes. That same hesitation that she had noticed that night. As though the entire space around him was somehow taking a breath; and, in truth, she felt it in herself too, felt herself taking a breath more deeply when she saw him, felt that she had, now, always to get something settled in herself, put aside in herself, before she could actually talk to him.

And when she had said that she was going down home for the weekend, had she imagined it, or had he reacted to that? Had he sort of blinked more quickly, or done, anyway, something rapid and distracted with his eyes? And was she going *mad*, counting and parsing the blinks and the eye movements of Emmet Doyle? Had she lost it completely?

Oh, Catherine, Catherine, James responded in Catherine's mind now, because of course it was James she was addressing, James to whom she was writing an imaginary, long juicy letter, as she went through all of this, as she turned it all inside out and back again. It was James she was moaning to, James to whom she was presenting the ever-more-convoluted elements of her case, and James who was absorbing it all, and James whom she was causing to frown thoughtfully, and James whom she was causing, now, to crease up with laughter, delighted with her latest drama, full of attention for this, the latest fine mess she had got herself into.

Except, of course.

Except.

And at Connolly station, as she walked towards the platform, she passed the bench where on another Friday evening, she had sat pressed up against James, listening to *OK Computer*. But it wasn't 'Exit Music' she was hearing now, as she went through the gates; it wasn't the mumbling, monotone Yorke singing of escape, singing of a chill. It was the jangled nerve endings of 'Lucky', its wary promises, its leaden warnings: *I feel my luck could change.*

7

James's new flat was on Thomas Street, near O'Brien's, and also near the art college, which explained why the flat had been laid out as a studio by the previous tenant; what little furniture there was in the big sitting room had been pushed back against the walls, and the floorboards were speckled with paint drops. James's landlady had not wanted to rent it to another artist, but he had persuaded her, promising that there would be no paint, and no smell of turpentine, and no smell of hash, either, and no loud music.

'My God, James, you've signed up to a very boring existence,' Aidan said, laughing. James had invited a few people around for a housewarming dinner; Amy and Lorraine and Cillian were there, and Zoe, and Lisa, the girl Catherine had met in the PhotoSoc office, and Aidan's friend Liam was due to call in on his way home from work in the Buttery. James had cooked a huge Bolognese, and they had eaten it sitting around the room, James and Aidan and Cillian on the floor, the girls on the kitchen chairs and the couch. It was James's second week in the flat now, and he had made it his own; his books were on a low shelf in the corner, and on the walls he had tacked up dozens of postcards and magazine images of artworks he loved. Warhol's blue-toned Jackie O was up there, and a shot of Vito Acconci panned out under the platform in *Seedbed*, and one of Walker Evans's pinched-faced sharecroppers, though James had explained to Catherine that that image was not actually Evans, that it was a piece that another artist, an American artist, had made by taking a photograph of the Evans. There was a postcard of a Matisse nude, a woman, one leg slightly bent, her hands clasped in front of her crotch, the space behind her seeming to explode with dark browns and blues. There was a whole row of Wolfgang Tillmans photographs, all of beautiful, thin people staring at the camera, their expressions as hard, in their way, as that of the Evans sharecropper; in the largest of these images, which was in black and white, a guy with a shaved head stood in front of a wall from which graffiti seemed to have been ineffectually scrubbed. He wore ripped camouflage trousers, and Doc boots, and a shiny bomber jacket of the type that Catherine could remember boys on the school bus having worn a few years ago; his arms were folded and in one hand he had a cigarette, and in the other what looked like a small stack of magazines for sale. His cheekbones were sharp, one of them marked by a mole. His eyes were two dark, unreadable dots.

Also there was one of the William Scott still lifes of pans and bowls – Catherine had told James about Scott's work in one of her letters – and a postcard of a piece by a Japanese artist – she had forgotten his name – which consisted just of a date, *April 12 1975*, painted in white on a black background, and a photo of a photographer making a daguerreotype, and a Cartier-Bresson portrait of Samuel Beckett, his face a clutch of long, deep wrinkles, his mouth pursed, his eyes sharp and fixed on something out of frame. Also, a postcard of three young black boys, naked, running, kicking and splashing into the sea. Their thin arms were outstretched; the soles of their feet were lifted to the camera, smooth and calm. Catherine was staring at them, her mug of red wine in one hand, when James came up behind her, putting his arms around her waist and resting his chin on her shoulder. She jumped at his touch, but in the next moment settled back against him. She felt the same flood of guilt that she felt every time he hugged her now, every time he cuddled her and nuzzled her in the way it came so naturally to him to do; she felt the wretchedness of wanting him not to stop doing it, not to detach from her again and open back out to a space which was shared with other people. The others, chatting and laughing on the other side of the room, were paying them no heed, but Catherine felt as conscious of their presence, and as bothered by it, as though they had been standing here at James's wall of pictures as well, pulling at him, pulling him away from her. She closed her eyes, willing the feeling to pass, to lift off her, like an insect or a virus, and decide on somebody else instead; she felt exhausted from the turmoil and shame of carrying it with her everywhere, at every moment.

'Hello,' James said softly, sweetly, and he tightened his grip around her. 'What are you up to, loitering over here like you're up to no good?'

Her heart pounded. She picked an image at random and pointed to it. 'What's the story with this one?' she said, the sentence not even sounding like a question, her words sounding limp and uninterested and tired.

But James did not notice. He responded happily and eagerly, telling her everything he knew.

Later, Lisa from PhotoSoc persuaded James to show them some of the photographs he had been taking himself over the last couple of weeks, and some of the photographs he had taken in Berlin, and he resisted for a few minutes, but then caved, grinning and shaking his head, going to the drawer where he kept his folders. Cillian, who had had more wine than anyone else, cheered loudly, and Amy and Zoe cleared a space in the middle of the floor so that James could lay the photos out for everyone, crouched and kneeling around him, to see.

The first few were from Berlin, and as James started to leaf through them, Catherine hung back a little, because she had seen them before; they had been taken in Malachy's studio, of Malachy, pot-bellied and bearded, at work, standing behind a huge camera on a tripod, and of the people who were posing for him; several of them were naked, which caused Cillian to cheer again, and to elbow past Aidan for a look at the women. James's angle on Malachy's subjects was, by necessity, not the angle for which the subjects, gazing towards Malachy's lens, were prepared, and the effect was disorienting; often, the faces were hidden, the limbs jutting out at odd angles. In a photo which Catherine particularly liked, a woman had, while twisting herself in a pose for Malachy, spotted James with his own camera, standing well off to the side; he had captured perfectly the moment of surprise and self-consciousness on her face. James did not comment on the photograph this time, but turned to the next, which was of another naked subject of Malachy's, this time a young man, dark-haired and striking, one arm raised high over his head. His legs were long and muscular, his buttocks high; from the side angle, his dick was a small, protruding blob high on one thigh. Like the woman's, his gaze was to the side, latched on to that of James's camera – but, unlike the woman, he did not look shocked or embarrassed. He stared.

Catherine stared too. She had not seen this photograph before. James must have added it to the folder only recently; it had not been there when he had shown her his Berlin photographs in Baggot Street.

'Who's that?' she said, crawling forward, but at the same moment Cillian, who was on his hunkers beside her, let out another cheer.

'Wahoo, Jimbo,' he said, clapping James on the back. 'You were fucking *well in* there, what?!'

James smirked. 'I don't think so, Cillian,' he said, going to turn the page, but Zoe put out a hand to stop him.

'He's bloody *gorgeous*,' she squealed, craning her neck to look at the photograph more closely.

'Who is he?' Catherine said again, a jump of urgency in her voice now, which James seemed to catch; he glanced at her cautiously.

'That's Florian. A young friend of Malachy's.'

The way he had said *book* that afternoon looking at the guy in Hodges Figgis was the same way in which he had now said *young friend* – as though it was something despicable, something laughable, something the very taste of which he wanted to wash out of his mouth. As Cillian and Zoe and the girls made further comments on Florian and James's photographing of him, James went again to turn to the next sheet, but now something came to Catherine, the realization of it hitting her like a wall of sound, and this time she was the one to reach out and stop him.

'Wait a minute,' she said, her fingers tight around his wrist. 'You mentioned Florian to me in a letter, didn't you? Wasn't Florian the guy who asked you out to the pub?'

The reaction to this from the others was loud and delighted; Cillian roared as wildly as though he was at a football match, and Zoe and the girls made noises like police sirens, and Lisa laughed, and Aidan sat back on his heels and watched James, grinning, seeming almost proud. But James shook his head hurriedly, irritably, and swatted Catherine's hand away.

'No, no,' he said, moving to the next image. 'That wasn't Florian. You must be mistaken. You must be mixing up the names.'

'I'm *not* mixing up the names,' Catherine said, offended. 'I wrote to you about Florian. I told you that you should have gone with him. I told you that you—'

She stopped, feeling suddenly almost dizzy with confusion. Was this the same Florian? How many guys with that kind of name, after all, could there have been? Had James said anything more about him in that letter? Could he have told her about taking his photograph, taking his *naked* photograph, for Christ's sake, and could she have missed it, skimmed over it, ignored it? She had, the uneasy truth was, skimmed over plenty in his letters, looking for the funny parts, the parts that were responses to her own life, the parts she had preferred to read; but could she possibly have missed such a detail? No, she did not think so, did not believe so; which meant that James was lying to her. And what did that mean? How much else, then, did that mean James was concealing? And yet, all that he was denying was what Catherine knew to be the case, which was that this guy – this gorgeous, naked guy, his skin glistening, his muscles taut – had asked James to come for a drink, and James, in James's nervous, frightened way, had stupidly declined. And Catherine had chided him for that. So what was she feeling so awful about? What was this panic, this – it felt almost like anger – rushing through her? As James moved to another folder now, seeming to have decided not to risk showing any more of the photographs from Berlin, as he started to show the new Dublin photographs, the strangers from Grafton Street, the familiar faces from college, what Catherine was reeling with felt absurdly like a sense of betrayal. What was wrong with her? She got to her feet, stumbling across Aidan as the others turned to him, laughing and exclaiming, in reaction to James's sullen, sharp-eyed portrait of him; standing, frowning, against the grey stone of the Campanile, his hands thrust into the pockets of his army jacket, Aidan looked like the guy in the Wolfgang Tillmans photograph.

'Brilliant shot,' Lisa was saying, nodding approvingly at James.

'*Smokin'*,' Zoe was saying, poking Aidan in the ribs.

'Oh, now, he was a right handful in front of the camera, I can tell you,' James was saying, which of course just made Cillian whoop and cheer all over again, and it occurred to Catherine that for her own sake, for her own sanity, she should really call it a night and go home to Baggot Street, to bed, and that maybe everything would be clearer in the morning, that maybe in the morning, everything would be OK; but no, the last thing she could do, the last thing she was able to do, was to go out of here and leave everyone else with James. What she wanted, rather, was for all of them to go, and for the two of them to be left alone together, and then maybe she could stay over, snuggled up warm and cosy beside him. Guilt and dismay accosted her again at the thought of this, or rather at the realization that she had, once again, allowed herself to be so sucked in, rendered so wistful and so hopeful and pathetic, by that thought; but it was there. It was in her. What was she supposed to do with it? she thought, watching as the door to the hall opened and Liam walked in, guitar case on his shoulder, six-pack of beer in his hand. What was she supposed to do with it, when it was not even something she could understand? From the middle of the room, James was coming, smiling, to greet Liam, hand out for a shake, then arms around him for a hug, and the horrible bird of jealousy thrashed against the walls of Catherine's chest again, and she poured herself another mug of awful, bitter wine.

———

And it was later that Catherine understood.

It was after several other conversations that had made her feel rattled, and baffled, and dreadful; a dreadful, horrible friend. Lisa, for example, telling James that there was a new exhibition by Ed Dunne coming up at the Gallery of Photography, and that she could get him an invitation to the opening, and James saying that they could go together, and happening, at that moment, to catch what must have been an injured look in Catherine's eye, and saying, abruptly, *We'll all go!* And everyone had agreed, and Zoe had said that they'd make a night of it, but that had not made Catherine feel any better – that had only made Catherine feel worse, because she wanted it to be only her and James who were going, her and James, glossy and sophisticated at an art opening – she would wear her black wool Oasis dress, the one she had worn to the English Ball – and she did not want any of the others there to get in the way of that, to diffuse that glow. And then Liam, talking for a long while about Dunne's photography and what he thought of it, because of course Liam, being from the North, had an opinion, because Dunne was from Belfast originally and his work was always in some way about the Troubles; Liam had plenty of opinions, and they were smart and they were reasonable and they were, at moments, quite angry – he did not think that Dunne, who had lived in America for years, had a right to pontificate, as he put it, about things he did not have to live with, or to worry about personally, or to experience. Liam's uncle, it turned out, had been killed early in the Troubles, shot at a checkpoint close to his home in Tyrone – and surely there was no worse feeling than the feeling Catherine had at that moment, of hating Liam for having a story which made him so interesting, so much the object of James's fascinated, sympathetic attention. What was wrong with her?

'Do you think the talks up there at the moment will come to anything?' Zoe asked him, and Catherine hated her, too, for being so earnest and worried about things that affected other people, not them, and for the way that James, in response to this, frowned, and looked, also, worried, and launched into a long exchange with Liam about whether the deadline just imposed on the peace talks at Stormont could really bring anything about. Catherine watched him as he spoke, and she thought about how, when she had watched him working earlier that week, taking photographs of Zoe on the lawn outside the Pav, she had felt jealous not just of Zoe but – this was insane, this was intolerable – almost of his camera; of the deep care it was getting from him, of the locked, intense focus. She could not understand herself. She could not *believe*—

And when the conversation had finished, Cillian and Liam took their guitars out, and the singing started, and it was after perhaps twenty minutes of their singing that Catherine understood. Cillian was singing, for the most part, though Liam joined in for a few songs, and everybody else did as well, and they were making their way through all the usual things – 'Blackbird' and 'Hallelujah' and 'Suzanne' – and then Cillian had started into a U2 bender – 'Pride' and 'Bloody Sunday' and 'When Love Comes to Town'.

'Oh, enough bloody U2,' Catherine said to James, who was on the floor across from her, smoking some of Cillian's hash and sitting back against the wall; he had one arm resting on the top of his head, bent at the elbow, and she thought of Florian in the photograph, and she chased the thought of him away. And James laughed, and said something that Catherine could not make out about Bono, and he passed her the joint, and their eyes met, and they were both smiling, and it was just lovely, Catherine thought – it was just the way it should be, with all of the earlier nonsense melted away. And by now, Cillian and Liam had started another song, a song it took her a moment to place, as Liam strummed it into the room, but it was more of the same: the same corny, heartfelt appealing. And she was actually laughing about it, thinking of how she and James would mock its lyrics, its diamonds and its cradles and its graves, when it hit her.

It was a song she had never really listened to before, though she had heard it so many times, heard its hoarse, desperate chorus. It was a song that had always just been there; always just part of the world's background noise. And now – now, it seemed, it was hers. Because now she was singing it, in her fucked-up mind. James was sitting across from her, whispering to Zoe, and she was here, with its words coursing through her, with its words in the place where her breath was meant to be. Where her sense was meant to be. Her reason.

You. And *you.* And the guitar chords slamming down like blows; Liam really going at the guitar chords, and Cillian, really pulling the arse out of the lyrics, roaring one word over and over, giving it two syllables, making it roll on, roll over; making of it a haunting.

And *fuck*, Catherine thought, as she watched James, as she watched the smile of him, and the lean of him, and the way his skin looked in this half-light, and the way his eyes looked when they fastened on Cillian and on Liam.

Fuck, she thought, *you cannot feel this. You cannot feel this for him. You cannot.*

On the jacket flap, Ted Hughes looked unkempt, his hair in wild flyaway strands. But dignified, still: a dark tie, a V-neck under a herringbone jacket. His eyes just darkness. His mouth in a half-smile.

She knew what she wanted her essay to be about now: she wanted to write about his presence in Plath's poetry, and her presence in these new ones of his. About autobiography, and how it never showed itself in the work in the lazy way that readers expected it to. She stared at the book's cover, its abstract reds and yellows and blues. She opened a page at random; 'Wuthering Heights'. She pulled it to her. Planted an elbow on each page and pushed her fingers into her hair.

> *Writers*
> *Were pathetic people. Hiding from it*
> *And making it up.*

Their trip to the Brontë ruins. The imagined ghost of Emily, and what she would have made of Sylvia's giddy presence in the house, her huge hope. Her 'huge / Mortgage of hope'.

Catherine was there with them. The wet, rotting beams, the stone floors covered with sheep droppings. In her mind's eye, it was her father's shed, the shed where he fixed farm machinery now, the shed that had been a home to someone not long ago. The moors she had never seen; but she could imagine them. Could imagine their whirling eddies of harshness and indifference. The winter sky, stern over a couple driven to be tourists in this place which, to them, ought to have been only too familiar – and must have been to one of them, at least, to Ted – and she could see it, Catherine could, the near blackness, the low ceiling, the shadowed corners, the sky leaning low. The stones, and the grass, and the animals looking in.

'Reilly. Where were you this morning?'

Emmet. He was crouching by her desk, holding on to the side, and he was grinning. He was reminding her that there had been a *TN* meeting that morning; Catherine had not bothered to go.

'Forgot about it,' Catherine said, and shrugged. 'Did I need to be there?'

He clicked his tongue. 'No loyalty.'

'No energy,' she said. 'I'm knackered after the weekend.'

'And what were you doing at the weekend?'

'Probably the same thing you were doing,' she said.

'Well, I was trying to convince Derek Galvin to go skinny dipping in the canal. So I hope you weren't doing that.'

'Skinny dipping with *you*?'

'No!' he said, looking horrified. 'By himself. Why would I want to go skinny dipping with Galvin? Jesus Christ.'

'OK.'

'What are you reading?' Emmet said now. He tipped at the book like a cat with a toy. 'Sorry,' he said then, quickly, with a wobbly smile.

'Ted Hughes,' Catherine said, unnecessarily, because in the same moment Emmet had reached over, closed the book and pulled it to him; he was examining the cover.

'Oh, yeah, I read something about this lately. Your one was his missus, wasn't she? Who topped herself?'

'Sylvia Plath.'

'Yeah,' he nodded. 'See, I know about poetry.' He opened to the description on the inside jacket flap. 'Oh. These are *about* her, are they?' he said, after he'd read for a few seconds.

'Yeah,' Catherine said. 'He wrote them for her.'

'For her birthday?'

'Kind of. Every year, like. She's been dead for thirty-five years now.'

He nodded. 'It's sad, isn't it? The way she died.'

There was this aspect to him, Catherine had noticed lately: this bluntness and frankness that startled her. These questions or statements he came out with, as unvarnished as a child's.

'Yeah,' she said. 'It was sad.'

He had settled on a page and had begun to read the poem. '9 Willow Street', she saw.

'It's about when they went to Boston,' Catherine said. 'He was teaching at Harvard.'

'Jesus,' Emmet said, after he had been reading for a few moments. 'They sound like a right barrel of laughs, the two of them.' He assumed a deep, plummy voice. '"I folded / Black wings round you, wings of the blackness / That enclosed me, rocking me, infantile / And enclosed you with me." Jesus.' He shuddered.

'He doesn't sound like that,' Catherine said. 'He didn't go to Gonzaga.'

'Signs are on him,' Emmet said, and he kept going. '"And your heart / Jumped at your ribs, you gasped for air. / You grabbed for the world, / For straws, for morning coffee, anything / To get airborne."' He looked at her. 'Could he not just make her a fucking coffee?'

'Give me that,' Catherine said, and she snatched the book from him.

'Are they all that melodramatic?'

'Are you going to stay here and torment me all morning?'

'I might,' he said, grinning in response, but he looked distracted. He was looking at her but he was not, she knew, concentrating on what she was saying as she told him now that she was on a deadline with this essay. He nodded, but he was doing the thing she had known other guys to do – it had taken her a while to work it out, but she knew what it was now – which was the thing of letting her talk, encouraging her to talk, even, so that they could use it as an excuse to look at her more closely. He was studying her face now, she knew, instead of listening to her. And he was grinning. And he was cute when he grinned like that, there was no denying it. And he was cute, there was no denying it, when he didn't grin.

But he wasn't James. Nobody was James.

'James,' he was saying now, and Catherine stared at him. 'What?'

'Did you see James this weekend?'

And that was another first: blushing at the mention of James's name; and she blushed harder as she talked about the dinner he had thrown, and she saw Emmet noticing this, and thinking about it, puzzling over it; tracking the blush across her face as it spread.

'And, em,' he said, picking up the book again, 'what's your favourite poem in this?'

'"Robbing Myself",' Catherine said immediately. She opened the index and found the page, pushing it towards him. 'It's about Hughes driving to their house in Devon after they'd left it. They'd split up by then, and he was going back to check on his potatoes and apples.'

'His *potatoes*?' Emmet said, incredulously. 'What a fucking culchie.'

From across the library, someone shushed them.

'You're incorrigible,' Catherine said. 'I'm not going to let you read it if you're going to slag it off.'

'No, no,' Emmet said, pulling the book to him. 'I'm sorry.'

'It would have been a couple of months before Plath died,' Catherine said. 'He says December. The December dusk.'

'"Over fallen heaven",' Emmet said. '"For snow". That's good.'

'Yeah,' Catherine nodded. 'That's good.'

He read on. 'He likes his potatoes all right,' he said, raising his eyebrows.

'No talking,' Catherine said. She watched him read.

'"Pigs' noses",' Emmet said with a smirk, and she rapped on the table beside him.

'Sorry,' he said, and he kept reading. And she watched him, as he came to the passage where Hughes crept through the house, the silent house, listening to the absence of his family, of his wife and children, feeling like a trespasser, seeing their books, the walnut desk, the Victorian chair he had bought for five shillings – '"Love, love, I have hung our cave with roses."'

'Shit,' said Emmet, at the line now, she could see, about Plath's tears, her last lonely weeks in the house. Did she imagine it, or did he shudder, reading about the house closed up again, tight as a casket, the stained-glass windows glowing? And then Hughes was back on the road again, and Emmet's eyes were climbing from the bottom of one page to the top of the last, and to the image she loved so much that seeing him read it for the first time, she knew she could not trust herself to speak:

> *I peered awhile, as through the keyhole*
> *Into my darkened, hushed, safe casket*
> *From which (I did not know)*
> *I had already lost the treasure.*

Emmet exhaled long and deeply after he had finished.

'Fuck,' he said. 'That's fairly depressing.'

She laughed. 'Yeah.'

'So she wasn't dead yet?'

'Well, she was when he wrote this.'

'Fuck.' He closed the book again, looked at it in his hand.

'Well, nice cover, at least,' he said, and she burst out laughing. He was laughing too, as he looked at her, but she could see that he was confused too, or hurt, even, by her laughter.

'His daughter did that painting,' Catherine said, pointing to the splodges of colour, the rusty reds and yellows.

'Did she?' Emmet said. 'When she was little?'

Catherine laughed again. 'No,' she said, and Emmet looked at her, disbelieving. 'When she was an adult. She's an artist.'

'Fair enough,' Emmet said, puffing out a breath.

'Here,' Catherine said. 'Give it to me.'

But it was too late: he had already seen the inscription.

'Oh,' Emmet said. 'That's nice. He has nice handwriting, doesn't he?'

'Yeah.'

'Mine's a fucking disaster.'

'I know,' she said. 'And so does my mother.'

He looked at her, bewildered for a moment, and then he got her meaning, and he laughed. 'So, em,' he said, rocking back on his heels, 'is James seeing anyone these days?'

'James?'

He nodded.

'No.' Catherine shook her head firmly. 'No. For James it's not that simple.'

'Oh?'

'No. Not that straightforward.'

'Well,' Emmet said, seeming to cast about for a response. 'It's not straightforward for a lot of people, I suppose.'

Catherine gave a little laugh, a laugh which might suggest that this was a cute idea. 'Yeah. But *slightly* more so for James.'

Emmet nodded. The book was in his hands again, turning and turning. He swallowed. 'Yeah. I can imagine.'

'Can you?'

He looked at her as though this was a test. 'I think so.'

'I don't know if anyone can imagine it, really,' Catherine said, feeling her throat swell with the importance of the statement. 'He's had some terrible things said to him.'

Emmet frowned. 'By who? Not people in college?' He looked almost angry.

'Just people,' she said, shaking her head as though it was something she could not possibly go into. 'You know.'

He shook his head now too. 'That's fucking appalling,' he said. 'Poor James.' He looked at her. 'You're such a good friend to him,' he said then. 'He's lucky to have you.'

There it was again: the openness, the plain-spokenness. Few people she knew would speak like that. Aidan, maybe, but with him it was somehow harsher. It was, with Emmet, the blush that made the difference, but it was also the way he said things. Like he meant them. When he was not joking, he was utterly serious. Was that true of everybody? She tried to think. Maybe. Probably. But no, she did not think it was. She glanced at him. He was not even looking at her, did not even seem interested in, or heedful of, her reaction. He was looking at the Hughes book again. He opened it at random, and quite astonishingly – or maybe it was just the way the spine was now, from her own use of the book – it fell open at '9 Willow Street' again. But he did not look at that poem – which reminded Catherine so much of Baggot Street, so much of the flat, the cosiness in which they all lived – but across the page, to the end of another poem. It was 'Child's Park', she saw; Plath in the park, going nuts at the girls who were pulling up the azalea flowers. Yet more than that. Always more than that.

'"What happens in the heart simply happens,"' Emmet

read. 'That's all right, as poetry goes. That's at least not as dreary as fuck.'

'Don't read the rest of it, then,' Catherine said, with a laugh that, she saw, came as a relief to him.

'Here you go,' he said, handing her back the book, and as he did so, his hand touched hers, and he let it stay there for a moment – for just long enough for her to know that he meant something by it. He glanced at her, like a child in trouble, his eyes cautious, the mischief only around the corner, the blush high on his cheeks again. 'Right, I have to head off,' he said then, and he stood. 'I've already missed a meeting with my Politics lecturer, talking to you.'

'Don't be blaming me, Doyle,' Catherine said.

'I will if I want to,' he grinned, and he walked away.

'What on earth was that about in the library with poor little Emmet Doyle earlier?' Zoe said. They were having lunch outside one of the lecture halls; Catherine had been having a sandwich by herself when Zoe had come up to her.

'Nothing,' Catherine said, shrugging.

'And thanks for letting me know you were going out for lunch. I was waiting for you to come over to me for the last half an hour.' She ripped open her sandwich: chicken and stuffing, the same thing they had every day. 'I'm bleedin' *starving*.'

'Sorry,' Catherine said again.

'Well?' Zoe said, her mouth full. 'I mean, you say you're not going out with him, but to me it looked like the two of you were in the process of breaking up.'

'What do you mean?'

'Well, it looked very serious. Did Emmet get his mid-twentieth-century poets mixed up or something?'

'Emmet Doyle doesn't know mid-any-century poets,' Catherine snorted, feeling immediately guilty, remembering how Emmet had looked so closely at the Hughes poems.

'I was talking to Conor earlier, by the way.' Zoe fixed her with a look. 'And he was telling me that you two aren't talking at the moment. He told me you had an argument in the Buttery a couple of weeks ago. Over James. I thought I was hearing things.'

'Did he tell you what he *said* about James? Did he tell you what he called him?'

'Camp, I think.'

'Yeah,' Catherine said hotly.

'Which,' Zoe said, raising her eyebrows, 'James kind of is. I mean, I think *James* would admit that.'

'Oh, fuck, don't you start.'

'Start what?' Zoe said. 'You're the one who took it upon yourself to tell Conor and me about James. And others, for all I know.'

'I *didn't* tell others,' Catherine lied.

'Well, fine. But my point still stands.'

'What point?' Catherine almost spat.

Zoe did not flinch. She rarely did. She regarded Catherine steadily, and sipped from her coffee, and put the cup down. 'You can't protect him, Catherine.'

'Protect *who*?'

Zoe actually laughed, though it was not really a laugh. 'Oh, please. You know who I'm talking about. You're too involved, Cath. Aidan and I have been meaning to bring this up with you for a while now.'

'Aidan and you?' Catherine spluttered. 'What are you, a crack team of fucking meddlers now, or something? Or, wait, are you sleeping together?'

217

'No, Catherine,' Zoe said in a warning tone. 'Look, I don't want to have a fight with you. I'm just saying. You need to give James some credit. You need to stop trying to protect him all the time.'

'I'm not trying to protect him! How could I protect him?'

'Well, that's kind of my point.'

'I don't want to talk about this anymore,' Catherine said, and she began to gather up her lunch things.

'I know you're his friend,' Zoe said quickly. 'His closest friend, I know that. But you have to let him fight his own battles. You know?'

'Oh, yeah,' Catherine said bitterly. 'Because that's really worked out so well. For so long. Leaving people like James to fight their own battles.'

'That's not what I'm talking about,' Zoe said, pointing at her. 'Don't paint me as some—'

'Saying nothing, instead of standing up and taking a stand?' Catherine said, hearing immediately how ridiculous the sentence sounded. 'Instead of doing something to make things easier?' she said.

Zoe stared. 'What are you *talking* about, Cits? Nobody is trying to make things difficult for James. If anyone is making things difficult for James, it's himself. And you, I might as well tell you, are not at all helping by hanging around him like an overprotective mother. Or like his girlfriend. Or like his fucking *wife*, actually. You do realize that people are assuming that you two are a couple?'

'I don't give a fuck what people assume,' Catherine said. 'What the hell am I supposed to do about the things that people assume? What can I do about it?'

'You could stop holding hands with James in public, for one thing.'

'We don't hold hands,' Catherine said. 'We link arms.'

'You look like you're holding hands,' Zoe said, shaking her head. 'It's the closeness. The physical proximity. It has the same effect.'

'Oh my God. Are you serious? Are you seriously talking to me like this? Fuck *off*,' she said, and she jerked her hand to the side, and this was how she spilled Zoe's coffee, which went all over the table. 'Oh, *shit*,' she said, moving to get things out of the way of the spreading brown liquid.

'Here, here,' Zoe said, already soaking up the spilled coffee with a wad of napkins she had produced from somewhere. 'It's all right,' she said, and she glanced up at Catherine. 'Is your book OK?'

Catherine just nodded; she had knocked *Birthday Letters* down onto her lap as soon as she could, but she was pretty sure some of the coffee would have got at it.

Zoe sighed. She reached across and took Catherine's hand, patted it briefly.

'Emmet touched my hand in the library,' Catherine said.

'Oooh,' said Zoe, and she raised her eyebrows. Then her face changed; something seemed to occur to her. 'Does Emmet know about James?' she said.

Catherine said nothing for a moment, weighing up her options, or trying to. Then she nodded, a short, sharp nod.

'Well, thank goodness for that at least.'

'What's that supposed to mean?'

'I mean, at least you're not pretending to *him*.'

'I am not pretending to anyone!' Catherine exploded. 'I told you! What am I meant to do about what people assume? James is my friend. And I'm worried about him. I'm being as good a friend as I can to him so that he doesn't feel—'

'So that he doesn't feel gay?' Zoe cut in.

Catherine stared at her. 'I can't believe you said that.'

'Well, I did say it, Catherine. And I'm not sorry I said it. I mean, if you don't care about yourself, and what people think about your availability . . .'

'Availability! What is this, a fucking matchmaking festival?'

Zoe shrugged. 'At this stage of life, yes. That's what it's meant to be.'

'Maybe for you,' Catherine said contemptuously.

'Maybe for James, too, if you'd let him.'

'You don't know *anything* about him. You met him a month ago, for fuck's sake!'

'I know that, and if I'd met him three hours ago, it would still be crystal clear to me how much you're potentially fucking things up for him. What do you think this is doing to James, Catherine? Parading around with a girl on his arm virtually every time he's out in public? What kinds of opportunities must this, this *illusion* of yours be wrecking for him?'

Catherine scoffed. 'There are no opportunities,' she said.

Zoe regarded her for a long moment. 'And why do you think that is?'

'Because he's not ready,' Catherine said, slamming her hand down on the table. 'Because he doesn't feel ready for someone. When he's ready for someone, someone will come along. Until then, I'm his friend, and it's my job to look after him.'

'To look *after* him?' Zoe said disbelievingly.

'To look out for him, then,' Catherine said. 'I don't care about the semantics. Put it however the fuck you want to put it.'

'Jesus Christ, Catherine,' Zoe said, shaking her head. 'On second thoughts, you should stay well clear of Emmet.

He doesn't deserve this bullshit. He doesn't deserve to find himself involved with someone like you.'

'Going to go after him yourself?' Catherine sneered. 'Another notch?'

'I don't know what's happening to you, Catherine,' Zoe said, and she got up and walked away.

10

Ed Dunne's opening was on the Thursday before Easter, as it turned out, so few people were still around to come to it with Catherine and James; Amy and Lorraine had already gone home for the weekend, as had Aidan and Liam, and Zoe and Lisa, who both had part-time waitressing jobs, were working that night. James himself had found it difficult to get the night off from O'Brien's; with every pub in the country about to close for twenty-four hours, the place would be teeming with drinkers, but he had managed to get someone to cover for him. Catherine, meanwhile, was meant to be in Longford already, helping to prepare for her grandfather's eightieth birthday party, which was taking place that weekend; she had managed to fob her mother off by pretending that her essay was due much earlier than was actually the case.

In Stormont, the peace talks were rapidly approaching their final deadline, which was, as a piece in the *Irish Times* had put it that week, 'the best possible publicity' for Dunne's show. His work had always reflected obliquely on the Troubles, even though he had been gone from Northern Ireland since the 1970s, living first in London and now in New York; over a period of many years, he had kept up with the news from there by making weekly phone calls to friends in Belfast. When news of a particular event struck him, he would go out and make a piece by photographing whatever happened to be in front of him. He had a home upstate as well as in Manhattan, so just as many of the images had a rural setting – a setting that looked almost Irish – as an urban one, and each one bore the date on which it had been taken. The new show would bring together works in this series from the past decade.

She and James had a drink in the Stag's before going to the gallery. James was disappointed that none of the others had been able to join them.

'It would have been a bit of craic with a few of us,' he said sadly.

'It'll *still* be craic,' said Catherine.

'Oh, of course, of course it will. I just meant, the more the merrier. You know?'

'Yeah,' she said quietly. 'You ready? It's almost seven.'

When they reached the gallery, James walked upstairs to the exhibition space ahead of Catherine, stopping short as soon as he got to the landing.

'Balls,' he said under his breath.

'What?'

'We're nearly the first ones here,' he said, sounding mortified. 'We should leave and come back again. What was I thinking? Nobody turns up at the time on the invite.'

And it was true, they were among the first people there; four or five people stood chatting in the centre of the gallery floor, among them Dunne himself, recognizable from the photograph which had run beside the *Irish Times* piece. He would turn sixty later that year, the piece had said, and the journalist had described him as looking younger, but to Catherine he looked about that; he was bald, and wrinkled, and as tanned as if he lived in the Caribbean, and he wore a dark suit, the jacket of which had a closed collar coming right up to his neck, and bright blue glasses, the frames very round.

In his hand he held a glass of champagne, as did the other people standing around him: a couple of grey-haired men, a woman in a tight red dress, a younger, dark-haired man in a more traditional suit and tie. As James and Catherine stood, frozen, at the entrance to the space, Dunne noticed them and beckoned them in.

'Oh, fuck, *fuck*,' James hissed out of the side of his mouth. 'What should we do?'

'Come *in*, for Chrissakes!' the younger man exclaimed. He was American; he looked, Catherine thought, like a Kennedy. He came towards them now as they walked – shuffled – into the space, both blushing – how Catherine hated to see this in James; how she wished he, at least, had managed to look unflustered – and the American smiled, showing his white, straight teeth. He was, Catherine thought, thirty or thirty-five or something, with a high, clean forehead under his tight dark curls.

'Sorry we're early,' Catherine said as they reached him.

He frowned. 'You're not early.'

'Sorry, sorry,' she blurted again.

He smirked. 'Oh, I forgot that about you people. The apologizing.' He extended a hand. 'I'm Nate,' he said. 'I'm here with Ed. And you two?'

'We're not,' Catherine said, ridiculously, immediately closing her eyes with the shame of it, so that she could not see the expression on Nate's face as he reacted to this.

'We're . . .' James said, seeming to cast about for a description. 'We're students. Art students. We heard about the exhibition through a contact.'

'Through a *contact*?' Nate said, visibly smothering a laugh.

'Well, a friend, really,' James said hurriedly. 'Another, you know, artist.'

'Hmm,' Nate said, nodding slowly. 'You still haven't told me your names.'

Seeming to have decided now to take charge, James stepped forward, his hand outstretched. 'James Flynn,' he said briskly. 'And this is Catherine Reilly.'

'Very formal,' Nate said; his handshake was firm. 'So have you met Ed before?'

'Oh, no,' they said in unison. Catherine blinked rapidly.

'We're just here to see the art, really,' she said, and she swept her gaze wildly around the gallery walls. 'Looks great,' she said, and then, as though propelled, she lurched away from Nate and James and practically ran to the piece which was furthest away, right across the room, a huge photo of a red-bricked block of flats, clothing hanging from many of the balconies, the reflection of a sunset glinting in a swathe of the windowpanes. She stood in front of it as though it was an actual building, and one to which she desperately needed to gain admittance; she stood there, clutching the strap of her new Oxfam evening bag, as though she was prepared to queue outside this building all night. Behind her, she could hear the sounds of Nate introducing James to Ed Dunne and the others: James's *Love your work*, Dunne's rote, bluffing professions of modesty, Nate's loud, confident interrogations, and the polite laughter of the people around them, the people who had turned up first to this exhibition and yet seemed not to have any desire to look at the work.

Gradually, more people began to arrive, filling the gallery space, standing in front of the photographs. Whenever Catherine glanced around, James was still deep in conversation with Dunne and his group. In the pub he had expressed a determination to network at the opening, and she had encouraged him, telling him to make sure that people knew that he had a show coming up himself, but now she could not help but feel the sting of being abandoned by him like this. It was her own fault, she knew; if she had not fled the exchange with Nate like she had, she would presumably also be a part of that chatting, smiling cluster of people now. She was comforted by the thought that James could not talk to them all evening, but in the next moment it occurred to her that he was very capable of doing just that; of getting so caught up in the excitement and the stimulation of being in the middle of things that he could completely forget that she was waiting for him elsewhere in the room. She pushed the thought away, because it threatened to make her miserable, and because she had resolved not to be miserable tonight; she had resolved to be normal, and easy-going, and a friend. She fixed her attention on the photograph in front of which she was now standing: it was a scene shot by torchlight in what looked like a field; blades of grass were visible, yellow and bright in the beam against the darkness. In the *Times* article, Dunne had talked about these photos as 'guilt-pieces', works saturated with the consciousness of the place he had left behind thirty years previously.

Bovinia, NY, 19 June 1994, the piece was titled. Each piece corresponded to an atrocity which had happened in the North, to an event which had claimed a life or lives. 19 June 1994; Catherine tried to think, now, what had happened on that day. She would have been in school, third year; it had been the month, she realized, of her Junior Cert, which had happened at the same time as the World Cup about which the entire country had gone insane. There had been a mass shooting in a pub up there the evening of the first Ireland match, she remembered now; the IRA, or the UVF, or whichever of the bastards it was, had walked into a bar and murdered several men who had been just sitting there, watching the football. Had that been the date? It seemed likely, but then there had been so many dates. Any one month could have had twenty of them. It was incredible to think now that all of that might really be over, that in a room up there, right now, people were possibly finding a way to make it end. It had been around as long as she could remember – her grandmother and her mother gasping and clicking their tongues in sorrow and disbelief at the news on the radio; her father's angry, downcast eyes. It had been always the choked, frightened air of the country, so Christ knew what it had been like actually to live up there, over the border; Catherine could not imagine. Her family had never even travelled there; it had simply always been a place to which you did not go. She thought of Liam; his father had a pub up there, she remembered him saying, though she could not remember in which town – Enniskillen or Armagh or Derry or one of those places; they were all the same, in honesty, to Catherine; they were all scary, forbidden places, the inhabitants of which she felt somehow in awe of. To live with that, and yet to get on with things – she simply could not imagine. *Daddy, I love you very much*, a dying girl at the scene of the Enniskillen bombing had said to her father, and Catherine, aged nine or ten then, had been unnerved and shaken by it, by the thought of a girl, her life about to be taken from her, having that much courage, that much thought for those who would mourn for her, to be able to say that to her father, to be able to speak those words.

She was growing morbid, she realized; she shook her head vigorously, to shake herself out of it, and moved on to the next photo. This one was of a young black girl sitting on what looked like a footpath; it was grey and stained and cracked. She wore denim dungarees, and red sandals, and her knees were scuffed. In her hand she held a bracelet made of brightly coloured plastic balls. *Atlantic Avenue, 8 May 1991*, the piece was called. Her eyes were huge. From the top right-hand corner of the image, a hand reached down, its palm pale and deeply scored.

'Spirited-looking child, isn't she?' a man to Catherine's left said. She turned, startled, and there was Michael Doonan, looking not at her but at the photograph.

'Oh,' she said, blushing instantly. 'Mr—'

'Mick,' Doonan said curtly, and then he turned slightly to the woman who was, Catherine realized, with him, and he put a hand to the small of the woman's back, and he nodded towards Catherine.

'This is the young lady who interviewed me for the Trinity paper,' he said. 'My wife, Julia,' he said to Catherine.

'Oh! Mrs—'

'*Julia*,' they both said almost chidingly, Julia shaking Catherine's hand warmly. She was beautiful, Catherine thought. She looked younger than Doonan, but it was hard to tell; it might just have been that she was so glamorous. She had an ash-blonde bob, and sharp blue eyes, and skin that was almost unlined. She wore a white shirt with a high, sculptural collar, and slim black trousers, and on her shoulders was a cropped brown wool cape, and three slim gold bracelets glinted on her right arm.

'We *liked* your piece,' she said, the word *liked* climbing steadily in a way that Catherine could not read.

'Oh, God,' Catherine shook her head. 'It was chopped to death by the sub-editor.'

'Ah, the eternal refrain of the journalist,' Julia said, laughing. 'I'm a publicist,' she added, by way of explanation. 'For my husband, not to mention other, more media-friendly clients.'

'I've never pretended to like interviews,' Doonan said with a shrug. 'I am what I am.'

'Which is bloody awful, most of the time,' Julia said, glancing to Catherine. 'Was he awful to you? He came home and told me he'd been awful to you. Which of course means he was actually twice as awful as he'd admit to having been.'

'Oh, no,' Catherine murmured. 'I mean, really, *I* was the one—'

'Well, you managed a good write-up in the end,' Doonan said, seeming unbothered by his wife's teasing, if that was what it was. 'Silk purse from a sow's ear, as my darling wife put it.'

'From a hog's arse, more like it,' Julia said, rolling her eyes at Catherine, and with one hand she made a playful swipe at Doonan. 'Go over there and get us a couple of glasses of champagne, Mick, will you, for heaven's sake. Make yourself useful.'

'Right so,' Doonan said, running a hand through his hair, and he trotted off.

Julia watched him go, a fond smile playing on her lips. 'I like to torment him,' she said, nudging Catherine gently. 'The fact is, I know well what a cheeky article he's capable of being with young women. I first met him when I was assisting with publicity for *Let Her Go* all those years ago. He was incorrigible.' She gave a short laugh, a jump of mirth. 'And still I married him.'

'Oh! Right! Well, he was fine,' Catherine said brightly. 'Really. Fine.'

'Oh, he's a brat,' Julia said, laughing again. 'Now, he's not Naipaul, I'll give you that. You read that interview that the woman from the *Independent* did with Naipaul?'

Catherine shook her head.

'*Well*,' Julia said, raising an eyebrow. 'Beg, borrow or steal it. Sir Vidia decided that the questions weren't worthy of him, and he stood up in the middle of the interview and said,

"I don't have time for this, it'd suit you better to be doing an interview with my wife." And he called her down from the kitchen or wherever the poor woman was, and he walked out on the journalist.'

'Jesus!'

'And I don't think he meant that his wife was a spokesperson for his fiction.'

'*Jesus.*'

'Then again, here you are, talking to Mick Doonan's wife,' she said, shrugging off her cape now, and folding it over her arm. 'Anyway, what brings you here this evening, Catherine? Are you writing about Ed's show?'

'Yes, probably,' Catherine lied, though maybe, she thought then, it was not a lie, after all; actually, she would quite like to write an article about Dunne's photographs.

'He certainly struck lucky with his timing,' Julia said drily, eyeing the photograph in front of them. 'Any other week of the year, this stuff would look exactly like the forced, stretching pedanticism it is. But the jammy bastard's opening night turns out to be the night of the peace talks deadline, and so here we find ourselves, bang in the middle of the most blazingly relevant cultural phenomenon of the year. I mean, look at the size of this crowd.' She gestured around the room, now full to capacity. 'I don't know how Ed does it. He always does, you know.'

'God,' Catherine said faintly.

'I mean, they're so bloody opportunistic. I mean, *Oh, bombing three thousand miles away, in the country I left thirty-odd years ago; oh, I'll just pop out with my camera and take a snapshot of the first sweet little black child I see.*'

'You're not Ed's publicist, then?' Catherine said.

'I am not,' Julia said, raising an eyebrow. 'And if you think I'm negative about them, you should hear Mick. But, that said, Ed is a very old friend of ours. He and Mick have known each other since London in the seventies. And I'm sure that he'd have some choice opinions of his own on Mick's work. These things are just better not spoken about sometimes, you know, if a friendship is to survive.'

Catherine laughed, unable to believe her ears. Doonan hated Dunne's work, and Dunne hated Doonan's, and they said horrible things about one another, and yet they were still, after twenty years, good friends? The idea of it staggered her. She looked for James, but he was hidden in the crowd. Twenty years from now, would they be like this, lying to each other, or not telling everything to each other, so that they could maintain the facade of being friends? It seemed impossible. Why would anybody bother?

'And as for our American friend,' Julia was saying now, with a sardonic twist of her mouth.

'Oh, Nate?' Catherine said, relieved for the change of subject.

'Nate from Brooklyn,' Julia said, giving the 't' and the 'k' a sharp, clipped sound. 'He's a handful in his own right. We thought he'd have long since moved on by now.'

'Yeah, my friend's talking to him,' Catherine said, craning her neck again to try and find James. 'He introduced him to Ed.'

Julia looked confused. 'Your friend did?'

'I mean, Nate introduced my friend to Ed. He's a photographer too. My friend. He has an exhibition coming up himself soon, actually.'

Catherine was blushing, she knew, and she was furious with herself for this, and she could see that Julia had noticed; she said nothing, but stood looking at Catherine with a strange, tolerant smile.

'Oh!' Catherine said, suddenly seeing James as the crowd parted for a moment. She pointed. 'There he is!'

Julia squinted. 'The redhead?' she said, sounding surprised.

Catherine nodded, swallowing.

'And you say you two are just friends?' Julia said doubtfully, studying James more closely.

'Well, yeah,' Catherine said. 'Good friends.'

'Ah,' Julia said, as though she understood perfectly. 'Well, the two of you will have to come to the little party we're throwing for Ed after this. It's back at our house. The American over there will have the address. Can you make it?'

'Oh God,' Catherine said, stammering. 'Really?'

'Of course,' Julia said, shrugging as though this was a stupid question. 'If you want to, that is. If you can be bothered with all us boring elders. Now, where did that gom go for our champagne?' She looked around. 'Oh, hark at him,' she said, pointing. 'He's given them to Moira bloody Donnelly and her *lover* over there.'

'Ha,' Catherine said.

'*Lover*,' Julia repeated, rolling her eyes. 'As though the rest of us are only going to Mass together.'

'Ha.'

'Anyway, what else are you writing about these days? Apart from Ed's photos?'

'Well, I'm writing an essay, mostly, at the moment,' Catherine said. 'For one of my English courses.'

'Oh, of course,' Julia said, her gaze drifting away. 'You have to get your *degree*.' She gave *degree* the same intonation she had given *lover*: a low drawl of derision. Catherine hesitated to go on.

'Yeah,' she said, then. 'I'm writing about Ted Hughes and Sylvia Plath.'

'Oh, *Jesus*,' said Julia, in the manner of someone who had just heard a very unfortunate piece of news. 'What's possessing you to do that?'

'The new book,' Catherine said, adding 'His', then, hardly necessarily.

'Oh, that book is insane, isn't it? *Insane.*'

'It's pretty intense, all right.'

'Intense? It'd give you nightmares for a month,' Julia said, shaking her head. 'What was he thinking, writing those poems?'

'Well . . .'

'God, he's such a fine figure of a man, though. Physically, I mean. We met him at a festival where Mick was reading a few years ago. Honestly. The whole room would weaken when he'd walk into it. Men, women, the lot of us.'

'I'm sure,' Catherine said, laughing nervously.

'But really, are you not just depressing yourself, writing about those two? I mean, it's a terribly sad story. An awful waste.'

'I know,' Catherine said. 'But really, I'm interested in the poems rather than in the lives.'

Julia smiled that same strange smile again. 'I believe you,' she said, after a long moment. 'Thousands wouldn't.' Then she nodded at something over Catherine's shoulder. 'Oh, about bloody time.'

Then Mick Doonan was upon them, muddle-handing three glasses of champagne.

'Here we go, ladies,' he said, a little breathlessly. 'Sorry about the delay. Forced diversion to Lesbos.'

'I'm sure you minded.' Julia cut her eyes at him. 'Catherine here is just telling me she's writing an essay about Ted Hughes.'

233

'Hughes?' Doonan said, as though Julia had just mentioned a difficult neighbour. 'Huh.'

'Hughes and Plath, really,' Catherine offered, in response to which Doonan made a face of droll horror.

'Oh, Jaysus,' he said, rubbing a hand over his mouth. 'Hughes. Hmm. Ever interview him, did you?'

'God, no,' Catherine said through a splutter of disbelieving laughter. 'I'd *die* if I had to interview him. I mean, I'd love to. I'd never be able to, though.'

'Now, make up your mind, darling,' Julia said.

Doonan was looking at her archly. 'Is that what you were like about the prospect of interviewing me?'

Catherine stammered. 'Well . . .'

'Oh, leave her alone, Mick,' Julia said. 'Sure you couldn't blame her.'

'I'd say he'd give you the runaround and all,' Doonan said, sipping his champagne.

'I'm sure he'd be a perfect gentleman,' Julia said. 'What do you think, Catherine?'

'I don't know,' Catherine said, sweating now. 'I mean, it's hard to believe that he's still actually alive. That's he's out there, writing something.'

Doonan gave a snuffle of protest. 'For Christ's sake, he's only eight years older than me!'

'Well,' Catherine shrugged, 'I meant in terms of, not age, but—'

'I know what you mean, Catherine,' Julia said, putting a hand on her arm.

'You mean stature,' Doonan said grouchily.

'Oh, shut up, Mick. You have absolutely nothing to complain about.'

Doonan clicked his tongue loudly and switched his attention to the photograph behind them. 'What in the name of fuck is this, anyway?' he said, apparently to himself.

'Mick,' Julia said in a warning tone.

'What's this lassie meant to stand for? The Black Kesh, is it?'

'Mick, *please*,' Julia said, still more sharply. 'You're making Catherine uncomfortable. And me, I might add.'

'*Atlantic Avenue*,' Doonan snorted. 'Atlantic Ocean would be the best place for this stuff.'

'I love the way you're wearing that cameo, by the way,' Julia said suddenly, and she reached out and touched the brooch with the cracked surface that Catherine had used to fasten her scarf. 'So clever.'

'Oh, thanks. I've had it for ages. My father gave it to me.'

'*Very* nice. Does he collect?'

'Oh, no, no,' Catherine said, laughing, thinking of how her father had found the brooch one evening while he was out foddering the cattle; it must have fallen from a car, he had told Catherine, or maybe – he had preferred this idea – it had been buried for years and had only just come to the surface. It was almost intact, but not quite; part of the bone had fallen away.

'Where's the rest of it?' Doonan said sceptically.

A ditch in Longford, Catherine was tempted to say, but she just smiled in what she hoped was a mysterious manner.

'That's the point,' Julia said.

'Oh, you're a deconstructionist, are you?' Doonan said with a theatrical shudder. 'Well, keep it to yourself, darling, will you please.'

'Hello?!' she hissed two minutes later, grabbing James by the elbow; he was still part of the same group of people, which had expanded considerably, now forming several separate

235

clumps, but still with Dunne at the centre of it all, beaming, chuckling, receiving compliments, delivering evidently hilarious replies. James, as she marched up to him, had been watching Dunne reverently, as though making careful mental notes. He turned to her now, and when he smiled, it was blissful and radiant; he was high on champagne, obviously, but also on the thrill of having been included by these people, folded in by them, of having received their attention, their interest, their apparent respect.

'Hello, darling,' he said, moving to make room for her, but Catherine indicated with her eyes that she wanted him to step away; reluctantly, he did so. 'I've been looking for you,' he said. 'Have you met—'

'Thanks for abandoning me,' she said, and it came out more angrily than she had in fact intended, but it was too late to do anything about that now. James, an empty glass in his hand, seemed to reel with confusion for a moment.

'I'm sorry,' he said. 'Did I abandon you? You were the one who walked away from me when we were talking to Nate.'

'Nate from Brooklyn,' she said sarcastically, pronouncing the words the way Julia Doonan had.

James frowned uncertainly. 'Yes. Nate. Ed's assistant.'

'Yeah, well,' Catherine said sulkily. 'I've been on my own for the last twenty minutes.' It was an outright lie, and it surprised her, but it had worked; James was moving towards her, looking remorseful.

'I'm sorry, darling,' he said plainly, and he put his arms around her, and he kissed her on the cheek, and he kissed her – giving, then, his usual little growl – close to the ear, and Catherine felt it in her spine, and she felt it in her crotch, and she forgave him; of course, instantly she forgave him.

'I got us invited to the after-party,' she said, still using the same sulky tone, which made no sense, but she found that she was not quite able to snap out of it.

James scrunched up his face. 'I thought you were on your own for twenty minutes?'

'Well, apart from Michael Doonan and his wife,' she shrugged. 'And they're throwing the party. And we're invited.'

'Oh, yeah,' James said casually. 'Nate told me about it. He said the three of us can walk there together, quite soon actually, because he and Ed are staying with Michael and Julia, and he has to make a call to New York before the working day ends there.'

'Oh, OK,' Catherine said, feeling robbed of her prize now. 'Or we could go back to the Stag's for a few drinks before heading up there? I don't want to be the first people to arrive again.'

'No, no,' James said, waving this suggestion away. 'We'll walk up with Nate. It'll be grand.'

The Doonan mews was off Harcourt Street. It looked small from outside, but inside it immediately opened up into two levels: an elegant hall gave way to a huge central room with a ceiling two storeys high; the upstairs floor was a mezzanine, with some rooms closed off behind doors and one whole side given over to what looked like another open space. The walls were hung with art – Catherine recognized a Brian Bourke in the main room, a sharp-boned woman with blacked-out eyes, and a piece in gold and linen that could only be a Scott – and though the night was not cold, a fire burned in the high stone hearth. She, James and Nate were indeed the first arrivals; the Doonans, Dunne and a slew of others had been still taking their leave of the gallery when the three of them had slipped away, Nate teasing them, calling them 'the terrible two', and slipping his arm into James's other arm in an imitation of how Catherine was linking with him. Here, the front door had been opened by a girl in a black-and-white waitress's uniform, and others, dressed in the same way, were busy setting up long tables with dozens of glasses and bottles of wine. From a kitchen at the other end of the house, there came a spicy, delicious smell.

'Nice, isn't it?' Nate said, as Catherine and James stood in the entryway, gawking. 'I'm just going up to make this call. Make yourselves at home.' He glanced back imperiously. 'Within reason.'

'Ha,' James deadpanned. But as soon as Nate had disappeared upstairs, he turned to Catherine, his eyes wide, his mouth open with amazement. 'Fucking hell,' he said. 'Where *are* we?'

'I know.' Catherine shook her head. 'It's amazing.'

'*Imagine*, Catherine,' he said, and he went over to a long white leather sofa and sat down. 'Imagine living like this.' He patted the seat beside him. 'Home sweet home, darling,' he said, and he laughed.

One of the uniformed girls came over to them, smiling, her hands behind her back. 'Can I offer you a drink?' she said.

'Oh, Jesus,' James groaned. 'We're in heaven, Catherine.' He looked at the waitress. 'Is there any way you can barricade the door?'

She laughed. 'I don't know about that,' she said, looking at them uncertainly; she was around their age.

'Ah, try, though,' James said, mock-pleadingly. 'Won't you? We're just going to have a quiet night in. Myself and the little woman here.'

'Eejit,' said Catherine, through waves of longing and confusion, and as they heard the rattle of the front door, she asked the waitress for a glass of red wine.

Very quickly, the house was full, and James had once again

vanished into the fray; he had gone looking for the bathroom ten minutes previously, and had not come back, but Catherine was too concerned with trying not to look lost and pathetic to think about how angry she was with him. At first she drifted around the edges of the big sitting room, looking very closely at the paintings, studying them as though she was thinking of making a purchase; as well as the Bourke and the Scott, there was a McSweeney bog pool that she loved, and a little drawing that she could not identify, but she thought it might possibly be an early Jack Yeats.

'Oh, probably,' said the first person to whom she got talking, a woman in a flowing, peasant-style dress, with very long black hair; the woman had been standing alone at the mantelpiece, surveying the room, and Catherine, taking a deep breath and knowing that she had to take this chance to have a conversation, any conversation, had gone up to her. She was the journalist who had written the *Irish Times* piece, it turned out, and she had many long, dreary pearls of wisdom for Catherine about avoiding the nightmare that was a career in journalism. A man from the Abbey Theatre came up to talk to the journalist, and in that way Catherine got talking, for a while, to him, and a man who taught English at UCD came up to interrupt their conversation, and after a minute the Abbey man made his excuses and slipped away, and so Catherine was left with the lecturer, which was another fifteen minutes of talking to someone, and even though what he was saying to her was mainly unasked-for advice, Catherine did not mind, because talking to him, or being talked at by him, was preferable to standing around on her own again, and after him there was an actor she had never heard of, and after him a woman who had just finished a book about Michael Doonan's books, so Catherine was able to talk to her for a long while, drawing on all the research she had found herself unable to use in the actual interview with him; then there was the man from the Abbey again, a little more tipsy and flirtatious now; then there was a young guy who wrote for the *Independent*, and who was actually quite cute, which reminded her to go and look for James, and by this time she had had two more glasses of champagne and maybe three glasses of wine, and talking to people was, by now, easy, talking to people was, by now, just, for heaven's sake, what you *did*, and when she turned around next, David Norris was standing behind her, the actual David Norris, and she got into a conversation with him about American poetry, and he quoted at her a couple of lines from a poem he loved – *Shoot, if you must, this old gray head / But spare your country's flag* – and she nodded, as though she knew of the poem, as though she had heard of it, and he smiled back, as though they did not both know she was lying, and Catherine was feeling delighted with herself, feeling she had discovered, at long last, the secret of being a grown-up, and she had seen several other people she wanted to talk to – the Doonans, for one thing, and she had spotted one of her English lecturers – when she found herself standing face to face with Nate. *You look like one of the Kennedys*, she had an impulse to say to him, but she managed to restrain herself. Nate, meanwhile, holding a tumbler of whiskey, seemed, for some reason, delighted to see her.

'Where have you been all night? Your sidekick and I are in the kitchen.'

'James?'

'James,' he confirmed, taking a mouthful of whiskey. 'That guy can talk. What's that thing?' He frowned. 'That you Irish kiss?'

'We kiss?' Catherine said, thinking that she had misheard him.

'The stone,' Nate said. 'The stone . . .' He arched his head dramatically backwards, staggering a little, the tumbler jerking in his hand.

'Oh! The Blarney Stone,' Catherine said, and then shook her head quickly. 'Irish people don't kiss that. Just tourists.'

Nate burst out laughing. 'Whatever. Your friend James must give head to the Blarney Stone every morning. He doesn't shut up!'

'Yeah. He's never short of something to say.'

'And you're the quiet one,' Nate said, sceptically.

'Well, compared to him.'

'Where's your drink?' Just at that moment, a waitress passed with a tray, and he grabbed a bottle and poured a dark torrent of wine into Catherine's glass. He pointed to a couch which had just come free. 'Take a load off?'

He sat, giving a loud sigh of relief as his limbs sank into the leather cushions, and then he went still, suddenly, and frowned. 'Oh, that's bad.'

'What?' said Catherine, taking a seat herself.

'Saying *Aaaaah* when I sit down. I can't believe that's happening already.' He glanced at her. 'How old are you?'

'Eighteen.'

'*Eighteen?*' he spluttered, and shook his head. 'Man, eighteen. You kids.'

'What do you mean?' Catherine said coyly.

'You know what I mean,' he said, grinning at her. 'I see it at every opening. Kids like you, showing up impossibly young and cool and beautiful, sucking all the oxygen out of the room. But –' he tipped his glass to hers – 'thank you. It sells the art.'

'So,' she said, feeling she should show an interest in Dunne's work, 'how many hours a day would you usually spend in Ed's studio?'

Nate looked at her blankly. 'How do you mean?'

'Well, James probably told you about when he was working for Malachy Clark in Berlin – he used to work twenty-hour days in there sometimes. Is it that bad in Ed's?'

He looked no less baffled. 'Why would I work in Ed's studio?'

'I . . .' Catherine blustered, already feeling the blush climb her cheeks.

'I work in my own gallery,' Nate scoffed. 'Ed's studio? No, thank you.'

'I thought you did. Sorry.'

'*No.*'

'So you're not his assistant?'

Amazement spread across Nate's features; his mouth dropped open, his eyes locked onto hers accusingly. Then a shout of laughter took him, and he slammed a hand down on the couch cushion. 'His assistant? His *assistant*?!' To Catherine's horror, he leaned forward, now, and shouted out to Ed, absorbed in a conversation by the fireplace. 'Hey, Ed! Eddie! I'm your assistant now! You hear that?'

Ed Dunne made his face into a mask of horror and turned away.

'Yeah, the feeling's mutual,' Nate said, sinking back into the couch. 'Christ,' he said, squinting at Catherine. 'Ed's assistant. Do you know what kind of torture Ed puts his assistants through? What in Christ's name made you think *that*?'

'Well . . .' Catherine said, mortified, but Nate's expression had already changed. He had worked it out, she saw from the way he was holding up one hand, nodding and laughing; he had understood.

'James?' he said. 'Well, that explains the conversation I just had with him in the kitchen. For one thing, it explains why he kept wanting to talk about Ed's darkroom.' He laughed again. 'Half an hour of me being expected to take orders in

Ed's fucking darkroom and the only photographer in that studio would be from the NYPD.' He shuddered. 'Christ. Our relationship only survives because I stay the hell *out* of his studio.'

Catherine's breath did something, then, so that she had to make an effort to find it. She knew that it was important, in this moment, not to look directly at Nate; not to let him see reflected in her eyes the rapid calculations and realizations and rearrangements that were clicking and whirring and snapping through the channels of her startled brain. 'Yeah,' was all she could possibly manage in the way of speech, and as soon as the word was out, she knew that she had botched it.

'Oh, fuck,' she heard Nate say, through a laugh of incredulity. 'Oh, fuck me. Ed and I are partners. Life partners, I mean. You didn't know that?'

'Oh,' Catherine said, as though Nate had just reminded her of something she had been meaning to do. 'No, of course.'

He gave a short laugh. 'Of course?'

'No, it's just . . .' She shook her head, laughing; going for carefree and landing on crazy. 'Just James. James said you were Ed's assistant. That's all.'

'Um, I have my *own* assistant. I'm a director of a gallery in Chelsea.'

'Ah.'

'Which is how I met Ed. We've been together now for nearly seven years.'

'Wow. That's,' Catherine said, stammering, 'brilliant.'

'Yeah,' Nate nodded. 'And because you're probably trying to work it out right now in your addled little brain, the age difference is thirty-two years.'

'Wow.'

'Yeah. He's ancient. But I love the old son of a bitch.'

'*Awww*,' Catherine said, which came out sounding unhinged; which came out sounding more like disappointment, actually, than like the sound of someone who was touched or moved.

'So there you go,' Nate said. 'God, I really thought everyone knew that by now. Or, at least, everyone who knew Ed's work.'

'Well,' said Catherine, wanting, suddenly, to defend herself. 'There wasn't anything about it in the *Irish Times* piece.'

'Oh, for Christ's sake,' Nate said, with a wave of his hand. 'Everything that dumb bitch could have got wrong about Ed, she got wrong. I'm surprised she didn't have him down as married and living in rural Pennsylvania with his wife and family. And Amish. And *dead*.'

Catherine laughed raggedly. 'I'm sorry,' she said. 'I'm embarrassed.'

'Well,' Nate said, smiling at her now. He put a finger to her cheek and hissed a long breath through his teeth to mimic the sound of sizzling flesh. 'I could tell that. But it's all right. You don't exactly talk about this over here.'

'Yeah.'

'Christ's sake, first couple of years we came here together, it wasn't even legal.'

David Norris is here, she almost said then, but she stopped herself; probably, that would just give him another reason to laugh at her. She felt young – so young and so stupid.

'So,' Nate said, settling his wine glass on his knee. 'Tell me about James. I can tell the two of you are close.'

'Very,' she said, nodding fervently.

'You're the friend, then,' he said, nodding knowingly. 'That's good. Every fag needs his hag.'

Catherine was speechless. She stared at him, her heart

pounding. Had he actually just said that? Was saying that even OK?

Nate, noticing her consternation, gave an uneasy laugh. 'Hang on a minute. You do know about *James*, right?'

'Yes, I know,' Catherine cut across him sharply. 'For fuck's sake!'

'OK, OK, just checking,' said Nate, holding up a hand, but he was laughing at her; he was really enjoying himself now, Catherine saw. She tried to think of something clever to say to him, something very cutting and very clear-eyed, but a second *For fuck's sake* was all she could manage, which just made Nate laugh harder, for some infuriating reason. Then she looked up, and there, making his way in their direction, was James – clearly plastered, smiling and waving as though he was meeting her off a train. She scrambled to her feet and got to him before he got to them.

Many drinks later, people began to sing. Was this a new thing in Dublin now, Catherine wondered, that every time a group of people were together in a house they had to start singing? Unlike the evening in James's flat, though, there were no guitars, and no joints going around; instead, people were taking it in turns to stand by the fireplace and sing mostly ballads of the mournful Irish variety; 'Boolavogue', a woman was wailing her way through now, which was a song that Catherine had not heard since being forced to learn it in primary school.

This was a tradition at the Doonan parties, Nate informed Catherine and James, coming up to them as they stood, catching up on each other's evenings.

'Well, nobody told us, Nathaniel,' James said, wincing in mock-horror.

'Consider yourself told,' Nate said. 'Ed takes it so seriously, he made me learn a new song. He tested me every night for a week.'

'You're codding me,' James said, laughing with his hand to his mouth.

'No, I am not codding you. Whatever that is. It sounds painful. Is it?'

'Sometimes,' James said, suggestively.

'Oh, for fuck's sake,' Catherine cut in irritably. 'I'm not bloody singing. I don't have a song.'

'What's your song?' James said to Nate, and Catherine felt a stab of jealousy at his having responded to him rather than to her.

'Well, the one Ed *made* me learn is not the one I'm going to sing,' Nate said. 'The one I'm going to sing is a surprise for him.'

'Awww,' James nudged him.

'What are you two going to sing?'

'We don't have songs,' Catherine said.

'Ah, no,' James said lightly. 'I think I can find something.'

Catherine looked at him. 'No, you can't. What can you sing? What song do you have?'

'Catherine,' he said, laughing at her, 'I have *lots* of songs.'

'Oh, for fuck's sake, James, we're not singing,' Catherine said.

'Ah, Reilly. Don't take it all so seriously,' James said, and he pressed his forehead to hers. 'Come on, darling. We can come up with something. Do it for me. Go on.'

'You could sing a duet,' Nate said, clearly enjoying the moment. '"I Got You, Babe". Or "I Loves You, Porgy".'

'That's the spirit,' James said, and he put his arm around Catherine, and if it did not melt her anger completely, it confused it, this gesture; she leaned into him, glad of his touch. In a high, gleefully corny tone, he sang the first line of

'Islands in the Stream'. He looked at Nate. 'What's the rest of that?' he said.

'Don't ask me.'

'Come on, Reilly,' he said, squeezing her. 'We'll dazzle them.'

'I'm *not* singing,' Catherine said.

Nate got up to sing his song soon afterwards, and as soon as he started, with no preamble, just a look – a tender and, it seemed, intensely private look – at Ed, something in the room went still. He had not even finished with the first line – it was not a line that Catherine recognized, though she could tell it was another of the old Irish ballads – and it was as though the entire room of people, thirty or forty of them standing and sitting, had caught their breath and then drawn it in more deeply, a deep, slow breath of sadness and gratitude. Nate's voice was strong and clear, and he was well able to hold a note, but that was not the reason; it was something else, she knew. Behind her, James sighed heavily, and she turned to him.

'What is it?' she whispered, tugging at him. 'What is this?'

'"My Lagan Love",' he whispered back, his eyes locked on Nate. 'Amazing.'

The Lagan; that was in Belfast, where Ed was from, and where the talks were, of course, happening tonight, and that was of course it; that was why the room had reacted that way. And listening to the lines – *the night is on her hair*, he was singing now, and something about lovesickness – Catherine felt herself yield to them too, felt herself becoming wistful and emotional and pleasurably, gratifyingly swollen with the momentousness of it all; that while this very song was being sung here in Dublin, history was maybe being made a couple of hundred miles to the North. What a moment this was!

247

The *Irish Times* woman should write about it and put it in the next day's paper. Although it was too late for the next day's paper now, of course, it was almost two in the morning, but Saturday's edition, maybe with a description of the dazzling people who had been at the party, Catherine and James named among them—

Across the room, Ed was watching Nate with tears falling, shining on his cheeks. Her arm moved, to nudge James, but she found that she could not do this – that she did not want to, she realized, in the next moment. She did not want him to see Ed there, crying, as his lover – *lover*, she heard in the voice of Julia Doonan, who was sitting close to Ed, looking as though she might cry as well – sang the song that he had learned for him as a surprise, as a gift.

For love is lord of all, Nate sang.

And afterwards, they cheered him to the skies.

'Holy shit,' James kept saying, clapping, clapping harder and harder. His eyes were damp too, Catherine saw, feeling dizzily, unhappily anxious at the sight of them, even though her own eyes were the same. 'Holy shit,' he said, then shouting it: 'Holy shit!'

But that was still early. Comparatively, that was still early. And later was later, and booze was everywhere, booze was in the very veins of the house, and an hour later, maybe two, there were not thirty people at the party but maybe fifteen, and they had all sung. And James had sung – a song Catherine could not now remember, because Catherine was drunk, very drunk, and Catherine was sitting on James's knee, and Nate had sung again, the song he had pretended to Ed to have learned, and Ed had sung, a song called 'Peggy Gordon', and Mick Doonan had sung, even, and the woman from the *Irish Times* had sung some kind of gospel song, and had wanted people to clap along and nobody had clapped, or maybe they had, or maybe some of them had and some of them had not; and everyone, everyone, everyone had been at Catherine, had kept at Catherine, to sing. *Oh, come on, love*, they had said, *you must have a song in you*, and Nate had said it and Michael and Julia Doonan had said it, and Ed had said it, and James had said it, and Catherine had resisted, because she did not have a single verse of anything, except of the pop songs which refused to leave the very molecular structure of her brain. Why did she retain that rubbish, and nothing worth knowing? All those suitable songs she had been forced to learn in school – where on earth had they gone?

'Come on,' Nate said to her again; he was crouching by James's knee, now, for some reason. He was prodding at James's knee, as though it was going to prompt Catherine to sing. 'You two kids,' he said, almost fondly; but was it fondly? Or was it mockingly? 'What are we going to do with you?'

'Do whatever you want with us,' James said from behind her, and he squeezed Catherine, saying whatever it was he was trying to say to her; what was he trying to say to her?

'What?' she hissed, wanting, suddenly, a translation, but not about to get one; she knew this in the moment that she twisted around to James and saw that he was grinning not at her but at Nate.

'I liked yours,' James said, and Nate gave a little bow, which caused him, because he was crouching, almost to topple over, and this made the three of them laugh, but James laughed hardest of all, so much that to stay on his lap, Catherine really had to hold on to him, had to hold on to him like they were moving, like they were on a sledge or something, speeding, bouncing down a snowy hill.

'I liked yours too,' Nate said, when he had recovered, and still Catherine could not remember what it had been, James's song; not even now, as they talked about it, he and Nate, not even now as Catherine shoved him and asked him, and maybe he was ignoring her, or maybe he was telling her and she was forgetting it again in the next instant, but she simply could not remember the name of it, that song.

And then it was five in the morning, or near enough to it, and still they were singing. Someone sang 'The Parting Glass' – maybe Doonan, or Julia, trying to get rid of them, trying to drop them a hint? But nobody went anywhere, and then it was 'Hard Times', at which people were damp-eyed all over again, which just seemed indulgent, somehow, which seemed just to be wallowing in things; none of them had had their legs blown off, after all, at least not as far as Catherine, from her perch on James's legs, could see. And Catherine was, by now, very, very drunk. And although the singing now seemed to be over for the night – 'The Parting Glass' once more – still Catherine, with the encouragement of James and the even more enthusiastic encouragement of Nate – stood up by the fireplace and she sang the words of a song she had learned in school, and which she had forgotten that she still knew, and which was a song in Irish, and the words of it seemed to flow beautifully back to her, but then, all of a sudden, the words were gone from her, completely and utterly gone from her, and she realized that she did not have a clue, that she did not have this song, not anything more than the tune of it, at all, and so she made them up, the words; she made up not only the words, but the sounds of them. Because they were in Irish, and she could not, any more, speak in Irish; who could? And who would notice? All Irish words sounded the same, once you were singing them in that low, sweet, melancholy way, after all – and she knew other Irish words, and she added other Irish-sounding words, and she wove them together, and she made them into the song. If the song had been in English, she would really not have been able to do this without sounding ridiculous, she thought, so she complimented herself, congratulated herself, as she sang, on having had the foresight, really, to have chosen this one. And she got as far as the chorus – or her version, anyway, of the chorus – and the sounds slid to a stop, and she bowed her head the way she had seen all the other singers do, and she said, *Thanks, thank you, I think I'll leave it there*, and they roared – they roared in appreciation, and they roared in admiration, and they roared, it struck her a moment, as she staggered back to James and James's lap, a horrible moment later, in hilarity – someone actually howled with laughter – had that been James? Would he do that to her? No, no, it had been someone else, someone they did not know, some fucker, some old fucker; *Die*, she thought. *Go away and get on with just fucking dying* – and someone cheered – and she loved this person, though maybe not – and someone held up their hands, clapping. *And everything holds up its arms weeping*, that came to her; that was a poem – Hughes, the new book. She shook it away. There was clapping, there was cheering; she needed to concentrate on the cheering. She needed to concentrate on James, on his beautiful, laughing face – no, just laughing face, that was the rule, just his laughing face – as he stood up, now, to take her in his arms – no, to hug her, just to hug her; friends hug, that was what friends did – and to laugh his kisses into her ear, into her hair, and to pull away from her, shaking his head, as though thinking of the wonder of her, of the wonderful wonder. *Wonderful wonder*; that was *not* from the Hughes. And Nate, beside her now as well, and someone shouted, *Who cares about the bloody words*, and Julia Doonan came over to her and said, *Inspired, darling, delightful*, and the room was getting back to itself, and part of Catherine felt very embarrassed about what had just happened, part of her wanted to curl up and die, but that was a part of her, she knew, that she would not have to face up to until the next day, and all that mattered was that she was here and she was now, sitting so cosily with James, bundled up on his lap; the armchair they were sitting on was in a kind of alcove, so it was as though they were hidden, protected, secreted away from the rest of the room, draped with a blanket that had come from somewhere – *Love, love / I have hung our cave with roses* – and as though this space, in which they were talking, was made only for them, only for their closeness, and their laughter, and the stories they had to tell each other and the things they had to discuss, and they went over everything, *everything*, not just the party and the stuff about Ed and Nate, but the whole evening, the opening, and how it had felt, the way they were looked at, the way they were here, the youngest, the kids, people thinking them interesting, thinking them beautiful, and wasn't it funny, weren't they a pair?

'I'll be back in a minute,' James said, after maybe half an hour of this, or maybe an hour, and he kissed her on the cheek and went to the bathroom, or wherever, and he did not come back in a minute, and when Catherine went to look for him, she could not find him, and she could not work it out, how this place worked, how it was laid out, Michael and Julia Doonan's mezzanine and Michael and Julia Doonan's split-level kitchen and Michael and Julia Doonan's little balcony out onto the street; might James be on it, the little balcony out onto the street? So she stepped out there, and she looked at the moon, which was still out, stubborn against the sunrise, which was coming, which would be beautiful. But fuck it, all sunrises were beautiful. Who had time for sunrises? And someone took her elbow, and she was frightened because she was on a balcony, and because the fresh air – fresh air, she now remembered, was the worst thing for drunkenness; it was like taking drunkenness and jeering at it, so that it became riled up and driven to do its very worst – had made things pitch and spin, had made them unpredictable, but it was James, thank heavens, and James was telling her something about a goat.

'*Coat*,' he said, urgently, shaking his head. 'Coats, Catherine. Where are they? Where did that girl put them when we got here?'

A girl had put things somewhere; that was right, the girl who had allowed them, for a few minutes, to pretend that this was their home; the home in which they sat and listened to music and were served wine by girls in white shirts and black waistcoats.

'They must be in the downstairs bedroom,' James said. '*Fuck*.'

'Why fuck?' Catherine said, almost dreamily.

'You're going in to get them,' he said, steering her down the wooden staircase, steering her towards a door – she had not seen it until now – at the end of the corridor leading away from the big central room.

'OK, Mother Superior,' she said, sniggering at him, and then they were at the door, and he was opening it, and pushing her into the room.

Nate was there, asleep on the bed, fully dressed, asleep on top of a pile of coats, which made her snigger again: he looked so untidy, lying there, so unkempt and so undignified. One arm stretched out towards the head of the bed, and his legs spreadeagled; Catherine felt the irresistible urge to take off his shoes. Not out of kindness, not out of consideration, or wanting to help him to be more comfortable; just out of mischief. She would put them, maybe, on top of the wardrobe, or she would find, in the wardrobe, a pair of Michael Doonan's shoes and replace Nate's with them. But as soon as she kneeled to reach Nate's shoes, he woke up, and sat up, and planted his feet firmly on the ground, and there she was kneeling in front of him, and he blinked at her, looking almost scared.

'What the fuck?' he said, gasping. 'Were you in here all the time?'

'No,' she said, frowning at him. 'All what time?'

'Where's James?'

'He's outside,' Catherine said. 'We don't go *everywhere* together.'

'Outside the house?'

'Outside this room.'

Nate stood, rubbing his hand across his mouth. 'OK.'

'I have to get our coats,' Catherine said.

'Yeah, there are some coats,' he said, and he gestured sloppily to the bed behind him. He looked at her. 'Why are you kneeling on the floor? Are you praying?'

'That's right,' Catherine nodded, slowly, deliberately, keeping her voice low and even, and she watched him, kept her eyes on him, as he left the room, and as he did so he was looking at her as though she was completely and certifiably insane.

In the sitting room, the dregs were left: Ed Dunne, and the Doonans, and two or three other people, and James, who was standing on the other side of the fireplace, the side closest to the door, talking very intensely to Julia.

'Coat,' Catherine said, and she handed James his coat, and Nate appeared to help Catherine on with hers.

'Oh, what a gentleman, isn't he, Catherine?' Ed said drily.

'Catherine and James,' Julia said, with a huge smile. 'It's been such a pleasure. Do you want me to show you where to get a taxi?'

'No, no,' James said. 'It's not far. At least not for Catherine.'

Catherine stared at him. Sobriety seemed to jolt through her. Would he not come back to Baggot Street? It was so close. It made no sense, surely, for him to go all the way back to Thomas Street, not for the sake of a couple of hours – and besides, it had been so nice, cuddled up to him, cosied up to him in the alcove of rugs and roses – would he not, would he not, come and stay?

They called goodbye to everyone, and Julia said she would walk them out, and as she left the room, James went with her – not, Catherine noticed, saying goodbye to Nate, which made her, in turn, want to say to Nate a much more effusive, pointed sort of goodbye.

'I'll keep praying for you,' she said, putting her arms up to be embraced by him.

'Pray hard, Catherine,' Ed said from the sofa. 'Pray long and hard.'

And then she was at the front door, with James and with Julia, and Julia, her new friend, was so nice to her, and seemed to really like and respect her, and told her that she had a beautiful singing voice, and that it mattered nothing at all about the words.

'James,' Nate said, from behind them; from the middle of the big, now empty, central room. They glanced around at him, all three of them, and he beckoned to James, who muttered, to Julia presumably, his apology, and stepped towards Nate with, Catherine thought, something almost businesslike in his eyes. And left alone together now, Catherine and Julia could chat a bit more, and so they did, and Julia was so friendly, so easy to talk to, and when she smiled at Catherine, Catherine felt so much approved of, and when, in the next instant, her gaze travelled over Catherine's shoulder, and caught on something there, and decided on something – made a very obvious and conscious decision – to come back to Catherine, but looked different as soon as it did so, looked full of something else, some wariness or wryness; when her gaze did this, Catherine knew that it was telling her not to look around, not to look to the middle of the room. Julia's eyes were fast on hers; they were full, Catherine thought, of the sentence *Stay here*, and Catherine was so very proud of herself then, because she was quick enough, in that next moment, as she turned towards James and towards Nate, to turn her inward gasp into a noise of amusement, of enjoyment – the noise of someone who took everything in her stride.

'The art of goodbye,' Julia said, from behind her, and Catherine dug up a laugh, and laughed it low in her throat where it sounded so much in control, and she took the movement her shoulders wanted to make, which was to slump, and she made them shrug.

James's mouth on Nate's mouth. James's hands on Nate's arse. Nate's hands in James's hair. Tongues; even in that brief glimpse she could see that there were tongues.

'Well,' Catherine said to Julia, shrugging again, and again Julia smiled. It was probably best now, Catherine thought – how utterly sober she felt, now, how capable, if she had had to, even of driving home – to talk about the weekend, and about what she was doing for the weekend, and that in a few hours, she would take the train home, and yes, she was so much looking forward to seeing her family, and yes, and yes, and yes, and then, once again, Julia's gaze shifted, and something in it told Catherine she could turn around, now, and there was James, coming towards her, looking past her, and there was the space where Nate had been.

11

In the street, she turned to him. Smiling; she had decided that she would be smiling about it. That this would be her tactic. Laughing, as though what a jape! What a whirl! Parties, who could be up to them? Parties, what silly things happened at them, what comical things, what things, so much fun at the time, but ultimately meaningless, ultimately—

'Don't, Catherine,' he said, holding a hand up, and her heart, she thought for a moment, actually stopped.

'Don't what?' she said, forcing herself into a giggle; out it came, like a brace of bells. 'James. You *snogged* him. You—'

'I can't, Catherine; don't,' he said, and his hands were to his temples, his fingers pulling at his brow. 'Don't, *please*.'

'James,' she said, still laughing, but then he looked at her – he blinked at her – and she stopped. 'I don't understand,' she said, trying to take his hands; he shook her off. 'I don't—'

'That was madness,' he said, leaning, with one hand, against a windowsill; possibly the windowsill of the room in which the Doonans and all their remaining guests were still sitting. With a light touch to James's shoulder, she steered him away, down past the other little houses, all their curtains closed against the dawn.

'Don't worry about it so much,' Catherine said. 'I mean, I know it was mad – it was mad. I mean, you snogged Ed Dunne's boyfriend!' She tried again for laughter; tried to get him – jostling him gently – to join in. Her heart was hurtling;

she did not want to laugh, she wanted to cry, but she could not cry. She could not show. 'James,' she said, and she put her hand on his arm again. 'You snogged Nate from Brooklyn!' She gave the words, again, Julia's enunciation. 'In Michael Doonan's house! This is mad!'

He spun around in her grip, then, it seemed to Catherine; he did something – shook her off, she realized, a moment later – the force of which set his whole body moving, and hers, and they stood there like this, jolted apart, in this narrow lane off Harcourt Street, in the half-light of morning, and James stared at Catherine, and Catherine stared at James.

'It's not fucking funny, Catherine,' James said, and his breath was coming raggedly, and Jesus Christ, he was crying. Crying. A tear betraying him at the corner of one eye.

'James,' she said, and it was so selfish of her, so self-centred, but what she felt, in that moment, was jealousy; she had wanted to cry, and had fought it back, and now here he was, doing it, and she could hardly join in – could hardly storm in on top of him; and she envied him that, too, she realized. His moment. His crisis. Whatever it was.

'James,' she said again. 'I mean, it was just a kiss. It was just a drunken kiss.'

'It should never have happened,' he said, his mouth grim. 'It should *never* have gone that far.'

'You were drunk,' she said, hearing that the pleading was coming through clearly in her voice. 'Nate was too. It meant nothing. It meant—'

'Nate,' James said, shaking his head bitterly. 'That fucking prick. That arrogant, self-satisfied, fucking prick.'

'Well, you kissed him,' Catherine could not stop herself from saying. 'You're the one who—'

'I do not want to talk about it, Catherine,' he shouted, holding up a hand. 'It is so fucking *vulgar*.'

259

'James!'

He stared at her. 'You don't understand, Catherine. You don't understand what it feels like to humiliate yourself in this way, to realize that you have behaved so carelessly, so stupidly, so visibly.' He looked at her, seeming suddenly to have thought of something.

'What?' she said weakly.

'Who else was still there?' he almost spat, as though she worked for him, as though she had not got the figures to him in time, or the documents, or the percentages; she felt, as she tried to summon to mind the faces of those who had said goodbye to them in the Doonans' sitting room, as though she was circling a desk, trying to get it in order; a phone was ringing, a pile of pages was collapsing.

'Ed, obviously,' she said, the words tumbling. 'And the *Irish Times* woman. And that bald man. And some woman, maybe from the gallery, maybe from some other gallery, I don't know.'

James's hands were over his face. 'This cannot be happening,' he said, faintly.

'I'm sorry. I don't know why it's so terrible. It's not as though—'

It's not as though they saw the two of you, she was about to say, but in that moment, Catherine realized something, and for a reason that, also in that moment, she forbade herself to think about, she made a decision. James, she realized, was unclear about the order of things; he was unclear on the question of who had been in which room, when, as he and Catherine had said their goodbyes; who had stayed in the sitting room, and who had trailed through to the main room with them, and who had been there, standing around the main room, leaning against doorways, watching them as they went. Watching him as he doubled back. Watching what came afterwards, observing it like the piece of news that it was, acquiring it like the nugget of gossip that it was, perfect for sharing, perfect for laughing over later.

'It's not as though it matters to these people,' was what she said, and instantly on his face she saw how little this had helped; how, somehow, this only made matters worse. 'James,' she said, reaching out to him again, but again, he shook her off. 'You barely even . . .'

'No, Catherine. We were fucking messing, talking, flirting, I don't know the fuck what, in the corridor, and the next thing we were shifting, and we went into that downstairs bedroom and we—'

'The bedroom?' she said, staring at him. 'You didn't—'

'No, we didn't, Catherine,' he said acidly. 'We just, messed around, I don't know, and then . . .' He shook his head. He looked, she thought, utterly furious.

'What?'

'Then someone came in for a coat, that woman who sang that never-ending bloody song earlier, and she saw us. And I got out of there.'

'And Nate fell asleep on the bed.'

'I don't fucking know what he did. And as far as I was concerned, that was an end to it. To be seen once was, for God's sake, enough. And he's such an arrogant prick, and such a cocksure fucker.'

'So how did it happen again?'

He laughed, but it was not the kind of laugh Catherine wanted to hear. It depressed her: it was sunken with irony, collapsed into anger. 'How did it happen again is right, Catherine?' he said, and he shook his head. 'How *did* it happen again?'

'How do you mean?' she said, and her voice was like a child's.

261

'Nothing,' he said, and he thrust his hands in his pockets and walked on towards Harcourt Street.

'You're not going home?' Catherine said, rushing after him. 'You can't go home in this state.'

'Where else am I going to go, Catherine? The George?' He laughed, the same empty laugh. 'It's closed. Even its clientele know when to call a night a night.'

'James,' she said, and she grabbed his elbow, and she did not care, this time, if he tried to shake her off; she would hold on to it, and she would take hold of it again and again, if she had to, would take hold of both his elbows, in fact, which, in the next instant, was what she found she had done, so that they were facing each other, his face wrenched in irritation, and hers in Christ knew what. Pleading, probably. Always with him now she felt as though she was pleading.

'Please don't go home on your own, James.'

His lips twitched towards a laugh, but did not go there. 'What, should I bring someone with me?'

'I mean, come back with me to Baggot Street. It's only ten minutes away. Thomas Street is miles.'

'It's not miles.'

'It's far,' she said, which she knew was stupid – it was only up Grafton Street, around Dame Street; he would be home – she glanced at her watch – by seven. Then she saw her opening. 'Your landlady will be up,' she said, shaking her head. 'Are you seriously going to walk through the door like this while your landlady's eating her breakfast?'

He said nothing; he looked to the ground as though it might have a solution for him, as though it might offer a way out.

'James,' she said, and she grabbed his wrist. 'Just come on. You can go home later. When she's at work.' She walked ahead of him, her heart racing, and she turned right onto

Harcourt Street, and after she had done so, she glanced behind, and she saw him, coming after her, his head down, and he had not turned left, in the direction of Grafton Street. He was coming home.

'Come on, slowcoach,' she said now, and she beckoned to him. 'I'm freezing. I want to get home to bed.'

And when he caught up with her, she took his hand, and he let her; he did not shake her away. And on Baggot Street, the news stand was open for business already, and the headlines were trying to be hopeful. And when they got home to the flat, it was empty, and there were plenty of empty beds, but these beds were not even mentioned. They went into Catherine's bedroom, and they got into Catherine's bed – James still in his jeans and his T-shirt, just as he had been when they had shared a bed before, only his feet bare; Catherine in her thin woollen dress, reaching quickly through the armholes, while James's back was turned, to unfasten her strapless bra and pull it free – and James faced the wall, and Catherine put her arms around him, and in the half-light, as they went to sleep, she tried to tell him, with her arms so tight around him, and with her lips pressed to the nape of his neck, that there was no need to worry.

Her lips to his neck: a kiss, and another, the language that was theirs by now, the language of affection and closeness and reassurance.

'It's getting bright,' she said, though she knew she should not be speaking; knew she should be letting him drift off, and should be drifting off herself. But she spoke, and she let her lips touch him in that spot again, where his hair trailed off, where the soft skin of his neck began.

'I know,' he said, and probably she was imagining it, the tremor in his voice, but in case she had not, she held him tighter; she gripped him to her, one hand on his ribcage, the other on the sharp jut of his hip.

'It makes me think of being little in the summertime,' she said, and this time when her lips met his skin, she left them there a moment, as he had done to her so often, and then she moved them, so lightly, just a whisper, just the lightest circle on the downy skin.

'Having to go to bed before it was dark,' she said, and she thought of it: long evenings leaking in through the curtains, the window and sill behind them seeming such a high, glorious box of light. Ellen asleep in her cot, and the sound, from outside, of tractors, or a lawnmower, or a visiting neighbour, allowed to stay up as long as they pleased.

'Yeah,' James said, with a breath of a laugh, and it almost startled her, to be brought back to him again, back to here. She had been drifting. But her hands were on him, her lips were on him, and when she moved her left hand, she felt his ribcage under her fingers, and more than that, she felt him go entirely still.

'I can count your ribs,' she said, and she counted them: two, four, eight of them. He laughed again, the same hesitant wheeze, and this time, when she put her lips to his neck, she let her tongue touch on his skin as well, and he gasped. He said her name. It was a question, she knew; maybe, she knew in some part of herself, it was a warning.

'Catherine,' he said, and she let her hand go lower.

'Catherine,' James said again, but now his hands were moving too, and he was not asking her anything anymore.

And just the touch of him made her come.

And she knew why it was working for him. She knew why it was that he was able to do this. He did not stay hard the whole time, and she knew why this was, but it did not take him long to recover, and she did not mind – it did not occur to her to mind – that he did so looking not at her, but elsewhere: at the ceiling, at the wall, it did not matter. Nothing mattered. She knew what this was. It was touch; he was desperate for it. With Nate – she pushed him instantly back out of her mind – it had been more than he could deal with, more than he could bear, but with Catherine, it was different. With Catherine, it was a deal.

And everything was such a relief; that was what struck her. Everything, as they kissed, as they touched, as they fucked. Everything was a relief, and everything was like the end of something, the end of a problem or a misunderstanding that had gone on, now, for far too long. And she did not think, lying there afterwards, that she would long for this with James again. She did not think it would be necessary. She thought, the fever had been broken now; the madness had been purged. And she thought that later that morning, or early in the afternoon, she would wake and she would be able to get on with her life now, now that this business was out of the way. She would catch her train home, and tomorrow night she would go to her grandfather's party, and she would come back to Dublin on Monday, or on Tuesday, and everything would be fresh, and everything would be clear. She lay there – laughing about it, really, the way that James, in the moments after they had finished, had been laughing about it too. Because what fun. What a lark. What divilment they had proven themselves capable of; what new knowledge they had of one another now.

And then Catherine woke up early in the afternoon, and nothing had gone away after all.

12

Her mother, smiling from the car. It was almost dark, but it was possible to make that much out: her mother's smile. Her mother leaning over the wheel a little, as though she needed to come closer to the windscreen to get a proper look at Catherine. And, Catherine could see now, in the space between the front seats, Anna, the blonde mop, the happy wave, and now she was scrambling, as she always did when they met Catherine at the train station, to get out of the car. She tumbled through the door, and she was out, and she was coming, running, and – *oooof* – Catherine picked her up and told her how heavy she was.

'I have six Easter eggs,' Anna said solemnly, and Catherine said that this could not possibly be true.

'Eight, because I'm sharing two.'

'*Eight*. That's unbelievable.'

'And you have two for you just on your own.'

'Hello, pet,' their mother said, coming around from her door to open the boot of the car; she leaned in to give Catherine a kiss.

It could not be shown. Under no circumstances could it, or anything close to it, anything that was even a shadow of it, be shown. So the thing to do was to talk yourself, to ask questions, rather than to be asked them.

'All set for Granddad's party?'

'He doesn't want a bloody bit of it,' said Anna from the back seat, and both women erupted into laughter at the child's pitch-perfect imitation of what she had so clearly been hearing all week at home.

'Stop that, you,' their mother said, as firmly as she could, and Anna gave a self-satisfied snort.

'So is there much left to do?' Catherine said, as Anna sank back in her seat, singing to herself.

'Oh, you'll be kept busy, don't you worry,' her mother said drily. 'Monica and Fidelma are up to high-doh with the preparations.'

'You'd think it was a wedding,' came another echo of her mother from the back.

'Anna!' their mother warned, before turning to Catherine. 'So what is it you've been so busy with?'

She slowed the car, now, for Mulligans' cattle; the large herd was walked to the farmyard twice daily for milking from a field further on down the hill, sixty or seventy Friesians filling the road to the verges, weaving lazily through the stalled cars, nosing windscreens, swatting tails against wing mirrors.

'They're late out this evening,' Catherine said.

'Good Friday,' her mother said. 'They were probably at late Mass.'

'The cows?' Anna said, delighted with herself.

'You settle down, now,' Catherine said over her shoulder. She wanted to get off the subject of Good Friday as smoothly as possible; she was cursing herself, now, for having walked right into it. 'Just this essay for English,' she said, seeing from her mother's slow blink that she had clean forgotten her question of a few moments earlier. 'It's a big one, so I want to do a good job.'

Her mother nodded. 'Where did you go to Mass today, in case you're asked?'

'At Mass?'

'If you're asked. I presume you didn't go.'

'I didn't get . . .' Catherine said, trailing off.

'Well. Pick a church,' her mother said briskly, and eased the car back onto the open road.

The yellow square of light on the hill as they drove towards the house. Inside, a figure moved past the window: Ellen. Catherine would have recognized the shape of her, the movement of her, even if she had been looking at a stranger's house from a stranger's car in a country she did not know. She was heading for their bedroom, where they would meet to talk, as they always did the moment Catherine arrived home; they would confer on the events of the weeks since last they had seen one another.

'Ellen's very worried about this bloody Leaving Cert,' their mother said now, clearly seeing the same thing. 'Give her some reassurance, would you?'

'But it's ages away yet.'

'That's what I keep saying to her. She can't go on like this for the next two months.'

'She's got exam stress,' Anna clarified. 'She needs to take a break and do an activity.'

'Where did you hear that?' Catherine said, laughing; it did not sound like their mother.

'The radio,' Anna shrugged, clicking herself free of her seatbelt.

'So who was at the party?' Ellen said, sprawled across her bed. 'Was Robert Emmet there?'

She had heard, on a previous visit of Catherine's, of James's nickname for Emmet, and had approved of it.

'No,' Catherine said. 'Nobody from college was there.'

'What were you doing there, then?'

'James.'

'Oh,' Ellen nodded. 'Cool.'

Ellen was the only one in Catherine's family who knew that James had returned to Ireland; Catherine had told her in a phone call that first Sunday, warning her to check, first, that there was no way their mother, much less their father, might be within earshot. James was still an unmentionable subject with her parents; James would always be that way, Catherine suspected. He had gone to Germany, far away and unable to influence their daughter, and that was all that mattered to them. That weekend the previous summer, when Catherine had stepped over the line so astonishingly, simply, now, had not happened; the shouting had not happened, and the arguing had not happened, and the aftermath, the weeks of creeping around under a cloud of anger and trouble, simply had not happened. With Ellen it was different, obviously; Ellen liked the sound of James, laughing at the things Catherine told her about him, at the lines of his that Catherine quoted to her, as though they were lines from films. But none of what had been happening over the last couple of weeks could be told to Ellen; she and Ellen had always told each other about the boys they liked, and the boys they had been with, but this was different. This was, Catherine felt, somehow shameful; that was what this was. This was not something that Catherine could stand for her sister to know. Which made it a first, yes – but some things needed, surely, to be that way. They were getting older. They were moving on, on their separate streams.

But then Catherine sighed, and Ellen could read Catherine's sighs, Catherine's every sound and gesture, as though they were her own. She leaned forward on the bed, suspicion alight in her eyes.

'What?'

'What?' Catherine said, shaking her head. 'No, nothing.'

'Did something happen? Something happened.'

'Nothing happened.'

'You're blushing. You're *puce*. What happened?'

'James,' Catherine blurted, and then panicked. No, no, she could not tell this; she would have to take a different tack. 'James shifted a guy.'

'*Cool*,' Ellen said, sitting up. 'Who? Was it Robert Emmet?'

'No,' Catherine said scornfully. 'This American fella. And I'm not sure if it's actually cool.'

'Why? It was his first shift with a fella, wasn't it? That's good.'

'He's older.'

'Well, you can't talk. Yer man Aidan was ancient.'

'Yeah, well,' Catherine shrugged. 'He's just not really suitable, or whatever.'

Ellen pulled a face of disbelief. 'You're not James's *mother*.'

'I know I'm not his mother,' Catherine shot back. 'Believe me, his mother wouldn't be talking about this.'

'Yeah, but you don't get to rule his life.'

'How am I ruining his life?'

'Rule! Jesus! Get over it! It's fucking well for you, going to posh parties and watching fellas shift other fellas. What do you have to be moaning about?'

'It's just more complicated.' Catherine shook her head.

'Why?' Ellen said, her suspicion sparked again. 'Did something else happen?' She looked at Catherine more closely. 'Did *you* shift someone?'

Catherine was silent.

'You did,' Ellen said, not with surprise but as though this was a fact which had merely been overlooked thus far in their conversation. 'You shifted someone. You're puce again.'

'I'm not fucking puce. Will you quit saying that?'

'Your face looks like you're after running up the lane from the bog. Who did you shift?'

'*Nobody.*'

'You shifted someone. I know by looking at you. What the hell is the big deal? Was he married or something?' Then something else occurred to her; her eyebrows shot up. 'Was it a girl?'

'No! Don't be fucking ridiculous.'

'*You're* being ridiculous.'

'It was the artist,' Catherine, her heart racing now, heard herself saying. 'The guy whose exhibition it was.'

'Wow,' Ellen said. 'Seriously?'

'He's Irish, but he lives in New York.'

'Cool. Maybe he'll take you to New York with him. How old is he?'

'Thirty, probably,' Catherine said, plucking the number out of the air.

'Thirty? Do you ever shift anyone your own age?'

'I was drunk. It was just a drunk thing. He pushed me up against the wall. I didn't even know—'

'Wait,' said Ellen. Her expression had changed. 'You mean, he made you?'

'No, no,' Catherine said impatiently. 'Look, these parties. You don't know. They're just sort of mad. Everyone's plastered, and everyone's sleeping with everyone. You'll see.'

Ellen stared. 'You slept with him?!'

'No, I didn't fucking sleep with him!' Catherine snapped, and at that exact moment, the door handle turned, and both sisters screamed at one another with their eyes, and switched instantly into the mode that this situation required.

'Yeah, she's so mean to Peter,' Ellen said, leaning back

against the wall. 'But I actually didn't see that episode. I can't believe she said that to him.'

'Yeah, I know,' Catherine said, shaking her head, and then they both looked, with perfect, calm-eyed innocence, to the door, where their father stood.

'You're home,' he said, with a nod.

'I'm home.'

'What do you think of your new room?'

'Oh,' Catherine said, looking around; Ellen had been so eager to get all of her news that there had barely been a chance to examine the new space that the extension had made of their bedroom, or to remark on it. It was much bigger than their old room had been, and painted in more sophisticated, adult-looking colours, and the bunk beds had been split apart, and were single beds now, covered in quilts of a diaphanous fabric, and Ellen's desk, neat and ordered and piled with notebooks and folders, stood in one corner. 'It's lovely,' she said, and their father nodded again.

'Very good. Well, I think your dinner's ready up here,' he said, and he stepped back out of the room and closed the door again; they heard his tread on the corridor.

'I hear you're havin' sex with ould fellas now, Catherine,' Ellen said, in an imitation of their father's low, careful tone. 'Very good.'

'Oh, God, shut up,' said Catherine, laughing, her head in her hands.

*

The following night, in the kitchen of Murphy's, her grandfather's local, Catherine and her mother and her aunts made hundreds of sandwiches, and from her seat in front of the television, old Mary Murphy kept one eye on *Kenny Live* and the other on the women who were slicing tomatoes and going through packets of ham. Like everyone who Catherine met with down home now, she commented on how much Catherine had changed, on how she had grown, as though this was an achievement in itself, and she asked the same questions that people down home always asked.

'You'll marry in it, so,' she said, nodding to the television, after Catherine had confirmed that, yes, she did like living in Dublin. Catherine coughed out a laugh, and looked to her mother for a mirroring of her own amusement, but her mother was not looking at her; her mother's hands had, for a moment, gone still, and she was staring at the bread piled in front of her on the chopping board.

'You'll marry in Dublin,' Mrs Murphy said again, but this time it was not Catherine's mother who reacted, but her aunt Fidelma.

'Oh, do *not*, Catherine,' she said, wrinkling her face into a grimace. 'If you know what's good for you.'

'Sure you don't know Dublin,' her other aunt, Monica, said.

'I'm not talking about Dublin,' Fidelma said, working a bread knife through a tower of salad sandwiches. 'I'm talking about riding.'

'Fidelma!' Monica and Catherine's mother spluttered in unison.

'Ride all around you, Catherine,' Fidelma said emphatically, 'and don't bother your arse marrying any one of them. That's my advice to you.'

'Jesus tonight!' Catherine's mother said, but along with Monica and Mrs Murphy, she was creased up now with laughter.

Fidelma pointed her knife straight at Catherine. 'Don't mind these ones, Catherine,' she said. 'I'm not joking you.

When you're my age you'll know that I wasn't joking you. I mean it. Ride. All. Around You.'

Catherine tried for laughter herself, to match the gasps and shudders of the other women, but she was too mortified, felt too paralysed in the spotlight; all she managed was a wheezing noise and a jerking of her shoulders. 'It's not really an option,' she said.

'Make it an option,' Fidelma pointed again.

'Jesus, Fidelma,' Catherine's mother said. 'Will you concentrate on the bloody sandwiches.'

'This is what you'll find yourself doing, Catherine, I'm warning you,' Fidelma said. 'Concentrating on the sandwiches.'

'Young people have great options these days,' Mrs Murphy said almost dreamily from her armchair. 'Great opportunities above in Dublin, I'd say, Catherine.'

Which started them all off again, really roaring laughing this time, bent low over the table, and Catherine standing in the middle of them, staring at a bowl of hard-boiled eggs. 'Well,' she said, to Mrs Murphy, 'I suppose, there's always something going on.'

'Ride them backwards,' Fidelma interjected.

Dancing. They all knew how to dance. Waltzes. Foxtrots. Jives. There was a confidence to them as they spun each other, moved with each other. But they never, Catherine noticed, looked into one another's eyes. They did not seem awkward in this; they seemed, on the contrary, quite happy. They talked to each other without looking one another in the eye, and they laughed together, and they met the eyes of other dancers, other couples, but never one another. Catherine remembered her mother coming home, once, from a dinner dance, giving out yards about the parents of a boy Catherine had gone to school with – they were rich, they lived in an enormous house on the outskirts of the town, they always sat, after Mass had finished, in their pew and talked to one another, the whole family, gossiping and chattering like people who were very glad of the chance to catch up with each other. When this couple had danced, apparently, they had looked at one another, smiling, as they did so, and Catherine's mother had considered this a deeply ridiculous, almost tacky, display; in the kitchen the following morning she had made Catherine and Ellen laugh by mocking them, grabbing Ellen and dancing her around the kitchen, pretending to be Jarlaith Byrne staring deep into his wife's eyes. Here, on Murphy's dance floor, the couples all observed the unspoken rule – her father with her mother now, to 'The Gambler', her grandfather with a neighbour woman, Uncle Matt with Fidelma, who was looking content and serene now, not at all like a woman who harboured a longing to go back to her unmarried years and fuck every man she saw. They moved quickly, with great skill, and they kept their eyes fixed on a point in the middle distance, which could not have been easy, since the pub was so small and so cramped; how, then, did they all find a point in the middle distance? And moving as fast as they were?

But they found it, and they fixed on it. They touched hands, but they did not hold hands; that was not what they were doing with their hands. With their hands, they tipped and they glanced and they slid, loose and confident; they knew when to fasten and when to let go. They stepped and they spun, locking and pivoting; they linked and they turned and they released. Often, Catherine had been hauled out onto this very dance floor, and it had always been mortifying, the mess she had made of dancing with whichever neighbour of her grandfather's had thought it a friendly notion to give her a spin; always, it had been a disaster of knocking limbs, and sweaty hands, and of her inability to understand when it was time to twirl and when it was time to stay, and her arm wrenching at the wrong time, and her feet shuffling against his, and no rhythm, no glide, and a hectic, wincing farce, then, when it did come time to twirl, and the dissatisfaction in the man's face, that she did not know the steps, could not give the pleasure, could not be relied upon even for the three minutes of forgetting that a good dance could allow. A young one who had not been taught to dance, she could see it in their eyes; what was the point of that? Forget college. Forget Europe. Forget everything that was coming, everything that had been promised yet to come. If a young one could not jive, what was the use of sending her out into the world?

*

Three hours later, they were back in her grandfather's house. Catherine's mother was in the kitchen with Monica and Fidelma, making tea and pouring lagers and pushing cloves into half-slices of lemon for hot whiskies. Her grandfather had decided that he wanted a bowl of soup; Catherine's mother, complaining about him, was making it out of a can from the press. Catherine walked through with drinks to the sitting room, handing them out and settling beside her grandfather a moment.

What was James doing now? Catherine checked her watch again: it was ten to three. They had been in Murphy's until two in the morning, and then the natural thing to do had been to come back here. So here they were, sitting around the room, her grandfather's sheepdog asleep under the table. Often, she noticed, her grandfather glanced towards the slumped form.

'Shep's tired,' she said. 'He's not used to company at this hour.'

ROMANCE

1

Love set you going like a fat gold watch—

Was there any line as magnificent?

That had been about the newborn Frieda, that poem. Frieda, who would grow up to send the red and yellow blisters across the cover of her father's book.

The children were very cold but quite safe.

None of this was any of Catherine's business.

*

Hughes, in 'Epiphany', his own poem about that same new-born, written that same London spring, described how he had almost bought a baby fox. A man on a bridge had the animal stuffed down his coat front, the tiny face staring out between the lapels.

Bereft
Of the blue milk, the toys of feather and fur,
The den life's happy dark. And the huge whisper
Of the constellations
Out of which Mother had always returned.

Cheap enough at a pound, the man with the fox said.

But no.

*

New slate – clean slate – but already the pressure of precedents. Her cry takes its place 'among the elements' – and shadows and blankness and 'own slow / Effacement' = dissatisfaction, anxiety. Mirror image is not actually mirror image, because the child has been born. The reflection untrue.

What is the 'far sea' that moves in her ear?

*

Inevitable.

What happened between herself and James was inevitable.

Was that true? Was that a reality?

Was a reality something you arrived at, or something you made?

Or something you just forced onto things?

2

Lovers.

As though – what was it Julia Doonan had said?

As though the rest of us are only going to Mass together.

And now, it seemed, they were *lovers*. At least in private.

At least, that was, where other people could not see them.

And, well, at the end of all, all love was private, wasn't it?

*

(This was what Catherine told herself.)

*

Catherine wanted him every minute. Catherine wanted him
to fuck her and fuck her until she dissolved.

James—

*

James was another story.

3

Once, as a small girl, she had gone with the wrong mother from the shop. She had not realized it was the wrong mother. The woman was tall, and moved with purpose, and wore boots and carried a handbag and had a winter coat. Her mother, on that day, had also had all of these things.

Catherine walked along, chatting and chatting.

The woman did not even notice the child at her knee.

How could you not even notice?

Her mother, calling and calling from the door.

*

James laughed at her when she told him that story. James was right to laugh.

'You knew damn well what you were up to, Reilly,' he said, stretched out on her bed, smoking. 'You liked the cut of that other woman's jib.'

His hand resting on his naked stomach. His nipples pink and pricked and hard. His dick, ten minutes earlier, had kept making her gag, but the throat was where you were meant to take it, wasn't it? The throat was how you had the best chance of getting it again.

And anyway, why on earth was she telling him that story now?

*

James had made it happen, the second time. Catherine not quite able to believe it. His hands, the way they changed from stroking fondly to stroking slow—

His tongue, full and supple against hers. The hardness of him, already waiting, already there—

And surely *that* meant something? Surely that said—?

But no.

Because the way they got through this – got away with this – was by laughing about it.

Their great joke.

Their great mischief.

Their great addition to the long, long list of things that, together, they could do.

*

And afterwards: the slagging. The innuendo. Like they were meeting for breakfast after their separate, hilarious one-night stands.

'You're terrible, Muriel.'
'*You're* terrible.'

*

And where does the blood go when it is making you weak, when it is making you want to fall? Does it go to the brain first, and from there to the cunt, or is it the other way around? Is it the brain or the cunt that says it to you, over and over, no matter how you try to reason with it, no matter how you try to roar at it; is it the brain or the cunt that hisses those words?

Hissing, Get him. Bring him here.

*

His hands. His tongue. The fullness of him, tensed and pleading in her hand.

His eyes, closed. The lids the colour of sand.

Packed sand, trodden over.

(Why did such things come to her mind?)

*

And for Catherine, just the touch of him was always enough. Just the fact of him. That this was *James*.

He was a long, low shudder that started deep in her spine.

And yes, probably, when he put his hand to her there, it should feel different. Yes. Probably, it should not feel like it felt: like he had lost something down there, like he was searching down there, impatiently casting about. And yes, probably, when he put his mouth there, probably he found it—

All of that – how would he think of it?

Architecture?

*

And was it her fault, if he looked to her more beautiful every day?

Was it her business?

Because it was only a lark.

Only a plunge.

Catherine and James. Catherine and James.

And the things they could do.

4

'What are you up to these days, Citóg? I never see you anymore.'

'Busy.'

*

Nothing that was not him was anything that she could see.

*

And James's gaze in the street now: not something of which
Catherine could afford to allow herself to be aware.

Still walking the streets as they were, the taunting bastards;
still everywhere, with their untouchable, insolently beautiful
stares—

(This was how she thought of them now: as stares, not as the
stared-at. Dublin, for her now: the house of the stare.)

And so if, beside her, he saw someone – if, beside her, he
sighed or muttered in that way – well, Catherine simply had
not heard. Catherine simply had not noticed it, that pulse of
pain and longing, that shrapnel through skin of what could
not be had—

*

From 'Tulips': *I am nobody; I have nothing to do with explosions.*

*

Amy, wanting to know if she should add Catherine's name to the pot one night for dinner.

'No. I'll be at James's. I'll probably crash on his couch.'

And Amy nodding, saying nothing. Amy, who had heard Catherine and James, the noise of them, through her own bedroom wall.

You know, I was always close to Amy, he had said to her, that day by the canal. *You know that.*

*

(That day now so long, long ago.)

*

Because nobody knew.

Amy, and that dividing wall just chipboard, really – and nobody knew.

Lorraine walking in on the two of them in the sitting room, one night – and nobody knew.

Zoe, and whatever it was that Zoe saw, or Zoe intuited – and nobody knew.

Because silence. Because pretending.

Because these were the things they all knew, so well, how to do.

*

Zoe:

> Dear Citstytis,
>
> You are not at your desk, a.k.a. Dead Poets Society, and you are not having coffee anywhere that I can see. Hopes of shaggage with Young Emmet also dashed, as I see him strutting in his peacock fashion around the lawn. Cartier-Bresson also nowhere in evidence, so I assume you are with him, discussing Important Art Matters, a.k.a. preying on v.v. pretty boys.
>
> Aidan, Lisa, Nordie Liam and I are going to the Alpha at 16.00 hours for fried animal pieces and many pots of tea. Please come if you get this! Bring Cartier-B! Fried animal pieces! Pots of tea!
>
> Yours in perpetuity,
>
> Z

*

Zoe, growing friendly, now, with PhotoSoc Lisa and with Nordie Liam, as she called them, always off for coffee or lunch or pints.

'You can't call him Nordie Liam,' Catherine told her, but Zoe just laughed.

'He doesn't mind. He's a sweetheart. I'm trying to get him and Lisa together. They'd be so cute, the pair of them.'

And what would that be like? To be so cute, the pair of you?

*

Everything was jealousy. Everything was longing for a life that she could not have. It was as though she had taken his pain, the pain he had talked to her about, and inverted it.

No. It was as though she had been jealous, even, of his pain. That was what it was.

That was how far it had gone with her.

*

Aidan, one day on the ramp pretending to eye them suspiciously as they passed, Catherine's arm locked in James's:
    'Where are *you* two sneaking off to?'

And Aidan, it struck her as James peeled away from her, going over to him for a brief, laughing exchange about something – she did not even pay attention to what – Aidan – was Aidan, after all, to be trusted, really?

And probably not.

Because he was older, Aidan; he was worldly, wasn't he? He had told her, hadn't he, that night that she had been with him, during the course of their long, snuggled-up conversation (how far away that conversation seemed now, how unbelievable) that he had done everything there was to do? Catherine had assumed that he was talking about travel, about the fact that he had been to South America, and Australia, and the fact that he had lived in London for years – but no, probably, it had been sex, actually, that he had been talking about that night – probably it had been his way of letting her know that he had been with not just women but also men—

And James had said he was sexy, Aidan. James had said it to her, that first day she had introduced them; James had mouthed it to her, making her cringe with his obviousness, with the way that Aidan could so easily see him—

And, so, had that been James's intention, then, that day?

And, so, was there any way she could trust them, the two of them in such close, dangerous proximity?

*

'We have to go,' she said to Aidan, and she pulled James, still laughing, away.

*

And:

'James, baby!' said PhotoSoc Lisa, greeting him one day, her arms thrown open at the sight of him.

Catherine's eyes became, suddenly, blades. Rounding on her, staring at her; unblinking. Lisa, maybe noticing; seeming to stumble in confusion a moment, before James hugged her, seeming to stagger a little with the worry that she had done something wrong—

Which she had. Which she *very* much had.

James, baby! Catherine mimicked in her head, angrily, all night. *James, baby!*

Because how could Lisa be trusted either?

No.

Nor woman neither.

Though by your smiling—

*

(Everyone could fuck off with their smiling.)

*

Emmet, one day up in the publications office, gave her a heart.

Joke heart. A discarded, forgotten-about charity heart. One of those lapel pins sold on the street to make money for the Irish Heart Association; he had found it, probably, in a pen tray or a drawer. Red velveteen blob of it scuffed now, stencilled, smiling face faded.

All of his polished, grinning irony, as he handed it to her.

All of hers, taking it as casually as though it was a memo or a fax.

She put it in the drawer of her bedside table.

(She said nothing about this to Zoe.)

(Nothing about this to James.)

*

A cigarette, tipping against the darkness. The sound of his breath, languid and weighed. His skin pressed to hers, damp, as they fell asleep together.

*

And in the morning, they made a joke of it, because that was the only way, Catherine knew, to make sure that it could happen again.

*

(Thinking of him all day. Thinking, *What now?* Thinking, *When next?*)

*

Thinking, *Love, love—*

*

Dreaming that she could make them a cave.

*

She was a miner. The light burning blue.

*

She wrote: *Plummet. Breakage. Loss.*

*

She wrote: *He must have been a beautiful boy.*

*

Down home one weekend, and so tempted to spill everything to Ellen.

But no.

(And how was it even possible, to miss a sister you already had?)

Or her mother's sigh; her mother's sigh that said, *I know damn well you're up to something, but I don't know what.* Sensing something, like a cat hunting, moving from garden into field. Blind hedge, and she could not see beyond it, but she had the scent. She had the sigh.

But the sigh could not get at Catherine now.

'No news,' was all she said.

5

Two or three weeks in, there came the night when James talked, in her bed, of a boy.

Of a particular boy – Zoe's new boyfriend, Lucien – and of how very nice he must be to fuck.

Catherine staring at the ceiling. Feeling as though her heart was dropping down a well.

And ordering herself to ignore this feeling. To ignore this hollowness, huge in her.

Because she was getting what she wanted, wasn't she? She was getting him.

She was holding him.

*

A line of poetry she tried:
Now every holding is a holding on.

(But not really. She was not really writing poetry anymore.)

*

The photos James was taking now: they felt like her poetry.

Four men by the side of a road, none of them looking at the camera.

How had they not seen him?

The bones in their faces so sharp and so fine.

The rain about to plunge from a sky the colour of stone.

Or a boy, around their age, huddled in the corner of a bus shelter.

Not homeless; she did not think he was taking shelter in that way.

But tired, and curled in on himself, his hands flung like things no longer useful.

His runners scuffed and filthy.

His eyes tightly closed.

*

Zoe and Lucien; Catherine had not quite noticed this happening.

Lucien was English. Tall, and cheekboned, and shabby, the way all the English boys in college were. Hair like an ancient settlement, which only served to make the English boys look even posher, for some reason; the Irish boys with that kind of hair just looked slightly unhinged, looked wild. Why was that? What, exactly, was that difference in them?

(These were the kinds of things she had once loved to discuss with James.)

Lucien lived in a big, rambling house with a couple of other English boys, and Lucien's room had a big double bed.

'In which,' Zoe said to Catherine, 'he teaches me everything a girl needs to know.'

And what would that be like? Catherine imagined it: the huge, wide bed. The space of it. To have all of that freedom. All of that acreage. And to have someone in a bed like that, looking at you, and to look at them, looking at you, looking all the length of you, the truth of you—

*

So wet, muttered James, one morning, and he sounded like someone stepping in out of the rain.

*

And well, was she stupid?

Was she so pathetic?

Because she knew his reasons for this were different from hers.

*

His reasons:
1. Touch
2. Forgetting
3. Fear
4. Convenience, now becoming Habit

5. The dark, unbearable cluster growing every day larger in his mind

Her reasons:
1. Him

*

So, yes, to Question 1, and yes to Question 2.

And no to Question 3, which was, *Does knowing make any difference?*

*

She tried to find it, the song that would be their song.

The one about the drifters, going to see the world?

No, that was not them. That was not their song, either.

None of the songs were for them.

And, well, did everyone need to have a song?

Not everybody needed to have a song.

*

Staring, one lunchtime, at Zoe's lips. Zoe's lips, as they smacked loudly on a yoghurt spoon, getting at every last trace of the stuff, wiping the plastic clean. Because what did those lips do to Lucien? What did Lucien look like, when those small, pink lips closed around his big, English dick? Because what would it be like, to be with someone, to do that for someone, and to know that just the sight and the fact of you doing it for them was amazing, was blissful, was – what was the word?

Enough.

That was the word.

Was enough.

*

And later that week, in Jenny Vander's, trying on a dress she was considering for the ball. James with her, of course – James had not been allowed not to come with her – standing, arms folded, by the mirror.

'It's nice,' he said.

Was it nice?

An old woman, going through the rails, stopping what she was doing and coming closer for a look.

'Buy it for your girlfriend,' she said to James. 'Buy it now. She has the height for it. She has the colouring. She has the mouth.'

*

It would become another of their phrases, Catherine knew. Another of their hilarious, ironic toys. *She has the mouth.*

*

And James would not hear of coming to the ball with her. James was not a Trinity student, he pointed out coolly and calmly; James was not going to spend fifty pounds on a ticket for a student ball.

300

But—

But—

But, coloured lights, making all the familiar old buildings unfamiliar; but, the night-time sweep to Front Gate, surrounded by so many other people looking so well. James in a tux – *I don't think Armani does a navy-blue taxedo*, and they would laugh over that line again – and Catherine in the Jenny Vander's dress, and they would walk in together, and they would dance together, and – yes, yes, boys, yes, boys, they would look at boys together, yes, of course, at all the beautiful, tuxed-up boys – but he would leave with her, that would be the important thing, and he would come home with her—

But no.

*

Emmet: 'Reilly! Does the Longford County Council grant cover a ball ticket?'

And she looked at him, for a moment.

Quite lovely, actually, now; had that happened only recently, or had he always been that way?

The bright boy's grin on him. The fresh, perfect clearness of his skin.

The blush, betraying him, the way a blush always did.

But he was impossible.

He was unthinkable.

He was an entirely different world.

*

Or, even an ordinary boy.

Nordie Liam – *Liam* – sitting on a bench with Lisa, just as Zoe had wanted it, smiling, laughing, chatting.

He was not someone Catherine would ever be attracted to. He was slightly short, and slightly shaggy – not in the Lucien way, in the Irish way – and he wore T-shirts with video game characters on them, and he was just the kind of boy you would not even see, really—

But he would see you, wouldn't he?

And then you would see him.

And then you'd be off, the pair of you.

Off to see the world—

But no.

*

Because her day, now: wake, already drowning in him. Not that moment of precious oblivion; not for her that child's empty instant before fully coming to. Her eyes opening, already fixed on the thought of him. Her mind bobbing up into morning, already logged and tangled with him. Her heart—

302

Fuck her heart.

She had a constant sensation of hunger, which only grew worse when she ate.

Even brushing her teeth, she was thinking of him.

Even locking the door of the flat, turning the key, feeling its clunky, stubborn resistance, its tiny attempt to refuse.

Even stairs made her think of him. Even stones under the soles of her shoes. Even rusted bicycles, propped up against wire fences; even the dour tones of a security guard, asking to see her ID card at the entrance to the library; even his dimpled, stubbled chin as he waved her through. The books on her desk, forget it:

> It was May. How had it started? What
> Had bared our edges?

*

That was from Hughes's 'The Rabbit Catcher', that line.

Plath had a poem of the same name.

They were both about the same day, the day of a picnic in Cornwall. Walking on the clifftops, Hughes had found a rabbit snare: ready, primed. Plath, furious, had tossed it useless into the trees; then had marched on ahead and done the same to another.

Then another.

Then another.

Hughes writing of her temper, of the rage in which she had simmered all morning; of his own forbearance in the face of it. And now, of how, as she destroyed the snares, the things he understood, the things people who were his people needed for food and for money, she was 'weeping with a rage / That cared nothing for rabbits.'

Plath, in her poem from probably twenty or thirty years earlier, writing of the force of the wind, and of the blinding light from the sea, and of the gorse, its 'black spikes', and of how the snares 'almost effaced themselves – / Zeroes, shutting on nothing.'

> *And, we, too, had a relationship –*
> *Tight wires between us,*
> *Pegs too deep to uproot, and a mind like a ring*
> *Sliding shut on some quick thing,*
> *The constriction killing me also.*

*

And, 'Catherine,' James said one night afterwards – said her name seriously, said it soberly, so that at first her heart leapt hopefully, at first her eyes thought they would meet, in his, something they wanted, something new—

But no.

'Catherine,' he said, and he looked at her, and seriously, soberly, he shook his head. 'What are we doing? What are we messing at, at all?'

And Catherine: 'No, no. Don't ever say that. Don't ever ask that. We can do whatever we want to do, James. We can do whatever we like. It's *us*, James. We're *us*.'

And his silence.

But his silence, by then, was as good as his loving word.

*

Because there was nobody like them. There was nobody else who had what they had.

6

Aidan, interrupting their morning coffee in Café en Seine far too often for Catherine's liking, now. Just showing up, just by some kind of happy coincidence, to sit down at the table beside them. Often bringing others; often bringing his little friend, Liam.

It was just not good enough.

Catherine picked for herself and James a different, further-off cafe.

*

And what did they talk about?

Everything.

Because they were still them. Still Catherine and James.

Because he was still the one she wanted to talk to, listen to, more than anyone else in the world.

And was she still that person for him?

He said she was.

'Oh, Catherine,' he would say, holding her, the way he did; the way he always had. 'Oh, Catherine. We're an awful pair of eejits, do you know that?'

His arms tight around her. His breath so close to her face. His skin and her skin: nothing made more sense to her than this.

*

Summer just around the corner now. And there was a thought. So many of the others going away – Zoe on a child-minding job somewhere in Italy; Conor and Emmet to America on the J1; Amy to work in a beer garden in Germany; Aidan, hopefully, on a five-year mission to Mars . . .

Such peace and quiet, they would have, the two of them. So much time to be together, alone. She thought about baking. She thought about dinners, having them ready at the end of their respective working days.

She applied for a summer job. It was temping work, advertised on the English department noticeboard; no specifics but a request for good typing skills, and lateral thinking, and an ability to work with permutations and combinations—

'Porn, obviously, Citóg,' said Conor, when she told him about it.
  'Ha.'
  'Doyle says his next column was inspired by you, by the way. What have you been doing to that poor lad?'
  Catherine stared at him. 'His next what?'
  'Well, I think he meant *Muck*. I don't think he meant "column" as a euphemism. But then again . . .'

*

What happens in the heart simply happens.

She gave James that line.

On a stall in the gift shop of the National Gallery, she found a postcard, a photo of Hughes taken by Cartier-Bresson in 1971. Hughes's coat was unbuttoned, his tie askew; his head was slightly tilted, his gaze serious and clear. He was standing in front of a bookcase, the books piled on top of each other; closed in, like specimens, behind glass.

She bought it, and she wrote the line on the back of it, and she gave it to James.

Because it had become their line, in her mind, now.

It had become them.

*

'Hello,' said James, smirking, when she gave him the postcard, looking at the photograph, and then he turned it over.

His face changed.

'Oh, Catherine,' was all he said.

*

Nordie Liam – *Liam* – telling her that he was having people round for drinks before the ball on Friday, and could she come? Could she, and James too, come?

Hair like an ancient settlement – an Irish one. Apples of colour high on his cheeks. His eyes a dark brown; she had not noticed that before, and she had always liked brown eyes. His accent, so quiet and so careful. 'Cath-er-ine': the three rolled syllables he gave her.

But no.

But no, no. No party. Aidan would be there, after all; Aidan in a tux. Aidan in a bow tie. Plenty of people in bow ties. So, no. They would not be going to Liam's. They would not be going to any party before the ball.

7

The summer job was horoscopes, it turned out. A woman setting up a new website, a subscription service that would email users their daily, custom-made horoscope, which meant that by the site launch in September, there needed to be five thousand freshly written horoscopes banked and ready to go. They would not be *entirely* fabricated, the woman explained at Catherine's interview, flicking her bleach-blonde hair back over her shoulder; the writers would use a code book to generate 'atmospheric and thematic guidelines', based on the given combination of symbol and star sign and shape and shade churned out, for every individual horoscope, by the database her team had designed.

'Right,' Catherine said doubtfully. 'I—'
    'I'm offering a pound per horoscope,' the woman cut in.

*

Love will come in the form of someone wearing the colour blue. Be attentive to its appearances.

An acquaintance, possibly a Pisces, needs to be watched carefully. Share with them nothing precious.

Do not despair if a plan is not proceeding. Venus says that persistence will reap rewards.

'Yes, exactly that sort of thing,' the woman said, and hired her.

*

(James, laughing so hard when she told him that he started, actually, to get on her nerves. That she snapped at him to stop.)

*

(He did not stop.)

*

'*Ouch!*' he said, after she had pinched him.

*

Shock on his face. Disbelief on it.

And could she be more terrible than this, this person who felt only proud, in this moment, of having been able to get right at him in this way?

*

And more: the next time he talked of a boy he wanted to be with, Catherine did not look at the ceiling.

The next time, Catherine did not just lie there, and lie still.

Cillian, Lorraine's Cillian, he talked of, and Catherine snatched the cigarette from his hand. She held it a moment, his eyes looking at her in confusion; then she pointed it, the glint-grey head of it only a fraction away from his white, naked skin. He jerked back from her, astonished, but she followed; she stared.

311

'Catherine,' he said, his voice just a breath.

She held his gaze for another second, and then she bent and stubbed the cigarette out on his bedroom floor. Into the carpet, its dirty threads; let the little smother of it leave a brand mark, round and black and hard.

'Catherine,' he said, clambering across her, incredulous. 'My landlady! Are you—'

'Your landlady would probably approve,' she said, and she turned to the wall.

*

And, *Catherine*, he said, the next night, and she knew what was coming, she knew it was another attempt to call a halt, but she pushed the words away with her hands. She pushed the words away with her mouth.

And his eyes stayed closed, as they always did.

But she could manage without his eyes.

8

MUCK

by Emmet Doyle

8 May 1998

Campus Benders Take Over: What Have We Done To Deserve This?

Five years after decriminalization, the full reality of 'equality' is beginning to show its face on campus – and college citizens are speaking out about their suffering.

IT HAS BEEN five long years since Ireland's First Gay, former college English professor Senator David Norris, convinced Ireland's Biggest Culchie, then-Taoiseach Albert Reynolds, to make it legal for gays and lesbians to live their homosexual lifestyles openly and without fear of being arrested, discriminated against or kicked to death in an alleyway without anyone even thinking it necessary to ring the Guards.

At the time, the people of Ireland were assured that decriminalization was a mere formality, and that everything would continue as normal. A few brazen gays would surface here and there in the initial months, but like all attention-seekers, they would slither off again, we were assured.

'Normal', after all, equals silence and invisibility in any civilized society, and it was taken for granted that Irish gays would toe this line if they knew what was good for them.

However, this scenario has not come to pass, and here on campus we have found ourselves the unhappy Petri dish for what is becoming an increasingly sinister social experiment. Being, as it is, a default hothouse for a proportion of the first generation to come to maturity since the change in law, college was perhaps inevitably going to bear the brunt of the resultant explosion in what the Equality Mafia so laughingly term 'freedom', but *Muck*'s intensive investigations today reveal the shocking full extent of this crisis.

*

There were quotes from 'Luke', a student union insider who had been shocked by the sight of two men sitting with their knees almost touching in the library, and from 'Mary', a first-year Irish and History student who was suffering the crippling social repercussions of having been spotted by an old schoolmate standing at the LGB Society stand during Freshers' Week, lured there by the promise of free rainbow-coloured M&Ms. To illustrate 'the profound damage inflicted on normal campus relations between the sexes', there was a quote from an unnamed senior lecturer, who reported that it was now almost impossible to extort blow jobs from female colleagues and students by threatening to expose them as lesbians; there was simply not the same level of fear, he said. More than one student had quite cheerfully told him that she actually *was* a lesbian. A senior *TN* source, meanwhile, revealed that he had been deprived of the location in which he had always sold pills when LGBSoc had been granted larger rooms at the start of this college year. And a college counsellor complained that she was experiencing a severe downturn in gay and lesbian students who wanted to kill themselves. It was just not on, Emmet wrote in his concluding paragraph. Freedom was one thing, but this was getting out of hand. He was calling on the Provost to institute a college-wide Straight Week as a matter of urgency. Awareness needed to be raised. Order needed to be restored.

*

James loved it.

James read it over and over, and the first time he almost cried with laughter, and the second time he laughed more quietly, and the third time and the fourth time and the fifth time, he did not laugh at all.

'It's really good,' he said to Catherine, nodding over it again. 'It's really very, very good. It's clever, I mean. This line about what's normal . . .'

He read her the line.

'Yeah, yeah, I saw it,' Catherine said.

'It's brilliant.'

'It's all right.'

'No, no. I have to say I didn't think he had it in him, young Robert Emmet.'

Catherine said nothing.

He glanced up. 'Did anything ever happen between you two, in the end?'

*

She slammed the door.

*

She was tempted to write it on the wall of the publications office, what she thought of Emmet's column. She was tempted to leave it there, in huge black letters.

But she said it to his face instead.

Strain in it. Hurt in it, as he tried to keep grinning his grin.

But his grin would not stay with him.

And that was the first time she had seen that, she realized: Emmet's face, without any kind of smile.

Something in his eyes that made her heart want to give in to something huge.

But, what, was she supposed to account for other people's feelings now as well?

*

James was going home for the weekend, he announced. His parents had known for a while now that he was back in Dublin, and he could not put it off any longer, the visit. It would be fine, he said. It would be fine. It would be his mother pretending nothing had happened, and his father not knowing that anything had happened, anyway, and he would try to take a few photographs around the place, maybe – because he really needed, by now, to start preparing properly for Lisa's show – and he would have a couple of pints with his brother, and he would be back on Monday or Tuesday, and he would see her then.

And she should go to the ball, he said. He knew she still had her ticket. She should go to Jenny Vander's and buy that dress.

'With *what*?'

'You have the mouth,' he said, laughing.

*

'Oh, *fuck* off.'

*

But no, no, she should go to the ball, he said, and she should have a good time, and she should do whatever a good time entailed.

And he would see her Monday. Or Tuesday. And he would call her at some stage. Of course, of course he would call her. Sure he would have plenty to tell her. He would have plenty to report.

*

He took the morning train.

By evening:

The train now boarding on Platform Four is the 19.45 service to Sligo. Calling at Maynooth, Enfield, Mullingar, Mostrim, Longford, Dromod—

Carrick-on-Shannon station, a quarter past ten. Around about now, the others would be walking through Front Gate into the square and the cobblestones lit up in all the pinks and blues.

Fifty pence in her pocket for the payphone. James's mother answered; surprise and then delight in her voice as she called out to him.

Jem! Jem! You'll never guess who's here!

'Oh, he'll be thrilled,' she said, coming back to the mouth-piece, to Catherine. 'Oh, he'll be only thrilled.'

*

(Her accent making Catherine think, for a second, of Liam.)

*

Because how could she have got through a whole weekend?

*

(James's face, as he beckoned her from the car twenty minutes later, was something, but it was not thrilled.)

(But no matter. No matter. She would bring him right around.)

*

(And he looked beautiful even when he was angry. He looked beautiful even when he was grim.)

*

No, his day had not been a good one, he said as he drove back to Carrigfinn. No, it had not. His mother, interrogating him all day, that was why. About what? Well, about everything, really. But mostly, since Catherine had asked, about Catherine.

About Catherine and him.

*

318

(If Catherine had been in the driving seat she would, at that moment, have run the car off the road.)

*

'About *me*?'

(No response.)

'But why? You mean, about why I came here tonight?'

(No, no. These questions had come long before James and his mother had known of Catherine's arrival. Catherine's arrival had only consolidated, for James's mother, all the grand ideas in her mind.)

'I don't . . .'

(She did not *what*?)

*

Him, banging on the steering wheel.

Her, making herself sound small and vulnerable and frightened, so that he would not continue to talk to her in this way.

*

Because, it turned out, his mother had been praying for Catherine. Yes, *praying* for her. Praying for her, or for someone like her; it was not personal – it did not need to be her. No offence.

(A tone which said, *Take as much offence as you like*.)

Yes, his mother had been praying for this. Praying for James to find himself a girl, a girl who would shake himself out of himself; who would bring him out of the terrible, hopeless place into which he had wandered. And his mother, because she had met Catherine the previous summer – no, no interruptions, really, this was worth hearing all the way through – his mother had had high hopes for Catherine, and his mother had made Catherine the forerunner. The *forerunner*. For what, did Catherine *think*? For everything that mattered. For the only things that mattered, obviously. For what was normal.

(That word spat, like a seed, onto the dash of the car.)

And so all day, James had faced questions about Catherine: about whether he had come back to Ireland because of Catherine, and about whether it was because of Catherine that he had not come home until now, and about whether he saw Catherine often in Dublin, and about whether he enjoyed her company, and about whether he had *thoughts* about her, or *desires* for her – yes, *desires*. Yes, *desires*; yes, she had used that fucking word. The sound of it, in his mother's mouth. And, worse again, asking him if he wanted, in any part of himself, to *lie with* Catherine, and had he ever lain with her, and he would not lie to his mother about this now, would he? Would he? He would not lie to his mother, if there was any chance, if there was any way, because she had prayed so hard, she had prayed so constantly—

Because I'm your mother, Jem, and I'm the one knows what's true of you, deep, deep down.

*

And Catherine hated herself, in that moment. For wanting to ask what she wanted to ask. For needing to. She tried to stop herself; she tried to bite it back, beat it back, this swelling in her: this awful, unforgivable surging of hope.

But she could not. She could not harangue herself out of hoping.

And so she looked at him. Her heart a frantic drum.

'And?' she said, her voice tripping, slipping on the word. 'And? What did you say?'

*

(Hoping *what*, exactly? Hoping that his reply would have opened the way to something different? Hoping it would show that his eyes had been opened, somehow, to something *new*?)

*

She was an idiot. She was a child. His long silence, before speaking, told her everything she was.

His top lip curling.

'I said, "Mother, we're not discussing this again." What do you think I was going to say to her? I said, "We've discussed this before, Mother, and nothing has changed; nothing has changed about me, and nothing is *going* to change."'

Catherine, nodding, agreeing, with all of her might.

And James saying that he was leaving again in the morning. That he did not even know why he had come home at all.

'I'll go with you,' Catherine said eagerly. Wanting to show her support. Wanting to show—

His laugh, high and angry.

'Oh, you don't fucking *say*.'

*

Who has dismembered us?

SYLVIA PLATH AND TED HUGHES: THE RESPONSIBILITIES OF LANGUAGE

Catherine Reilly, SF English (TSM) Trinity Term, 1998

> *And still the heaven*
> *Of final surfeit is just as far*
> *From the door as ever.*
> (From 'Blue Moles', 1957)

*

Twenty-five pages of it, and writing it exhausted her. Almost twenty hours in the computer labs at the back of campus; she finished it with only minutes to go to the deadline.

Afterwards, all she wanted to do was find him. Was fuck him. Was sleep with him, sleep tucked and hidden in his arms.

His arms around her. His arms, making her feel she was home.

But no.

No more.

*

Songs that had the exact shape of your heartbreak: they were the songs you had to cross the room to turn off.

*

Because he was suddenly nowhere she could find him. Not in the darkroom when she expected him to be in the darkroom. Not in O'Brien's when she expected him to be on a shift there. Not in Thomas Street: she called the number, she knocked on the door, but no, his landlady said, she had not seen him this morning / this afternoon / this evening, she had no idea when he would be home—

*

And the ball had been absolutely *brilliant*, Zoe said.

And Liam's drinks party, before the ball, had been very interesting indeed.

*

'*Very* interesting,' Zoe said.

*

And how had Catherine missed this? How had she not seen it, this danger right in front of her eyes?

Because she thought like James about these things now, was the answer.

Or rather, the way she thought that James thought.

323

Because she had looked at Liam all these weeks and seen –
well, go on, be honest . . .

Nothing.

No threat.

Just an ordinary boy.

9

'I'm *not* suggesting him because suddenly now I know another gay guy and so I automatically think he and James should be together. You're being far too small-minded about this, Catherine.'

*

She should have seen this. She should have—

*

'Though now that you mention it, that is precisely what I think should happen.'

*

Panic hammering in Catherine's chest all day now; by now, it was when her heart stopped racing that she noticed it at all.

*

Waking and saying to the morning, *Please do not get any worse.*

But you could not reason with a morning. A morning was not a thing that had to give anything beyond what it was.

*

Working only in the farthest, most hidden reaches of the library. Law. Philosophy. Theology. The places where she reckoned herself least likely to be found. By Zoe. By Conor.

By anybody. The desks in these sections hemmed in, on all sides, by bookshelves, and nowhere near the windows, and so nowhere in sight of the summer as it descended now: smug, thinking itself so generous, shining down on all the happy bodies, all the happy smiles.

*

Thinking, *Might not*. Thinking, *Need not*.

Might not ever find out, that was.

Need not ever be told.

Or Liam told, come to think of it, about him. Because Zoe had not told him about James; Zoe, it turned out, on that score, was a lot more discreet than Catherine had ever been. Saying, *We can let them work it out for themselves. We can help them – we can nudge them – after the exams are over, we can make it so that they're both in the right, same place, at the right, same time—*

(And Catherine would see it again in her mind's eye, as clearly as though it was unfolding right here in the library before her: James's smile meeting his smile. James's eyes softening at what they saw in his. A greeting, shy, and a conversation, nervy, and a knowledge, an understanding, sparking at every atom of the air; and a suggestion, a conversation, an invitation – something casual, something light . . .)

(And what, though, was actually *wrong* with her? What kind of friend would ever try to block this for him? Would fantasize about how to stop this ever from being?)

(But those were questions for other people. Those were questions for people who lived in some other, simpler realm.)

*

And of course she should never have left her hiding place. Of course she should never have gone out of the library, that lunchtime, for food. Standing at the arts block railing, eating her sandwich, and keeping her eyes on the ground, and nearly there; just on the last bite of bread—

And then Liam. Of course.

Lifting his hand to her: a shy greeting. Smiling at her, striding over to her, calling out her name—

Giving it those three long syllables. What would James's name sound like in that mouth?

She has the mouth.

Those fucking Northern accents: so dangerous. So fucking attractive. How had she not copped at least that before?

Telling her they had been missed at the party. Her and James.

And so that was how James's name sounded when he said it. Sweet and lifted. Quiet.

She told a lie; she told a lie about James's father, about how he had been sick at the weekend, about how James had needed to go and see him.

And so had she, obviously. Obviously – and she let the implication hang there, let it sit on the air between them and do its insidious, straining attempt at work – obviously she had needed to go there, as well, with James.

(Cursing herself in the next moment for having caused Liam's face to become so filled with worry for James; to become so softened by concern for him, so tender with it—)

*

'Well, we'll all have to get a few drinks, now, when these exams are over,' Liam said, once she had assured him that James's father was fine, now, that there was no cause for alarm.

(*Or for caring*, she said to herself.)

Yes, a few drinks, Liam was saying; a few drinks after the exams. But Catherine shook her head.

'Well, James is pretty busy,' she said. 'I mean, with this exhibition he has coming up at the end of the summer.'

'Oh, aye,' Liam said, laughing as though she had said something funny. 'Ah, well, we'll try. I'll be around Dublin all summer.'

'Why?'

'Ah, you know, a bit of independence. Up home is fine, ah, but it's a quiet old spot. You know yourself. Have you something lined up?'

'I'm staying here.'

'Aye, but I mean, like, a job?'

And laughing again when she told him.

'But what kinds of things are you going to write for people? What kind of thing would you write, say, for me?'

*

> *As if a sober star had whispered it*
> *Above the revolving, rumbling city: stay clear.*

*

'What?!'

'Nothing. It's nothing. It's just a line from a poem.'

*

And all the time she had been talking to him, she realized afterwards, she had been trying to see it in him. Studying him; staring at him through their conversation, as through a strip of gauze. Trying to see: where was it in him? Was it that softness, that sweetness, in his voice? Was it that slight unsteadiness, always, in his smile? Was it that restlessness in his hands, their constant motion, their darting as he spoke to people? Was it in his brown eyes, the eyes that – yes – she could imagine James finding beautiful? Was it somewhere to be seen, to be read as though it was a kind of notation, in his clothes? In his video-game T-shirt? His baggy corduroys? His scruffy Vans?

And yet, so many of the boys in college dressed just that way—

And no, she could not believe she was doing this. She could not. She could not believe that this was what she was trying to do. That this was what she was, actually. That this was what she had revealed herself to be carrying. That she had so much fooled herself, flattered herself, into thinking that she was good. That she was so open, and so loving, and so all right with everyone, in every way—

Many things in the world have not been named; and many things, even if they have been named . . .

Because that was what she was looking for, wasn't it?

Because that was what she was trying, in Liam, to see.

*

UNIVERSITY OF DUBLIN

TRINITY COLLEGE

Faculty of Arts (Letters)

School of English

Senior Freshman Examination

English Studies / T.S.M. Trinity Term 1998

ROMANCE

Saturday, 23 May 1998   Regent House   9.30–12.30

Answer three questions
Candidates are warned against repeating material

1. Can it be claimed that medieval romances offer a significant comment upon and engagement with reality?

2. Write on images of divine activity in medieval romance.

3. 'Many romances are so episodically structured that they are more like collections of stories than one story, and consequently often appear to have no overall meaning.' Discuss.

4. 'Description of place in romance can carry all the excitement of furious action.' Do you agree?

5. 'A self-portrayal of feudal knighthood with its mores and ideals is the fundamental purpose of courtly romance.' Discuss Eric Auerbach's statement.

6. Write on the importance of episodes and interludes of delay in Romance narrative technique.

7. How significant is the title . . .

*

Dear Cit-Bag,

EXAMS ARE OVER. Therefore, leave the library at once. The pleasure of your company is requested at Le Pav RIGHT THIS MINUTE for some v.v. pleasant boozing, which will take place on the lawn, in the company of every single other person who attends this university, along with quite a few who do not, beneath the lovely rays of the lovely sunshine.

If you do not come, I will send Aidan to get you.

You are DULY WARNED.

Z

P.S. I know that James is around, because Liam – ☺! ☺! – tells me that they bumped into one another this morning – ☺! ☺! – so please inform him that the pleasure of his company is also required.

P.P.S. If you do not snog Little Emmet this evening, I will be very cross.

P.P.P.S. I may already be slightly drunk.

*

'Just look at them all!' Aidan said, as he walked her down from the library. 'It's like Milton, the fallen angels!'

Green sweep of the cricket lawns. Evening heat of the sun. All the hundreds of people stretched out, free now, drunk and happy and grateful, the whole, glinting summer before them.

Drop your bags. Lose your notes. Buy your cans, and slip off your sandals, and feel the grass cool on your callouses, on your unpainted toes. Sweet smells of several smokings. Lazy strummings of several guitars. Sunburn being nudged back to life on so many faces, freckles springing back to the surface on so many arms.

*

And James was already there.

*

'Howaya,' he said drowsily, and he waved to her, from where he lay, which was with his head in Zoe's lap, with Amy on one side, and Lisa on the other, his legs stretched out in front of him, his jeans rolled up. He was barefoot.

'Hiya,' Catherine said, standing over them. Aidan had gone in to the bar.

'Sit down, Cath,' Lisa said, patting the ground beside her, and Catherine sat down. Her limbs felt stiff. She did not know what to do with them. Lisa handed her a can.

'I must give you that photograph you took of James that day up in PhotoSoc, by the way,' she said. 'I finally developed that roll of film.'

'Oh?' James said.

'Yeah. Most of them were rubbish, but Catherine's one of you was lovely, actually. Really nice. You look like you're dreaming, or something.'

'Now, Reilly,' James said, as though this proved some point, and he sat up to take a sip from his own can. 'Anything I can do, you can do better.'

*

And Catherine could not even look at him. What had he meant by that? Had he meant it as some kind of comment on her? Something snide. She felt sure of it – her heart was pounding with her sureness of it – but she could not understand what it was he had meant; had he intended for her to understand?

332

But now he was laughing. Reaching across to her, actually, Catherine saw with a start – and touching her. Clasping her.

'Happy anniversary, Reilly,' he was saying, and she was staring at him, her mouth gone dry. Was she losing her mind? What was he talking about? Had he even said it, that thing that she felt quite sure that he had? *Happy anniversary?* What was he talking about? She stared at the date in her mind, but it meant nothing to her: the twenty-third of May? Was he taking the piss out of her? How drunk was he?

He was watching her, a smile on his lips, and the girls were laughing.

'Happy anniversary?' she said. 'What anniversary?'

'Ah, Reilly,' he said, and he came over to her, clambering across Lisa's legs. His breath was sharp with beer. 'The day after your exams finished last year was the first day we met. I was just telling the girls.'

'About you and your pea fetish,' Zoe said. 'And your hangover from trying to fall asleep in Conor Moran's arms. *State* of you.'

'You're an *eejit*, Reilly,' James said, and he put his arms around her, squeezing her, and her breath was gone. 'I'm so glad I met you,' he said, over her shoulder. And then, much more quietly, into her ear so that the others could not catch it, 'I'm sorry about everything.'

'*Awwww,*' Lisa was saying beside them; the sound of her had almost drowned out James's murmured words. But he had said them; Catherine saw from his eyes now, as he pulled back from her, that he had said them.

'James—'

But Zoe was scrambling to her feet now, a commotion. 'Hey, Liam! Liam! LIAM IS HERE!' she shouted, jumping and waving as though to a rescue helicopter. 'Liam! LIAM! We're OVER HERE!'

'Yeah, I think he hears you,' James said. 'I think all the Liams can hear you.'

'There's only one Liam I'm interested in,' said Zoe, as Liam, his cheeks pink and his hair a tangle and his smile wide and delighted at the sight of them, ambled over.

*

And they talked about everything, the two of them. Once they got going, there was nothing that they did not seem to cover.

They were drunk, Catherine knew, which helped – but still.

They stretched out on the grass, not beside each other but opposite each other, his feet alongside James's shoulders and James's feet alongside his, and the evening blazed down on them, and they talked on for hours. The others wove in and the others wove out, and Catherine was among them, the weavers, the contributors, the consulted, but the spine of it was the pair of them, laid out across from one another. Their voices climbing easily across the way.

*

And later, Zoe's argument, set out loudly and firmly and drunkenly.

*

Because she had heard it was the only place in town to go if you wanted to really, really dance.

Because it was a Saturday night, and on a Saturday night, everywhere else would be awful.

Because Conor and Emmet had at some stage joined them, and Conor and Emmet were making outraged noises about the idea of it, but Conor and Emmet would go where everyone else was going – 'I resent that!' Emmet said – and it would be such fun – 'I resent that!' – to watch them squirm.

Because Zoe had heard that the DJs there always played Madonna, a lot of Madonna, and Madonna was precisely what this occasion called for.

Because none of them – could this be possible? – not even Aidan, had ever been there before.

Because the sun had gone down.

*

Because James.

That was the actual reason.

Because Liam.

*

And maybe there were other gay clubs in Dublin, but this was the one everyone knew about. This was the one everyone used, after all, in jokes.

*

And Catherine could go with them or she could go home now, alone, to a house that would be empty, because Amy was here, and Lorraine and Cillian were out elsewhere; she could go back to a house that would come at her every instant with new panics, new versions of what was happening a mile away, of what was being forged.

That was the choice.

And as they crossed Front Square, somebody was whooping and somebody was turning cartwheels on the cobblestones, and somebody was hoisted, wobbling, onto Aidan's shoulders, and someone was puking, and someone was laughing, and the blue face of the clock was looking, watchful, down on them all. *Seen it all before*, it would say, if it could say, but it was a clock.

Tick-tock

Tick-tock

'The fucking drink better be cheap in this place,' she heard Emmet grumble behind her. 'That's all I can say.'

*

The drink was not cheap.

All these men, so handsome, so smiling—

(All these women, smiling that way too.)

'Fantastic,' Aidan kept saying, looking around as though in wonder, looking over the railings to the dance floor below. '*Fantastic*.'

Emmet, leaning back stiffly against the purple walls: 'Do you want binoculars, Murphy?'

*

Purple walls, and long velvet curtains, and velvet couches in bright reds and blues, and gilt edging on all of the furniture – everywhere was gilt, everywhere, and all of this oversized faux-Baroque, so that you could see the irony, you could see the confidence, you could see the gleeful wink and nod.

Tiny, twinkling lights strung down from the ceiling, all over the stairs.

And downstairs, in the lower part, was where the music they could hear now had its centre; the bass was reaching up here, full and determined and languid, but the heart of whatever was happening was down there, still out of sight, and the tune playing was one that Catherine could not place just now, but she knew it, she did—

('Jesus Christ,' said Emmet, as another guy in a white vest went past, smiling at him.)

'You love it, Doyle,' said Catherine, without enthusiasm; her eyes were on James. James, who was bundling, with Amy and Lisa and Zoe, onto one of the huge velvet couches. James who was falling into the cushions now, all elbows and knees and giddy laughter, something manic in the look of him—

Something scared.

So, safe enough yet?

That was what Catherine caught herself thinking. That if he was scared, if he was nervous, about being here, that then she was safe enough yet. That she might not be losing him just yet; that he might not be ready to go from her, after all—

In the next breath, despising her mind for the things it said to her. The places it allowed itself to go.

(But, safe enough yet?)

*

Conor and Emmet lasted twenty minutes, and then they left for the Stag's.

*

'Look at us,' Catherine said to James. They were standing in front of a wall covered entirely in tiny shards of mirror. Everything glinted in the countless tiny mirrors; everything shivered.

'So many of us,' James said, and he was waving.

'Come *on*!' said Zoe, and she was grabbing them, marching them downstairs, and they were rushing, then, into the opening swell of the song that began with seagull calls, and with waves crashing, and with the mock-up chords of a tune that had come to mean a smiling bride on her father's arm, and as they all clattered downstairs to the dance floor, there was the sound of the cymbals, and the keyboards, and as the light soared and swirled over everyone, over all of the upraised arms, there was the sound of the men's chorus, low and even and stern.

And there was the first word. The word pulling them together.

And then their feet hit the floor.

*

Bodies pulsing everywhere. Voices roaring out every syllable. Chests and hips and shoulders—

338

Lips and hands and tongues—

And the music like a shimmering, oceanic wall.

*

And this, *this*, now, this was a *really* brilliant song—

Everyone on the dance floor shouting for joy as they recognized it.

The people dancing on the stage actually dropping down, for a moment, to their knees—

*

Singing of mystery, of the mystery that life was.

*

And no, but really, had all these songs always been so brilliant, all along? These songs that had been only tinny radio rackets in your childhood, and only things you thought embarrassing in your teenage years, and now – now they were genius. Now they were perfect.

Was this just irony, this dancing, this sheer, sheer happy love, now, or was this honesty?

*

Were you meant to actually know which one it was?

(She could not work out anything; she could not work out anything about how things were meant to be.)

And full throttle now.

*

And on the dance floor, on the balcony, on the stairwell: full capacity. All the bodies, reaching; all the bodies, arching; all the bodies, surging in an imitation of prayer—

(Except: no imitation.)

And sweating, and singing, and hands held high, and the song was sweeping them up now, the song was bringing them home, and again there was a choir in the background, but this time it was a happy choir, this time it was a choir and you could hear that they were smiling—

*

And yes, it felt like . . .

*

And on the stage, the dancers were incredible. The dancers were heaven. Their bodies like angels. Their smiles like light.

Like this was another country.

That was what Catherine saw.

Everyone chanting now. Everyone, now, just part of the chorus.

(And how many other songs were there from your childhood that turned out to be so much about your life? Not just your life, but everybody's life? Everybody's happiness? Everybody's love?)

And so, so beautiful, James's face now; so, so beautiful, his body, with his arms in the air. Sweat dark under the arms of his T-shirt, now, and sweat shining on his forehead. And a twist of something on his face, now: pure pleasure, and pure joy—

(Nothing, it hit Catherine, that she had seen before.)

He opened his eyes, and he smiled at her.

And Catherine reached out her hand.

And around his waist at that moment, other hands came, and other arms, and James leaned back into them, smiling, and James let fall; James let go.

*

James let everything go.

*

And the girls whooping and cheering as though they were at a concert, and as though James and Liam were the stars. As though, just by touching each other, just by dancing together the way they now were, they had walked out on stage, smiling at everyone—

(But they were only smiling at each other, Catherine saw.)

And the girls – the girls were smiling at each other, as though together they had achieved something, together they had brought something into being—

Slipping away from the two of them now, melting away discreetly from the group they had been, so that the group became a smaller one, and so that James and Liam were in a space all of their own—

*

And who could not be happy for them?

Who could not want to smile, just at the sight of them?

*

Five minutes later, Catherine was walking through the door of the Stag's.

Conor, standing at the bar with some people she did not recognize. He studied her as she walked towards them. Her skin, she knew, still slick with sweat. Her hair still damp. Her eyes must have been wild.

Emmet—

'He's gone, Citóg,' Conor said. 'You couldn't expect him to just keep waiting around for you.'

'No,' she said, her voice small and hollow.

'Do you want a pint?'

'No. I think I'll go home.'

'Have a good summer, Citóg,' he said, and he gave her a hug.

10

And now: be good.

Now: be so, so good. Be good the way you had to be good; be good the way you told yourself you could be good, before—

Be good. Be good and then be still more good. Love is patient, remember. Love is kind. Love does not—

Love does not—

*

'We're just friends, for God's sake,' James said to Catherine, when he called around to Baggot Street the following evening. 'It was just a bit of dancing, was all it was. It was just a bit of saying hello.'

'Oh-ho, Jimbo!' said Cillian, upon seeing him in the kitchen, and he put his hand up for a high five. James obliged, blushing, shaking his head, on his lips a shy, half-hidden smile.

'Good man, Jimbo,' said Cillian, slapping him hard on the back. 'I hear the seal is well and truly broken. Fair fucking fucks to you. Literally.'

'About fucking time!' said Lorraine, as she came in, now, and she threw her arms around James. 'Well!' she said, holding him back so that she could get a good, interrogative look at him. '*Well?!*'

*

(Love does not do any of the things that you ask it, nicely, to do.)

*

And James, constantly smiling now. Even when he was not actually smiling, it was there; he had become, somehow, a smile.

'I'm telling you, *we're just friends*,' he said to Lorraine again, when she teased him.

Something so content, so utterly delighted with itself, in his eyes.

And Catherine standing right there beside him, feeling as though she was choking on all of the questions that she did not dare to ask.

*

Mars enters your house of love today. This brings on a highly romantic time, a time for meeting new people. If attached, you may find your relationship deepening. If single, you may find that someone wearing blue is the key to future possibilities. This person may be from another place, geographically or emotionally, and you may not, at first, think of them as a likely candidate for your affections; but be open, Aries. Change is a positive thing. Be aware, too, that hot on the heels of Mars, in the same sector, is the planet Saturn, the planet of work and responsibility, which may seem to present an obstacle to the pursuit of love; but it does not have to be so. This person may be the key to a future change of career, or to other possibilities which will open your eyes and fill your heart with happiness. Tuesday is a particularly auspicious day for you.

Mars enters your house of love today. This brings on a highly romantic time, a time for meeting new people. If attached, you may find your relationship deepening. If single, you may find that someone wearing blue is the key to future possibilities. This person may be from another place, geographically or emotionally, and you may not, at first, think of them as a likely candidate for your affections; but be open, Pisces. Change is a positive thing. Be aware, too, that hot on the heels of Mars, in the same sector, is the planet Saturn, the planet of work and responsibility, which may seem to present an obstacle to the pursuit of love; but it does not have to be so. This person may be the key to a future change of career, or to other possibilities which will open your eyes and fill your heart with happiness. Tuesday is a particularly auspicious day for you.

Mars enters your house of love today. This brings on a highly romantic time, a time for meeting new people. If attached, you may find your relationship deepening. If single, you may find that someone wearing blue is the key to future possibilities. This person may be from another place, geographically or emotionally, and you may not, at first, think of them as a likely candidate for your affections; but be open, Cancer. Change is a positive thing. Be aware, too, that hot on the heels of Mars, in the same sector, is the planet Saturn, the planet of work and responsibility, which may seem to present an obstacle to the pursuit of love; but it does not have to be so. This person may be the key to a future change of career, or to other possibilities which will open your eyes and fill your heart with happiness. Tuesday is a particularly auspicious day for you.

*

Some evenings he met with her after work, but some evenings he was not available to do this. Now he emailed her, something he had only ever done, before, when he had been chasing her; when he had been lonely for her letters in Berlin, wondering where she was, what she was doing instead of writing to him.

But now he was not chasing her. Now he was not lonely for want of word from her.

> Spending the evening in the darkroom, darling. Love to the others. See you tomorrow, maybe?

Love to the *others*?

*

But be good.

Be so, so good.

*

In the backyard of Baggot Street, a feral cat close to giving birth. Dragging herself around. The noise of her. Trying, as they watched from the steps, to burrow into a tangle of ivy.

'She's trying to get away from the pain of it,' Cillian said. 'She doesn't understand it's inside of her.'

Catherine stared at him. Could that be true? Could that possibly, possibly, be true?

*

The kittens, a few days later: tiny grey clouds of mewling, already with the pus on their eyes.

'Get, get,' Lorraine said, scattering them with the snap of a tea towel. Her face, tense with guilt when she came back into the house. 'There's no point,' she said to Catherine, though Catherine had not said a word.

*

Yellow will be your colour to watch for in the week ahead.

Do not run from the things it comes to you most naturally to fear.

A letter from a friend may bring you to see old situations in a radical new way.

*

She missed him. She missed him so much that the city did not feel like the same city anymore. It felt like the trace of a city, into which she had blindly wandered. Without him beside her, what were these streets?

*

Darkroom again this evening, I'm afraid – Lisa has been asking to see some possible photos for the show. You free for lunch on Saturday, maybe? Maybe get some food and bring it to the Green?

Lunch was for people you had tossed down to the *Sometime* pile. Everyone knew that.

*

Dear Cosmic Cit

GREETINGS from L'Arse End d'Italia!! I am very, very sunburned and very, very tired of running after these monsters, and I am at all times within moments of snapping several very small necks and spending the rest of my life in an Italian jail, but apart from that, life is good here. The young men are very forward and many of them ridiculously pretty, and that is quite enough to be going on with for now.

Speaking of pretty, any promising correspondence from Young Emmet? Any flirtatious little missives from Chicago? I must say, I am still teeming with impressedness (<u>should</u> be a word) re: your decisive march on the Stag's that last evening, even if it <u>was</u> a bit of a flop. But never mind. We will live to fight another day. Or you will. And he will. And there will be no fighting, just snogging. And I will be waving pom-poms from the sidelines.

Which brings me to JAMES! Not pom-poms, but snoggage, namely, with Nordie Liam. Has there been any? Has there been plenty? Please send updates asap! I have had one very coy, very no-news-here postcard from James, but the front of the postcard did show a whole lot of boys running naked around a beach – which, let's face it, seems like a rather good sign, does it not? I hope that the matter is progressing nicely. They are v.v. cute together, and I am not even saying I Told You So. But. I did. So write and tell me everything, because James is stubbornly refusing to.

Do I have any news for you? Not really. Life here is very hot and very worky. I am up with my charges from before seven in the morning, because the little buggers refuse to sleep any longer, and after that it is a long day of feeding and changing and cleaning and trips to the swimming pool and trips to the gelateria and brushing off Papa's unwanted advances, which, of course, just has the effect of making Papa all the more determined.

Anyway. Speaking of jobs, you are probably currently in your nightly communication with the stars and the planets to replenish your astounding astrological wisdoms for tomorrow, so I will not keep you any longer with dreary tales of other people's children and pathetic wonderings about other people's sex lives. Write me a PROPER LETTER, please, Cits. No postcards. I want one of those big fat envelopes you used to send to James. I need something to read other than crappy Italian bedtime stories.
TELL ME WHAT YOU HAVE BEEN UP TO.

    ZOE

*

She missed Zoe, she realized. She had not expected that to be the case.

She missed everyone. Even Emmet, who she did not think would be sending her any emails from Chicago, flirtatious or otherwise. Missing him surprised her. Everything surprised her.

And yet nothing did.

Because what had she been up to?

Sleep, as long as it lasted. Which was not – which was never – long enough.

And then the waking. And with it the thinking, *Maybe this time it will be different. Maybe this time it will not be so bad.*

But then the other waking. Then the second waking, the real one. Because how it worked, she had discovered, was this: body woke first, but body was innocent, body contained within itself space for some kind of oblivion. Mind; when mind kicked in, mind put a stop to that gallop. Mind; mind got to. Cranked it up. Piled it on; piled it down. Not just thoughts; they did not feel like just thoughts. They were whole life forms, living in the crevices; they were real things, happiest in the mornings, when they could pulse and they could roam. They were of her, but so much more than that, they were about her, and they were things – she felt sure of this – that she would not necessarily have come up with, herself, about herself, left to her own, small devices—

So much energy they had, the thoughts. Seemingly boundless, endless energy; she almost had to admire it in them.

*

And to have tried to drag Emmet down into this shit: unforgivable.

*

The skin on her arms, those mornings: so alive with the desire to be cut.

Tingling with the want of it. With the love of it.

But skin was dead, though, wasn't it?

Skin was the part of you that was already the leftovers of the past.

Or most obviously the leftovers, maybe; most visibly. Maybe that was what it was.

*

Do not push yourself past your limits.

Do not test yourself more than you can need or bear to be tested.

Do not take for granted those things you have been lucky to have—

In work, they were delighted with her. They raised her pay another ten pence a script.

*

A dream. More than once, the same dream. A bed pushed into the corner of a room. Boxes piled high around it, so that its warmth became a hiding place, and within that hiding place was the still deeper, still warmer cocoon of his arms. She curled into him; she smelled his smell. She dozed, blissful; woke to the sound of his voice saying, *Catherine, you're—*

Never the end of the sentence. Never what it was that he thought she was, what it was that he believed of her. She tried playing it over to herself during her waking hours: sitting on the bus, staring at the cursor, drinking the powdered coffee the factory machine made—

But it never finished itself. And Catherine could not finish it either.

11

What conversations they had now seemed only rubble.

Sitting, barely remembering how to talk to each other, over a half-touched picnic on the Green.

The look in his eye: as though she was the one who had gone from him.

As though there was so much he had to tell her; had, now, to share with her—

But no.

*

How are things?

How was your week?

How are your fake fucking horoscopes that are just as useless and empty as you?

How are our friends who are so relieved that I escaped you?

(The last two would have been honest, at least.)

*

Small talk as insult.

*

How are you?

That was the question he seemed to know it was better not to ask.

And the question she would not ask him:

How is your boyfriend?

*

Because there was little doubt but that a boyfriend was what Liam was, by now.

'I really *like* him, Lorraine,' she overheard James say in the kitchen, one of the nights he came round to visit them. 'I mean, *really*. I mean, a lot.'

'Bring him round to meet us, for Christ's sake,' said Lorraine, her voice so soft, so tender. 'Bring him for dinner on Friday night. You can stay. You can have my room, the two of you; Cillian and I can sleep in the sitting room. Why not? Make a night of it. Bring him round.'

*

The panic breaking over her. The idea of it. The two of them, just on the other side of the chipboard wall. The noise of them—

*

She took the train home for the weekend. Her mother eyeing her, suspicious. Ellen pretending, in the room at night, not to hear her cry.

(This was a deal she and Ellen had long had.)

Sunlight on the mid-July hayfields. All the local farmers out driving tractors as though they were racing cars. Anna turning cartwheels on the lawn.

*

'How's James these days?' her mother said, on the drive back to the train station. 'Is he back from Germany?'

Catherine stared at her. 'James?'

'Yes, James,' her mother said with exaggerated patience. 'I presume he's back for the summer again, is he?'

'I . . .'

'Listen, Catherine, I should have said this to you long before now, but it was a pity, what happened last summer. You know?'

She could not speak.

'It was just a pity you had to say anything at all. If you'd said nothing at all, it would have been fine, sure. Sure you know that. Sure I know you have to have your pals.'

'Yeah,' Catherine managed.

'So, whoever it is has you in the state you're in, forget about him, for God's sake, and enjoy yourself with your friends. They're the ones who are worth your while in the long run. James and the rest of your friends.'

*

Was she imagining, now, *everything* that people seemed to be saying to her?

355

A man at the train station, asking her for the time; she fell back from him, frightened, thinking he was asking for a kiss.

Two girls, walking alongside her on Talbot Street, and Catherine could not shake the skin-prickling suspicion that they were bitching about her.

The bus driver on the number 10, saying goodnight, but had he actually accused her, rather, of not paying the right fare? *I'll see you, now* was what he had seemed to say, but was he actually saying *I see you*, meaning *I saw you*, meaning he thought that she had done something that she had not done?

She stared at him as the bus drove off again, and sure enough, he looked at her—

Sure enough, he had his eyes on her—

And then there was someone walking too close behind her on the walk back to the flat, and she broke into a run, and when she got there, she was so worked up that she had not even prepared herself for the possibility of James and Liam.

*

'Oh, they never came round,' Lorraine said, shrugging as though she had been asked about a football match she had not even known was on. 'I think we're doing it next weekend instead.'

*

Do not go blindly into a new business relationship.

Pluto, the ruler of your fifth house, turns direct this month, and things will become clearer.

A child will bring wisdom and surprise.

*

'You're as *thin*, Reilly,' he said, hugging her hello at Front Gate one evening. 'What's your secret?'

That skin on his face. She could strangle him.

His lips as he smiled. She hated him.

But she loved him more than life.

*

Love. Was this really love? Love set you going. Love set you going.

(But what else could it be?)

(And yes, there were times.)

(But even if you went into the farthest waters, from the farthest tip, someone would find you eventually. And then someone would have to see.)

*

Matters of the wallet are important today. Do not let go willingly of something you really need to keep.

The new moon of the 23rd will brighten your house of home; positive changes are afoot.

Where a friend is concerned, do not let them out of your mind for a moment.

*

An email from Emmet.

Cheerful. Cheeky. Teasing her about all the usual things.

Unanswered.

*

Lorraine: 'They're so *cute* together, Catherine. You should see them.'

*

Thinking, *Might not.* Thinking, *Need not.*

Might not last, that was.

Need not mean as much as it increasingly seemed to mean.

*

> July has been a busy month for you. It is time to
> sit back and take stock of what you have. A close
> relationship may seem to be suffering, but do not
> despair; close care and attention will bring you the
> results you desire. If a rival is in the picture, assess
> your options, but do not act rashly; remember that
> everything happens for a good reason. The new
> moon suggests that a new path is about to open up,
> and that you will be able to find solutions to old
> problems that have bothered you for a long time.
> Green is the colour to wear in the weeks ahead, as it
> will shroud you in the aura of new beginnings and a
> new, stronger sense of how things are meant to be—

It was such shite, such nonsense, and it was so easy to pro-
duce. She rigged the autocorrect function so that she could

get through them even more quickly; she programmed it to substitute whole, long phrases for certain words or abbreviations. The sentences rolled out in front of her eyes. The lies kept coming. The money kept coming in.

You will enjoy unprecedented prosperity this month.

Your abundance will bring you happiness.

*

The thing in her spit, in her gums. The dull taste of hating the day.

*

Every morning, the first thought was what the day, for them, would bring.

What the day, for them, would be.

What the light on his shoulder looked like in the minutes after waking.

Whether another person would even notice that.

What it felt like to walk Thomas Street in the ten o'clock sunshine with him, hands not touching, but hands wanting, so badly, to be touching.

What it felt like to say, on a street corner, *See you later*, and to know that those were not only throwaway words.

That those were not just words you said to someone to send them on their way.

Late afternoon, thinking of them thinking of each other. Thinking what their thoughts would look like; thinking what the shape of them would be.

And then the evenings.

The empty evenings.

*

Times when it was so hard not to pick up the phone.

Saying, *Liam? Is this Liam?*

And telling him – telling him—

*

Telling him what?!

She had nothing. She did not even have that.

*

She would do such things—

*

You will meet a very important person this week.

You will have a very meaningful dream this week.

This week will be very lucky for you. This week will be like no other.

*

Ellen was coming up to Dublin for the day. Looking for a flat for college.

'Can you meet me? Say six o'clock outside Trinity? Can I stay with you?'

But that was one of the James evenings. Ellen would have to take the last train home.

*

'James and Liam are coming round for dinner on Friday,' Lorraine said to her the next evening. 'Is that OK with you?'

'What?' Catherine said, staring at her. 'Here?'

'Yeah,' Lorraine said slowly. 'I told you they were coming some Friday evening. They'll probably stay. It'll be nice to have them around for the weekend. You don't have any plans, do you?'

*

Dear Callous Cit,

Why no love from you? Have you been so swept up into a transatlantic cyber affair that you have forgotten your sunburned, Italo-groped friend entirely? I am very sad not to have heard from you. You have caused me to look at the postman with such pathetic hope that he, along with every other man in this kip of a village, thinks he is in with a flying chance of a shag. Thanks v. much.

James, however, has been a little more forthcoming. Is this not v.v. exciting, this rapidly developing non-cyber, real-life-actual-boy love affair? James seems to be properly smitten. I am SO smug. Isn't the story about the photo and the line from the poem the sweetest thing you've ever heard? Very cute of James. Very—

*

She knew nothing of a photo. She knew nothing of a line from a poem.

*

She put this information with the other scraps of information. The things she knew it was better that she had never heard at all. The things she knew it was better for her to ignore.

*

But it refused, like all the rest of them, to leave her mind alone.

Thinking, *What poem?*

James did not read poems.

James did not harvest lines and gather them.

So what line had James taken from a poem?

*

It ran through her mind in the night-time and in the daytime, and it would not leave her be.

12

But she knew.

13

A voice calling out to her as she cut through campus.

PhotoSoc Lisa. Smiling, waving, happy-looking; why did everyone look so bloody happy?

Wanting to talk to Catherine about the photo she had been keeping for her; the photo of James that Catherine had taken with the Rolleiflex. Apologizing; walking towards Catherine, Lisa was already apologizing, already explaining; she had kept it, she was saying, for weeks, had been carrying it around in her bag, even, in the hope of bumping into Catherine just like this. Imagine! And now she had, and she didn't have it with her—

And it was all right, Catherine said, shrugging, wanting to be free of her; she could give it to her another time.

But Lisa, shaking her head, holding up her hands as though surrendering, and saying no, saying Catherine didn't understand: the photo was already gone. She had the negatives, of course – she could do another copy – but the photo was gone. It was just that she had bumped into Liam, one day – right here, in fact, just a week or so ago – and she and Liam had been chatting, and naturally, James had come up in conversation – wasn't it just *so lovely* about Liam and

James? – and she had taken out Catherine's photo of James, which she had still had on her, to show to Liam, and, well, it was just that Liam had loved it so much, had been so very taken with it—

And she had the negatives, she said again, and she could make another copy.

And as for that *amazing* portrait that James had made this month of Liam—

Had Catherine seen it?

It was beautiful, really beautiful; he was going to give it to Lisa for the John Street show, of course – it would be the centrepiece of the whole show, even, possibly—

Catherine *was* coming to the opening, wasn't she? James had passed on her invitation?

*

The *name* of the photo? Oh, yes, it had some name – some name from a poem – wait, now, until she thought of it; wait until she got it—

The heart is a thing that happens, would that be it?

The heart is where it happens?

The heart, anyway. She knew that much. She was certain of that much. It was *the heart* something, *the heart* – something to do with the heart.

The heart—

The heart—

*

Fuck the heart, Catherine said, and Lisa stared.

14

And of course she would not always do this, Catherine assured herself.

Of course, in the future, there would be others, and by then, Catherine assured herself, it would be fine. There would, by then, be no need. No problem. Everyone would get along swimmingly, and nicknames would be bestowed, and fondness would only grow with each golden, gorgeous evening—

A perfect future summer.

I really like him, Catherine. I mean, really. He's—

And James would say what he was. Whoever he was. James would say the sentence about him. James would finish the sentence.

And Catherine would listen, and smile.

*

Liam's voice as he answered the phone so confident, so bright. Expecting someone else, by the sound of it. Expecting someone who would bring something else to him.

Not this story that it was Catherine's only choice, now, to bring.

Her only option.

And yes, yes, said Liam, sounding bewildered, he could meet her that evening in O'Brien's. But would James—?

*

No, James would not be.

This would be just them.

*

And so what of it, if it was not happening in reality anymore, the thing Catherine told Liam was happening – the thing she told him was happening often, happening whenever the circumstances could allow?

What of it, if that thing was not actually, any longer, taking place?

Because it had happened. It had happened often.

And because it was happening. It was happening, every minute of every day still, in her mind.

*

His hands. His lips. His eyes.

His tongue, full and supple against hers.

And already waiting – already there – and surely that meant something? Surely that meant—?

His breath. The sound of it. The sound of what happened to it.

His hands. His lips. His eyes.

The way she wanted him to fuck her and fuck her until she dissolved.

*

The way he obliged.

*

The way he did not seem able to help himself; the way he was – and this was so *normal*, after all, she stressed, so *understandable* – so unsettled, so confused. Because, she said to Liam, these things were, after all, complicated, weren't they? These things – she was sure that he himself had had his doubts . . .

'My *doubts*?' Liam said, looking at her almost wildly, and for a moment Catherine thought he had said *My dice?*

(That accent. That accent which should never, ever, have been trusted.)

'No, Catherine,' he said, and he did it to her name again, rolled it out as though it was a name in another language. 'I've never had my *doubts.*'

*

(Well, that was his business.)

*

Well, it was just that she thought he deserved to know, was all, Catherine said, turning the beer mat over and over in her hands.

Pieces flaking and crumbling off of it. The thick square of it, soggy with the Guinness she had spilled, sitting down.

It was just, Catherine said, that she had decided that – for both their sakes – this could not go on any longer.

This deception.

This lie.

Did he see what she meant? Did he understand why she had had to tell him?

(Dates, all stored up and ready to give to him. Evenings, and mornings, and weekends; because she had known every moment of that summer. She had known, every moment, where James was, and she could remember every evening that he had been with her, and every evening that he had not, and so, she could list them out.)

*

'I can't believe this, Catherine,' Liam said, but she could see that he could.

The trouble in his eyes; she could see the trouble she had put there.

And she had never had any doubt, really, but that he would believe her.

Because, when it came down to it, really, how could you ever be sure of knowing any other person?

Really knowing them?

And Liam knew this, she saw. Liam understood this.

*

On the way home she stopped at Patrick Kavanagh's bench.

The bronze face glared.

*

And even if it was not true now, the thing she had told Liam, then still it was true in the core of her, and the core of things was, wasn't it, what mattered?

The core of things was what counted.

And it was just that it was not Liam's time for James, she told herself.

Not yet.

*

'You're looking better,' Lorraine said to her, that evening. 'You've been looking so tired lately.'

    'All those bloody horoscopes,' Catherine said.

    Lorraine smiled. 'Exhausted from seeing what lies ahead of us.'

*

In a day or two you will know where you stand
in relation to something important to you.

This week will bring closure.

This week will bring a return.

*

And no, of course Catherine had not thought it through.

What James would or would not say; what he would or would
not be able to say to Liam, to undo the things Catherine had
told him, to turn Catherine's truths into fictions with a wave
of his hand—

She had not yet come to that part of the thinking.

Because she had not been thinking at all, actually.

She had only been doing what her every bone and every blood
cell had ordered her to do.

*

The knock on the door. The knock, loud; loud and angry.

Lorraine going to answer it, and Lorraine's cheery hello, and
Lorraine's cheery hello faltering into concern, into confusion,
as James walked past her, calling Catherine's name, giving
Catherine's name two syllables, and both of them ugly, and
both of them sharp—

Catherine went to meet him.

His face, leached of light.

372

His eyes, in them nothing she had seen before.

And still her stupid heart leaping at the sight of him.

*

And everybody hearing. Lorraine, Cillian, the friends who were over at the time, visiting them – everyone. The people in the flat upstairs; the people downstairs; the people in the houses on either side, even. They would be hearing them; they would be hearing James as he roared at her. What would they make of him, Catherine found herself wondering – worrying – as she stood there, in the path of him? What would they think of the things he was letting them hear?

'People can hear you, James,' she said, at one point. 'Everyone can hear.'

He looked at her. She had stopped him, at least; she had stopped him mid-flow. At least there was that; at least there was this silence, merciful between them, for these moments.

(Even if there was that look in his eyes.)

And then he spoke.

'Christ,' he said, 'You learned your spake from the best of them. *People can hear?* Christ, you were taught and taught well.'

(His spittle, as the words formed, landing on her cheeks, landing on her lips as they opened to try and form words of her own.)

(She did not wipe it away.)

*

That she was devious, controlling, manipulative.

(Well, she knew that.)

That she was insane.

(And she knew that, too.)

That she could not bear to see him happy. That she could not bear to see him have something, someone, of his own. That she could not stand not to get her own way, when her own way was what she had always made damn sure of getting; that she was a spoiled child, a self-absorbed child; that she was a madwoman, that she was hysterical, that she was out of her disturbed and unstable mind. The way she had clung to him – followed him home to Carrigfinn – the way she had gone behind his back with his boyfriend, or tried to; what was fucking *wrong* with her, for Christ's sake? Why would anybody want to go on in that way?

(Why, indeed.)

And that she was wrong, too. That was the greatest irony of it. That was the laugh, almost; that was almost the laugh. That she was wrong about Liam. Wrong about him. That she was wrong if she thought that it had been so easy, that any of this was, for James, in any way easy; in any way just something into which and through which he just wandered, easily, blissfully, as though he was just as much of a child as her. That none of this was easy for him. That so little of what he had

374

brought home with him from Berlin had gone away. That Liam had made things easier, had made things feel lighter, but that Liam had not just wiped all slates clean. That every day was still difficult, that every day there was still the fear; not being able to hold his boyfriend's hand in the street, for instance – did she have any idea what that felt like? And even though they were not holding hands, seeing the way people looked at them, knowing that people saw them, and knew, and hated them – did she have any idea what that was like? Probably not, because she was one of those people, actually, wasn't she? She was one of those people who begrudged them every precious scrap of what they had? Wasn't she? Yes, she was. Yes, she was, no matter what she tried to tell herself – well, then, if she was not, then why had she done what she had done? How could she have done what she had done? How could she ever have thought—? What kind of *fool* had she taken Liam for? Did she honestly think that Liam would believe something like that of him? No, he hadn't; no, he hadn't, no matter what it had looked like to her; no matter what Liam had looked like to her in the pub. And what did she think she was doing, anyway, arranging to meet his boyfriend in the pub? Arranging to lie to him? What was actually wrong with her? What had she turned into? Had she always been this way? Was it just that he had not seen it? Because, when it came down to it, they barely knew each other really, he and she; they had barely even known each other a year, if they were being honest. Writing those fucking letters to each other, like children, like penpals – his letters that – he knew, he knew fucking well – she had barely even bothered to read. Because they had not fitted with her nice, light, college-girl lifestyle. Because they had not fitted with her boys and her parties and with all of the things that she had wanted to do more than she had wanted to bother with the trouble of being a friend to him. Until he had decided to act the same way, of course. Until he had decided, himself, to strike out on his own, to stand on his own feet. Oh, *then* it had stopped being all right for her, not to have him where she could see him, not to be aware of his every breath, his every move; *then* it had stopped suiting her.

Well, this was an end to it. This was the end of it; this was the fucking limit of it. Because it was laughable, *laughable*, what she had done, what she had tried to do – as though he would want to touch her. As though he had ever, *ever* wanted to touch her; did she really think otherwise? Did she really delude herself so badly? No – no – she was not to touch him, now, she was not to even *try* to touch him – she was to keep her hands well and truly clear of him, that was what she was to do, and she was not to come near him again, and she was certainly not to come near his boyfriend again, and she was to leave them the *fuck* alone, and get her own life, not this pathetic, clinging shit she was up to now, acting like someone who was actually insane – no. No more, Catherine. He was not doing this anymore; he was not putting up with this anymore. He would not be coming here anymore; he would miss seeing Amy and Lorraine and Cillian, but they would find other ways to see each other; they would find other ways to maintain the friendships that had been in place long before she had come along, and that would be in place long, long after.

And as for Liam – he and Liam – he and Liam were getting out of the city this weekend, up to stay with Liam's parents, because Christ knew they needed to get away for a couple of days after the shit she had put them through; Christ knew they needed to get out of the city and somewhere they could

376

relax without worrying about bumping into her, or about being stalked by her – because that was what she had been doing, did she not understand? Stalking them? Stalking them like some kind of fucking psychopath?

They were *gone* – did she understand that? They were getting on a bus in the morning, and they were *gone*.

Did she understand that?

Fucking nutcase. Fucking *limit*.

*

(And God help her, what she most wanted to know, in that moment, was whether Liam's parents knew about Liam and James. Whether Liam had told them. Whether, when they arrived up there for the weekend, would it be as a couple, would James be there as Liam's boyfriend, and would Liam's parents have no issue with that? Would Liam's parents be happy for them to walk around the town, whatever town it was, and for anybody who saw them to see them? And maybe to know?)

(This was what she found herself thinking, as she watched the front door slam.)

(Which meant that he was right, didn't it?)

(*Christ, you were taught and taught well.*)

*

'Don't even talk to me,' Lorraine said, when Catherine walked back into the sitting room, shaking, the tears finally, frantically beginning to fall. 'Don't even look at me, Catherine.

377

I can't believe you. I can't believe you would try to do that to him. After all that he's gone through. After all we've seen him go through. He's finally happy, and you try to – you try to – I can't even understand you. I don't *want* to understand you. I have to be honest with you, Catherine, I think you should go. I think you should leave. I don't think there's any place for you here anymore.'

(*He never said he was happy*, was what Catherine thought.)

*

And she did not expect that Lorraine would talk to her again.

She expected that the silent treatment she was given that evening, and the next evening, and all of Saturday morning, and into Saturday afternoon – Lorraine and Cillian ignoring her, talking to one another as though she was not there – would continue, and that it would be a full weekend of silence, and a full week of it, and another, until she managed to find another place in which to live—

And she was fine with that. Or she was growing fine with that. She had cried all the tears she had to cry. She had hoped all the hope she was going to bother with. She had no use for it anymore. She needed to leave no room for it. This was not, it turned out, a terrible feeling. This numbness, this emptiness, was not the worst way to feel. She watched a lot of television, and she did not move from the armchair which was farthest from the sitting-room door, so that, if someone came in, she would find herself less tempted to look at them, less naturally inclined—

It was golf on the television all that Saturday afternoon, which she did not understand even in the slightest, but which she let herself watch for hours anyway. Slumped in the armchair for two days. No horoscopes on the Friday; they could do without her, she had decided. She had made a couple of grand out of them, and that would keep her going for a while, that would give her the deposit and the first month's rent on a new place, and someone else, some other robot, could create lies about how people's lives were going to turn for them, about how people's days were going to be—

Her poems; maybe she would go back to her poems now, or maybe – *what happens in the heart* – maybe, actually, probably not. Something else. Something with a cleaner, blanker kind of slate. *Putt* again of the golf ball, and murmur of applause from the crowd so genteel that they did not even need a cordon, the crowd who stood there like good boys and girls, trailed the golfers across the course like a sea of chaperones. *Putt.* And applause. And the sun was streaming hot through the big bay window. And the picture on the television was filtered through its dusty, heavy haze. A red band running around the bottom of the screen now, but Catherine could not make it out, Catherine could not be bothered to squint at it; *putt*, and applause. *Putt*, and applause. Walk, and the crowd goes with you – stop, and the crowd stops too—

Then a clatter from the hallway. The clatter of someone tripping on the way from the kitchen, and then, over the clatter, someone calling her name. Someone coming closer; someone up on their feet again, coming towards the sitting room, calling – shouting – Catherine's name.

Lorraine.

Catherine almost laughed at the sound of her; *that didn't last long,* was what she thought. Probably, Lorraine had discovered that all her cigarettes were gone, and had made the assumption that Catherine had helped herself to what was left of hers. But she was wrong, and Catherine looked forward to telling her. Catherine looked forward to—

Lorraine at the sitting-room door now.

'Catherine,' she said again, and Catherine saw; Lorraine had the transistor radio from the kitchen clutched in her hands.

Her voice, when she said Catherine's name, sounded at once very old and very young.

And her face. It surprised Catherine that faces could actually turn that pale. That they could be so drained; drained of every drop of blood. And yet, still, the freckles as dark as ever; seeming darker, even, and more vivid, even, against the whiteness; spilling across the whiteness like tarnished stars.

And her hands. Her hands, trembling so violently, Catherine saw now, that the radio should surely have fallen. That the radio could not stay—

And in that moment, the radio fell. Bouncing off the carpet; the battery cover knocked off, the batteries spread—

The voices silenced.

'Catherine,' Lorraine said, 'Have you heard from James today? Have you heard from Liam?'

Catherine stared. Was this some kind of joke?

'*Catherine*,' Lorraine said, and now a sob had leapt into her voice, and her hands, which had been hanging, went to her temples, went to her hair. 'Catherine,' she said, and she said a sentence that Catherine did not understand. Some of the words she understood, and one of them she could not but understand – it was not a word you could ignore – but another of them, the most important of them, she could not understand; not just what it was, but how it was relevant, how it was relevant to them. Relevant to Lorraine, standing, really crying now, crying ragged, frightened tears in the doorway, the parts of the radio scattered, useless, at her feet; relevant to Catherine, sitting, still half hearing the *putt* and applause, in her big soft armchair in the afternoon sun. Relevant to James, or relevant to Liam, who were up with Liam's parents in Enniskillen, or Derry, or wherever it was—

And then Catherine understood the other word.

Ah, a quiet old spot, she heard Liam's voice saying, from a day when Liam had not yet been Liam.

Except, she had been wrong about that, as well.

'Catherine,' Lorraine was saying now, trying to pull herself together; dragging palms across her streaming eyes, pushing wrists against her streaming nose. Gathering the batteries of the radio, as though that mattered; as though hearing those voices, and the news they were bringing, would change a single thing. 'Catherine. We have to do something. We have to—'

But Catherine could only stare.

Because what was it, exactly, that they were meant to do?

What was it that they, two people standing in a sitting room, could possibly do?

UNTITLED

James gave the same name to every portrait he took that day.

Untitled
Gelatin Silver Print, 1998
178 x 120cm

Untitled
Gelatin Silver Print, 1998
178 x 120cm

Untitled
Gelatin Silver Print, 1998
178 x 120cm

Untitled
Gelatin Silver Print, 1998
275 x 180cm

Untitled
Gelatin Silver Print, 1998
178 x 120cm

Untitled
Gelatin Silver Print, 1998
178 x 120cm

Untitled
Gelatin Silver Print, 1998
178 x 120cm

Liam was the larger portrait. Liam: not the portrait of him that Lisa had expected as the centrepiece, but a newer portrait, and a starker one. The *Irish Times* review a few days later described how people at the opening had crowded around the portrait; how they had asked whether anything was known of its subject; whether he had recovered; whether he would be OK.

But then people had probably wondered that about all seven of the portraits, Catherine thought, about all seven of the subjects: about the three other men, one of them very elderly, staring gravely at the camera; about the three women, one of them pregnant, one of them crying, the tears glistening on her face.

The series was titled simply *Omagh*, and it was shown in its entirety at the show on John Street, a month and four days after the bombing. Which was too soon, some people said, especially given that most of the subjects were either still in the hospital where James had photographed them, or only recently discharged. Not to mention that so many others had never even made it to a hospital bed.

But James would not care for what people said, Catherine knew. James, she knew, would be very, very clear about what he was doing with the photographs, and why.

James. Who had escaped injury. Who had escaped worse. Who had separated from Liam for half an hour that afternoon to go to a camera shop on the other side of town, leaving Liam to run an errand for his mother. Milk, it had been. Just milk. To buy the milk, he had headed for a supermarket down the town, taking his time in getting there, calling in to the record shop on the way, to the bookshop, to the shop where, occasionally, they had in some decent-looking jeans. But what did any of this detail matter? Liam gave it to a journalist a few weeks later – the journalist, in fact, who had been at the party for Ed Dunne – and the journalist, writing a story on James's show, had worked the details up into a narrative stark and unsettling in its simplicity, in the simplicity of a twenty-year-old man going out, on a Saturday, to buy his mother a carton of milk—

What did any of the details matter? A red Vauxhall, a Cavalier, the explosives packed into it like things needed for a trip. The number plates changed; the two men who had parked it gone, long gone, and the warnings phoned in to three different places, so that the overall effect was one of confusion – deliberately, accidentally, who knew? Who would differentiate? It was half past two on a Saturday afternoon. Liam was already on Market Street, weaving through the crowds of shoppers and tourists, when the evacuations began, when the police began cordoning people into the area, people who were complaining, but not particularly worried; laughing and chatting, many of them. Long grown used to this kind of drill: the threat, the scare, the all-clear shortly afterwards, the afternoon interrupted and the groceries yet to be bought.

Ten past three.

And for a few seconds after the explosion, said the next day's newspapers, there was a silence, a frozen, disbelieving silence.

And then the screaming.

*

James, on the other side of the cordons, frowning down towards the other end of town, asking people around him if they knew any more than he did.

And then the noise of it. A noise like nothing he had ever heard before, he told the journalist, but a noise, still, that he could not but recognize. Not like a thunderclap, no, no. Nothing like a thunderclap.

What had it sounded like? It had sounded like the thing that it had been.

And then the silence.

And then the screaming. Except that James described it as wailing. James described it as wailing that rose from the streets in front of him and climbed, twisting and growing, into the blackened, burned air.

*

(Although maybe that had been the description of the journalist. The journalist who so loved the look of her own words; so loved the shapes they made, the rhythms of them.)

*

Catherine was not at the opening. Catherine knew that it was not her place to be there.

But she went to see the photographs, the next day, when the gallery – not even a gallery, just the stripped-down floor of

388

what had until recently been a shoe factory – was quiet, when the only other person there was the attendant, a girl her own age, who did not give her a second glance.

After the reviews began to come, the gallery would not be quiet anymore. But on that day, it was just Catherine, and just the attendant, and then the attendant slipped out, and it was just Catherine, and just what James had seen. What James had understood.

They were the photographs which made his name.

FRIEZE
(2012)

'Astonishing piece, isn't it?' said the gallery assistant, thin as a hatstand and with the face of a John Currin child, as she joined Catherine in front of the new Zhu Wang. The piece was enormous, its thickly sludged canvas taking up almost the entire back wall of the Lewis booth, and it was astonishing, all right, but for all the worst possible reasons: its gimmickry, its sloppiness, and the artist's very obvious hunger to be done with it so that he could move on to its equally high-earning successor. Catherine shook her head slowly, to suggest that words could not suffice in the face of such artistry, and let her gaze scan them again, the red and scarlet clumps of oil paint, the rusted nails pressed into them like twigs crushed underfoot.

'It's really a masterful one of Zhu's,' the gallery assistant said. She was straining, Catherine knew, to read the laminated name tag hiding itself between Catherine's jacket lapels; though it was the second afternoon of the fair and the grabbing and slavering of the big collectors was therefore over with, still Catherine – well-dressed, passably well-groomed – could be somebody it was important to greet – as the girl, finally making out the dangling name and affiliation, realized that Catherine indeed was.

'Oh my goodness, you're Catherine from *Frieze*?' she said, and her smile took on its full Manhattan wattage – although they were not in Manhattan, actually; they were on a small island to the east of Manhattan, Randall's Island, which, because it had space for the giant marquee, had been chosen as a site for the first New York edition of the Frieze fair. 'It's so good to meet you! I really want to come to your criticism panel later! I'm Ashley – I work with—'

'Nice to meet you too,' Catherine said, extending a hand. 'We're all so glad the gallery could be part of our first New York fair.'

This was disingenuous, and both women knew it; even the uncovering of a forgery operation in Nate Lewis's back rooms would scarcely have been enough to block his gallery's participation in the fair. As soon as it had been decided that there would be a Frieze fair here, it was assumed that Lewis would not only take part but would be assigned one of the most prominent booths; today, Catherine had spotted the Wang as soon as she had walked through the huge tent's glass doors. The other pieces in the booth were also by big-name Lewis artists: the Lucas Borga dot drawings, the long, low marble Falken, the Michael Woyzcuk metal frames with the stones suspended in them like mutated bell tongues. There was a piece from the Wittenborn archive, and a very delicate, actually quite beautiful little Clara Long, and in the middle of the space, on a pedestal, a yellow Meccano structure which revealed itself, as Catherine came closer to it, to be a miniature camera tripod; a small Diana camera had been painted exactly the same yellow – the case, the lens, everything – and was perched atop it.

'That's a Noh Ritter,' Ashley said, following behind. 'She just joined us in March, as you might have heard.'

'Mmm,' Catherine said.

'We're all very excited about her new show. If you're still in town, the opening is—'

'Oh, no, unfortunately I'm really just here to do the panel, and then I have to get back to London. The July issue is about to go to print.'

'Oh, that's such a pity. Nate will be so sorry to have missed you, too. He was here earlier, but he's in LA now until Tuesday.'

'What a pity,' Catherine nodded.

'And you actually *know* Nate a little, right? From Ireland?'

'Well, not really. I mean, we met, but that was a long time ago. A very long time ago, really. I'm surprised he remembers.'

'Oh, he remembers everything,' Ashley said with a theatrical little lift of her eyebrows.

'Yes, I'm sure,' said Catherine, trying, with her laugh, to achieve the same tone.

'Of course, you're Irish,' Ashley said, tilting her head now. 'But to be honest your accent sounds English to me.'

'Well. I've been living in London since I was twenty. That does things to your accent.'

'Oh – there! I can hear it!' Ashley trilled, pleased as a child who has just heard the first cuckoo. 'Yeah! *Does things*,' she said, in the ridiculous Hollywood brogue always used at such moments. But it could be worse. Ashley could be interrogating her further about her connection to Nate, and putting two and two together, with the glue of the Irish accent, and coming up with—

'Wait, so do you know James Flynn?' Ashley said then, more quietly, leaning in as though the matter was a confidential one, as though the knowledge of James and Nate's now long-ended relationship was not as public, at least within the art scene, as these things could be. The rising young star just arrived in the city and the dapper young gallerist just opening his own space; the sell-out show and the affair that was an open secret; the older lover, wronged and betrayed and with his career on the skids and, a year and a half into the whole business, found dead in his loft on West 26th Street. Ed Dunne had in fact suffered a massive heart attack, as became clear with the coroner's report a couple of weeks later, but this was 2005, when Gawker and the other media gossip sites were climbing towards their gleeful zenith, and the circumstances of Dunne's death were the tinder for several posts about James and Nate and the tragedy to which their glamorous liaison had led. In London, Catherine, then still freelancing, had called into the internet cafe on the corner almost hourly for updates; she had pored over the photographs of James and Nate at openings, of Nate and Dunne in their loft, of the glass-and-steel exterior of the new Lewis gallery, of James's works on display there, that portrait series for which he had got so much attention – the high-school footballers, the bodega men, the hipster boys with their tattoos and their mullets, their four-hundred-dollar skinny jeans. James looked almost like one of those boys himself now, which Catherine found, out of all of it, almost the hardest thing to believe; there was a photograph of him standing outside the main entrance of Lewis at an opening, smoking, a bottle of Presidente in his hand, and his lip was curled like someone she had never known, and his clothes were shabby and expensive, and his eyes were sharp with cynicism and dark with something deeper.

He and Nate had lasted another couple of months after Dunne's death, and then there had been the break-up, and the swoop of Jonathan Greene to snatch James away from the Lewis Gallery; by then, Catherine was an assistant editor at *Frieze*, and could track the story from the comfort of her cubicle and her high-speed broadband, and still call it work.

At Jonathan Greene in early 2007, there had been the collaboration with Ryan McGinley; in 2008 the *HO-HO-HOPE!*

show, which had got the *Artforum* cover, and soon afterwards, the Infinity Award. On each of these occasions, Catherine was tempted to send a congratulatory note to James; she knew the magazine stationery would get any correspondence marked *Personal* past the gallery's gatekeepers and on to his apartment in (she knew this from a *Vogue* profile) Bushwick. But she never knew what to say, or rather, how to go about saying it. She tried; she wrote the sentences; always, she ended up crossing the office to the industrial-sized shredder, and watching to make sure that they had turned into off-white ribbons. When, in June 2010, the civil union announcement appeared in 'Vows', with its language of almost comic combinations and formalities – *James Flynn, 32, the son of Peggy Flynn and Michael T. Flynn of Leitrim, Ireland, will commit Sunday to Christian Brandt, 33, a son of Denise C. Brown and Dr. Arthur D. Brandt of Stamford, Connecticut* – Catherine had actually gone to Paperchase and bought a card with two little, blue-tuxedoed, grooms – *I don't think Armani does a navy-blue taxedo*, she had written inside it, across from her fondest wishes for many, many years of happiness and love, and that card was still in her desk on Montclare Street, just waiting for the office franking machine – just the office franking machine, that was all.

That was not all.

(Things, with her own groom, beginning to go so depressingly, irretrievably south during that same summer; that had not helped matters either, although it had also, arguably, been completely beside the point. *Catherine M. Reilly, a daughter of Patricia M. Reilly and Charlie F. Reilly of Longford, Ireland, and Lucien F. Gordon, the son of Appalled Alexandra A. Gordon and Flare-Nostrilled Thomas E. Gordon of Lancashire, et cetera, et cetera, were married Saturday and separated Monday, or near enough as makes no difference . . .)*

'Oh no, not really,' Catherine said to Ashley now, with an apologetic wince. 'I mean, I *know* of him, but Ireland's funny like that. You'd be surprised the way that with some people, your paths never cross.'

'Oh, I can *really* hear your accent now,' said Ashley, staring at Catherine's mouth in seeming wonder.

'Ha.'

'Well, anyway, if you're interested, there's a big Flynn in the Greene booth across the way,' Ashley said, pointing to the booth opposite, which was equally spacious, equally well-appointed, and equally equipped with a young blonde assistant and a Russian bank vault's worth of pieces. 'I really like it, actually, though I'm not always sure about his work.'

'Oh, I know what you mean,' Catherine said, and with a smile and a thank you, she said goodbye.

*

The glass-walled auditorium in the centre of the tent was full to capacity for the criticism panel. That was down to the participation of Hal Foster and Roberta Smith, though Dan Franks had his own groupies, too, Catherine suspected, and she noticed that while when Foster or Smith spoke, there was respectful silence, contributions from Franks set a restless sort of charge ticking in the room, not the kind which made people want to get up and leave, but the kind which made them want to stand up and demand to hear more. Franks was in his late thirties, and was the founding editor of *Mauve*, a quarterly magazine dedicated to the crossover of contemporary art and fashion, the art content of which consisted partly of unsigned, notoriously snipey reviews, but mostly of photo essays of beautiful girls lying naked and spreadeagled across rusted fire escapes in Bushwick and long, possibly ketamine-fuelled Q&As with high-end photographers or artists who had connections to the designers whose ads comprised most of the rest of the magazine. Though this was unfair, Catherine reflected now, half listening as Franks defended the particularly savage review of the Lucas Borga show which had run in *Mauve*'s winter issue; the magazine had alerted her to the existence of countless younger artists she would never have found out about from the pages of *Artforum* or indeed *Frieze*, much less the *New Yorker* or the *New York Times*.

Under her blazer, the short sleeves of her silk blouse were soaked through with sweat; she widened her elbows a little more on the table in an attempt to distract herself from the discomfort, and prayed that Foster, beside her, was too caught up in his evident bemusement by Franks to notice any odour there happened to be. She looked down at her notes – *Maintaining Independence, Making Decisions, Dangers of Celebrification, Pissing People Off*, one of her checklists read, and she underlined the last and began to mentally prepare a follow-up question for Smith, bouncing off of Franks' remarks, when her gaze, floating languidly over the audience as she chewed over the words *enemy* and *adversary*, seemed, all at once, in the same moment, to clamp down and yet swerve maniacally. The room was not spinning, but slamming off of itself, like a rubber ball off a set of narrow walls, and she blinked as his face came into focus and then into yet another focus that was so sharp, so visceral, that the first instant of focus seemed only some kind of dreamlike meandering – and he was not looking at her, but now he was, and the eyebrow lift and half-smile he gave her before turning his attention back to Franks was as shocking to her, as much of a jolt to her whole being, as though he had stood up and somehow sung out her name.

Beside her, Foster cleared his throat, and Catherine realized that she had let hang onstage a moment of awkward, unshepherded silence, and into the microphone she let slip an awkward, unshepherded sound: the exhalation of someone who has just been obliged to run up several flights of stairs. Foster looked at her with an enquiring smile, and she turned to him with the follow-up question that was specific only to the coverage of the *Times*, and he took it like the fuck-up it was, and he babysat it for a while and then he handed it, smoothed out and newly layered, on to Smith, and by the time it came back to Catherine, ready to become the segue that would bring the whole discussion to a close, she had determined two things: firstly, that the audience was not a thing that needed to be looked at again, not even glanced at, not even during the long questions-from-the-audience part of the event which she would now have to moderate, and secondly, that her new Isabel Marant blouse was now ruined beyond repair.

*

The cheerfulness with which she would bestow her greeting would be immense. The warmth would be like a late-evening sun. The affection would be clearly of old, and deep-seated, and barely needing words, even, to settle its amber glow on the heavy air between them, and her smile would be so easy, so natural, and yet so full of knowledge, so full of understanding, of the things that had never been spoken, of the years that had marched through them, and over them, uninterested in the nature of their participation, uninterested in the way it had fallen apart like wet paper, their bond—

(Not wet paper. A tear. A craft knife, its triangular blade

down a strip of cardboard, cleaving it so neatly, with such apparent symmetry, the trace of the wound visible even on the surface beneath the space where the parts had joined—)

So many times she had visualized it, dreamed it: their meeting again. At such moments, in such places that she was often ashamed, felt almost diseased with guilt at her own thoughts; even walking up the aisle to Lucien, she had imagined it: his smiling, well-wishing face in the crowd. Only a flash, only the fraction of a moment, but still, it had been there. Yet such moments were uncontrolled; when she daydreamed, when she steered and directed her reveries, they were like this: she saw James first, in enough time to get a hold of herself, get a hold of her face and the expression in her eyes, before he saw her. Thus composed, thus arranged, she would be waiting, and in the street – it was always Dublin, it was always Wicklow Street, for some reason, within view of watching, fascinated people in the window of Cornucopia or one of the other restaurants – when he turned, or when his face, lost in thought, registered the trace of her, the whisper of her, the first, freighted sighting, around them the traffic of cars and shoppers would seem to hush and to become a gentle blur, and they two, two friends, two lost ones, two people who had once again found one another, would stare—

'Hi!' Catherine said instead now, almost squawked it, like a person hanging helplessly out of an upstairs window, having to attract help from below. 'Hi, hi!'

'Hi, hi,' James said, a deliberate – probably, yes, mocking – echo, as he leaned in, with that same half-smile, and kissed her lightly, quickly, on each cheek. She lifted her arms, jerked her body forward, for a hug, but he was already straightening up again, so she pulled herself back, and staggered a little, her lips moving too much, too madly, a stiffness already at the base of her skull as she gazed up at him. Had he always been so tall? Well, yes. You did not grow in your twenties. Not physically; not upwards.

(Had his eyes always been that startling shade of blue?)

'So, I saw you were moderating a panel,' he said, in an older, rounded-off version of the voice her memory so often thrust at her, 'and I thought—'

'I thought you were in bloody Venice!' Catherine interrupted him, having remembered, as soon as he opened his mouth, the bantering, art world line with which she had decided, soon after spotting him from the stage, to begin any conversation which might ensue; having used it now, though, it sounded unduly aggressive, not to mention stalker-ish; yes, someone in her profession would naturally know that James was about to represent Ireland at the Venice Biennale, but they would not necessarily know, from James's Twitter stream, that he was to spend this weekend there taking the measurements of the appointed space. 'Didn't I hear something,' she said now, scrabbling for ground, 'about you being there?'

James nodded. 'Well,' he said slowly, his gaze sliding to the side. 'I was there, actually, until around eight o'clock yesterday evening.'

'And now you're *here*?'

'Now I'm here. And so are you.'

'Well.'

'Well indeed,' he said, indicating the auditorium exit. 'Do you have a bit of time?'

Probably, it was the fancy artificial light in here, futuristically white and almost breathlessly clear, that made his eyes seem that unfamiliar blue, Catherine thought, as they walked towards the front of the tent, making jumpy small talk about the panel, James's strides long and hurried in his red jeans and scuffed leather work boots, a pair of green braces looped over his blue oxford shirt. The braces, or rather the look which involved brightly coloured braces, she had seen before, in a studio visit streamed on the Greene website and from recent photos on Scene & Herd; it was even more surreal to her in reality, but that was just how things worked; years passed, and the surreal, more and more, was simply the real. James had a beard now, and his red hair was fairer, but also with strands of grey at the temples and in the beard, and his skin, like hers, was now just skin, its textures on show, its pores like dirt flecks, its creases and their tributaries beginning. Probably, if someone's eyes had been that shade of blue always, that would be the thing, or at least one of the things, you would remember about them most strongly; that would be one of the things you carried with you, wouldn't it?

That would be one of the things you had, for instance, noticed. What with living your every breath for that person. What with being in love with them.

(The real became the surreal, and the surreal turned its impossible face towards you, and was the real.)

(Emmet's eyes: they had been blue.)

'Good flight?' she said, because it was the thing you said in these situations, marching along beside someone, with a folder of notes under your arm, in your jacket pocket your BlackBerry buzzing – but she would look at that in another moment, she would deal with that when she had dealt with this.

'Well,' James said, and he gave a short laugh, 'it was the kind of flight you'd feel guilty complaining about.'

'Oh,' Catherine said, confused.

'Seen those?' he said, pointing to a trio of Alice Neel portraits as they passed the Zwirner booth. 'They're so perfect.'

'Oh, yeah,' Catherine said, blinking at them; the dour faces in their exaggerated play of shadow and light, the vivid red lips, the bare-chested man with the dark circles around his eyes and his partner by his side. 'I can see why you like them,' she said, not even knowing what she meant.

'I love them,' James said, his eyes still on the paintings.

'And that photo of yours in the Greene booth is amazing.'

'I want to stop by there for a minute now,' James said, nodding as though she had said something obvious. 'Is that OK with you?'

'Sure.'

'Oh, and thanks, I should have said. I like that piece too. I wanted to keep it back for the show next week, but they wanted it for here.' He glanced at her. 'Will you still be here for my show?'

'I fly back Monday night, unfortunately.'

He said nothing, his attention seeming snagged by another piece, or perhaps by someone he recognized in one of the large German booths; his hand went to the back of his neck, she noticed, and rubbed it.

'I'll just be a minute here,' he said, turning left into the long rectangular space given over to Greene; at a beautiful Danish modern desk, two gallerists were tapping on their laptops. As was the case in many of the booths, a bottle of champagne was open on the desk, and a couple of half-empty flutes stood nearby; nobody ever seemed to be drinking the champagne, but its visibility was crucial, signalling that the gallery was celebrating an already successful fair.

As they came further into the space, one of the women at the desk lifted her gaze, and on seeing James, who was now standing with both hands out as though demanding an answer, a broad grin on his face, she shrieked his name, jumped out of her swivel chair and rushed over to hug him.

'You're not supposed to be here!' she scolded him, her arms still around him, as the other gallerist, waving madly, came over to do the same. 'No artists at the fair!'

'I know, I know, I'm an awful fucker,' James said, and it was so strongly in the accent and the intonation of fifteen years previously that Catherine stared at him.

'I thought you were still in Venice,' the second gallerist said, her hands on his face now, patting his cheeks like those of a baby. 'Your Twitter says you're going to the British Pavilion this morning!'

'Keep the bastards guessing,' James said, in the same accent, which made the women peal with laughter, and then he shook his head. 'No, no, I'm only joking. Jonathan was taking the plane back last night and he offered me a lift.'

'Oh, right,' the first woman said, as if to something which made utter sense.

'I was worn out from trying to work with those bloody Italian technicians, to be honest,' he said, and he extended a hand towards Catherine. 'Meghan, Veronica, have you met Catherine Reilly from *Frieze* magazine?'

'We've met,' Catherine said, her words echoed by the two women as they shook hands. 'I was in earlier.'

'How'd your panel go?' the first woman, Meghan, asked.

'Super,' Catherine said automatically. 'A really good conversation, I think.'

'They all know how to tell us what we should be doing, but they're not so keen to talk about what they should be doing themselves,' James said drily. 'Is, I think, what Catherine means.'

Everyone laughed, Catherine watching James out of the corner of her eye; had he really been offended by something in the discussion? She could barely remember a single thing that had been said. Should she have asked him, as they had left the auditorium, what he had thought? Had it been a grave lapse on her part, a grave professional lapse, not to steer the conversation that way, to have assumed that what was between them as they walked was somehow, instead, personal? She realized, with an almost bodily jolt, her assumption: that James had come to the panel, indeed possibly come to the fair, to see *her*, to have a chance to meet with *her*, talk with *her*. When, actually, he was an artist, at an art fair. Yes, the gallerists had flapped at him for being here; yes, they had made all the expected noises about how artists should steer clear of these things, so crude, so commercial, the collectors lurching between booths like drunks between dive bars, but the fact was, plenty of the artists wanted to keep tabs on things just as much as did the people with the chequebooks. That James should be one of those artists: that did not surprise Catherine. That did not surprise her at all. She stepped away from him, pretending a sudden deep interest in the small set of Nielsen photographs on the side wall. She moved her face close to them. She did not permit herself to focus on what was reflected from behind her in the glass of the frame.

'And then, of course, it's Christian's birthday,' James was saying now to Meghan and Veronica. 'That's the *actual* reason I had to come home.'

'Oh! You're surprising him!'

'You're *such* a good husband.'

'I don't know about that,' James said wryly. 'Would a good husband force his husband to pose for the likes of that thing over there?'

Catherine's whole body spun towards the portrait on the side wall. She had seen it earlier, but had not realized it was Christian; he looked nothing like the man from the photographs online. The pose, she realized, was actually very like a pose from an Alice Neel painting: Christian was sitting on a quite formal armchair, a velvet-upholstered thing with burnished wooden arms, and one bare leg was drawn up over the other, ankle almost to knee, and he was looking, seeming bored or resentful, to the side. Though maybe his expression was just neutral, or thoughtful, or distracted; with every passing second, Catherine felt less and less certain about what kind of expression it was, and after all it was a photograph, and not a painting like the Neel, and therefore just a moment, not a considered state, not even necessarily a caught mood. It was just one of the many, the countless moments a married couple spent in one another's company, noticing one another, or not noticing one another; both things they were free to do, both options they were free to stretch into, to enjoy, and this man, this dark-haired, fine-boned man, with his lips that were still full, and his arms that were strong and muscled from his mornings or evenings at the gym, and his cargo shorts, army green and faded, and the dark hairs on his legs and the silver metal watch on his wrist; this man was – had been – in one of those moments. Over his shoulder, through a window, a flash of green: a field. Blue sky, no clouds in view. Somewhere, Christian had been passing time in a sitting room, a summer afternoon waiting for him to go back out into its warmth.

'That's Carrigfinn,' James said, leaning closer to her. 'I took it when we were visiting there last summer.'

'Oh,' was all Catherine could say, and she stepped closer, and she tried to see the very grass of the field.

'It's such a great piece,' Veronica said, and Meghan gave a long, low sigh in agreement. 'Such a great photo of Christian as well.'

'Christian's not mad about it,' James said. 'I told you that, didn't I?'

'I think you mentioned – he thinks he looks old, or something?'

'Something like that,' James said, shaking his head. 'If he wanted to look good in photographs, he should have married Juergen.'

The women laughed. 'Not really an option,' one of them said.

'Ah, now, you wouldn't know that either,' said James. 'Don't forget Christian is *very* persuasive.'

Then they were leaving, James having talked Meghan into telling him the name of the collector who was likely to be buying the portrait; as was often the case, there were a number of offers, and it was up to the gallery to decide on the most desirable buyer.

'Oh,' James had said, looking impressed. 'OK. He'll do.'

Meghan widened her eyes. 'Right? But I didn't tell you that.' She poked him in the chest. 'I did not tell you that.'

'He'll give Christian a good home. Possibly better than I do.' He checked his watch. 'I need to get into the city to get him a gift.'

Meghan reached for her iPhone. 'Do you want me to get you the car?'

'No, no,' James said. 'It's a beautiful day. I think I'll walk over the thingy, the footbridge.'

Meghan made a face. 'Are you sure?'

'Yeah, yeah. It'll be nice by the water. I can take a cab at First Avenue.' He looked at Catherine. 'Will you walk me? Or do you have to be somewhere?'

They were looking at the East River, James explained, and the brown high-rise buildings on the other side were East Harlem, and the highway frantic with yellow cabs was the FDR. She was struck by the sounds of these names in his mouth, how thoroughly they seemed to belong to him, how he talked now about needing to get down to the Sixties and then down to Orchard and Hester for a meeting. Catherine had been to New York several times on business, but still the street names and the neighbourhoods seemed so exotic to her, seemed somehow unreal; she felt self-conscious using them, and always expected others to be the same.

'Do you live near here?' she said to him. 'Or, rather, where do you live? Not in Manhattan, right?'

No, not in Manhattan; she knew that. She knew that from the articles. He lived in Brooklyn, in a house for which he and Christian had paid $1.8 million.

'No, not in Manhattan,' James said, shaking his head as though she had mistaken him for someone else. 'In Brooklyn. Fort Greene. Do you know it?'

'No. Sounds nice.' *Sounds nice?* What was she saying? She was gabbling. With every sentence, she was hissing at herself to stop, to slow down, to let him do the talking, but always already the next sentence had fallen out of her helpless mouth. James must surely have noticed. But he gave no sign of it. He paid, now, for the two iced coffees he had ordered for them from a truck parked at the tent entrance.

'Thanks,' she said, as he handed her the plastic cup. 'I meant to say, I like the braces.'

'Oh.' He gave a short laugh, glancing down at himself.

'*Bejaysus, you're like old Barney Rodgers of the mountain.* That's what my oul' fella said when he saw them.'

'Have they been over?'

'Oh, yeah. A few times. For the' – he nodded backwards, as though at something they had just walked past – 'wedding, and then a few other times besides that.'

'That's lovely. Congratulations, by the way.'

'Thanks.'

'On everything, really,' she said, feeling a sudden impulse to shove a great many things together into a hole. 'I meant to write—'

'I was sorry to hear about you and Lucien,' he said, talking over her. 'I'm still in touch with Zoe on Facebook. She mentioned it.'

'Oh, thanks,' Catherine said with a shrug. 'It's for the best, probably.'

'Still, it's hard,' he said, and he pointed to the path down by the water, to indicate that they should go that way. 'I don't remember Lucien very well, I have to admit.'

'Well, he was with Zoe when you would have known him. It was years later when I met him again in London. He's with the *Guardian*.'

'Yeah, I've read a few things. He's good.'

'He's brilliant,' she nodded. 'We're still friends, you know, it's just . . .'

'Yeah,' he said, unevenly, and that hung between them, the brokenness of it, the awkwardness. How had she steered them, so quickly, into that water? Because she had kept talking, she told herself. Because she had obeyed, as always, the temptation to elaborate.

'My mother loved him,' she forged on then, immediately, without any idea of where she was going with this – this anecdote, she realized, this completely unnecessary and not even entirely true anecdote. 'The two of them used to sit in the conservatory, when we were over visiting, and watch the tennis.'

'Tennis!'

'On the TV, obviously. As opposed to out in the garden. The Celtic Tiger wasn't *that* good to them at home.'

'Still, though, a conservatory. Mammy Reilly at least got something nice under the tree.'

'She'd rather her nice English son-in-law, I think, and no conservatory.'

'Ah, well,' James said, raising his eyebrows. 'Sure you can get her another one.'

'I don't think so,' Catherine said, more darkly than she had intended.

'And how's your father doing?'

'Oh, great,' Catherine said, shrugging. 'He voted for David Norris in the presidential election last year. He was raging he didn't win.'

'Oh, yeah?'

'Oh, yeah. All change.'

James said nothing, but gave a short nod. They passed fishermen waiting by the water's edge; were passed by cyclists, dog walkers, a woman on rollerblades, a child on a narrow red scooter. The gravel crunched as they walked. The grass on either side of the path was patchy, humiliated-looking; with borders of daffodils and other plantings, attempts had been made to make this into a pleasant municipal space, but the ground seemed unhealthy, exhausted; polluted, probably, by the river. It looked like the ground at the edge of one of the abandoned housing estates she had seen at home: scraggy, brownish, littered with stones. Those were dandelions underfoot now, and beer caps. To their right, the drop to the water was marked with large square boulders set into the earth. The river was grey. On the other side, she could make out some of the brand names emblazoned on a building: CostCo, Target. The next building looked like a courthouse, and beyond that more of the high-rise brown blocks that must have been apartments; *projects*, the word came to her suddenly. It could have been any city. It looked to her nothing like New York; there was none of the familiar glint and soar of the skyline, none of its narcotic, cinematic glow.

'Zoe's kids are cute, aren't they?' she said then, reaching for an easy, airy tone. 'I love the photo she put up last week.'

James made a noise of agreement, a fond sort of grunt, and took another slug of his coffee. Seeing this, Catherine did the same, although the sharp coldness of the liquid baffled her; it was so aggressive, somehow.

'Why do Americans drink this stuff?' she said, shaking her cup in front of her. 'I never understand it.'

'Are you still in touch with any of the rest of them?' James said, not seeming to have heard her; he was frowning at his straw, fiddling with it; the friction of plastic on plastic made a dull clicking sound. He looked at her.

Catherine felt the need to swallow. 'Not really,' she said, afterwards. 'Facebook, a few people. I hear from Conor now and then. He's a big-shot playwright now, you know?'

'Oh, yeah,' James said, raising his eyebrows. 'I read about the Tony nomination. Didn't win though, did he?'

Catherine shrugged. 'He'll win yet.'

'And Robert Emmet?'

'He's in the Dáil, believe it or not.'

'What?!'

'Not as a politician, obviously. But working for one. He's a speechwriter for the Minister for Justice.'

'Oh, for fuck's sake. Are you joking me?'

'No. I suppose someone has to do it.'

'I suppose a satirist is better qualified than anyone else.'

She laughed. 'Yeah. But I'm not in touch with him. And anyway, I transferred to Goldsmiths in my last year, so I fell out of contact with most people. I'd sort of fallen out of contact with most of them anyway. Afterwards. You know.'

And there it was. 'Afterwards'. Bringing with it the 'before'. Surrounding them, now, in their very breathing, as though it were a cloud they had walked into, a cloud of chemicals or a cloud of tiny things that were alive. The low hum of it. The oscillation; a disturbance. Catherine inhaled slowly, deeply, almost warily, as though she could protect herself from its poison, but she could not; she had, after all, been the one to exhale it. A sightseeing boat ploughed the river's centre; from this distance, the crowd packed onto the top deck seemed unmoving, resigned, like refugees, and it occurred to her to point this out to James, to make a joke of it, but James, she thought then, might very well not see the humour in it. Wherever the humour was.

'You know, I wasn't completely honest with Meghan and Veronica back there, Catherine,' James said now. 'About my reasons for coming here, I mean.'

'Well, it's Christian's birthday,' Catherine said, hurriedly.

'No, no,' James said, shaking his head as though explaining something to a child. 'Christian's birthday is why I came home last night from Italy. But here, I'm talking about.' He gestured behind him in the general direction of the exhibition tent. 'The fair, I mean.'

'Oh.'

'I don't give a fuck about what they sell and what they don't sell. Well, I do, but there's no need for me to be in there checking up on them. They're right, a fair is no place for an artist. They're just bloody rackets.' He glanced at her. 'No offence.'

'None taken,' Catherine said, a little too eagerly.

'Yeah. Well, anyway, I was saying. It wasn't the booth. Jonathan had a programme for this on the plane last night, and I saw you were giving a talk.'

'Oh.'

'I've read lots of your articles, you know. Obviously. They're good.'

'Thanks,' Catherine said, feeling awkward.

'No poetry anymore then? All journalism?'

She shook her head. 'Oh, no. The poetry was just, you know. A teenage thing.'

'You were good at it, as I remember.'

'Not really.'

'Anyway. I mean, I'm sure this isn't the first time work has brought you to New York,' he said, more briskly. 'And obviously I'm in London a good bit.'

'Oh, yes,' Catherine blurted, 'I saw your show at the Frith.'

'Arrah, that,' James said, shaking his head. 'That was a rushed show. I shouldn't have done that.'

'Oh, no, I thought—'

'I was going through some stuff then, I wasn't right in the head, I don't think. I was still drinking.'

'Right, right,' said Catherine, as though she was well acquainted with the fact of his sobriety, or indeed the fact of its opposite having been an issue, a problem, for some past version of James, who was at the same time somehow still – to her – a future version of James, since he was the James he had become in the time afterwards, in the time after she had stopped knowing him, been forced to stop knowing him, and she had never had the chance, in those years, to know him, and now that version of him, those years, was utterly gone. And the drinking must have been bad, then, if he had had to give it up. And had she done that to him as well?

'Anyway, you probably heard about all the stuff with Nate, and then Ed Dunne had to go and die of a heart attack in his bathtub, and "dead in the bath" was all anyone wanted to hear, and that was – well. You can imagine how that was.'

'Yes,' Catherine lied.

'I mean, it was madness. Absolute madness. Some journalist rang my mother in Carrigfinn. Can you imagine?'

'Oh my God.'

'Frightened the fucking life out of her. She thought *I* was after dying in the bath.' He made a face. 'Or worse, I'd say. I'd say she thought worse.'

'Oh, James.'

'And Nate.' He looked at her. 'Have you crossed paths with Nate through the magazine?'

'No, actually.'

'Well, you remember him?'

She nodded, not quite able to get the word out.

'And he became even more full of himself once he started up his own gallery.'

'I'm sure,' Catherine said, not having to work hard at all to call up an image of Nate Lewis, a composite made from all the photographs she had seen of him online: the suits, the tan, the carnivore's smile. Gone the boyish head of brown curls; he kept his head shaved, presumably to hide the places where the hair had refused to stick around. If he had been in the booth earlier today, what would she have said to him? She had gone in there feeling blasé about the possibility, feeling that the years could not hurt her, that the years, the traces of what they had brought with them, meant nothing, meant less than nothing, even, but if Nate had been in the Lewis booth that morning, what would she have said to him? Ridiculous, to feel herself almost panicking now, almost shuddering, at the thought of the thing that had not happened, and about the prospect of which she had not even been worried in the first place, but the sight, the fact, of James had changed everything. James here, and James walking with her, and James telling her, now, that he had come here to see her, and 'afterwards', and 'before', and this coffee in her hand, so cold and heavy and pointless, and these joggers, these strollers, these art crowds in their Acne and their Watanabe and their Demeulemeester, and this New York heat beating down, through this overcast sky—

'Didn't stop me being in a relationship with him for nearly two years, though,' James was saying now, and he shook his head.

'Well,' Catherine began, 'Everyone—'

He looked at her. 'Everyone has to start somewhere, is that what you were going to say?'

'No, I meant—' she said, and stopped; this was, in fact, pretty much what she had been going to say. She chewed on her straw.

'Because I didn't start with Nate, did I?'

'No,' she said, into the straw.

'Did I, Catherine?' he said, his voice more urgent.

She lifted her chin. 'No.'

'I've wanted—' He sighed. 'I've wanted to be in touch with you. For a while now.'

'Oh,' she said, and her heart seemed to be trying to elbow its way out through her chest. They were nearing a park bench; if she suggested that they sit down, would that make things better or worse? Was it better to be moving? Better for your legs to be out from under you?

'I shouldn't have cut off contact the way I did, Catherine,' he said, his voice jumping. 'That was the wrong way to go about it. Whatever "it" was.'

'Well,' Catherine said. '"It" was Liam. What happened with Liam. What happened *to* Liam, because of what I did.'

James nodded slowly. 'I'm still in touch with him, you know. Facebook, needless to say.'

'Oh,' Catherine said, more brightly than felt appropriate. 'How is he?'

He nodded again. 'He's good. He teaches in Belfast now. He has a partner.'

'That's nice.'

James said nothing.

'And is he—' She stopped. What had she even been going to ask? 'What does he teach up there?'

'History,' James said, with what could have been a beat of irony in his tone, but the word had come and gone too quickly for Catherine to tell.

'That's nice,' she said, and immediately winced. 'He was always so smart.'

'The scarring is not really visible anymore,' James said then, as briskly as though he was delivering test results. 'At least I don't think so from the photographs he puts up now. A bit' – he put his hand up to his jawline – 'a bit of something around here still, maybe, where it was bad, but nothing major. The doctors up there, you know.' He nodded. 'He looks good. He looks much the same, actually.'

'Good, good,' said Catherine, in the same tone of absurd brightness. *Tell him I was asking after him*, she almost said, so efficiently had she whipped herself up, now, into this state, into this welter of refusal and pretending. This was not happening. This was not real. She was not on a scrap of scrub-land off the coast of East Harlem, gripping a ridiculous plastic beaker, sweating into her fancy clothes, being pulled by the quiet, serious voice of James Flynn into the summer of fourteen years before.

'Catherine,' James was saying now. 'You know, what happened was terrible.'

'Yes,' she said faintly.

'I don't just mean Liam. I don't just mean' – he cleared his throat – 'that day. I mean the whole thing.'

'Your photos, the photos you took that day, were unbelievable,' she said. 'They were so moving.'

He shook his head. 'What was I doing, taking fucking photographs?'

'James.'

'No. What was I *doing*? Taking photographs in a *hospital*, for fuck's sake?'

'They were important. They were very powerful. They still are.'

'I don't know. I can't look at them. I don't know if I'll ever be able to look at them.'

'You should be proud of them.'

'I don't know.'

'I'm proud of them for you,' she said, and she reached out to him, and she touched his arm, but it all seemed to happen in slow motion, and it all seemed stilted, stunted; it all seemed strange. James drew back a little at her touch – she did not think she was imagining this – and so the sentence that she was already rolling out to follow the first one, the one in which she said it to him, the one in which she told him, seemed ill-judged now, seemed like an ugly, distasteful flare. But, 'I'm proud of *you*,' she said it anyway, had said it, before she could stop herself, and in response to that, James actually stopped in his tracks; James froze, and James looked at her.

'Don't, Catherine, please,' he said.

'I'm sorry,' she said, horrified, mortified, not even sure what she was apologizing for. 'Never mind me, never mind me.'

'It's not that it's not nice of you to say something like that.'

'No, it was stupid. Of course it was stupid. We don't know each other anymore. It's not my place.'

'No, it's not that,' he said, walking again now, shaking his head. 'I mean, yes. Of course yes, we don't, you know – it's true. We don't know each other anymore.' He sighed. 'Which makes me sad, actually.'

'Me too.'

'But, you know,' he said, 'this is how it is. Time moves. It takes you with it. Life changes. You know?'

There was far more to it than that, Catherine thought, but she did not say this. She nodded. 'I'm sorry about what happened, James,' she said. It seemed hopelessly inadequate, but it had to be said. It should have been said many years previously. She had tried; she had started the letters. But his own letter, written to her a week after what had happened, had been clear. No more. No contact. No way; no explanations; no point. It had been unfair to keep Baggot Street from him, to keep the girls from him – they had been his friends first, after all – so she had found a flatshare with some other people from college in Ranelagh. Zoe had come home from Italy; Zoe had been her friend. Emmet had come home; Emmet had been more than she could ever have believed Emmet could be to her. Heartbreak, in the end, too; heartbreak enough to make up her mind about moving to London; heartbreak, in its way, far worse than it had been, a year previously, with James; was that irony? Was that a justice somehow served? Was that just life?

Yes, yes, probably that was just life.

'I'm sorry,' she said again. 'It's not enough, it's not even a beginning, but it's true, James.'

'It wasn't your fault.'

She stared at him. 'What?' she said, and she almost laughed. 'Of course it was my fault. If it wasn't for me—' She shook her head. 'You shouldn't even have been up there. Either of you.'

'No,' he said firmly. 'You see, that's not true. We should have been able to be anywhere we felt like being, anywhere we wanted to be. Everybody who was there that day should have been able to be there. Without that. Without being blown to bits by a bunch of fucking psychopaths.'

'But that's different,' Catherine said, frowning. 'That's a separate thing.'

'No,' James said, shaking his head. 'You didn't do that to us.'

'I did part of it. I did enough.'

'No,' he said firmly. 'There's no point in telling yourself that. If you want to tell yourself, that's another matter. That's, however you put it, a separate thing.'

He was not trying to comfort her, Catherine realized. He was not trying to take something painful away. It was as if he was trying to tell her that something painful had never been hers to hold on to at all.

'You were supposed to be in Baggot Street that weekend,' she said, 'the two of you. You were going to come for dinner, stay the night . . .'

He made a noise of disbelief. 'Why would we need to stay the night? We didn't need to use someone else's house. We would have gone home to Liam's place, or to mine.'

'It was something I heard Lorraine suggesting. That you would stay. Make a weekend of it. And then there was the photo.'

'What photo?'

'The photo of Liam.'

He squinted at her. 'The photo of Liam was taken afterwards.'

Not that photo, she wanted to say, but there was no point – there was no point in raking this over. It was so long ago. It had been, anyway, such a small thing.

But James was still frowning, still shaking his head. 'You must be misremembering, Catherine. That doesn't make any sense.'

'I think the idea was—'

'Because we weren't hiding,' he said over her.

'Yes, you were,' she said quietly.

'No,' he said sharply. 'No, we weren't. Hiding from you, maybe. But that was different. That was' – he changed his intonation – 'a separate thing.'

'So you do blame me.'

'*Blame?*' he spat. 'I blame the bastards who parked that car. I blame the bastards who stole it, the ones who drove it up there knowing—'

'But you were up there because of what I did,' Catherine said, and she saw, then, a bin, and she threw her coffee into it; it landed with a slosh.

'You weren't really into that, were you?' James said, and she was astonished to see that he was almost laughing. She stared at him.

'Do you even know what I said to him? What I told Liam that day?'

'You told him we were fucking,' James said, in the same vaguely bemused tone. 'And you said I was – how was it that your mother put it that time?'

'My *mother*?'

'Troubled,' James said, nodding in evident satisfaction at having remembered the word, or at having had the chance to present it. 'Troubled, that's what you said I was. Which he had no trouble, so to speak, believing. The rest of it, though' – he shrugged – 'sure, all he had to do was ask me.'

She stared at him. The collar of his denim shirt, fluttering slightly in the breeze. The grey in his beard. A freckle high on his cheek, maybe a mole; he should get that checked. But that was not something she should even be noticing; that was not something it was her place to notice.

'Well, I'm sorry,' she said again, feeling the need to insist on it.

He shook his head. 'You don't need to tell me that, Catherine. That's your business. The being sorry, I mean. That's part of *your* life. I don't mean anything harsh by that. I don't mean that it's worthless or anything, your being sorry, or your apology, or sorrow, or however you'd put it. I just mean, it's yours.'

'Yeah,' Catherine said, her voice hollow. She felt she was being fobbed off, somehow; she felt as if, all over again, she was being refused.

'I have my own things,' he said, and he gave a short laugh. 'Fuckin' plenty of them.'

He sighed. 'That's the walkway,' he said, pointing up ahead. A bright green lane for cyclists and pedestrians arched across the river, pinned at two points by tall, thin towers at the top of which sentry windows were visible. It was a strange structure, looking like something out of a graphic novel against the clouds, against this city which seemed, dourly, to have turned its back to them. As they watched, a cyclist whizzed down the platform and onto the island path, disappearing behind the scraggy trees.

'People come out here to get a bit of headspace,' James said. 'It's a weird old spot.' He pointed to the city. 'Look, there's the Chrysler, look, peeking out between those two lumps of things. Can you see it?'

She squinted. 'I think so.'

'Well, you wouldn't mistake the Chrysler. It's beautiful. Where are you staying?'

'The Standard.'

'Oh-ho,' he said, gleefully. 'Sex with Michael Fassbender up against the plate-glass windows?'

Catherine made a face. 'I wouldn't complain.'

'Well, you're a free agent now,' he said, and he took her arm. The touch of him, the solidness of him; for a moment, Catherine could not breathe. He swayed into her, and she swayed against him, and then they were in step; then they had their rhythm. The path, and the yellow flowers, and the grass verging scruffy against the gravel, and the water's edge, and the bridge was coming, and the bridge would take him away.

'You trusted me, and I don't think I did the right thing with that, James,' Catherine said. 'I don't know why I did what I did with it.'

He shrugged; she felt it, against the arm he was holding, as a tug. 'I wasn't that good to you, either.'

'Not deliberately.'

'Neither of us was acting deliberately. Maybe that was the problem.'

'Maybe,' she said doubtfully.

'We were kids, Catherine. We were wains, as my mother would say. It's all a long time ago now.'

'Not *that* long.'

'Are you joking?' he said, and he pointed to his face. 'Look at these wrinkles.' He made a show of examining the skin around her eyes. 'You're not doing too badly, actually. Fuck you anyway.'

She burst out laughing; he was laughing too. It was a performance, of course; a performance with which he could steer them out of dicey territory. It was what he had always done, and he was still doing it now, only now he was so much better at it – Catherine saw it, the smoothness, the quickness, the practice he had had. He stuck out his bottom lip now, in a mock-sulk, and pretended to glower at her skin again, and she laughed again, like he wanted her to, like he needed her to do.

'You're terrible, Muriel,' she said, in an Australian accent.

'I'm terrible, Muriel,' he said, in exactly the same twang. He gripped her arm very tightly for a moment, and then he let it go.

At the entrance to the walkway, they hugged goodbye; not a long hug, but not a short hug, either, and as he stepped back away from her, James sighed. Nothing had been said about keeping in touch, or about meeting up again during the rest of her stay here; they had not exchanged email addresses or phone numbers, had not said anything, even, about finding each other on Facebook. Catherine would have felt ridiculous suggesting this, even though it seemed to be staring them in the face as something obvious now, something natural; they had, after all, mentioned it several times. But she could not do it; she felt that the move, if it was to be made, was up to him. And what was it anyway, only staged photos and inane ramblings? They were better off without it, probably. They were better off just bumping into one another whenever the world sent them one another's way.

'Listen,' James said now, and he glanced towards the city. 'This show of mine, Catherine. In the gallery.'

'Oh, I can't,' Catherine said. 'I thought I mentioned – I'm flying back to London on Monday night.'

'I know, I know, and the opening's not till Tuesday,' he said. 'But if you wanted – if you were able – I mentioned to Meghan there as we were leaving that I'd like for you to be able to call in for a private viewing on Monday during the day sometime, and could she arrange to have someone there.'

'Oh?'

'Yeah. It'll be mostly installed by then.'

'And will you be there?'

'Oh, no,' he said, flinching as though he had been stung. 'I couldn't – I can barely stand to look at them when they're up myself, never mind to watch someone else looking at them.'

'Oh, sure, sure.'

'But I'd like you to see them. Just, you know. To see.'

'Sure,' Catherine nodded, and, feeling the need to make this somehow businesslike, she took her BlackBerry out of her jacket pocket. She toggled the screen randomly; the weather icon was what opened up. 'What time?' she said, her eyes on the screen. 'Ten thirty or eleven?'

'It's up to you,' James said. 'They'll be there all day. Just go when it suits you. If it suits you.'

'Of course it suits me. I'm really looking forward to it.'

'OK,' James said, and he smiled at her.

'Thanks, James.'

'I'd better go,' he said, pointing towards the walkway as though it was something waiting for him. 'I'll chat to you?'

'I'll chat to you,' Catherine nodded, and she watched him walk away. And when she walked away, she looked back at him, at his form going over the strange green bridge, his rucksack on his back, his arms swinging, like a tourist going to see what he could see.

But he was not the tourist, of course. The tourist was her.

———

His name was already printed on the frosted glass of the gallery window, low down, to the left of the entrance: James Flynn, and the name of the show, *Twenty of You*. Catherine pressed the buzzer and waited. The street was almost eerily quiet; on a Monday, the galleries were all closed to the public. The door opened a crack, and a young woman peered out; seeing Catherine, she smiled and ushered her in. She was Alice, she said, and James had called that morning to let her know that Catherine would be coming to see the work – could she get Catherine anything: coffee, water, anything?

'I'm fine, thanks,' Catherine said, glancing around the space; they were in the reception area, where a large desk – presumably Alice's – faced a wall of catalogues of James's work; the large hardbacks of the last two shows at Greene were there, along with the magazine-bound editions he had made with McGinley and the others, and the softbound catalogue from the first Lewis show. Catherine moved towards them, but then realized that the girl – Alice – was holding something out to her; a list, on an A4 sheet, of the works in the new show.

'Oh, no, it's OK,' Catherine said, shaking her head. 'I'd prefer just to look at them head-on, if you know what I mean. I always prefer to do it that way at first.'

'No problem,' said Alice, and she put the list back on the desk. 'Well, the show starts in the next room and continues into the back room,' she said, pointing. 'I hope you like it.'

All of the faces greeted her; all of the staring men. Young, most of them. Striking, all of them, each in their own way, but then that was James; that was what James did. And then, not all of them were staring, she realized; some of them were looking right out at the viewer, a sort of reckoning, but some of

426

them were refusing, or simply not feeling obliged, to meet the viewer's eye; glancing to the side or to the ground, to something other, something out of frame. Or maybe to nothing at all; maybe only to thought, to where a thought led.

Shaven-headed, the first of them – from the entrance, she moved to the right, to the man with the buzz cut and the vaguely disapproving mouth, the touch of bloodshot at the sides of his eyes. She did not like him, she decided; she was, somehow, afraid of him. Ridiculous, but that was her reaction, and she had learned, in all of these years walking around galleries, to realize that the reaction was the thing really worth looking at, was the place where the interesting, uncomfortable stuff was to be found.

The next boy was beautiful, the boy with the wax in his hair; more wax than he needed, but it did nothing to interfere with his beauty; nothing could. He was probably twenty-five, she thought, but he looked younger, maybe because he looked startled; maybe because the camera had caught him by surprise, clicking at him as he busied himself with something that could not be seen, something on the other side of the rock on which he was seated; it was a summer day, and he and James had been somewhere, a park, a mountain, somewhere, and James had taken up his camera and the boy's head had turned. A bag at his feet. No trace of wariness in his eyes.

Smoking, the next guy. Not young. Standing at what looked like a bus stop. A check shirt, the sleeves rolled up. Blond hair on his arms. His fingers were stubby; the nails were flecked with something: maybe paint. He did not look like someone waiting. His eyes looking out to the street. He looked like someone who had not decided whether, when the bus did come, he would be getting on.

Long-haired and weary-looking, the fourth one. Dark

shadows under his eyes. This was another formal portrait, like the first one; there was nothing in the background, there was no everyday clutter, no everyday world. There were no props. The wall behind him bare. His shirt blue, his chin dimpled, his impatience seeming already to have propelled him out of the shot. He hugged himself. He wanted to be away.

Five looked Irish, she thought. Some kind of embarrassment in his gaze; some kind of awkwardness. *Ah, Jaysus, James,* the photo might have been called, she thought, laughing to herself; but he was handsome, the dark eyebrows, the high forehead, the shirt collars askew.

Six was black, stretched out on what looked like a beach towel, though fully clothed. She glanced around, seeing another black guy across the way, and felt immediately ashamed of herself – counting, as though it was something she should even be noticing, but the reaction was the whole point, she reminded herself, and anyway, nobody needed to know. Alice, for example, coming smiling towards her now, an iPad in her hands; Alice did not need to know that Catherine had looked around and had counted the black faces, and nor did anyone else.

'Superb, aren't they?' Alice said. She looked around the walls and nodded, as if in agreement with herself. 'I love the one of Christian,' she said, and she pointed towards the door.

'Oh,' Catherine said. 'I hadn't even noticed.'

'The pieces go from left to right, really,' Alice said, 'but I guess it doesn't matter which way you look at them.' She gave a short laugh. 'As long as you look at them.'

Catherine said nothing. She was crossing to the photo of Christian, which had obviously been taken on the same day as the one she had already seen; he was wearing the same clothes, the same sleeveless T-shirt and cargo shorts, and

428

there were his dark curls, and there were his full lips, and there was the light tan on his skin, the tan he had brought with him, surely, to Carrigfinn; you did not get a tan in a place like Carrigfinn. This photo had been taken outside, out in the greenness and the warmth which it had been possible only to glimpse over his shoulder in the other one; at his back were the rusted bars of a gate, a gate into a meadow, and in the meadow the grass was high, the sunshine was flooding it; it glowed like a field made of light.

'That must have been June,' Catherine said in a murmur. 'They haven't knocked that field.'

'Knocked the—?' Alice was saying from beside her now, sounding confused.

'It's nothing,' Catherine said. 'Just a detail I noticed. It's a beautiful photo.'

'*So* beautiful,' Alice said. 'I mean, the look on Christian's face. The way you can tell he's just about to smile. And the way he's leaning back onto that railing – something about the, sort of, playfulness of that, I love it.'

'Yeah,' Catherine said. 'I love it too.'

'And I *love* the one of you.'

Catherine stared. 'The—?'

'You haven't seen it yet?' Alice said, walking towards the second room, and beckoning Catherine to follow her.

'I'm sorry,' Catherine said, her voice closing on itself. 'There's a photo of me?'

'Oh yeah,' Alice said, glancing back. 'James didn't tell you?'

She shook her head. 'No.'

'Fuck!' Alice said, putting a hand to her mouth. She immediately looked horrified. 'Oh my God, I'm sorry. I shouldn't have said that. It's just – I assumed you knew – I didn't realize it was a—'

Catherine was already walking past her.

'It doesn't even look like you, really,' Alice said weakly, as Catherine passed into the next room, as Catherine caught her breath.

It was a photo of a photo. A photo of a photo in a bright blue wooden frame, standing on a bookshelf, books behind it; you could read the spines, if you wanted to, which Catherine did not, just at this moment; Catherine did not know, just at this moment, what she wanted to do, whether it was to stare at this small square of what had once been herself, or to turn her back on it and run. The photo had been taken at the kitchen table in Baggot Street that first day; not the first day, not the day they had met, but the day after they had first been together, the day after everything had changed. She was slouching, and straggle-haired – she was hungover – wearing her old flannel shirt, the shirt she had loved, the shirt she had bought second-hand from a market stall near St Stephen's Green the summer she was sixteen. In her hands was the Gary Larson mug Ellen had given her one Christmas, the one with the joke about Moses parting the waters, and the table was a mess in front of her: milk cartons, and tea towels, and the yellow plastic bowl for which nobody ever remembered to get any fruit. Somebody's empty Marlboro packet, crushed as though it had been stepped on. A newspaper; a newspaper, by then already ridiculously out of date.

She was staring right into the lens.

'*1998*,' Alice read from her iPad. 'Wow.' She cleared her throat. 'I love the shirt you're wearing.'
    'Thanks,' Catherine managed.
    '*From which I did not know*,' Alice said. 'Nice.'
    'What?' Catherine said, turning sharply.

'That's what it's called,' Alice said, offering her the iPad. 'From which—'

'Let me see that,' Catherine said, taking it, and Alice held up her hands, as though to protest that she had been giving it to Catherine anyway.

From which (I did not know), Catherine, 1998, the description read. Catherine pinched it with thumb and index finger, enlarging it, as though to test it, as though to make it somehow more real. The words grew huge against the white background; they seemed to come closer to her, until there was space only for *know* on the screen. Catherine stared at it. She looked back to the photo, to the cheap wooden frame around the moment of which she had no memory. How could she not remember him taking that photograph? How had it slipped so completely from her store of things, when what it had been made of – James's eyes fixed on her while she had her eyes fixed on him – had been what she had wanted so badly?

'It's kind of strange, the way the brackets are,' Alice said, sounding a little nervous.

'I know what it means,' Catherine said.

Alice waited a moment but then, realizing that there would be no further explanation, she nodded and took a step back.

There were eight or ten other portraits in the gallery, Catherine saw now, looking around; Liam was there on the adjoining wall, the photo of him that James had taken in the hospital. She had seen it before; she forced herself now, to look at it, not to look away from it. She looked at the pillow on which his head rested, and she looked at the softness of his hair, and she looked at his skin, his young, perfect skin, and she looked at his eyes again, and she looked at the bandages on his neck and on his shoulders, and she looked at his hands.

Her heart was pounding. Behind her, Alice was saying something, but Catherine did not know what it was. An adjective; it was always an adjective. As though an adjective could come close to this. As though an adjective could come close to any of them. Then she looked more closely, Catherine did, and she saw something she had not seen before, and she realized why the angle of the photograph seemed crooked somehow, seemed somehow haphazard; it was because the photographer was holding the camera only with his right hand, and because his left hand was covering Liam's; it was because that was the photographer's thumb, the photographer's index finger, there, in the bottom corner of the photograph, laid over Liam's hand. And that was why the frame was so tight. That was why the lens was so near. That was what explained that look in Liam's eyes.

Catherine heard Alice clear her throat now, and say something, and as she glanced her way she saw how Alice's expression jolted and then hesitated at the sight of Catherine's tears.

'I'm sorry?' Catherine said, wiping them away. 'I'm sorry, did you say something to me?'

Alice smiled apologetically. 'I was just asking whether you had any questions.'

Catherine shook her head. 'No questions,' she said, and she turned to look at the other faces in the room. 'No questions at all.'

Acknowledgements

My thanks to Peter Straus, Anna Stein,
Paul Baggaley, Kris Doyle and Lee Boudreaux.

Huge gratitude to my first readers John Butler,
Michele Woods, Jamila-Khanom Allidina, Philip Coleman,
Mark Doten and Kimberly King Parsons.

And to Aengus: thank you for this and all the rest.

Permissions Acknowledgements

Grateful acknowledgement is made to the following:

The epigraph on page *ix* is from *Light Years* by James Salter; it appears here with the author's permission.

The phrase 'Dreams fled away' is extracted from Thomas Kinsella's poem 'Another September' and appears here with his permission.

The extract from 'The Planter's Daughter' by Austin Clarke on page 57 is reproduced from his *Collected Poems* (Carcanet Press Limited, 2008).

Part of the exchange between Catherine and James on page 138 refers to a refrain in the animated TV show *Pinky and the Brain*.

'You're terrible, Muriel' is a reference to the 1994 film *Muriel's Wedding*, written by P. J. Hogan.

The 1998 Trinity College Dublin Department of English examination paper on Romance appears here with the permission of the copyright holder, Trinity College Dublin, the University of Dublin.

Extracts from 'Blue Moles', 'Morning Song', 'Nick and the Candlestick', 'Rabbit Catcher' and 'Tulips' are taken from *Collected Poems* © Estate of Sylvia Plath and reprinted by permission of Faber and Faber Ltd.

Extracts taken from 'Child's Park', '18 Rugby Street', 'Epiphany', '9 Willow Street', 'Robbing Myself', 'The Rabbit Catcher' and 'Wuthering Heights' are taken from *Birthday Letters* © Estate of Ted Hughes and reprinted by permission of Faber and Faber Ltd.

Lyric excerpt of 'Exit Music (For A Film)' by Radiohead. Written by Philip James Selway, Jonathan Richard Guy Greenwood, Edward John O'Brien, Thomas Edward Yorke and Colin Charles Greenwood. Copyright © 1997 Warner/Chappell Music Ltd. Reprinted by Permission of Alfred Music. All Rights Reserved.

Lyric excerpt of 'Shine' by David Gray. Copyright © 1993 by Warner/Chappell Music, Inc., Universal Music Publishing Group. Reprinted by Permission of Alfred Music. All Rights Reserved.

Lyric excerpt of 'Lucky' by Radiohead. Written by Mark P. Dombroski, Philip James Selway, Edward John O'Brien, Jonathan Richard Guy Greenwood, Thomas Edward Yorke, Colin Charles Greenwood. Copyright © 1997 Warner/Chappell Music Ltd. Reprinted by Permission of Alfred Music. All Rights Reserved.